To Jan

Best wishes

Rex Godbehere

Oct 2000

SEVENTEEN OF APRIL
SCUM

Ronald Godbehere

MINERVA PRESS
LONDON
MIAMI RIO DE JANEIRO DELHI

SEVENTEEN OF APRIL SCUM
Copyright © Ronald Godbehere 2000

ISBN 0 75411 265 9

First Published 2000 by
MINERVA PRESS
315–317 Regent Street
London W1R 7YB

Printed in Great Britain for Minerva Press

SEVENTEEN OF APRIL
SCUM

To Mo for her motivation
and
Phally for everything

The Wedding

For a young south-east Asian girl, there is nothing like her wedding day; it was as if her parents had been rehearsing Sokunthea for this event for years. Yes, her father had broken with tradition in the past and insisted that although his only child was a girl she would still go to school and study hard, but when it came to weddings, tradition had to be followed. She had studied hard and found that many suitors didn't want a clever girl, and now at twenty-eight she had been left a little too long on the shelf and had often wondered if this day would ever arrive.

Sokunthea Sen lived in a small wooden house in Phnom Penh's Deum Kor district with her parents. Her father, Kimbly, worked for the Ministry of Works as a gardener, a job that he enjoyed but didn't pay much, which meant her mother paid the bills. Her name was Rany and she worked for the Ministry of Statistics with the responsibility of registering marriages and this, her own daughters, was going to be a pleasure. Sokunthea's parents had lived in Phnom Penh for the last eight years; before that they had worked in the rural town of Takeo and before that in the rural village of Rhor Kar. This was where Sokunthea developed her tough spirit and determination to succeed. They had moved to Phnom Penh after her father's brother died and left the house to him; it was easy to get a transfer after the right people were paid the right amount as a bribe. Once in Phnom Penh, Sokunthea was able to concentrate on her studies and she developed a reputation as a hard-working intelligent girl who would make someone a good wife. Sokunthea was still considered pretty by Cambodian standards, even beautiful to some, but with the war many suitors came and went, never to be seen again, and others just wanted to marry any woman before conscription.

The war – well, that won't bother me today, she thought. This day, this seventh day of May 1972 was her long-awaited day. Her husband had seemed a little strange to her at first, often distant when they met. At first this was a little off-putting, but as they met over several months it was a feature she began to like. As usual, his family thought he was marrying below his station, a view which filled Sokunthea with anger when she first heard it. Piseth was from a part-Chinese family and had just qualified as a doctor; she had studied French and English at school and was on her way to being a professor at the local high school – look down on her indeed! Well, the wedding day was here; if his family did look down on her they certainly had not been able to dissuade him from marrying her. Sokunthea looked out from the second-floor balcony; her mother was behind her inside her bedroom arranging clothes.

'What was your wedding like?' Sokunthea called to her mother.

'It rained, all day,' came the reply.

'That's supposed to be bad luck, isn't it?' said Sokunthea.

'Well things turned out okay for us.'

Sokunthea had developed a good relationship with her parents and they with her, a spirit which had seen her through many years of hardship. As a child in Rhor Kar she had had to walk, boat-ride and bus many kilometres every day to get to school; before and after her studies she would have to work hard in the rice field and at home. Her father had always been demanding, never accepting second best, her mother had been sickly shortly following her birth, which was one of the reasons why Sokunthea had no siblings. By contrast her future husband, Piseth, had had it relatively easy with a prosperous trading family behind him. They lived in the town of Kompong Chhnang, situated north of Phnom Penh on the Tonle Sap. Many traders of all nationalities came to this riverside town and over the years interbreeding had occurred; this was the case with Piseth's family, for, although they could trace Chinese ancestry, their blood had been mingled with Cambodian for many years. Piseth had not wanted to be a doctor, in fact he hadn't known what he wanted to be when he left middle school, but a relative had offered to pay for his studies and it allowed him to get away from the family for a while and into Phnom Penh. This mild rebellion against his family's wishes had led him to Sokunthea. He had seen her at the university where she lectured, for a short time he had enrolled in her English class but gave it up when his medical exams got harder and harder. She left a lasting impression on him especially the way she stood up to the more unruly members of her class. His parents had chosen other women for him, two in particular more suitable to them because they had money, but the arrangements fell through, one because he was Chinese and the other because he would not buy his proposed bride a motorbike.

'Come on, how did you feel about marrying Dad?' continued Sokunthea.

'I didn't know him. Of course, I'd heard about him, my parents tried their best to describe him to me.' Her mother walked across the wooden balcony and looked out into the street.

'Heard about him?' inquired Sokunthea.

'He was a bit of a rogue, always getting into trouble, my parents only let me marry him because he bought a house for us to live in and a cow for my father.'

'Phally told me that Piseth had been asked for gifts by other suitors,' mused Sokunthea.

'I wouldn't worry about such stories, and anyway, gift buying is common in Cambodian engagements.'

'I don't want to be bought, it's hard enough marrying a man you don't really know without being bought by him.' With this, Sokunthea felt the usual rage rise up inside her and thought it best to change the subject.

'What was it like on your first night?' she said after a short pause.

'What do you mean?' said her mother.

'Come on you know what I'm talking about.' Sokunthea's mother searched for a way out of this conversation.

'I don't intend to spoil any part of your wedding day, so you will have to wait and see.'

Sokunthea's thoughts had repeatedly projected into the future and her sexual relationship with her future husband. Although her parents had talked freely about the benefits of this marriage, when sex was raised the subject was changed. Her mother had once told her that the man took care of all those things, a view that confused her even more. What things? Sokunthea's girl friends also viewed sex with interest but in what a woman on her wedding night should do or expect they were no more help than her mother.

'He's a doctor, he'll know what to do. I've heard they (the men) sleep on top of you; don't worry, you'll work it out.'

Sex education is not part of a young Cambodian girl's upbringing and, with an absence of magazines or books, introduction to this secretive activity occurs on the night. Her mother's final word on the subject was to have children quickly.

The early morning was beautiful with a clear blue sky with just a tinge of red and yellow, the kind of sky that foreigners, when they see it, exclaim at for its beauty while locals look up and can't see what all the fuss is about. Well, this morning Sokunthea was going to see and appreciate everything. My God, yes, the sky is beautiful, she thought. Although the war, which was raging in the rest of the country, had made things hard this was going to be a traditional wedding with the many changes of gowns, the food and drink. Not even the Vietnamese army was going to spoil this. Sokunthea didn't want to think about the war; her future husband had said that he may be conscripted now that his studies were over and this filled her with dread. Although she had no information about the war she had heard stories of many deaths. What a way to start married life and maybe a family, she thought. War, when will it end? As she looked across the narrow dusty road from her balcony the first signs of wedding activity began with the arrival of the *rong kar* erectors.

'They're early,' said her mother. 'I'd better get down there and sort them out.'

Sokunthea watched her mother depart knowing this was just as much her mother's day as hers. The *rong kar* would construct tents along the street with little concern for traffic. These would soon be followed by the chair and table delivery men; over four hundred guests were expected throughout the day, so food and drink had to be marshalled like a military campaign. Most Cambodian weddings occur this way: outside contractors who specialise in the wedding business would arrive at almost any location, erect tents and arrange and deliver food and drink for any number of guests. By Cambodian standards this was a small affair; richer families would invite up to a thousand guests with competition developing between families as to whose wedding was the largest, a competition in which Sokunthea was not interested. This was her day, a start to her new life, a husband and children, a new home in Phnom Penh, a life with a house and, she hoped, a garden to organise. As she watched the tents and tables going up her mother called to her from below the balcony.

'They seem to know what they are doing; I'll come up and help you dress.' It was time to begin a ritual of dressing and undressing. Throughout the day Cambodian custom would require her to change clothes on seven occasions as the wedding progressed from stage to stage. These stages in the wedding were the bride's delight, as she could demonstrate to all the wealth she would bring to the wedding, not just in money but in her own dressmaking skills and appearance, a prize worthy of wedlock. It was approaching early morning and she knew her husband and guests would be about to start their journey to her parents' house, the groom carrying coconut flowers on his head, as the sound of the first shell hit the city. The explosion, though some way off, jarred her thoughts. They'd shelled the city before and nothing had hit her street, nothing would happen, don't panic, she said to herself. Not American bombing, Vietnamese shelling or those other people – the Khmer Rouge – would stop her day, they couldn't, they shouldn't.

The procession appeared at the end of the street surrounded by the sound of traditional Khmei music; Sokunthea rushed into her small bedroom and with the assistance of her mother was ready in time to meet the people who were arriving carrying food, clothes, fruit and all kinds of drink perched upon their heads. As more and more guests arrived it was time for Sokunthea to change from her greeting dress to the dress for the gift ceremony. This required her to sit beside her future husband on a rug in the centre of a room while all the gifts were placed in front of them. The music continued and a traditional female singer sang while one of each gift was taken and placed within a basket. She looked at her husband-to-be and smiled; he appeared to be more nervous than she and had begun to sweat. The coconut flowers were taken away and later would be given to her parents. Then a teacher began a traditional story of the duty of marriage, its happiness and responsibility, then everyone ate of the fruits provided, taking a small piece as the basket was passed around.

By late morning it was time for the hair-cutting ceremony and another change of clothes for the bride. Sokunthea and her future husband sat behind a low table surrounded by flowers and dishes of water. A man and women danced around the table and encouraged her parents to cut Sokunthea and her future husband's hair; family and friends then joined in. As this occurred, the people cutting the hair would express their views with regard to the future happiness of the couple. Sokunthea and her husband-to-be sat close together and he tried to push his body closer to hers. According to custom Sokunthea did not respond, but she took this as a sign of his feelings for her.

It was time for Sokunthea to change again and, with her fiancé stand beneath the *rong kar* and greet their guests prior to eating. As they ate a young boy and girl danced around their table, then would move amongst the guests to collect money. On returning to the bride and groom's table, they would leave the money and then continue their collecting. With the meal coming to an end it was time for Sokunthea's fifth change in preparation for the monks. This was the religious wedding: they sat on a special pillow together and their parents and friends moved around them carrying seven candles. Then their wrists were tied together with a red cotton thread and a wise man gave them counsel as coconut flowers were thrown over them. The final ceremony was an eating ceremony where food was brought to them and they sat and fed each other. Although the official part of the wedding would occur in three days' time at the central registry, to them and their families they were now wed.

Only two more shells landed on Phnom Penh that day, well away from the wedding and of such little importance that no one heard them. The wedding, once started, developed a mind of its own and the bride and groom became just actors in a scene of their parents' pleasure. Sokunthea finally caught her breath as it all came to an end; her father had informed her that the wedding guests had paid more money than the wedding had cost so he was pleased. She could now stop bowing and smiling, changing and serving, greeting and departing. Weddings were hard work, she concluded. During this process her contact with her husband was fleeting as they both rushed to meet the needs of their own gender within the hustle which is characteristic of wedding receptions. Even when they had periods of close contact they hardly spoke and physical contact only occurred through occasional body rubbing. Now things were quiet they could sit together and talk, and for the first time he kissed her, a light delicate kiss on her forehead. She quickly looked around to see if any family members would object, then realised it didn't matter any more – she was married.

As more and more friends, guests and family disappeared she became aware of the event that was approaching. Surprisingly to her she suddenly became aware of her body; this frame that she had lived in for the past twenty-eight years was about to be shared with someone else. All the tales of her friends and mother were about to be exposed with regards to their knowledge and honesty. She could feel herself getting hot, her heart began to beat faster, it was time to sit down and have a drink. Her husband, who had wandered off to say goodbye to the last guests, returned and it was then that she noticed he was rather drunk. The great event of the night was therefore not going to happen; on arriving at the bedroom her husband quickly apologised and fell asleep, fully clothed, on the bed.

Sokunthea remained awake all night; after washing she lay beside her husband and stared at the roof. What an anti-climax, she thought but regained her positive thought by thinking that it was only her first married night – there would be many others. She began to think of their future together, the children they would have, the life they would lead. She was determined that she would continue working then relented, believing that she should put her husband first. Like all insomniacs she found the night lasting for ever; the harder she wished it to end the slower the time went. Her temperature again seemed to rise and a slight then greater pain developed in her abdomen; she knew what it was but it was early, at least a week early. As dawn began to break so did her period. Any hope of her husband consummating the marriage that morning had gone; just my luck, she thought. She rose to wash and find her mother who also couldn't sleep, thinking about

11

her daughter's first night.

'Are you all right?' said her mother.

'No, not really,' she said, then after a pause, 'he fell asleep, he was drunk and fell asleep.'

Her mother just laughed. 'Just like your father,' she said, 'only he was drunk for almost the first week, I thought he didn't like me.' They both began to laugh.

'Won't he be looking for you when he wakes up?' asked her mother.

'Well, that's the problem. I think it's me that will miss the first week – my period's started.'

'That's unfortunate,' said her mother.

The early beginning of her menstruation *was* unfortunate but, she thought, her husband was a doctor; he would understand. He did, partly due to guilt feelings for not having made the wedding night a night to remember, and partly enjoying the considerate husband role in understanding his young wife's problem. The delay in consummating the marriage for eight days was not to be discussed with other family members or friends at her husband's request, yet this period was to be a most educational time with female family members and married friends sharing with her their sexual experiences with their husbands. You had to join the club before you got the details, thought Sokunthea.

When the event finally took place the subtle planning and anxiety were what Sokunthea remembered. Although her menstruating had stopped several days earlier, her husband had made no approach towards her, and Sokunthea was occupied with their planned removal from her parents' home. She had worked hard most of the day packing and arranging for items to be transferred or stored, and it was time for a shower and to begin the preparation of dinner. Her husband appeared as if he had been waiting somewhere in the house; as she came out of the shower he was there. He placed his right hand around her and pulled her close to him. All she could feel was his hand across her shoulder and his lips falling onto hers, then she felt her *kroma* loosen and fall to the floor. She stood naked in front of her husband for the first time, in fact, naked in front of any man for the first time. Piseth stood back and looked at his wife.

'Beautiful,' he said. As he pulled her towards the bed she felt exposed, embarrassed by her nudity.

'What about my parents?' she blurted out.

'They're out, gone to the market,' was the reply. Sokunthea wondered if this was conspiratorial just to leave them alone. She climbed under the mosquito net and onto the bed, covering her naked body. Her husband undressed quickly and climbed in beside her. His hands began their travels across her body, sometimes smoothly sometimes hard. She lay on her back asking herself what she should do, how could she help, how should she react? She wished the advice-givers had provided more detail. His hands found her genitalia and she felt herself getting hot, he began to kiss her breasts while his fingers, gently at first, probed her vagina. It was then, with a short burst of pain, that his fingers entered her; he began to kiss her body, then her neck in a search for her lips. As he rose up her body with his mouth he penetrated her and for the first time she knew what having sex with a man was like. His body began to work into a rhythmic movement but she remained still. What shall I do, she thought, and engaged her husband in brief penetrating eye contact. She decided to respond to his body movements with her own, then worried that this might give her husband the impression that she may not be a virgin.

How, she wondered can I get more pleasure out of this without suggesting that I've done it before? Shortly after that her husband climaxed and rolled to one side. She looked at the ceiling and wondered what was next. Her husband moved through the mosquito net and headed for the bathroom; is that it? she thought. She felt the fluid between her legs and smelt the body odour of her husband upon her, but her thoughts were about how well she had done and what she should do next time.

Her husband returned. 'You'd better clean up before your parents get back,' he said.

'Did you arrange this with my mother?' she asked.

'Well, sort of; your mother said we needed some time together and I didn't disagree.'

Sex by appointment, thought Sokunthea as she stood under the shower for the second time.

'Have you and mother arranged other times for us?' she yelled from the shower.

'Don't be like that,' said her husband as she entered the bedroom. 'She was only aware that we hadn't… well, you know.'

After a pause, Sokunthea said, 'What do you want me to do in bed, I mean sexually?'

'I don't know, just like you were, I suppose, why, was it no good?'

'I just want it to be perfect I suppose,' said Sokunthea.

'I've no knowledge of sex you know,' said Piseth. 'I never went with prostitutes or any thing like that.'

'I'm glad to hear it,' said Sokunthea.

'It's not easy for me. I know all women expect the man to have all the answers, all the moves, but I don't. You are my first woman – I hope we can work it out together, positions and all that.' Piseth began to feel uncomfortable.

'Yes, we'll work it out,' said Sokunthea, glad to hear that she was his first woman but wondering how he would respond if she let her feelings enter her actions the next time. She dressed slowly and followed her husband downstairs. Her first experience of sex had not satisfied her but she didn't know what she could do about it. As if on cue her parents entered from their shopping expedition, her mother came over to help with dinner.

'Well?' she asked, with a large smile on her face.

'Thank you for the time,' and, as Sokunthea turned away, she added, 'but don't make it regular.'

Over dinner, while the two men were talking about the war, Sokunthea avoided her mother's eyes. Later she asked her daughter what the problem was.

'How can a Cambodian woman get enjoyment from her husband when, if she takes an active part, her husband may think she is not a virgin and if she just lays there, ah, that's not sex, not for me anyway.'

'You have to get involved slowly, let the man think he has taught you how.' Sokunthea's mother knew something else was troubling her daughter. 'What's the real problem?' she asked.

'It was just an anti-climax. I just expected… I don't know what I expected,' said Sokunthea with a shrug of the shoulders.

'You will have to guide him, but slowly, tell him what you enjoy him doing but don't pressure him or he'll find his pleasure elsewhere and you'll find yourself pregnant,' said her mother. 'There's a war coming; you don't want to find yourself with a baby.'

'I thought you wanted me to have children. As quickly as possible was your advice.'

'Well, I've new advice,' said her mother.

Phnom Penh

Following the wedding, Sokunthea and her husband Piseth moved into his cousin's house in Phnom Penh. The home they had hoped to share had been taken over by refugees and although the landlord offered to reduce the rent if they cleared them out it was a task they were not prepared to do. It was a small place, consisting of three rooms upstairs and two on the ground floor, but Piseth's cousin and his wife had not started a family yet so there was plenty of space for four adults. During the evenings the main topic of conversation was the ongoing war. Stories abounded in Phnom Penh about battles won and lost but all agreed that Cambodia must defeat the dreaded enemy, Vietnam. Occasionally stories about the Khmer Rouge would be spoken but nobody really appeared to know who they were. To everybody things were getting worse, this could be seen in daily travelling around the city. Refugees had appeared in their thousands on the streets and the price of food in the shops had rocketed upwards.

Sokunthea and Piseth were managing to survive by earning extra money outside their government jobs; Sokunthea taught English to the more wealthy members of the community while her husband had started a small private practice. Life, although growing in problems, was still tolerable even with the occasional shelling, but this was to be shattered by three major events. The first was of pleasure as Sokunthea realised that she was pregnant, and later, when it was confirmed, the pleasure spread amongst the two families. The second was the dreaded news that Piseth would be conscripted into the army of Lon Nol. The thought of losing her husband so soon after the wedding became too much for Sokunthea, with the growing baby inside her. She began to feel her marriage had been cursed. She hated this war more and more, she hated the shelling, she hated the growing number of refugees, she hated her husband for being conscripted and then she felt guilty about it all. If she was going to lose her husband, she decided, she would spend as much time as possible with him now, she would pamper him with his favourite foods and dedicate her time to him. This meant giving up her extra job and taking on more of the household work.

It was in pursuit of this goal that on one September morning she set off to the local market for the family food. Normally the housekeeper would carry out this chore but they had had to let her go due to the spiralling costs of domestic help. So, on this day Sokunthea set off determined to buy something special for her husband. As she walked to the market other forces were gathering in Phnom Penh that day: the refugees, who now numbered several hundred thousand, had decided that starving in the streets of Phnom Penh was not for them. The riots that developed began in a small way as all riots do, a spark was needed and an individual who would not accept or put up with the situation any longer, one whom people would follow but after the event not know his name or where he came from. Such an incident was to occur in the central market of Phnom Penh. Like all markets in major cities, this attracted customers of all social classes with a wide range of goods; it had its beggars and injured soldiers no longer able-bodied and therefore of no further use to Lon Nol. Some say it was begun by such a soldier who decided that he had fought and lost a leg for his country and now he was going to share in some of the food that was on show. It doesn't matter who started it – once it began many followers joined in. The market soon became a battleground of fighting shop owners and hungry refugees, guns appeared from shop counters as refugees smashed and grabbed what they could.

In the middle of all this were the usual shoppers; suddenly caught up in a nightmare; Sokunthea found herself trapped in a semi-closed area with shops on two sides and a high wall on a third. The local shop owners then barricaded the only exit deciding it was the best way to protect their property against the rioters, a plan that would have been sound if someone had not decided to use fire. Sokunthea and several shoppers and shop owners crowded back behind the barricade. They could hear gunfire and every time they did they retreated further until their backs were against the wall. The fire just appeared; later it was thought that someone had thrown a Molotov cocktail, but for the now-trapped group panic set in. Several individuals decided to run through the fire; the ones left behind did not know how successful they were although they could hear the screams, which seemed to accompany every exit.

Sokunthea decided that option was not for her; as the smoke and flames began to move towards them she crouched low in search of fresh air – she was not going to die here, not now. She stood up and noticed the iron frame that ran up the side of the end shop. Above it were the high ventilation slots, which are common in tropical buildings. If she could get that high she thought, she might be able to reach the top of the wall and then safety. Her fellow trapped companions were still too busy screaming and clutching each other to listen to her so she dropped her bag and began to climb. She had reached the top of the iron frame when others in the panicking group below realised there may be a way out. It was then, of course, that the urgency to escape was added to the state of panic, a terrible brew. Men began to scramble up the iron frame pulling and pushing each other, the notion of women and children first being abandoned in favour of male survival, and fights broke out as they tried to climb over each other. Sokunthea had just reached the air vents when the first hand from below grabbed her leg; she kicked out, mainly to free herself for the next move up but from below it was interpreted as a hostile act. The hand slipped slightly, dislodging her shoe, then grasped again, this time below the knee. She could not move, it was useless to resist as the man below pulled himself up alongside her, then pushing against her levered himself onto the top of the wall.

'Bastard!' she yelled at him, and, as if awakened from a dream, the man turned, looked down at her and offered his hand. She took it and he hurled her up beside him. Within seconds Sokunthea and the stranger were hurtling through the air, backwards down the far side of the dividing wall. When she opened her eyes her husband was the first person she saw. She realised that she was in a hospital bed.

'How did I get here?' she asked.

'You were brought from the market, what happened?'

'I remember the fire and the man on the wall.'

'He's dead,' said her husband. Tears then swelled up in both their eyes and they just held each other.

Her fall had been caused by a gas canister exploding in the fire; of the people trapped, five had died and nine were seriously injured. Her stranger on the wall had broken his neck when he fell. The food rioting that day was to cost over fifty lives and, although all lives are special, Sokunthea was to discover later that fifty-one had died, including the loss of her baby. The self-incrimination began slowly for Sokunthea and grew and grew until her discharge from hospital. On her arrival back at her cousin's house her mother was waiting and she became the target of its release.

'It's all my fault, I'm a curse to the marriage, if only I'd carried on working,' she told her mother.

'No one is to blame and Piseth doesn't need you falling apart at this moment,' her mother replied.

'Right from the beginning this marriage has had problems and it's all because of me, Piseth doesn't deserve this.'

'And neither do I,' said her mother angrily. 'I planned this marriage because it was right and I don't want these ideas about who's to blame. If there is blame to be given then it's me who got it all wrong.' She began to cry.

Sokunthea knew that by criticising the marriage she was also criticising her family for arranging such a bad marriage. 'It's not you it's me,' she said. 'I'm just feeling sorry for myself, I want Piseth here to tell me it's all okay. Your choice of husband was great.' She tried to console her mother.

'There are more people than you hurting, you know. Just because we don't show it, it doesn't mean we don't have pain.'

Sokunthea's need for understanding had started a feeling of guilt now so she changed the subject. 'I'm just sorry that you won't have a grandchild soon.'

'The grandchild can wait. Remember what I said about the war – your father said things are getting worse, more and more refugees, less and less food.' She began to cry again. 'Phnom Penh is becoming a prison. Nobody can get out and every day more arrive,' she said.

'Well, that's one advantage of Piseth being conscripted into the military, we do get food.'

'For how long?' her mother replied.

Later that day her husband announced that he had been ordered to report to Neak Loung, an important supply route for Phnom Penh based on the Mekong River. Sokunthea had already heard about Neak Loung – many battles had occurred there with many deaths and she was afraid. Was this the final piece of bad luck in her marriage?

'Aren't you afraid of the fighting?' she asked him one evening.

'Of course, but I won't do any fighting. I'm a doctor, I just clear up the mess,' he said.

'But what about the shelling? That doesn't discriminate with regards to doctors and soldiers.'

'Nobody sets out to kill doctors and wounded soldiers, there are rules, even in war.'

'What rules?' she said.

'You don't kill wounded soldiers, what's the point? They can't fight and where there's wounded soldiers there's doctors, and anyway, after all wars they need doctors so there's no point in targeting them and trying to kill them all.'

His point seemed reasonable.

'But if you're in the middle of Neak Loung and they start shelling…'

'Look,' he cut her off, 'they know where the hospital is sited, nobody just kills doctors.' She realised he didn't want to talk any more, but knew she could use his argument against him when she decided that she would face the war with her husband. Their time together had been so little that she felt if it were to end it should end together. Her husband at first thought it was a reaction to her fall and bad news; he later thought it was just plain stupid and refused but Sokunthea was adamant she would go even if she walked there herself. Her husband relented and said he would inquire about the possibilities of her accompanying him. He was to discover that the army of Lon Nol did not mind who the soldiers took with them providing they went, they fought and they died.

Sokunthea's fears were to be put on hold for a while as the

military decided they needed a young doctor at Phnom Penh airport; although she knew that the airport was a target for Vietnamese and Khmer Rouge shelling she felt safer because her husband would be nearer home. Life became a little improved. Her husband, now in the military, was able to obtain enough food for all the family and his regular salary bought the extras, yet, as if the good times could not last forever, Sokunthea had noticed how following sex she would develop abdominal pains. At first she thought it was irregular period pains again but when they began occurring in the day also she knew something was wrong. She decided not to tell her husband and made an appointment at a private clinic in the city centre. The results confirmed her fears – she was unable to have children, the fall from the wall had extracted a greater toll than anyone thought. To the traditional Cambodian family such news was a real curse so she decided she would not tell anyone, but the night after she obtained the results she began to construct her defence mechanisms.

'Did you mind losing the baby?' she asked her husband as they prepared for bed.

'It wasn't planned,' he said.

'Do you think we should try again?' she inquired.

'Let's stick with the pills for a while – unless you are having problems?'

'No problems,' she said. 'I'm just concerned about this war, that's all.' Sokunthea knew this was a lie, the first she had told her husband.

'So am I,' he said. 'From a child's point of view, of course.' He didn't want to upset his wife. They climbed into bed and she rolled onto her side and held her husband to her.

'How many children do you want?'

'We Chinese want lots,' he replied and softly laughed.

'How many is lots?' as she dug her fingers into his ribs.

'Oh, one of each will do, and we can start after the war.' He rolled over and clicked out the light, a sure sign that sex was not needed tonight. Sokunthea didn't mind; after receiving the news from the clinic even her own sexual demands had been frozen. She lay in the dark on her back wondering if she ever wanted sex again. Without the possibility of children what was this twice

21

weekly, five-minutes-a-time activity all about?

As 1973 rolled on Sokunthea and her husband thought the war and the military had forgotten them. At night Piseth would tell Sokunthea about all the injured soldiers being brought in from the front line and how the rich of Phnom Penh were getting out. As food was provided directly by the military to Piseth, Sokunthea was not experiencing the spiralling cost and shortage of food within Phnom Penh, signs that the city was being starved out. By the middle of 1973 the Vietnamese began shelling the city regularly, at first targeting the airport then later the city. On these nights with their husbands away, Sokunthea and her cousin, whose name was Phally, would sit in a ground floor room and think of their husbands. This night the shelling appeared to be concentrated on their district, several times the house shook and tiles would abandon the roof and crash as they hit the ground only adding to their anxiety.

During these times Sokunthea would always wonder if her husband was thinking of her as much as she of him. Previously her husband had informed her that during the shelling of the airport the officers and invited guests would take to a deep shelter where Hennessy flowed like water. He had joked that if the enemy had invaded at that time everybody would be drunk and nobody would stop them. Now, in this dark room, she wished she had some Hennessy, then wondered what it tasted like. By the second night the shelling intensified but had no pattern, no rhythm – an explosion here then a long pause then two in rapid succession. The sound of the explosions appeared to be far off and Sokunthea was thinking that the airport must be the target when a loud crash occurred, followed by roof tiles and timbers crashing to the ground. Both women huddled together and screamed. When they realised they were not hurt they lit a small candle to look at the damage, Amidst the rubble and smoke they could see a round grey canister. Sokunthea immediately knew what it was.

'It's the bomb,' she said to Phally. 'Get out quick.' She grabbed Phally and dragged her out of the house. As they stumbled into the street neighbours appeared asking questions and checking the damage.

'Get back, there's a bomb inside!' she screamed.

The neighbours quickly turned and began running, screaming back to their houses.

'What about our things?' said Phally. 'We can't leave.'

'And we can't stay,' said Sokunthea. 'It could explode at any time.'

Phally began to cry. 'What shall we do?' she said. 'If only our husbands were here.'

'Well, they are not,' said Sokunthea. Sokunthea didn't know if it would blow up or not, she only knew she and Phally could not sleep in the street all night, so she went back into the house to collect some clothes, blankets and money.

'Where shall we go?' asked Phally.

'To my parents' house,' replied Sokunthea.

'But that's at the other side of the city!' and at this Phally began to cry again.

'Look, stop crying. We can't stay here all night and none of your neighbours seem willing to help us so it's walk or freeze. Anyway, we can take motodops,' insisted Sokunthea.

'They're so expensive now, I think we should stay,' mumbled Phally through her tears.

'Stay! Are you crazy? The bomb is still in there and it could explode.'

Sokunthea felt she was about to lose her temper.

'But my husband will not know where I am,' whimpered Phally.

'We'll leave a message for them both with a neighbour, if I can find one,' said Sokunthea through her teeth.

They found a neighbour three doors up who had decided to stay in their house.

'It could be dangerous,' said Sokunthea.

'We have nowhere else to go, and anyway if we move out the refugees will move in,' said the neighbour.

'That's it,' said Phally. 'I'm not leaving my house to refugees.'

'If we or refugees go wandering around that house there will be no house and no us.' Sokunthea's temper was beginning to rise.

Phally just cried. Sokunthea gave the message to the neighbours and put her arm around Phally and they set off. They decided to walk to Sokunthea's parents' house some three kilometres away, leaving behind a broken house and neighbours in panic. To Sokunthea it seemed strange that no motodops were active that night – people caught out when shelling occurs usually want to get home quickly. Phally said it was the war and a lack of gas.

On the following day Sokunthea's husband returned. A military policeman informed him of the dangerous state of the house. He asked about his wife and was told by a neighbour where she had gone. He arrived at Sokunthea's parents' house just as they were having tea, and although he would have liked to have taken his wife in his arms, protocol meant that he politely asked about her well being. Although she was glad to see him his news was not what she wanted to hear: he was going to Neak Loung.

'Well, that settles the problem of somewhere to live,' she said.

'What do you mean?' he replied.

'Neak Loung, there's no way I'm not going.'

'Sokunthea, it will be dangerous, it's the front line of the war!'

'Then we'll fight it together,' was her reply. Piseth glanced at her parents, hoping for support, but they just carried on drinking their tea.

'Has she always been this stubborn?' he asked of her father, who just nodded.

'Yes,' said her mother, 'and you won't convince her otherwise.' She looked at Sokunthea and winked. Piseth knew he could not stop her and thought it may not be a bad idea to have her around.

'Okay,' he said, 'we'd better start planning.' He smiled at her and drank his tea.

Neak Loung

His orders demanded his departure in two days. His wife could accompany him but she was not the responsibility of the army; her transport, accommodation and security was his responsibility. Piseth's original strategy of refusing her request to go on the grounds of her security had evaporated with the previous days' shelling. His arguments simply ran out, she was going. Even if she had to make her own arrangements she was going.

Neak Loung was a small ferry crossing on the Mekong River which had grown into a major tactical town as it supplied Phnom Penh. Everybody wanted it and if they couldn't have it they were going to make sure nobody else had it. In August 1973 the Lon Nol government of Cambodia held it, but only just. The Mekong above and below was regularly closed by the Vietcong or the Khmer Rouge and the hinterland around it was a stagnant battlefield with trenches, wire and minefields, a relic from the First World War. Access into and out of Neak Loung was either by boat on the Mekong or overland on the opposite bank and then crossing the Mekong by ferry. Both approaches were hazardous. To get river traffic in and out boats travelled in convoys and were supported by helicopter gunships strafing the river banks. These gunships were often provided by the South Vietnamese and Americans who realised that if Neak Loung was to fall then the Vietnamese could develop a supply depot to support its war in South Vietnam.

On August 6th, with the South Vietnamese riding shotgun, Lon Nol support troops arrived, many with accompanying wives and children. Travelling down the Mekong with helicopters swooping overhead Sokunthea thought this very exciting. No wonder men like their little war games, she thought. The passage was smooth and uneventful but on arrival she was tired, all that adrenaline pumped up on the way down had now collapsed into an anti-climax and she had collapsed along with it. Her husband was to join the medical team there and was shown to a small room with half of one wall missing. This would be their home for as long as Piseth's tour of duty lasted. Sokunthea gave thanks that she had not had to bring a baby here and then quickly felt guilty and abandoned the thought. Her husband's concerns were how his wife would cope within such a dangerous and unpredictable environment. Sokunthea seemed to lose her fatigue on seeing the living quarters, here she had a woman's thing to do – cleaning up. Her husband had to visit his commanding officer for instructions, which gave Sokunthea all the time she needed. On his return Piseth discovered the living area clean and the smell of *somla machu* boiling in the pan. Maybe having Sokunthea here won't be a bad thing, he thought.

Piseth had reason to agree with his assessment on the following day. The sky over Neak Loung was clear and the new military personnel were meeting in groups to be assigned their new duties. The experienced troops had already explained how the wet season meant that the Khmer Rouge would withdraw and that the North Vietnamese were planning to strike the Americans. Civilians and military alike were looking forward to several months where life could almost get back to normal. Then the first bombs hit. Piseth and Sokunthea had heard about the blanket bombings that the Americans had carried out in southern Cambodia and the horror stories that followed them; they now discovered that talking about them and experiencing them are two totally different things.

As the bombs hit, the ground appeared to leap into the air, buildings that were not hit shook violently and collapsed on their occupants, houses when hit just disappeared. Many people were killed through sheer panic, cars running over them as they ran into the road, running into dangerous buildings to save loved ones only for the remaining part of the building to fall on them. Yet it was the whistle that got to Sokunthea, as the bomb racing towards the ground came into earshot. Sokunthea and Piseth had planned to stay in their house and try to repair the hole in the wall. As the first bombs hit they both thought the shelling had started again from the North Vietnamese, then the patterns of explosions suggested it was something else. A line of bombs fell along the perimeter of the hospital grounds, their power and sound enough to send both of them crashing to the ground. A group of the new medical workers were out there exercising, an activity which Piseth had been given permission to miss due to his urgent house repair needs. Instinctively he ran towards them and Sokunthea followed. Like three footprints of a giant the ground had been eaten away in a neat row and along with them most of the garrison's medical staff. Piseth then appeared to freeze.

'What can we do, what shall we do?' he whispered.

Sokunthea grabbed him, pulling towards the surgical tent, but when they got there Piseth looked around as if in a daze.

'Medicine is not like this,' he said and then repeated himself, only louder. Sokunthea looked into his face and then did something that no Cambodian woman would ever do to her husband – she hit him, hard across the face.

'Take the emergency pack and get back out there, I'll find the stretchers.' He turned and ran towards the hole where thirty men should have been. After grabbing two canvas stretchers she ran after him. She hoped the bombing would not come back as she headed straight for her husband. He was sat on the edge of the crater holding the dead body of a friend.

'Leave him,' Sokunthea shouted. Her husband looked at her with tears rolling down his face.

'I went to medical school with him, I promised to look after him.'

'He's dead. Start looking after the living,' she said.

As other help arrived five people were saved from the crater. Sokunthea was involved most of the day and night organising the transfer of injured people to field hospitals and the dead to a makeshift mortuary. She helped with minor operations, bandaging and washing away blood, lots of blood. After help had arrived she lost track of her husband. She was too busy; only later did she discover him back at the crater where it had all started, looking into its depth. She took his arm and led him home. That night, lying in a small cot alone, she reflected on the day and concluded that she had actually enjoyed it. Even though so many had died she had for the first time been treated as an equal by the men, they'd even taken orders from her without question. If that was the world of men and how they felt, she wanted more.

The official figures state that one hundred and twenty-five people were killed and over two hundred and fifty injured through pilot error but Sokunthea and Piseth knew the number was much higher. For Sokunthea, the bombing of Neak Loung taught her many lessons as a save-yourself attitude prevailed. Senior officers and rich merchants who were still operating out of the town ran to their shelters and closed them to others; these same people Sokunthea would see encouraging and championing the poor soldiers as they prepared themselves for battle, a battle that if victorious would guarantee the wealth of these true dogs of war. No commonality or mutual sharing appeared to happen at these times, only the law of the jungle: look after yourself and be strong. Several people, including young children, had been found outside these rich mans shelters burnt to death by the afterblast of some terrible device; they were just swept away in the rush to start business going again.

Sokunthea's experiences in caring for the injured, laying out the dead and the skills that male health workers forgot, talking, listening and comforting the bereaved relatives, were buzzing inside her head. Even though many had died and there was much to do she continued to enjoy the experience and became more and more involved. Over the coming months she learnt about different drugs, how to recognise different wounds and conditions and how to treat them. She cared for grateful soldiers injured on the perimeter line, some dying and wanting to speak to their mothers before the end, a role she never could fulfil. Then, as all good Cambodian women, she would arrive home with her husband and begin the work of cooking, cleaning and comforting. As with all relationships where husband and wife work together then fracture into gender roles when getting home, Sokunthea began to review her relationship with her husband. At night usually after sex she would lie awake wondering about her future, working through plans if her husband left her. She justified these ideas by proposing that no Cambodian man will stay with a wife that can't have children, that has struck him, that has seen him face a challenge and fail. Yet the real problem lay with her: she enjoyed working and being considered on equal terms with men, she knew she could cope better with most situations than her husband. Her husband was kind, handsome and not sexually demanding although that did leave her frustrated at times; he was a kind, docile man. As Sokunthea worked all this through in her mind she realised that her experiences over the past eighteen months had changed her. Maybe when this war was over she would start again with someone else.

As the months rolled by Sokunthea and her husband grew further apart. After work he would remain back at the hospital under some pretext of work, but in reality he'd begun drinking with other colleagues. Sokunthea in part understood this; the wounded men were still coming in from the perimeters, some with appalling injuries, and her husband with his wounded pride had to show that he could cope with this. Dealing with such sights every day puts strains on the human spirit but when that spirit has been damaged or a weakness exposed it becomes an act of pride. Now the bombing was over Sokunthea was slowly relegated to a nursing role, no more treating patients or helping in theatre as before. She knew this was the action of her husband but couldn't decide if it was just professional pride or if he didn't want her to become any more hardened. Away from work they hardly spoke to each other and their sex life had come to an end. As Sokunthea's sleepless nights increased she believed her husband was only staying with her because of the war; he wouldn't abandon her in the middle of this war-torn depot town, but when it was over. She knew the answer already.

The experienced soldiers were right. Due to the rainy season attacks on Neak Loung stopped; only the river traffic remained as a military target. In Neak Loung there was an almost visible relaxation. Small bars and restaurants opened out on to the street and the markets grew in size. Due to the deaths from the bombing Piseth had been promoted within the military medical ranks and with promotion came improved food supplies and accommodation. This elevation in status appeared to have an impact on Piseth's overall confidence, he was now a senior officer, and people respected him, but unfortunately he believed that this did not apply to his wife. Their relationship over these past months had not improved and Piseth began to stay out all night.

Sokunthea decided she would not stay and suffer the embarrassment. Although Cambodian culture demanded that she stay by her husband's side no matter what he does, new cultures could be broken. After spending another night alone she decided it was time to face her husband. She washed, dressed and headed for the military hospital. She went straight to her husband's office, opened the door and walked straight in.

'We must find time to talk,' she said, trying to remain calm.

'I am very busy these days, you don't seem to appreciate that,' replied Piseth.

'Our relationship appears to have stopped,' she said.

'Has it?'

'Don't be difficult about this. You have stopped sleeping with me, stopped coming home – just stopped. I hear stories of you sleeping here in your office all night… well!' She began to get a little annoyed.

'I said you shouldn't have come here, us living together under such pressure…' he paused.

'It changes people.'

'It can help them understand each other more and bring them together,' she said.

'Or burst them apart,' he replied.

'Is that what you think about us, that we've burst apart?'

Piseth was looking down at his shoes. 'You know how I reacted, if we get any more like that – well.'

'You know how I reacted, and together we got the job done. All I learnt is that we're a team and can work together – you hear?'

He looked up at her and tears swelled in his eyes; he stepped across the room and held her close. That night Sokunthea and her husband had the best sex she had ever had with their bodies working together and their climax coming as one.

They concentrated on their jobs, Piseth at the hospital and Sokunthea working in the local orphanage and for several months their relationship appeared to get back to normal. Then in early 1974, reports began to arrive about heavy shelling and death in Phnom Penh. Sokunthea wondered about her parents and would go to the waterfront every day to gather further information. As March approached Piseth got some good news.

'I'm being posted to Phnom Penh,' he said.

'When do we go?' responded Sokunthea with obvious enthusiasm.

'Don't be so pleased,' he said. 'Phnom Penh is being shelled almost every day.'

'Well at least we'll be near my parents,' she responded.

'The army want us to move tomorrow.'

'Tomorrow! That's quick, what about our things, saying goodbye to friends?'

'They say tomorrow or never; they expect the Vietnamese to increase the number of attacks on the river, so we either go tomorrow or stay.'

This was no real choice for Sokunthea; after hearing about the shelling of Phnom Penh she was determined to get back there. That afternoon she spent her time packing and seeing close friends to say goodbye. Although she was against this war, any war, she knew she had learnt so much more about herself here in Neak Loung.

In March the river level of the Mekong is low, so the military had decided that large convoys supported by helicopter gunships was not affordable anymore. Boats had to take their chance and this had led to a reduction in river traffic resulting in almost every vessel being a target. A lucrative trade had developed with young Cambodians, army deserters and small-time crooks hiring out small fast motorboats. They would start before dawn and race the two-hour journey to Phnom Penh. The price was high so only the rich and the desperate could afford it. Piseth decided it was the only safe way out for him and his wife. It would mean handing over all the money he had saved whilst in Neak Loung, but what is money worth if you're dead? Piseth told his wife of his plan.

'I'm worried,' she said. 'Rumour is that when attacked they push the passengers overboard and return. It's even said that they are in league with the Vietnamese.'

'Look, there will be several military personnel with us. If they try any trickery we'll be able to deal with it.'

Sokunthea didn't want to be thought to be questioning her husband again. 'Okay, we risk the speedboat.'

They left their small military apartment while it was still dark and headed towards the waterfront carrying one bag each; that was all the speedboat people would allow. Sokunthea had noticed that Piseth was not in uniform; in fact, he had left all his possessions associated with the military behind.

'Where's your uniform?' she asked as they stumbled along the dark track to the waterfront.

'I was told it best not to wear it, in fact, when we get on the boat if anyone asks what I did in Neak Loung just say I was a doctor.'

'Why?' Sokunthea stopped; she had suddenly become very nervous.

'Don't worry,' said her husband, and, after a pause, 'a colleague told me that they don't like to ferry military people to Phnom Penh, they say it attracts the artillery.'

'Are the other military travellers going out of uniform?' she inquired.

'I don't know, just remember I'm just a doctor!' he insisted.

Even at this early hour the waterfront area was very active; boats of different size and type were unloading or loading. Groups of people were gathering, preparing themselves for departure. What struck Sokunthea as very strange was that, even with all this activity, everything was very quiet.

'This way,' said her husband. She followed him along a narrow dusty track, stepping over rice bags and what looked like ammunition boxes.

'Are they coming in or going out?' she asked her husband.

'What do you think?' he replied.

'But doesn't the army need all its ammunition here?' she continued.

Her husband turned and looked at her. 'The ammunition is paid to the Rouge in return for not attacking us.'

'But who do they attack?' she continued.

'The Vietnamese of course. Look, the Rouge hate Lon Nol but they hate the Vietnamese even more. If we give them arms and ammunition they leave our boats alone and stockpile their newly-acquired weapons for the day when they fight the Vietnamese.'

'But I thought they were all on the same side,' she said.

'We're all on the same side against Vietnam,' replied Piseth.

They got to the end of the track and Sokunthea could see a group of small fibreglass speedboats. Here the cargo appeared to be only people. She looked at the group and noticed one or two uniforms in the crowd.

'Remember,' said Piseth, 'I'm a doctor.'

A man dressed in various military fatigues and T-shirts approached. 'Got the rest of the money?' he said.

'When we make it to Phnom Penh,' said Piseth.

'Okay, but I need to see it; people have cheated us in the past.'

Sokunthea looked at the man and couldn't imagine anyone being so stupid as to try and cheat him. He was clearly an ex-soldier but on whose side she didn't know. He had lost his right leg and walked with that rolling gait so typical of amputees with artificial legs, but he was strong. He was tall for a Cambodian and his dark brown face showed he had lived out in the fields; his hands were strong and worn and his grip was solid. She felt this as he helped her into the boat.

'Not a man to cross,' she said to her husband as he climbed into the boat. Her husband looked up at the man then turned to his wife, smiled and nodded in agreement.

The boat filled up with six more people. Three were obvious prostitutes returning to Phnom Penh after a money-earning tour of the front-line troops and they were being accompanied by their madam. The other two were men; one was dressed in civilian clothes while the other wore the uniform of a captain. Surprisingly to Sokunthea, instead of telling the soldier to remove his uniform or cover it up, the boatman appeared overjoyed to see him, patting him on the back and offering him a drink of local wine.

The boat moved out of its berth slowly, and Piseth put his arm around Sokunthea and smiled. 'Two hours and we'll be in Phnom Penh; your parents will be surprised!'

Sokunthea, in all the rush to pack and say her goodbyes had forgotten that her parents would not know that were coming. 'I just hope they're safe,' she said.

The boat straightened and then the sound for which they had paid almost one year's salary became audible. They raced off up the river to home as the first streaks of light appeared on the horizon. The noise of the engine made talking difficult so Sokunthea decided to scan the banks and watch the daybreak. Her husband stared straight ahead as if he had many things on his mind, and the boat just glided on. The river had been straight for the first kilometre or two but now it began to twist and turn; this was in part to follow the river, but rapid movement was also necessary due to sandbanks and the sunken hulls of other unfortunate adventurers.

After thirty minutes of travelling Sokunthea noticed a change in the engine noise – it was slowing down. She looked at her husband and saw that he'd noticed too. As they came round a sandy bank they realised why; there, on the sandbank in the middle of this stretch of the Mekong was a small boat and five heavily-armed men. Sokunthea's heart began to race. This is it, she thought, and grabbed her husband's hand. The soldiers were all dressed in black, some with red *kromas* across their heads and shoulders; she could tell by their uniforms, the same uniforms she had seen in posters declaring that these were the enemy and had to be killed, that these were the Khmer Rouge.

The speedboat pulled in alongside the small, flat-bottomed boat of the Khmer Rouge. The boatman was the first off; as he walked up the sandbank he greeted one of the men like an old friend. The passengers were ordered off and told to line up on the thin sandbank; to Sokunthea's surprise the military officer walked up to the boatman and the Rouge leader and began to talk. The Khmer Rouge leader then turned to the assembled passengers. He walked past the prostitutes and stopped at the madam and, with great speed and precision, drew his revolver and shot her in the head. As the madam fell back into the water Sokunthea grabbed her husband's arm and battled to control the tears that were swelling up inside her.

'Scum,' the Rouge leader said and moved down the line. He stopped in front of the businessman. 'How much will you supply us with this time?' he asked.

'About four tons,' came the reply. 'The Americans are cutting back, they're not just throwing this stuff around like before.'

The Rouge leader looked straight at the businessman. 'Americans, I hate all Americans.'

'The delivery is on its way up now. It should be here in about one hour; the crew's been paid.'

'You will stay to check its delivery,' the leader cut in.

'No; I've got to get to Phnom Penh to arrange the next shipment, that's the deal.'

On hearing this the Rouge leader hit him hard across the face. 'You will obey the Ankor, if you do not you will be re-educated.' At this all the soldiers and boatmen began to laugh.

He moved to Piseth, then looked at Sokunthea. 'Well, what do we have here?' he said.

Sokunthea looked at the leader. Apart from his dark skin and large burn on his left cheek his most striking feature was his eyes. These were dark and cold, the kind that expose the message that the owner is looking at absolute filth. Piseth began to speak but the leader brought his fist up into Piseth's throat. He collapsed to the floor fighting for breath, then coughing and choking. Sokunthea reached for him but as she did the leader grabbed her hair and pulled her to her feet. The pain was excruciating as he twisted her head upwards and back; she was determined not to scream but couldn't control the rush of tears down her face.

'Why are you on this boat?' came the cold voice.

Sokunthea's mind was racing; if she told the truth they were dead. 'I need to get to Phnom Penh, I'm pregnant and there's a problem.'

He let her go. 'And who is this?' he inquired.

'My husband; we're trying to save our baby.' She began to cry. Her husband, who was still lying on the floor and unable to talk, was praying that she wouldn't mention that he was a soldier. The leader looked down at Piseth then shouted over his shoulder to the boatman.

'Do you know him?' pointing at Piseth.

'No,' said the boatman.

'Is he military?' he said to the Cambodian officer.

'Never seen him,' came the reply.

His cold eyes pinned Sokunthea. 'Will you return to Neak Loung?' he asked.

'Never,' she said.

He stared at her for what seemed like an hour, then turned

slightly, put his hand behind the neck of the businessman, grabbed his collar and pulled him out of the line and onto his face. 'On the boat,' he said.

The boatman began to usher the prostitutes onto the boat; Sokunthea grabbed her husband, pulling him up and moving him towards the speedboat where he stumbled aboard.

'You,' the leader's voice came from behind Sokunthea. She turned and as she did the butt of his pistol hit her hard and low in the abdomen. She buckled and fell back into the boat.

'Only Ankor will save the children!' he shouted as the boat pulled away.

As Sokunthea lay in the bottom of the boat holding her abdomen she knew she and Piseth were lucky to get away with their lives. She could hardly believe the scene she had just endured; it was as if the war were just a business with soldiers working for both sides and everyone fighting for money. As these thoughts were going through her head one of the prostitutes sat down beside her.

'Are you okay?' she inquired.

'Please don't move me, just let me lay here,' replied Sokunthea.

The girl just sat beside her. 'She wasn't that bad, you know,' said the prostitute. 'She looked after us and paid us well; I know people look down on us but I couldn't work in the fields any more, not with this war, and to get a job in Phnom Penh...' she stopped and slowly began to rise.

'It's okay,' said Sokunthea. 'I know it's hard.' There was a silence between them only broken when Sokunthea asked the girl her name.

'Touch,' she said.

'So what will you do when you get back to Phnom Penh?'

'Compete for soldiers like all the other girls.' This shocked Sokunthea slightly; she had never thought of prostitutes competing for custom between each other. To her prostitution was all about men seeking out the woman for pleasure. The thought of the woman seeking out the man for money just seemed strange.

'I wish this war would end,' said Touch. 'In the beginning all those soldiers meant extra earnings, but now, well, I hope it ends soon.' She began to cry.

The conversation had helped take Sokunthea's mind off her pain and she was able to sit up and look around. She found her husband being comforted by the other prostitutes and apparently enjoying it; she then glanced at the boatman.

'It's business!' he shouted. 'Just business!' as if knowing what was on her mind.

Touch put her arm around her and they huddled together in the bottom of the boat. Sokunthea began thinking about the effect this war was having on the people, rice girls having no alternative but prostitution, soldiers who would sell their loyalty and the Khmer Rouge who would try to kill an unborn child for some ideology. It was during this time that the first motor shell hit the water twenty yards ahead.

'It's a warning shot,' the boatman said, 'just a warning shot.' Ahead he saw a flag being waved and he slowed and pulled into the shore.

Immediately soldiers in combat uniform appeared and signalled for the boatman to get off. He climbed ashore and scrambled up the bank. Sokunthea and the others waited in the boat; two guards were training their automatic weapons on them, which encouraged everyone to sit still. Sokunthea noticed the guards looking in particular at the women and talking between themselves; she knew enough Vietnamese to understand what were their desired intentions. Again the boatman returned with what looked like an officer.

'You lot, out.' He pointed to the prostitutes, who began to cry.

'No,' said Sokunthea.

'Look, lady,' said the boatman, 'they wanted you as well, pregnant or not, they don't care, so shut up and get into the back of the boat.' Sokunthea noticed the fear in his voice and crawled back to her husband. She kept her head below the rim of the boat as it sped away, but the screams of the girls would stay with her all her life.

They arrived in Phnom Penh by late morning. As they slowed to cruising speed the boatman said, 'Don't tell anyone, you hear? If you want to live, don't tell.'

The tone of his voice and his face was enough to convince Sokunthea that he meant what he said. When they landed Sokunthea and her husband, who still had problems talking, climbed ashore. Sokunthea had no intention of making the final payment and none was asked for. They found a motodop and headed for her mother's house.

The house appeared to be just the same as ever with little sign of war damage in the neighbourhood. Her parents were happy to see them and made them welcome. As they sat down for lunch Sokunthea's mother informed them of the death of Phally and her husband.

'How?' asked Sokunthea.

'They went back to their house; the area was being slowly taken over by refugees, and when they got there they found that the army hadn't done anything – the bomb was still there and refugees were squatting. Phally's husband and some neighbours began fighting with the refugees and we think they disturbed the bomb-boom!' Rany began to cry.

'How could they be so stupid?' said Sokunthea, standing and beginning to pace the room in order to control her emotions.

'It's the shelling; we've been okay but in the poorer areas, there's no houses left,' said Rany.

Turning to Piseth, Kimbly said, 'Have you heard from your parents?' Piseth shook his head.

'There's no road routes out,' he continued. 'I hope they're all right.'

Piseth, who still couldn't speak properly, just nodded.

'So what happened to you?' asked Rany.

'It's just a throat infection,' interrupted Sokunthea.

'It looks serious,' said her father.

'We'll try the hospitals, tomorrow,' Sokunthea replied.

'We'll be prepared, they're full,' said her mother.

Sokunthea decided it was time for an afternoon sleep; she and Piseth were tired and a shower and familiar bed were a dream come true. As she undressed for the shower she noticed a large bruise developing on her lower abdomen and some dried blood on her inner thigh. Although her pregnancy story had been a lie she found it hard to imagine a man deliberately trying to kill an unborn child. When she came out of the shower she found her husband already lying on the bed with his hands to his throat asleep; it reminded her of her wedding night.

Home

After a couple of days Piseth reported to his new military base and was immediately sent home on sick leave. A soldier who couldn't shout orders was no good, even a doctor. Sokunthea had decided to try and get work with some aid agency; she'd heard they paid good money and in dollars. The Phnom Penh that they now saw was not the one they remembered. The streets were filling with new refugees every day, the central market had shrunk to only half its normal size and what was left was just a large warehouse controlled by the military. The food inside was supposed to support the refugees but the stories of night-time lorry convoys of food out of the city were common. Piseth still got his food ration but that too was smaller in amount and of poorer quality. Sokunthea's parents both continued to work, simply because there was nothing else to do, but with no pay and no real work to do the war was creeping up on them.

One evening, sat on the dark balcony with only a candle for light Piseth said, 'Were you really pregnant as you said to the Rouge soldier?'

Sokunthea saw an opportunity of informing her husband and her family of her inability to have children but she also recognised the consequences of telling the truth. 'I'm not sure,' she said. 'I could have been.'

'And now, what about now?' he asked.

'I still get pain down there, that's why I can't always manage sex.'

'Oh, that's okay don't worry,' responded Piseth.

'How would you feel if I couldn't have children?' she asked.

'Children are so important to us Chinese; who will remember us when we are dead if there are no children?' was the reply. 'I know you were hurt protecting me; it seems you've been protecting me ever since we were married but life without children...' he stopped and looked straight at her.

Sokunthea stayed calm on the outside but inside she was screaming; yes, she had protected him, supported him and now when she needed some understanding she was confronted with remembering the dead.

'You have never referred to your Chinese heritage before or the need to be remembered. I thought you didn't believe in these old religions.'

'Maybe it's the war, but of late I've been thinking about many things,' he whispered.

The silence was broken by the arrival of her parents bringing Chinese tea.

'I know you two would prefer to be alone but we can't afford two candles,' her mother said. She began to pour the tea. 'How is your throat Piseth?' she enquired.

'Much better,' he said, smiling at his mother-in-law.

'You'll be going back to barracks, then?' cut in Kimbly.

'I'll check in tomorrow, even if I can't shout I can treat patients,' he said.

'What about you?' Kimbly said to her daughter.

'Good news; I've got a job with the Swiss Red Cross.'

'Doing what?' asked Piseth.

'Translating, of course, and they pay two hundred each month, in dollars. I knew my languages would come in handy,' she said, grinning and hooking at her father.

'That's worth a celebration,' said her father, who disappeared downstairs. When he returned he was carrying a bottle of Hennessy and two glasses.

'Left over from the wedding,' he said, and poured out two drinks.

'Hey, where's mine?' said Sokunthea.

'This is not for women,' said her father, nodding towards the Hennessy bottle.

'Well, it's my celebration and therefore it's for this woman,' she said, grabbing the bottle and taking a swig. As the liquid inside hit the back of her throat her eyes began to water and she swallowed the drink amidst coughing and spluttering. The men laughed and her mother reached over and took the bottle from her.

'It's not for women,' she said, and they all laughed.

Next day Sokunthea was up early laying out her clothes for the first day at her new job; Piseth, who had come to bed drunk, having helped his father-in-law empty the bottle, was still asleep. She showered and dressed quickly, not wanting to disturb him. When she got downstairs her mother was preparing the traditional breakfast of rice soup and dried fish.

'What does this job entail?' she asked.

'Simple; the medical people speak French or English while the people speak Cambodian. Me, I fill in the gaps,' she smiled.

'Language, what a strange thing to earn money for. In my day growing food and cutting rice was the job for a woman.'

'And having children I suppose; well, I can't.' Sokunthea paused, realising what she had said.

Her mother glanced up and, with tears in her eyes, said, 'I know.'

Sokunthea felt cold. 'How do you know?'

'After Phally's house blew up the police brought some things around; in them was a letter to you from the hospital asking if you wanted further tests.'

'Who else knows?'

'Just your father.'

Sokunthea grabbed her bag and headed for the door. 'Don't tell Piseth, understand?'

Her mother nodded. 'What happened on the boat ride from Neak Loung?' she said.

Sokunthea turned and looked straight at her mother. 'I nearly died,' she said and left.

Due to petrol shortages and the high cost of motodops, Sokunthea walked to work; the journey was straightforward taking her along the wide boulevards of Monereth and Monivong. These were two of the major arteries of Phnom Penh; she was headed for the Phnom Penh municipal building where the Swiss Red Cross had started a shelter for refugees. Nothing could have prepared Sokunthea for what she encountered as she reached the gates of the municipal building where crowds of refugees, police and military personnel were gathered. She had been given a pass, which she showed to a group of soldiers who waved her forward and through the gate. Inside was no less crowded although the gender balance had changed, outside it was mixed gender while in here only women and children. She walked to the back of the building past a never-ending line of women with children; ahead was a large white tent erected by the Red Cross where she and the queue were headed. Sokunthea was glad to get inside; even at this early hour the sun was becoming unbearable.

'Good morning,' came a voice she recognised; it belonged to one of the doctors who had interviewed her, who had been introduced as Sue.

'Am I late?' she said.

'No, they always start this early,' she said, referring to the queue.

'What should I do first?' Sokunthea asked.

'Well, we have a tricky one for you.' Sue lead Sokunthea into a small area at the back of the tent, where before her sat a middle-aged Cambodian woman dressed in rags. 'We only offer a service to refugees and the street people but sometimes we find the more affluent members of the community think they are missing out on something free and try to cash in; we think this is one of them,' said Sue.

'What do you want me to do?'

'Find out,' said Sue.

Sokunthea sat in front of the woman. 'Good day,' she said. The woman nodded.

'Where have you come from?' Sokunthea asked.

'Kompong Chhnang,' was the reply.

'And what did you do there?'

'I'm a field worker, but with the bombing...' she began to cry.

'How did you get to Phnom Penh?' asked Sokunthea calmly.

'By boat, of course,' the woman snapped and began to cry more loudly.

'And when did you arrive in Phnom Penh?' she said quietly.

'Yesterday, why all these questions?' The woman looked menacingly at Sokunthea.

'We need to gather information about people's movements, that's all,' said Sokunthea. 'Where in Kompong Chhnang did you exactly work?'

'In the town,' she replied.

'But I thought you said you worked in the fields?'

The woman stopped crying and looked straight at Sokunthea. 'I worked in the fields and in town.'

'May I look at your hands?' she asked the woman.

The woman stared at her again, then after a short pause slowly stood. 'Who are you to question me?' she shouted. She then turned and walked out of the tent.

Sue, who had stood in the corner throughout this exchange, just looked at Sokunthea then said, 'You'll do. Come on let's get a drink.'

They went out of the rear of the tent and into a small concrete building where a few tables and chairs were scattered.

'Do you get many like her?'

'Quite a few,' said Sue. 'They think aid and see free and so they want it; no matter what it is they want their share. It's greed really,' she continued, 'but of course we aid people often encourage it.'

'I'm not sure I understand,' said Sokunthea.

'Never mind,' said Sue.

'Is that what you will want me to be doing?'

'Well, yes, but mainly getting details, information from the refugees, where they have come from, what the problems are; of course, there will be times when we will need you to explain to refugees who need medical treatment what is happening and talk to relatives, okay?'

'Fine, but I sure don't want to be a policeman all the time, checking hands and trying to contradict stories.'

'You won't be, don't worry,' said Sue.

After a drink Sokunthea was taken back to the registration tent and began work. That day she was involved in two other cases of investigation, both cases exposed middle class women trying to get something for free and both cases left Sokunthea feeling ashamed to be Cambodian.

'It's time for you to go home,' said Sue. 'It's four o'clock – that's enough for day one.' Sokunthea didn't argue she was tired.

'How will you get back home?' asked Sue.

'Walk,' said Sokunthea.

'Where do you live?'

'Deum Kor,' she said.

'I pass there, you can share my motodop,' said Sue. Sokunthea wasn't going to argue; a lift home was a dream.

That evening while helping her mother with the washing, Sokunthea told her of the day's events.

'Oh, it's easy to tell a rice girl from a city girl,' said her mother.

'How?' asked Sokunthea.

'Give her a glass of water,' she replied.

'A glass? Explain,' said Sokunthea.

'Rice girls are used to drinking brown-tinted water, field water; I remember you always said you preferred it to any other,' continued her mother.

'Okay, okay, but how does this prove anything?' asked Sokunthea.

'Well, silly,' said her mother, sounding a little impatient, 'city folk won't drink tinted water, they only want it clear. Stand the women in the sun for a while, then offer them a drink of tinted water. If they refuse, complain or even just sip it, you've got a city girl; rice girls, they just drink it down.'

'Where did you learn this from?' asked Sokunthea.

'Every rice girl knows it; you've been out of the fields too long.' Her mother laughed and turned away.

As 1974 continued, the war came closer and closer to Phnom Penh; the refugees grew and grew as food became scarcer and scarcer. Sokunthea continued her work with the Red Cross and while Piseth had returned to the army, her parents had both stopped work and remained at home. Piseth had started up a private practice again and, using Sokunthea's dollars, was able to buy drugs cheaply from a military source, as drugs like food were becoming expensive items. Although Sokunthea didn't like this black-market approach to acquiring drugs she knew Piseth needed to show her that he could compete on dollar terms; to have a wife earning more than a husband was not acceptable in Cambodia.

For security reasons Piseth would store all his drugs at his in-law's house; they were bought at random from the army or when a plane or boat managed to get into Phnom Penh. One evening Sokunthea noticed the drugs that Piseth had purchased that day had the Red Cross symbol on the side.

'Where did you get these?' she asked.

'From the airport,' came the reply.

'But they're for a charity, a charity which helps the poor, my charity!' Her anger began to rise.

'Look, nobody cares about the refugees, many of them aren't even refugees, and don't think the aid agencies don't know about this – they do, they're part of the business as well.'

'What do you mean?' asked Sokunthea.

'The aid agencies survive and get paid all those high salaries by inflating their figures; if they say there's two hundred starving children nobody in the West cares, but if they say one hundred thousand will starve the money rolls in. Wake up – it's all a sham.' He turned to stow the drugs away in a large trunk beneath the bed. 'I'm going out,' he said.

'Where?'

'To buy more drugs from those aid agency angels.' He stared at her. 'They're in a business, the suffering business, and they make it pay.' He stormed off, down the stairs. 'Don't wait up for me; I'll be late,' and he left.

The following day at work Sokunthea asked Sue about what her husband had said.

'There are corrupt people in every organisation,' she said.

'But how can people steal from what is helping their country?'

'Greed,' said Sue and the conversation ended.

As the year came to an end Sokunthea saw less and less of her husband and during this period her mother's health deteriorated. She was diagnosed as having hepatitis with bowel and lung complications. Sokunthea divided her day between work and caring for her mother; as to the whereabouts of her husband she did not know and realised she did not care. One evening after helping her mother to bed, a call came up from the street.

'Hey, Sokunthea, it's me!'

She knew the voice straight away; it was her husband. 'Come up,' she said.

'No, I want us to go for a drive.'

'A drive? Where? You've got a car?' she responded.

'Come on, we need to talk,' he said.

Sokunthea remembered using that line herself. 'Okay, I'll be right down!' She told her father she would be back in time to give her mother her nightly medication and went outside. The car, large and black, was sort of official-looking, Sokunthea thought. 'Why have you bought a car?' she said.

'Is that all you have to say?' he said.

'Okay, where have you been and why don't you come home any more?'

'We have a new home,' he said, 'We're going there now.'

Sokunthea sat back in the car seat in silence, then said, 'My mother is dying.' This was the first time she had spoken to anyone about her mother and her pain.

'We have to concentrate on the living, remember.'

'You bastard!' she said. 'You just don't care about anyone!'

'Look,' he said, 'this war is creating opportunities that I would have had to work for twenty years as a doctor to get; people are selling houses, cars, everything cheap just to get out, the war has really spooked them.'

'Is that where you're taking me, a cheap house, a house you've cheated out of someone?' came the reply.

'Listen, you may not like what I'm doing but it's for us, after this war ends whoever wins will need skilled professionals like us. I'm just making sure that we enter that new world with some basics behind us.'

'A house,' she said.

'Yes, a house and money, but above all, we'll be together.'

'I've not seen you for five weeks.' She stared at him.

'I've been busy,' he replied.

'With your drugs?'

'With business.'

The car stopped outside a large gate; Piseth blew the horn and someone opened it. It was the kind of house Sokunthea had always dreamed of, big, very big and with a garden. She knew her father would love the garden. Her father – with this she thought of her mother and her medication.

'I can't stay long; as I told you my mother is ill,' she said.

'Okay, just a brief look inside and then I'll take you back,' he replied.

The house was already furnished but scattered around were the empty packages of drugs, some with the Red Cross symbol while others stated MILITARY USE ONLY; even drugs for the front line are being re-routed, she thought. Upstairs it was clear that several beds had been slept in and the occasional item of personal clothing could be seen.

'Is this a hotel?' she asked.

'People have been staying over,' he shrugged.

'And this is yours, legally?'

'Legally,' he said.

'I don't want to know,' came the reply. 'I must return to my mother.'

'Okay, but I want you to move in; the house needs a woman and I need my wife.'

She stared at him and frowned. 'Take me home.'

As they drove back to her parent's house, Piseth appeared to become more nervous.

'What's the problem?' she said.

'I have a shipment coming in tonight and must make a pay-off,' he replied.

'How much?' asked Sokunthea.

'I'm not...' he blurted.

'Don't lie to me, this is why I'm here, right?' said Sokunthea sharply.

'It's business, it's for our future,' he responded.

'How much?'

'Five thousand dollars,' he whispered.

'All my savings, in other words.' She shook her head and stared out of the window.

'The deal tonight may be the last; we'll be ready for whoever runs the country after this goes down. I've got the rest but I'm just short; I need your help,' he said as the car turned down the track leading to her mother's house.

'Okay,' she said. 'Wait here; I'll get it now.' She left the car and walked into the house. Sokunthea hid her money in a large box beneath her father's tool box in the kitchen; she had saved over five thousand dollars over the years and like all Cambodians, was saving it for her old age. She opened the box and removed the black cloth in which the money was wrapped, then paused and wondered if what she was doing was right. 'You silly cow,' she said, slammed the lid, turned and went outside.

She returned to the house and was confronted by her father.

'I didn't think you were coming,' he said. Although very tired, she just smiled, shrugged her shoulders and headed for her mother's room.

'Have you been in?' she asked over her shoulder.

'I looked in, but she was asleep,' came the reply.

Sokunthea lit a candle and entered the room. She approached the bed and first shook her mother's shoulders gently, then a little more strongly. 'Mother!' she shouted, but her mother was never going to hear her.

Sokunthea's mother died on 27 December 1974 and, as custom demands, the ceremony lasted through first seven then thirty days. During this time and to her surprise her husband had been supportive, enough for her to move into his new house. The death of his wife had hit Kimbly very hard; he refused to leave his home and go with his daughter and son-in-law and often promised to visit, an event that never occurred.

As the new dry season arrived in Cambodia the communist forces began renewed attacks on government forces and as the number of refugees increased, the Red Cross announced it was pulling out. The pull out date was to be early February, with the refugee mission closing at the end of January. All Cambodian staff were thanked for their service and given three months' salary; Sokunthea went home in tears. That evening, with her husband not home, Sue arrived to say a private goodbye.

'I'm terribly sorry,' she said.

'But why? We're supposed to be winning!' Sokunthea blurted out.

'That's not our information; we've been told it's only a short time before the government falls.'

'But whoever wins will need help.' She began to cry.

'Look, they're flying us out tonight because it's so dangerous; I want you to take this money.'

'No,' Sokunthea said. 'The new government will need people like me; I'll survive.'

'Listen,' said Sue, 'these Khmer Rouge are different, we have reports of them committing terrible atrocities. I don't want to frighten you but they're different.'

'They're Khmei and I'm Khmei, we'll be all right,' she said.

'Your husband is an officer in the army, right?' said Sue.

'A medical officer, yes,' came the reply.

'Tell him, if things start to go wrong, to get out of uniform; Khmeis or not they kill Lon Nol officers.' Sue looked straight at Sokunthea, who realised she wasn't joking.

They said their farewells, with hugs and kisses and promises of meeting again, promises which both knew would never be fulfilled, and when Sokunthea returned to the study she found the gift of money on the table. Well, she thought, it may come in handy.

That night and for the following week Piseth didn't come home, so Sokunthea decided to go to the military hospital and find him. As she walked down the street approaching the hospital she became aware of a peculiar, dreadful smell. When she entered the hospital grounds she knew its source: the hospital was a scene of chaos with patients overspilling from the buildings into the grounds. Many were surrounded by their families, chickens, pigs and other four-legged creatures. The sight of blood splashed against walls and turning green grass red was mingled with the cries of people in agony.

Sokunthea just stared; she began to walk towards a building marked *Administration*, stepping over patients and animals. Every corner of every building or tree base was the site of human defecation, and human garbage was scattered everywhere with pigs spreading the waste. She arrived at the building and, stepping past more wounded soldiers, approached a makeshift counter.

'Is Dr Piseth Morm here?' she said. 'I'm his wife, Sokunthea.' She smiled.

The receptionist turned and looked at a young military officer sitting behind her, who stood up slowly and approached the counter.

'What is your name?' he asked politely.

'Sokunthea Morm,' she said. 'What's the problem?' thinking her husband had been transferred to the front, or, even worse, was dead, she asked, 'What's happened to him?'

'I have no idea,' said the young officer. 'Your husband has been thrown out of the army for failure to do his duty and black-market activities; we would be very interested in his whereabouts.' Sokunthea just stared at the soldier. 'When did you last see him?' he continued.

Sokunthea's mind was now racing ahead. 'Mrs Morm!' the officer shouted. 'When did you last see him?'

Sokunthea was shaken back to the present by the loud voice. 'Over a month ago,' she said.

'I don't expect you to turn him in but if we catch him we'll shoot him.' The officer gave her a shallow smile and returned to his seat.

Sokunthea went shopping in the old market for food then went to her father's house. On her arrival she was surprised to find her husband there. 'I've just been to your hospital,' she said, 'the military is after you.'

'I've finished with the military, bloody hypocrites,' he said.

'Their message was that if they find you they will shoot you,' she continued.

'Then we'll have to make sure they don't find me.'

'Why couldn't you have told me you'd left?' she pursued.

'Because of us, because of your mother, because they'll shoot me, because I didn't want you worried.' He rose to leave. 'Do you want a lift home?'

'No, thanks, I need to talk to my father, cook him a proper meal.' He nodded and left. 'How long has he been here?' she asked her father.

'An hour or two,' came the reply.

'Why? He's never bothered before,' she said.

'Oh, he needed the money I promised him.'

Sokunthea froze, then the red flush of rage burst up from her chest and neck and into her face. 'How much?' she said trying to remain calm.

'I've only got ten thousand,' he said.

'How much?' she repeated.

'All,' he said.

Sokunthea made his dinner and, before leaving, gave him all

the money she had. She arranged a motodop and paid on arrival at Piseth's home. His car was in the covered garage and he was sitting in the study.

'Don't say anything, he offered it,' he said as she headed for him.

'He's a poor old man who will need that money!' she screamed.

'Listen, you know I'm in deep with the racketeers. Well, now they're worried, I mean men who would kill you for smiling at them are worried, scared stiff.' His face was white.

'So what's…' she began.

'They're scared stiff of these Rouge guys,' he continued. 'The stories they tell about how they are treating people, their own Cambodian people, are scary and I want us out. You now how they treated you; you were supposed to be pregnant and he did that. I'm telling you, if these people win then we don't want to be here.' His colour started to return slowly.

'So you take my father's money to escape and leave him here,' she said.

'I'm trying to get us out, all of us.'

'And if we can't?' she replied.

'For God's sake give me some support here; I'm trying to get us into a good position so that when this war is over and it's safe to return we will be on top.' He stood up and stormed across the room looking for a drink.

'Why don't you discuss these things? Then it wouldn't be so bad.' She knew the answer already: in Cambodian tradition, men make the decisions.

Piseth found what he was looking for and took a long swig. 'The communists have closed the Mekong; we can't get out anyway.'

Sokunthea looked up at him, curled her fist and with all her strength punched him in the nose. He fell back, and she turned and marched off to bed locking the door behind her.

The following morning she woke to find her husband had already departed. As she looked out of the balcony she saw the ever-present security man standing under a tree enjoying the shade. She decided it was time to investigate what it was that he was guarding. She began in the lower rooms but found only dust and empty boxes, and then moved upstairs, checking every room – nothing.

'There must be something here,' she said to herself. 'He's not outside for my benefit,' nodding towards the guard. She went back into the master bedroom and sat on the bed. As she stood up, she glanced into the toilet and noticed some soil on the seat, so she wandered over. Around the base of the pan was more soil. 'Shoes,' she said out loud; she looked up and above her was a trapdoor leading to the loft. She changed quickly into trousers and T-shirt and, finding some stepladders in the storeroom, began climbing.

The loft held many large boxes of pharmaceuticals; these drugs were the property of everybody except her husband. Boxes for the Red Cross, the US embassy, the military, all full of the drugs desperately needed by wounded and dying soldiers. As she worked her way around the back of the boxes she noticed a small bed and several empty bottles of Johnnie Walker; he sleeps and drinks here, she thought. It was then that she heard a crackling noise behind her, the kind of noise she had heard many times when changing radio stations. She moved more slowly along the roof joists towards a small doorway in the main loft partition. She poked her head forward and as she did a crashing hand smashed down onto her lower head and neck. She fell to the floor further injuring her face and head; when she awoke she was lying on the small loft bed, and her husband was holding a handkerchief to her head.

'I nearly killed you,' he said.

'I think you did,' she said, trying to stand.

'Lay still,' he said, 'the hole in your head will need stitches.'

She collapsed back down. 'What were you doing?' he asked.

'Finding out why there are so many guards around this house when there's nothing inside, and if you say to protect me I'll punch you again,' she groaned and he laughed.

'So what do you think you've found?' he continued.

'I don't know, some big bully tried to knock my head off,' she said, staring at him.

'You didn't hear the radio?' he asked, looking straight at her.

'So that's what it was,' she replied. 'What's it for?'

'I report to the Americans.'

'Report what?'

'Traffic on the river, number of wounded coming into Phnom Penh, just basic data,' he said, shrugging his shoulders.

'Why do they want to know that?' she wondered.

'They know this war is finished and they've lost, they just want a few of us around when it all settles, to tell them about the Rouge, I suppose.'

'So from a doctor to a racketeer to a spy. I hate this war and what it's doing to us.' She tried to stand.

'Lay still. I'll have to put a couple of stitches into your head; it's a good job I've got all the stuff here,' he laughed. She lay still while the wound was treated. 'There,' he said when he'd finished, 'now get some sleep if you can.'

'What are these Rouge like?' she asked.

'My reports are that they are cruel, very cruel; what they will do to the likes of us I don't know.'

'I thought you said professionals like us would always be needed,' she responded.

'When the Americans pull out they will leave behind over one million refugees needing food. The southern rice fields have been bombed and mined into non-existence and this present government is only concerned with its bank accounts. Sinarth, the boatman who brought us out of Neak Loung, tells me the Rouge are using people as slave labour to grow rice, and the only professionals they want are rice growers.' He strapped a dressing over her cut. Sokunthea sat on the bed wondering what the future held for them. If we can't feed ourselves what the hell will we do? she thought. She slept on the small bed in the loft until her husband woke her.

'Come, let me help you down the steps, before I have to go,' he said.

'Where this time?' she replied.

'Listen, I go out every night to collect information, down on the waterfront,' he said.

'Aren't you afraid the military will get you?' she enquired.

'Don't you listen? I work for the Americans, our military

works for the Americans – nobody will touch me,' he said with some disgust.

'I want to go with you,' she said.

'Absolutely not. A woman down there is seen as a liability or a whore or both, so no.' He shot a hard glance at her.

'Then I will go as your whore; I know where the waterfront is and where the boatman berths his boat, so you take me or I go alone.' She glared back.

'Slut,' he said. 'Okay, but men rule down there, you start asking stupid questions and you may find yourself having to practise your new role.'

They ate dinner in silence then washed and dressed.

'What is that?' Piseth said on seeing his wife's choice of clothes. 'You're supposed to be a whore, remember.' Sokunthea had chosen a long traditional Cambodian skirt with a high-collared Chinese top. She looked up and down her attire, agreed and went back into the bedroom. On her return she wore a short blue skirt and a tight tank-top. Her husband looked at her and realised just how beautiful she was.

'I'm not sure this is a good idea,' he said.

'Why, is this no good?' she said referring to her clothes.

'Too good,' he said.

They drove towards the waterfront avoiding all the main roads. The journey took about half an hour, and when they pulled into a partially hidden driveway Sokunthea said, 'Where are we?'

'Sinarth's,' came the reply. They climbed out of the car and as she stared into the dark foyer she noticed Sinarth standing in the dark.

'Who's the whore?' he said, then he looked again. 'What's she doing here?'

'I don't know,' said Piseth.

'Well, we've no time to argue, we're late for the meeting already.' They all got back into the car, and Sinarth turned to Sokunthea and looked her up and down.

'She could be trouble for us,' he said to Piseth.

'She's my whore; providing she stays with me she'll be okay,' he replied.

'I hope so,' said Sinarth, looking at Sokunthea's clothes again.

They drove for another half-hour along the back roads, which seemed to gradually deteriorate the further they went. Nobody spoke and Sokunthea began to wonder what she was doing there. The car turned down a narrow road, which got narrower and narrower and then just before it seemed they would be squashed by the walls, Piseth turned the car into a hidden courtyard. As they got out of the car the gates were closed behind them and a voice directed them to another wall where a small gate opened through which they walked. In the dark they stumbled forward down a rough track then over a plank of wood acting as a bridge, then along more track. Sokunthea found this walk very difficult in her high-heeled shoes and stumbled several times.

Finally, they came to what looked like a roof covering the ground with music coming from it; as they got nearer she noticed steps cut away in the ground leading to a doorway. Sinarth knocked and a voice asked who was there and demanded a password. The door then opened and the three of them entered a large dimly lit room. Around the walls were booths where people were drinking and whores and punters cavorting; in the middle of the floor was a small stage where a number of young women at various stages of undress were dancing. The smell of alcohol, cigarette smoke and cheap perfume filled the place. This was why Sokunthea had come, this place was alive; no war, no refugees, no sitting at home being a good housewife while the men go out. If she was going to die she was going to live first. They were led to a booth away from the door; when they got there they saw their meeting companions had already arrived and settled in.

'Sorry we're...' began Piseth.

'Who's the woman?' asked a thick-set man wearing a military combat jacket.

'She's just somebody I picked up,' he said.

'Not bad,' came the reply.

'Let's get down to business,' said Sinarth, looking very irritated by the conversation based on Sokunthea.

They all sat down. With the original party was a young prostitute, who whispered to Sokunthea, 'Let's go to the toilet.' She stood and walked off. Sokunthea followed, but as she walked into the toilet the prostitute grabbed her arm and swung her around, slamming her into the wall and ramming her forearm into her throat.

'How long have you been on the game?' she said.

'Not long,' said Sokunthea, not daring to struggle.

'You've come to a very dangerous place,' the girl said, 'the men out there are killers.'

'Why are you here?'

The prostitute burst out laughing. 'To get fucked, of course, what about you?' The bluntness of the response shocked Sokunthea. Although she had known that prostitutes would be part of her husband's destination, when the stark reality hit her she wasn't ready.

'This is where the real money is,' continued the prostitute, 'and I don't need a new face for competition.'

'I'm not competition,' Sokunthea said. 'I've come with this one guy.'

'Are you blind?' the prostitute cut in. 'The way my guys were looking at you, you're in for an interesting evening. God you are green,' she concluded and released her grip. 'My name's Thea,' she said, 'and my advice to you is to get your man to take you home.'

'But this place is so – interesting,' said Sokunthea.

'Interesting?' Thea shook her head. 'For who?' she asked. 'The men drink and make their business, they add a few drugs to the cocktail, sometimes fight and sometimes kill each other – the river is just the other side of that wall – after that they grab a woman, any woman, and screw.' She engaged Sokunthea eye to eye. 'We'd better get back. Remember: don't say you're new to the game, it only attracts them; don't drink too much, don't smoke the dope and avoid the tablets at all costs. If you find yourself in a difficult position with a guy don't struggle; he'll beat you and it turns them on. Stay next to your fella and don't go anywhere alone with a man, they're all sharks.'

Sokunthea splashed some water onto her face and they exited the toilet. As they approached the booth the man with Thea and another man came towards them. They grabbed both women around the waist and lifted them onto the small stage.

'Strip,' they said, and pressed a hundred dollars into their hands. As they stood there in the dim lights everybody began to chant, 'Strip, strip, strip.'

Thea looked at Sokunthea. 'Do it,' she said.

'I can't,' she replied, and looked at her husband; he too was shouting the same message, strip.

Thea began unbuttoning her top while twisting and writhing her body to the orchestrated applause. 'Follow me,' she whispered to Sokunthea who had frozen. Sokunthea followed, slowly at first, but then got into the swing of it, peeling off her outer clothes and gyrating her body. The adrenaline was pumping through her body like never before. She looked into the semi-darkness to see who was looking and became more excited as she thought they were all looking at her. She began to rub her body against Thea's and both women embraced and kissed as they removed each other's bras. The noise from the watching audience increased as the two women removed their panties and Thea began oral sex with Sokunthea, then the two naked women, lying on the floor of the stage, began to simulate intercourse with each other.

Sokunthea had never felt this way before, her whole body screamed for Thea to kiss, bite and penetrate it and her head was swimming in emotions and memories of lost love. She had never felt this with her husband. As she lay there naked with Thea on top of her, her mind began to focus and she could hear the bedlam around her, then a man grabbed her and started to pull her to her feet. A bottle then crashed over him and he slid to the floor; another man appeared and, grabbing her round the waist, pulled her off the stage. She had no idea where Thea or her husband were, as fights appeared to be happening everywhere.

The man appeared to be dragging her towards a doorway when a chair smashed against his back and he and she crashed to the floor. She was then pulled up by the two men who had started this whole affair and they propelled her through the door and along a small corridor. They bundled her into a room and threw her onto a bed. Sokunthea screamed, for she knew what came next; the first man jumped on top of her and tried to pin her limbs down but she struggled and kicked out, ignoring what Thea had said. The second man appeared: he was naked and punched her hard in the abdomen then slapped her several times across the head until she felt dizzy and decided she could not resist any more.

She lay on the bed waiting for the first man to penetrate her but nothing happened. She rolled over and noticed one of the men lying over a small table, seemingly dead. She then felt someone climb on the bed behind her so she turned to look at her rapist and saw it was Sinarth. He kissed her gently and began to stroke her breasts. Whispering to her to relax as his mouth migrated down her body and as his tongue passed over her labia and entered her body the adrenaline fired again within her. Shortly after, when he entered her with his penis, which was hard and long, she stopped caring. Her head was awash with delight as his body would rise and then slam into hers; she felt he was reaching her stomach as well as her mind. She had longed for this; sex, real sex, the sex she wanted from her husband but didn't get, the sex of her relatives' stories and dreams. She screamed out softly but he just continued his rhythm.

She woke as the sun was rising and he was still lying by her side. She had taken her clothes off on the stage and therefore had none, until she saw the clothes of one of her would-be rapists and dressed in them. As she got to the door Sinarth spoke.

'He's no good, you know.' Sokunthea knew who he meant as she turned and looked at him. 'The first sign of trouble and he'll ditch you to save his own neck,' he continued.

'And you, what about you?' she replied.

He lay silently on the bed and Sokunthea turned to go. 'Hold it,' he said, 'it might not be safe. Wait; I'll get dressed.'

As they left the bedroom Sokunthea saw the body of her other would-be assailant, dead in the corridor. They walked back into the main room and she saw Thea's dead body on the stage; either before or after her death many men had taken advantage of an unprotected vagina. Sokunthea began to cry, and, picking up a tablecloth, covered Thea's body. It was then that she heard a groan from the booth where all this had started. It was her husband, high on some cocktail of drugs and alcohol. He had passed out and missed all the events; Sokunthea thought he was pathetic. They dragged him to his feet and Sinarth carried him to his car.

'I'll drive you back,' he said and she just nodded.

Piseth was sick four times on the return journey and on arrival at home they put him straight to bed. As they left his bedroom Sinarth reached for Sokunthea, pulled her to him and kissed her; she didn't resist.

'Leave him,' he said. 'I'm going to make a run for Thailand; my parents were born there. You could say it's home, it will be hard but not impossible.'

She stared at him. 'I can't,' she replied.

'Why not?' he asked.

'I have my father as well as him to look after; if the Rouge are as bad as they say they'll need all the help they can get.' She pulled away and walked downstairs.

'He was planning to leave you; it was all arranged, out on one of the last transport planes, ten thousand a seat,' he said. Sokunthea was not surprised by the news, she just shrugged her shoulders and walked into the study. 'I'm going to try tomorrow night, we can make it.'

'No,' she said.

'You are crazy; after what we did last night, you don't love him.'

Sokunthea snapped. 'What do you men know about love? Love to men is sex, a good screw; well, to women it's more about loyalty, tradition and respect for the family, and, yes that does mean taking on a downtrodden role where men do what they wish and women stay at home crying.' She began to fluster. 'Love is knowing someone is there, someone who has shared many experiences with you, not just sticking their penis inside you.' She stopped.

He stood up, wished her good fortune and left. She would never see him again.

Sokunthea and Piseth were to go on no more nightly trips; over the following weeks dark figures were to come to their home and remove the drugs. She and her husband never spoke of the nightclub experience, and their relationship developed into that of a sister and brother. Sokunthea spent her time visiting her father, praying to her mother and reading. The news that Neak Loung had fallen to the Rouge and that the Americans were running away was of no interest to her but a small passage in one of the last broadsheets being produced talked of two men shot while trying to escape the city; she knew who one was. One group leave us to go home, another is shot trying to get home and I'm living in a house that is not my home, she thought and decided she would go to her father, to her real home.

Exodus

'Come out, come out!'

Sokunthea stirred in her bed.

'Leave your houses, the city is not secure, come out!' continued the call from the street. Sokunthea and Piseth went onto the balcony, below they saw their neighbours vacating their houses and gathering in the street.

'Outside,' said a voice behind them.

They turned to find a Khmer Rouge soldier, who gestured with his gun towards the street. 'Out,' he said.

'I need to dress,' said Sokunthea and pointed towards the bedroom; the soldier nodded. Sokunthea and Piseth dressed quickly and began to pack a few items into bags.

'Only take what you can carry,' said the soldier, 'you have a long way to walk.'

'Where?' asked Sokunthea.

'Outside the city,' came the reply, 'hurry Ankor is waiting.'

Sokunthea took one last glance around the bedroom and left; as she descended the stairs she gestured to the kitchen.

'Ankor will provide,' said the soldier and nodded towards the door.

'But we've not eaten,' pleaded Sokunthea, 'and we'll need a drink.'

The soldier nodded. 'Be quick,' he said.

They both burst into the kitchen, Sokunthea attacked the fridge, stuffing two bottles of water into her bag while Piseth searched the pockets of his jacket which he had left hanging over the back of a chair the night before.

'Enough, outside,' said the soldier. Sokunthea looked around and saw a large box of drugs standing on the top of the fridge; she added them to her bag, while Piseth just smiled.

'Come on,' he said, 'I've got what we need.'

They left the house and entered the street, which was already full of people moving like a slow river. 'Keep moving,' they heard someone shout through a megaphone. Around them people of all ages, with heads slightly bowed, shuffled along the road. Unlike Sokunthea many were carrying large household items, pots and pans, bags of rice, children bringing a favourite toy and teenagers carrying radios. As she walked she thought about her father and how she wished she had returned home after her mother's death as she had originally planned. Of course, in the end her father felt she should give Piseth one last chance and had ordered her to be next to her husband. She, of course, had obeyed and continued in a marriage without love or affection, sharing the same house but not the same bed. Her thoughts were disturbed as she stumbled into a small group collected around an old man in a wheelchair.

'I will not go!' he shouted to what appeared to be his family.

'We must,' said his hot and angry wife, 'they say it's not safe.'

'Safe from who?' he barked back.

'Please don't be difficult, grandfather,' said a young girl.

'I will not go, I cannot go,' he continued as the family members began to cry.

'What is the problem?' came a stern voice from behind Sokunthea and a soldier pushed his way into the group.

'My husband is sick, he cannot travel in this way.'

'Do not worry,' said the soldier, 'Ankor will provide.' He looked around and waved to two soldiers standing on the edge of the crawling mass of humanity. 'Here,' he shouted, and the soldiers were quickly in attendance. 'Move the old man into that courtyard,' he ordered.

'But my husband, I cannot leave…'

'You may stay with him,' said the soldier, 'but the rest of the family must move on.'

'But how…' responded the granddaughter.

'We will bring him to you when you arrive at the safety area,' he responded. 'Now move on,' he said with a raised voice, and nobody argued.

The people continued to walk and when they turned into the main Phnom Penh boulevard of Monivong, Sokunthea was stunned by the mass of people all walking slowly south. Like a small tributary entering a larger river the flow of people wedged together without a word lowered their heads and walked on. By 7.30 the sun was hot and people began to wilt as the feeling of claustrophobia, exhaustion and dehydration began to take its toll. Sokunthea and Piseth had managed to migrate towards the edge of this flowing mass and began to notice the ever-growing pile of cast-off baggage and people resting, gasping for breath. Ahead Sokunthea noticed a small group of soldiers who would enter the body of the exodus and return with a radio, then promptly smash it on a wall or under a boot. As they got alongside this group they noticed a large pile of these smashed radios and, curiously, other items: walking sticks, incense sticks, religious objects and cameras.

After walking for several hours they had covered only about two kilometres due to the mass of people; as they approached another road junction where even more people were joining the main exodus, Sokunthea and Piseth left the flow and sat against a wall under the shade of a tree. Sokunthea pulled out one of the bottles of water and took a long drink.

'What did you bring?' she said.

'Money.'

'How much?'

'A couple of hundred, enough to see us through to our return.'

'You think we're coming back?'

'Sure, what else are they going to do with us?'

'Well, they're sure going to a lot of trouble just to let us come back.'

'I don't know if my family is coming back,' said a weepy voice.

Sokunthea and Piseth looked across at a middle-aged man sat on the other side of the shade. 'Why?' asked Sokunthea.

'They've gone the other way.'

'What... what way?' she enquired.

'They split from our road... I mean, when I came out of my house my family had been pushed one way and I another... they're on Norodom going north.' He began to cry.

Sokunthea looked at Piseth. 'All these people all going in different directions with all this suffering, just to come back again... I don't believe it,' she concluded.

Several other people had stopped and were seeking shade when Piseth said, 'I'm more worried about food and shelter.'

'Ankor will provide,' said a tall, thin man leaning against the tree.

Piseth looked at him. 'If Ankor had left us in our homes it wouldn't have to provide.'

'Your homes were not safe,' said the man, 'the Americans are about to bomb the city.'

'And why would they do that?' said Sokunthea, getting a little annoyed.

'They are the enemies of Ankor,' was the reply.

'If the Americans are about to bomb,' continued Sokunthea, 'why have you lined us all up in the street... we're sitting ducks.'

The thin man straightened up. 'You must learn to trust Ankor or be re-educated.' He smiled and walked away. Sokunthea and Piseth drank the rest of the bottle of water and began to doze.

'Up, on your way.' Sokunthea looked up to see a young soldier prodding his rifle into Piseth; 'Up,' he said. They staggered to their feet and re-entered the slow-moving human mass moving as one down the long straight boulevard. The midday sun was above them and human strength was waning.

'Keep near the edge,' said Piseth, 'and don't fall, you'll be trampled to death.' Sokunthea held onto him and felt glad he was around; her mind wandered again to her father – in which direction was he headed and had he managed to gather enough water?

They walked on for another three hours, covering even less of a distance, then the mass of people began to slow and stop. People vacated the road en masse looking for a place to rest and get out of the sun; Sokunthea and Piseth had stopped outside the old palace of Chamea Moen so they scrambled over the wall and headed for the palace pond.

By evening the palace was an island surrounded by a sea of people all together yet all in individual groups. Some were making fires in order to cook, others were collecting water from the pond while even more were just sitting and, for the first time, talking. Sokunthea and Piseth had settled with their backs against a small crematorium under a large tree and overlooking the lake and the palace grounds. They had already bathed which had helped bring their body temperature down and had satisfied their thirst by drinking half the remaining water.

'I'm hungry,' said Sokunthea.

Piseth looked at her. 'Ankor will provide,' he said sarcastically.

'Well, they'd better hurry up or there won't be anybody to provide to,' she replied.

'I'll walk around, see what I can get,' he said and walked off.

Sokunthea sat and began to reflect back on the day. 'It's crazy,' she mumbled, 'just crazy.'

'Is there room here?' said an old lady, looking at Sokunthea and then the space around her with envy.

'Well, my husband will be returning soon but... okay.'

The woman laid a large bundle on the ground and disappeared, only to arrive a short while later with two younger women, one heavily pregnant. Sokunthea helped lay the pregnant woman down and gave up a little extra space.

'Thank you,' the old woman said.

'Has she been walking all day?' Sokunthea nodded to the pregnant woman.

'Of course; when they emptied the city, they moved everyone regardless of their condition,' responded the old woman with bitterness in her voice.

'But the hospitals...' began Sokunthea.

'Emptied,' cut in the old woman.

'But the very ill...'

'Emptied,' said the old woman, 'you walked, were carried by other patients or you died.'

'Died, you saw them die?' Sokunthea could feel herself going cold with fear.

'You don't see them die, you're moved on, but who's left to care for them?' she asked. 'Look around, how many wheelchairs do you see, how many disabled people do you see? None. Phnom Penh had two million people; were none needing care, were none sick, were none pregnant?' She began to cry.

'Forget it, Mother, we'll be all right,' said the non-pregnant girl. 'My name is Li,' she said. 'We started off with our brother; he is handicapped and needed his wheelchair.' She began to cry quietly. 'The soldiers said he could rest and they would bring him to us but we think we'll never see him again.' She wiped the tears from her face.

'Well, we have guests,' said Piseth, who had returned unnoticed and sat down.

'This is my husband,' said Sokunthea, 'he's a doctor so you can relax.' She glanced at the pregnant woman.

'Don't admit to that,' said the old woman suddenly, 'they shoot doctors.'

Everyone fell quiet. 'I've got some food and drink,' Piseth announced, as if trying to change the subject. 'Maybe it's enough to go around.' He stared at Sokunthea.

'Oh, don't worry,' said Li, 'we have enough.'

'Well, we'll share,' said Sokunthea. To Piseth's rice and water the women added some dried fish and hard-boiled eggs. As the night began to fall Piseth asked about the pregnant woman.

'She's my sister-in-law,' said Li, 'her name is Roksunchandra and my mother is Chan Ly.'

'Is this her first pregnancy?' enquired Piseth.

'Yes,' said Li.

'And why was she in hospital?' continued Piseth.

'Oh, not for the pregnancy,' replied Li, 'we were with her husband, my brother.' The tears began again.

'And what happened to him?' Sokunthea cut in.

'He's dead, they're all dead,' cut in the mother.

'We don't know that, Mother,' said Li.

'You heard that officer, he said the soldiers of Lon Nol are the enemies of Ankor, and must be killed... I'm going to the pond.'

'Don't be upset by my mother, she's... tired, the walking has nearly killed her,' said Li.

'You seem to have experienced a lot today,' said Sokunthea.

'Your mother said they shoot doctors; what did she mean?' said Piseth.

'Nothing, don't worry,' said Li.

'Tell them,' said Roksunchandra, 'they need to know.' Everyone looked at her.

'When they emptied the hospitals,' Li began, 'they kept the doctors back; we thought it was to take care of the really ill patients... we were slow to leave, what with my mother and, of course, Radoo, our brother. Roksunchandra didn't want to leave her husband, the soldiers almost threw her out of the ward – anyway, we were slow to leave… then we noticed the doctors being taken into a small building at the back of the hospital. It seemed strange but we just headed for the gate, then we heard the gun fire… we don't know if they killed them,' she said, looking at Piseth, 'we don't know.'

Nobody spoke, and the group settled down; Roksunchandra was checked for comfort then everybody tried to sleep and, after the rigors of the day, found it very easy.

Sokunthea awoke early and, surprisingly, found her husband missing, so she stood up and looked around. There were early signs of life around the camp with some already making fires for cooking; the water carriers were active and the pond was attracting early bathers. Sokunthea decided to join them, so she walked over to the pond and entered the water where a group of women were bathing.

'Hello,' said Sokunthea, to a young bather, 'ready for the walk?' she enquired light-heartedly.

'I don't know what it's all about,' she said, 'all I want to do is get back to my market stall.'

'You're a trader them?' said Sokunthea.

'Was, I don't know what's happened to my stock.' She offered Sokunthea the use of her soap.

'I suppose the soldiers will take care of it,' said Sokunthea, naively.

'They'll steal it, you mean; war to soldiers is an excuse for robbery.'

'Are you with family?'

'My son and daughter; my husband was in the army so I've no idea where he is.'

'Do you have enough food?'

'No, and I can't spare any.' She became defensive and retrieved her soap.

'Oh, don't worry, I'm not after food, I just wondered if they had provided you with any, as they keep saying Ankor will provide.'

'I don't believe it, how are they going to get food to us when all the roads are choked with people? Nah, look after yourself,

that's my advice, look after yourself – that's what Ankor is doing.'
The woman wandered away.

Sokunthea walked back to her group, refreshed but dreading
the upcoming day. She was approached by Li.

'She's having it, where's your husband?'

'I don't know,' said Sokunthea, brushing past Li and heading
for Roksunchandra.

'Don't force, don't force,' her mother was saying to
Roksunchandra, 'only push when I tell you.'

'How can I help?' said Sokunthea.

'Try to get her into a panting rhythm and keep her calm.'
Sokunthea supported Roksunchandra's head and, following Chan
Li's guidance, began to encourage Roksunchandra to slowly pant.

'Push,' said the mother, 'slowly.'

Roksunchandra was caught between following the panting
rhythm and her mother's calls to push which often resulted in
panting when pushing was needed and pushing when panting was
in order, and the outcome was increased anxiety for the poor
woman. Sokunthea's soothing words of, Relax, everything will be
all right, only infuriated Roksunchandra more. For Sokunthea, the
shouted orders of Pant! and Push! appeared to be affecting her,
and, as she duly complied she wondered who it was having the
baby.

'It's coming, it's coming!' shouted the mother. 'Now stop
pushing, wait, wait, push, hard!' Roksunchandra and Sokunthea
duly obliged. The baby, when it appeared, seemed to explode into
the world and was quickly transferred from Chan Li to Li who
began to wash it and wrap it in a *kroma*. Like Roksunchandra,
Sokunthea was exhausted and as she sat back she noticed for the
first time the large crowd that had gathered around. Forget
privacy, she thought, everybody needed cheering up and there's
nothing like a new baby to do that. As she reflected on her efforts
she noticed her husband leaning against the tree looking at her; he
glanced to one side and as her eyes followed his she noticed the
tall, thin man from the previous day watching the scene. The
activity around the new baby had woken the camp and many
people came and left a small item for the new child, mostly rice.
Then the soldiers appeared and the new day's march began.

'Don't leave us behind,' said the mother to Sokunthea.

'But we have to go,' she said, 'they won't let us stay.'

'You'll never see us again,' she said.

'Come, Mother,' said Li. 'We'll be all right,' she said, turning to Sokunthea, 'they say we can rest for a day, we'll be okay' and she smiled.

Sokunthea and Piseth said their goodbyes and joined the great throng of people heading south. The day continued as the one before with the slow-moving mass of people shoulder to shoulder heading in the same direction. Sokunthea was the first to notice the increasing piles of more discarded possessions by the side of the road and then she noticed her first dead body. As they walked on the number began to increase and although she began to count them she stopped after reaching one hundred. By midday they had reached a petrol station where they were told to rest. Li had shared some of the rice they had been given with Sokunthea and they still retained some water, so they sat beneath the large petrol station canopy drinking and eating their rations.

'I wonder if they know what this is being used for?' said Sokunthea, nodding towards the Caltex sign. 'The first refugee petrol station.' She smiled to herself.

The group was allowed to remain at the station until the following day; people began to suggest that this was it, they'd wait here and then go home. Yet Sokunthea couldn't see this happening.

'Why walk us eight kilometres and then send us back? We're not even fully out of the city yet.'

'Let's hope it's true,' said Piseth. 'If we turn back tomorrow I could have a bath by tomorrow evening.'

'I don't believe it, I just don't believe it; what about the stories about the doctors at the hospital, how would they explain them if we go back?'

'You didn't believe them, did you?'

'Yes, I did, and so did you, that's why you didn't help that pregnant girl; you saw the spy and you didn't want him to hear, Thank you, doctor. You've been a great help, doctor.'

'Oh, stop it, you're sounding like that old woman… anyway, if these people think we are going back it might be a good time for business.' He winked at her, stood up and walked off. He returned several hours later with a large plastic bag.

'How was business?' said Sokunthea sarcastically, still smouldering from their previous exchange.

'Not bad... enough rice and water for a couple of days, and these.' He threw her a can of coke.

'How much did this lot cost?'

'Five dollars; people are willing to sell their surplus at a more reasonable price if they think they are going home.'

'If you're so convinced, why buy these?'

'Hedging my bets.'

Sokunthea drank the coke in silence; she had never understood all the hype about this foreign drink but knew it tasted wonderful. She looked at Piseth, 'What do you think will happen?' she said.

'I don't know, but we should prepare for the worst. I'll try the other groups later, see what else we can buy.'

'No, you rest; give me the money, I'll see what a woman can do.' Piseth handed over fifty dollars. 'Is that all we have?' asked Sokunthea.

'No, I've another couple of hundred,' he replied. She nodded and walked off.

The petrol station and all the roads around were crowded with people as Sokunthea picked her way through the groups huddled together on the ground. She was hoping to spot her father and wondered where he was.

'Careful,' said a voice.

Sokunthea looked down at a young man curled up on the floor eating handfuls of rice from a banana leaf. The young man looked at her up and down. 'Sorry, I didn't see you.'

'You can rest here if you like,' came the voice.

'No... I'm okay, I'm over there with my husband.'

'Why are you wandering around then?'

Sokunthea looked carefully at the young man; she didn't want any more involvement with spies. 'We didn't bring much food, so I'm hoping to buy some.'

'Are you crazy? People who are caught trying to buy food are re-educated.' He looked at her and made a gesture across his throat.

Sokunthea crouched down beside the young man and noticed he was only a boy. 'Where are your parents?'

'Don't know, we got separated way back.'

'You've not tried to find them?'

'What for? They're most likely dead anyway.'

'Why do you say that?'

'My father has a bad leg... polio when he was a kid, he can't walk very far or very fast.'

'That doesn't mean he is dead.'

'Lady, look around. Have you seen the dead bodies? – look at them, just look at them, all cripples and old folk; if you slow Ankor down you're dead.' Sokunthea had noticed that and it made her think of her father.

'They're taking the children as well,' the boy continued.

'What do you mean?'

'The children, they're taking the children.'

'What are they doing with them?'

'I don't know.'

'Why haven't they got you?'

'After the way they treated my father... I ain't going anywhere with Ankor.'

Sokunthea looked at the boy. 'Look, come with us.'

'No way... if you carry on showing money you'll be lying next to the road, too.'

'But how do we get food?'

The boy looked at her. 'Come back when it's dark; I'll meet you at the old diesel pump. Come alone.' He wrapped the rest of his rice in his banana leaf and, deftly stepping between groups of people, disappeared. Sokunthea returned to her husband and related her encounter.

'Don't go,' he said.

'I thought we should prepare for the worst.'

'Not if the risk is high, that kid could kill you and take everything you have.'

Sokunthea stared at the floor. 'What about his advice?' she said.

'About what?'

'People caught spending money.'

'Everybody's doing it… I've even seen soldiers selling.'

Sokunthea sat silently and reflected on the boy's observations. She had already decided, before she had told her husband, that she would meet the boy later; it wasn't the food that interested her but any information that he might possess. Piseth and Sokunthea began to eat some of the food purchased by Piseth; around them were family groups of all sizes beginning to prepare their food and it struck her how right the boy was. Where were the children and the old? The traditional Cambodian family appeared to have disappeared; her thoughts went to Li and Roksunchandra.

'Stop… get him!' The cry startled Sokunthea. The area around her seemed to be in turmoil and all eyes were following the escape of a small boy clutching a small basket.

'What the hell is happening?' she said.

'He's stealing food,' said her husband, nodding towards the commotion. As he said this a group of men cornered the unfortunate youngster.

'Step aside!' a voice shouted. Everyone looked across the petrol forecourt as three soldiers and the tall thin man walked towards the boy. They pulled the basket away from him and some rice fell to the floor. The thin man turned to the audience.

'There is no need to steal food, Ankor will provide.' Sokunthea was mimicking these words as he said them.

The boy was collected by the soldiers and all departed, along with the thin man and the rice, and as the groups were still discussing the disturbance and settling down into their territories a single shot rang out, and all communication amongst the groups ceased. Sokunthea had located the diesel pump earlier so as the sun went down she was able to traverse the sleep-bound groups and head straight to her destination. Piseth didn't want her to go, of course, and had even offered to accompany her but alone had been the demand and alone it would be. She stepped past small groups of men, some still finding time to play cards, and young couples with small children; the smell, smoke and noises of people huddled to the ground prior to sleep were everywhere. Above her the night sky was surprisingly cloudy with the moon only occasionally sneaking through.

'You came,' said the boy to a startled Sokunthea.

'Yes... I don't know... did you see the incident earlier?'

'With Chay?'

'Chay... was that his name?'

'Yes... he's mental, you understand what I mean.' The boy pointed to his head.

'Mentally handicapped, you mean?'

'Yeah, something like that... he doesn't know any other way.'

'So they shot him.'

'Yeah, of course, they've been after him for a couple of days. Come on,' said the boy, 'we can't talk here.'

Sokunthea followed him towards the garage maintenance area, which had been sign posted as a closed area by the Rouge: *entry on pain of death* read the welcoming notice. Inside they dropped down the maintenance trench and through a small trapdoor. As they came outside again two things struck Sokunthea; the first was a burst of clear moonlight and the second was a dreadful smell. The moonlight gave her a clear view of what the smell was.

'Bodies!' she said. 'Where have they all come from?' she whispered while holding her nose.

'Early arrivals.' The boy gave out a small chuckle. 'This way.' He headed towards the pile of corpses.

'I'm not going in there,' Sokunthea said.

'Then go back... there,' pointing towards the bodies, 'is the only place the Rouge won't go.' Sokunthea grabbed his arm and he led her into the ditch and its gruesome occupants.

'Is that you, Rom?' came a voice from the side of the ditch.

'Yeah.'

'Who you got?'

'Some lady who wants to buy food and drink and listen to a few stories.'

Rom and Sokunthea stumbled towards the dark shape. 'They finally got Chay,' Rom said to the shape.

'Poor bastard... well, lady, what do you want?' the shape said, turning to Sokunthea.

'Whatever you've got.'

'Okay, rice, roast chicken and a couple of bottles of water, real water not the rubbish they try to tell you is water.'

'How much?' asked Sokunthea.

'Fifty dollars.'

Sokunthea looked at the small pile of food. 'That won't last us two days,' she said, 'it's too much.'

'Okay, I'll sell it to someone else.'

'No, no,' said Rom, 'she's new, she doesn't understand the whole picture yet.'

'Well, tell her quick, there are many others who will buy this stuff tonight.'

Rom grabbed Sokunthea's arm and they both sat down amongst the bodies; the stench was beginning to affect Sokunthea.

'Listen,' he said, 'people think they are going back but they are not, the country has no food, the bleeding Americans left us to starve and the Rouge have decided that only a massive land labour approach can get the rice back. Anyone who opposes them is shot, anyone who disobeys is shot. They will shoot us all, why not? A dead body is one less mouth to feed. Listen, buy the food; you'll need it and more before this is over.'

Sokunthea didn't want to listen any more, she just wanted to get away from the rotting bodies and the dreadful smell, so she groped in her pocket and handed over the fifty. As Sokunthea rose the moon made another appearance in the night sky and laid its beams down the ditch. Although the stranger's face remained in shadow she instantly recognised the uniform of a Rouge field commander; she felt sick, grabbed the arm of Rom and was led away.

Rom and Sokunthea stumbled out of the ditch and through the maintenance area. Suddenly Sokunthea stopped; the glow of the cigarette as it was inhaled was unmistakable. 'Stop,' she whispered and pointed to the dark figure leaning against the old diesel pump.

Rom looked across. 'It's Thai,' he said, 'he points out to the soldiers the ones to be re-educated.' Sokunthea had finally got a name for the tall, thin man. Rom and Sokunthea crouched down beside the maintenance area wall and decided to wait it out; the moon was still under the cover of clouds and Thai didn't appear to be looking for anyone. Then another figure approached Thai. 'That's Radoo,' said Rom, 'we just bought the stuff from him.'

Sokunthea looked at Rom. 'You mean, Thai is involved in this as well?'

'Of course, he gets most of the food.'

'In what way… I mean, explain.' Sokunthea began to feel her anger rise.

'Look,' said Rom, 'Thai identifies the people with food and matches their food to people like you who are carrying money… it's business.'

'But he's Rouge… he's Ankor.'

'Forget the Ankor rubbish, that's just an excuse to steal things from the people. He identifies the older folk, the ones who plan ahead, who bring food, but they can't walk quickly, okay, so they re-educate them and drop them in the ditch behind us,' he paused, 'and you buy the food.'

Sokunthea looked at Rom. 'You bastard,' she said, 'you knew this and you still told me to buy.'

'Stop being stupid, stop being this kind, considerate, traditional Cambodian woman and realise that these people would kill you without remorse; they're taking you out of the city and stripping you of valuables and when you get to the fields they'll work you to death, so wake up, toughen up and stay alive.'

Tears began to fall down Sokunthea's face as she looked across the no entry area towards the diesel pump, where the two men were in conversation and sharing a smoke. She wiped some tears away. 'Thai will know about me.'

'He already does,' said Rom. 'Your husband has bought before, they know you have money so you're okay for a while… when it runs out or you flash it too much in front of the wrong people…' he stopped.

Rany and Thai finished their dealings and walked away, and Rom led Sokunthea almost back to where her husband was asleep. 'Take care,' he said.

'Won't you be going on tomorrow?'

'No, I'm the middleman, I deal with the next group.'

'And when there's no more groups?'

Rom shrugged his shoulders and paused. 'It's run or re-education.' He turned to leave.

'Where are all the children of your age?' she called after him.

'They're the new Rouge, they're being trained to control their elders,' he laughed and was gone.

Sokunthea sat beside her sleeping husband, all around were bodies curled up asleep on the ground, all afraid, all wanting to go home. The moon broke through the yoke of the clouds and she thought of the ditch and its sleeping occupants; they would never go home.

The following day the march began again, still south and still slow; their destination was to be the market of Chbar Ampov on the very outskirts of Phnom Penh. She had told her husband of the previous night's events and his only concern was the fifty-dollar price she had paid. He'd eaten all the chicken before he started to walk, ignoring Sokunthea's pleas for restraint.

Chbar Ampov was a large open-air market serving most of south Phnom Penh, where rural produce met urban money; in its heyday it had attracted over five hundred wooden-framed stalls with their grass roofs. The garbage would pile up throughout the day attracting all kinds of animals and along with beggars and motodop drivers, the scene of organised chaos was complete. When Sokunthea and Piseth arrived in early afternoon it was a sea of humans scattered upon the dusty clay ground; any sign that a market had ever existed had disappeared. The sun was still high and, having walked for several hours without rest many people simply collapsed in the unsheltered arena. Sokunthea and Piseth sat in the middle of this furnace covering their heads with clothing. They pulled out their water and began the process of re-hydration, around them hundreds of families followed suit. Sokunthea had not washed for two days and felt a growing need to get clean; she looked around the market arena and noticed a line of water barrels against the rear wall of the only building still standing.

'I'm going to check them.' She nodded towards the barrels and walked off. As she approached the building she realised it was occupied by the soldiers travelling with the exodus.

'Stop!' She turned to see Thai looking at her. 'Where are you going?'

'I was going to check the water,' and she nodded at the barrels.

'That water belongs to Ankor,' he said, and walked up to the nearest barrel. 'It's not for drinking, anyway.' He turned and smiled.

'Then why not let people wash with it, and keep cool?'

'Do you wish to bathe?' he said.

'It's hot, people are fainting... of course I'd like to bathe and so would they,' she said, pointing back towards the market arena.

He shrugged his shoulders. 'You, you bathe,' he said.

'I'm going back to my husband,' she said. As she turned he grabbed her arm and pulled her around to stand in front of the barrels.

'You will obey Ankor... you will bathe... if you need to bathe Ankor will provide.'

'I'll tell the others.'

'No others.'

'I'm a married woman.'

Thai looked at her. 'What do you think I'm going to do?' he smiled.

'I must get back to my husband.'

'Disobey Ankor and you may not have a husband.' He glared at her.

Sokunthea recognised that same cold look, so she tied back her hair and looking at Thai picked up the small water bowl floating on top of a water barrel and began to pour water over herself. The warm water felt wonderful; with every bowlful it raced down her neck and down her body, and soon her vest top and the *kroma* strapped tight around her waist began to cling. She glanced at Thai each time she poured, knowing that, as her clothes grabbed her body tighter and tighter, he was getting his satisfaction. As soon as she had started she stopped, loosened her hair, tossed the bowl back into the water barrel and set off back to her husband, Thai watching her all the way.

'Where did you manage to do that?' Piseth said on her arrival back.

'The barrels have water.'

'I'm next.'

'I wouldn't... the Rouge cleared me off, it's theirs now.'

'How are we for food?' he continued.

'Enough for two or three days, if we ration it maybe four.'

'But it's all rice and dried fish, isn't it?'

'There's some pork.'

'I'm going to see what I can find.'

'No… it's dangerous, they're watching us.'

'They're watching everybody. I'll just see what I can get, don't worry.'

Sokunthea watched him walk off then reflected back on the bathing; it's amazing how you don't appreciate simple things until you can't have them, she thought. Although the bath had been good she had been unable to loosen or remove her underclothes and she feared developing some fungal infection in her hot, damp state. She looked around and feeling unobserved removed her bra from within her vest top and quickly changed her panties for a dry pair from within her bag, laying the wet items out to dry. She drank a little more water and, as she lay back in the sun to dry further, she began to snooze.

'Your husband does not need to worry about me,' said the voice.

Sokunthea looked up, shielding her eyes from the sun, and saw Thai. 'What… what do you mean?'

'Come with me, your husband is in trouble.'

He helped her up by her arm and began to lead her to the Rouge building. 'Your husband is a fool,' he said. 'There are many soldiers here and he tries to buy food.' Thai shook his head. He marched her by her arm into the building and through a doorway; as her eyes became adjusted to the dark she noticed two men standing around an empty chair and a man lying on the floor crying. The two men pulled Piseth back to the chair and she noticed he had been badly beaten.

'Where is the rest of the money?' came the scream. Piseth just shook his head.

'He has none,' cried Sokunthea.

The nearest of the two men to Sokunthea took one stride and hit her hard across the face, she collapsed to the floor. 'Whore!' he shouted at her.

'Enough,' said Thai. The two torturers looked at him then left the room. Sokunthea began to climb to her feet.

'Take him back,' Thai said, nodding towards Piseth.

Sokunthea helped her husband to his feet and, supporting his weight, struggled out of the building and back towards the market arena.

'I told you not to go,' she said through her tears and blood.

'Whore,' he mumbled.

'What?'

'Whore,' he said again.

Sokunthea got him back to their space within the arena and helped him to the floor. She rummaged in her bag to find something for his bleeding face and her bleeding mouth, but as she tried to wipe away some blood from his face he pulled away.

'What's up?' she said.

'You,' he said, 'just look at you.'

Sokunthea glanced down her body and noticed her missing bra. She looked at Piseth. 'I come running to help you, get smashed in the face and all you're worried about is that I've no bra?' Her voice began to rise.

'No Cambodian woman would show herself to other men... unless she...'

'Unless she what?'

'Was a whore.'

'I don't believe this... I come running to save you and I'm a whore... you make me sick. You're just trying to change the subject because you know you should have followed my advice and not done business,' she continued.

He remained quiet and began to sulk, and Sokunthea grabbed her now dried bra and put it on.

'I'm going for a walk.' Sokunthea began stepping over people and walking around groups, many looking dishevelled and bewildered. The cries of loss could be heard from many quarters as the long march of the day had claimed more lives; families were being forced by soldiers to remove their dead relatives and friends as quickly and as quietly as possible. Looking to the faces of the weeping relatives she felt ashamed of her own feelings of loss and betrayal. How can they go on like this? she thought while watching people drag their dead loved ones away while others simply looked in another direction, not wanting to share or even see the pain. The Rouge are simply reducing us to animals, she thought. She arrived back at Piseth; he was still sulking and on her arrival just looked away.

'I'm hungry,' she said, 'where's the food?'

He pointed to her clothes bag. 'I've split it,' he said.

'Why?'

'It will avoid arguments about saving it and if we're split up, you'll be okay!'

She opened her bag and took out a small portion of rice wrapped in banana leaf.

'What's going on between you and him?' he began.

Sokunthea looked puzzled. 'Me and who?'

'Him… you know, the spy.'

'You mean Thai?'

'Whatever.'

'There's nothing going on… I loathe the man.'

'I was set up.'

'What?'

'Set up; a soldier approached me, said he had some food and was I buying, we walked down towards those trees and he offered me a bag of rice, and as soon as I showed the money your Thai and two thugs appeared, started screaming and dragged me off, they started to beat me senseless and saying I was dead, then he said only you could save me and disappeared, and next you're coming in the room with him half-dressed.'

'I was not… listen, believe what you will, but I hate that man and all he stands for and although we could hardly be described as husband and wife, by law you are my husband and we will live longer if we stick together.'

They both sat quietly. 'I think they're watching us,' he said, breaking the silence and nodding towards two soldiers standing looking at them.

'I think they are watching everybody. Look around: people are getting desperate, something is going to happen.'

As the cooler evening set in some of the groups again began to build cooking fires but these appeared to get less and less as the days went on, a sure sign that food was getting short. Sokunthea checked her bag again, two small parcels of rice remained and two bottles of water. Enough for two days, she thought. She looked at

Piseth who was casually drinking water.

'I'd save some if I were you,' she said, but he just looked at her and looked away.

'How are your cuts and bruises, anything broken?'

'I'm okay, I'll try those water barrels of yours, help take the swelling from my face.'

'They're Rouge; if they catch you…'

'We're not husband and wife, okay?' came his sharp reply, and he stood up and wandered off.

Sokunthea watched him go. 'All I need right now is for him to fall apart again.' She shook her head and began to sip some water.

She had no idea what time it was but it was dark and the sound of automatic gun fire was very close; she had fallen asleep and had been dreaming of Sinarth and how she wished he was here with her and not Piseth. Now awake she felt guilty, as her husband wasn't around. All around her people were hugging the ground but she could see some shadows running in different directions. Where is he? she thought. At first she began to crawl towards the water barrels, then rose up into a crouched running position; the gunfire continued but was coming from behind her.

She had left the main group and crossed a small, shallow stagnant pond when she saw her first Rouge soldier. She froze; her heart was thumping in her chest so loudly that she thought the soldier might hear it. It was clear that his attention was focused on something and, as Sokunthea watched him, she saw he was moving like a hunter slowly towards the water barrels. Sokunthea then noticed his prey: her husband, he was trying to hide behind the barrels but the hunter had clearly got him in his sights. More shots rang out behind her and she could hear distant cries but her sight was set on the events about to happen before her. She stepped forward slowly and quietly and soon came into hearing range as her husband, realising he had been spotted, cried to the soldier that he wanted to surrender. Sokunthea knew this meant certain death, so she crept closer then noticed on the ground a piece of wood, previously part of one of the stalls, which she picked up.

'Come out!' screamed the soldier. 'Come out… dog.'

'Don't shoot, don't shoot… I only needed water… don't

shoot.'

'Ankor decides if you need water,' he said. He then heard the sound behind him and turned quickly; Sokunthea hadn't noticed the large rusty nail sticking out of the wood but it was this that killed him instantly as it penetrated first his right eye and then burst into his brain.

'Let's go,' she said to her husband.

He didn't move, he just looked down at the soldier's battered face.

'Come on, let's get out of here!' He still didn't move, so she covered the ground between her and her husband very quickly and slapped him hard across the face. He collapsed to his knees and began to cry. 'Get up and get moving.' She grabbed him and, by pulling and pushing, moved him stumbling along. She could hear more shouts and shots all around them but she kept him going until they reached their rest area in the market place where they lay quietly on the ground.

Piseth, lying face down, began to mumble, 'We're dead, we're dead… why did you kill him? Sokunthea stayed quiet. 'They'll know its us… we're dead.'

'Stop grovelling… you were dead, he was going to kill you or, worse, hand you over to Thai's thugs… if we stay calm nothing will happen… stay calm.' She glared at Piseth.

Sleep was impossible that night as periodic gun fire and cries were heard; Sokunthea sat cradling her tearful frightened husband and when she tried to sleep could only see the face of the young Rouge soldier. As early morning arose so did the soldiers, once more ordering them on, and as they walked the stories from the previous night's events began to circulate. Several families had attempted to leave the exodus, hoping to find their way back, all had been caught, all had been shot. About the dead guard at the water barrels nothing appeared to be known.

The mass of people continued their journey; all travelling much lighter now as excess baggage had either been emptied of its food or discarded. With the food had gone the need for pots and pans, dishes and various other utensils associated with food; people were travelling in what they stood up in, and anything that added weight was ditched. The gruelling sun was again climbing up the sky and Sokunthea could see ahead more and more people fainting and stopping for rests by the roadside; some were quickly forced on by the soldiers, others shot. The road was wide, straight and dusty with little to no shade; it quickly changed from a tarmac to a sandy road confirming that the city was far behind.

'It was you, wasn't it?' said Thai, as he moved in beside her. Sokunthea continued to walk with her head down. 'It was you,' he repeated.

'I don't know what you're talking about,' she replied and, glancing at her husband, she noticed his agitation.

'The dead soldier,' Thai continued.

'What dead soldier?'

'We found one of our guards dead when we got back from our disturbance,' he chuckled.

'I don't know what you're talking about,' Sokunthea repeated.

'We didn't go near the water barrels,' Piseth cut in.

Thai smiled. 'Who said anything about water barrels?' He looked at Sokunthea.

He moved on ahead of them in the crowd, and Sokunthea looked at Piseth and wondered just how close he was to breaking down. The beating had obviously taken much out of him and she feared his behaviour may become erratic.

Again they walked all day with no rest as if amongst this apparent chaos there was a developing strategy. Speed had become important and Sokunthea noticed how the larger group had been divided into smaller, more manageable groups and allocated a soldier, whose orders appeared to be to move them on quickly. By the middle of the afternoon they began to slow down. Something up ahead was reducing the mass to a crawling pace and as people packed even closer together the rate of fainting and the urge to just sit down grew. As they slowly progressed forward the mass was suddenly divided into six queues, which stretched ahead like bug snakes; families were often split into different lines which increased the tension, the cries, the tears. The soldiers controlling the lines were becoming more and more brutal to family members who tried to deviate from their allocated queue in order to get back to the family. The number of people collapsing increased and they were forcefully dragged to the side of the road and left, family members were not allowed to stay with them. Family and social support is being destroyed at all levels and at all times by the Rouge, Sokunthea thought, what are they planning for us?

As they slowly shuffled forward hundreds of other people could be seen working in the rice fields on either side of the road; they were building what appeared to be an irrigation system of canals. Everything was being done by hand with no machinery, oxen or horses to be seen, and it reminded Sokunthea of a book she had when she was a little girl which showed drawings of the old Ankor temples being built by hand and by slaves in the ninth century. The queues moved on to reveal others digging up tree roots and yet more appearing to be preparing new rice fields. As Sokunthea observed more she noticed how everyone appeared to be working in silence and how periodic beatings would occur, yet these were not done by the soldiers but by what appeared to be teenaged children. After three hours of shuffling along in her queue Sokunthea noticed she was about to enter the village of Koh Krabei, the six queues were being targeted into six houses on the outskirts of the town; these were all fenced in and newcomers allowed in first had to sit outside until called into the building. Sokunthea and Piseth were ushered in and they sat on the floor waiting to be called.

'Are you okay?' she whispered.

Piseth nodded, but she could see he was suffering some unspoken pain.

'Thank God we're sat down,' she continued, then suddenly a child of about eleven whipped her hard across her face with a small piece of cane.

'Shut up!' she cried. 'Only Ankor speaks here.'

Sokunthea felt the blood roll down from a cut on her cheek, she glared at the child and imagined her as one of her students back in Phnom Penh. The child then looked across the enclosed compound and screamed, 'Nobody talks… nobody talks.' After a further hour Sokunthea was called into the building and followed a man down a dark corridor into a dark room, six feet by six feet. Ahead of her was a small table and sat behind it were two men; behind them was the only other exit, a closed door.

'Undress,' came the voice.

'I will...' and as she began to speak the small child with her whip appeared from the shadows.

'Undress,' came the repeated order.

Sokunthea looked at the child, ready to pounce, and quietly removed her vest and *kroma*.

'All,' said the voice.

Sokunthea looked around the room; with two men in front of her, one behind and a child ready to pounce she had little choice, so she removed her underclothes. One of the figures from behind the desk got up and came over to her.

'Lean onto the desk,' he said. She did, and he began without touching at first to look at her body.

'Are you a virgin?' he asked.

'I'm a married woman,' she replied.

'Hum... you have a soft body,' he said, 'you must be from a rich family in Phnom Penh.'

Sokunthea was unsure how to answer this and remembered some of the warnings she had received along the road. 'No, I'm a rice girl who had an arranged marriage.' He then reached under her extended arm and firmly grabbed her right breast; she instinctively turned and hit him across the face. The guard from the rear pushed her forward and she was pinned across the desk face down; she waited, wondering what these men would do, then thought of Thea and how she had found her. The first strike of the child's whip brought her mind back to the present, the second and third just instigated sheer pain, the frenzy continued as she began to cry silently then stopped just as suddenly.

'Get dressed,' a voice said. 'Hut four,' it informed a man behind her.

The guard escorted her out of the room down a small flight of stairs and into another courtyard which was full of more waiting people. He continued across the courtyard through guarded barbed-wire gates and into a small compound with a concrete building on all sides. 'Sit,' he said, pointing to the floor, Sokunthea sat and the renewed pain hit her, she lay on her side and wondered how she would treat something she could not see.

Around her, small groups of people were located outside each building, all sat quietly and staring at the door of their allotted destination. She took out her water bottle and began to drink. 'If they are going to kill me,' she said to herself, 'I'm not leaving them anything.' As she lowered the bottle from her face she noticed two men dragging her husband towards another hut; he had obviously been badly beaten. She stood instinctively and ran across to him but her efforts were in vain, as one of the soldiers grabbed her by the hair and swung her around.

'Back,' he said. Sokunthea thought her hair was about to be pulled out and as the soldier marched her back across the compound he grabbed her arm and twisted it violently up her back. When they arrived at her allotted position he threw her to the floor and kicked her hard; she was unable to scream as all the air had been forced out of her when she rolled over and over in the dust. The soldier then saw her bottle of water, picked it up and walked back to the house. Sokunthea lay on the ground, trying to regain her breath, force life into her painful arm and not acknowledge the pain in her backside.

'This way,' said the soldier standing above her. She looked at him, then the hut, then her husband still lying face down on the ground across the compound. She slowly staggered to her feet, picked up her bag and followed. The hut they entered was a single room with a large window; this allowed light to shine onto a large desk where two men sat.

'Sit down,' said one of them, and she obeyed. 'Where are you from?'

'Phnom Penh,' she said, after a pause, the pain in her backside increasing.

'Which part?' came the voice.

'Deum Kor.'

'A not so rich area... what did you do?'

'I was a housewife.'

'Children? came the response.

'None.'

'Where is your husband?'

'Outside.'

'Where did he work?'

Sokunthea remembered what Chan Li had said. 'He had no

work… the war…' she began.

'Don't speak of the war,' came an angered response from the second interrogator.

'You are the daughter of a rich merchant,' continued the first.

'I am a rice girl.'

The interrogator looked at her. 'Let me see your hands.' She held them out; he looked at her coldly then reached across the table and poured out a glass of water, brown water. Sokunthea thought of her mother, picked up the glass and drank it all.

'What was your village?' The questions continued.

'Rhor Kar.'

He began to write. 'Where are your parents?'

'Dead,' she replied.

'Hum…' he looked at the guard. 'Put her in the rice-growing compound for tonight, tomorrow she goes to Takeo.' As she rose and staggered to the door the interrogator observed bloodstains coming through her *kroma*. 'You have problems taking orders,' he said, and she turned and looked at him. 'Do not fight Ankor,' he said, 'you will die.' He looked straight at her; she lowered her head and left the room.

She half-staggered, half-stumbled behind the guard to wherever he was taking her; all she remembered was a high pitched voice screaming at her to get up. When she woke it was dark and all around people were asleep; her fever had just broken and her body was still covered in sweat. The pain in her rear was still there and she realised it was the source of her present problems. It was then that she remembered the bactrum; she rummaged deep within her bag and found the drugs, and opening her last bottle of water she washed the first dose down. As she lay on her side she began to think of Piseth and where he might be; she remembered he looked very bad when she had seen him in the compound, but at least he was still alive and the interviews had been pretty easy.

'Why?' she said to herself. 'Why did the beating stop? The child and the men were obviously enjoying it; why have I just been left here and not dragged off like other ill people, dragged off to die… thank goodness they beat me,' she thought, 'in doing so they forgot to search my bag.' She put another bactrum in her pocket for the morning and hid the rest in the lining of her bag.

She woke as someone was shaking her. 'She's not dead,' the guard shouted, 'get up, and go and help him.' He pointed across the rice compound. Sokunthea raised herself up on one elbow and looked across to where the guard had gestured – Piseth was curled up there on the ground. She staggered across to him, his face had been badly beaten again and his breathing suggested that he had a broken nose.

'Piseth... Piseth!' She shook him. 'Piseth, it's me... we have to go.'

He rolled over and looked at her, then grabbed her and held her close to him. 'Don't leave me,' he said, 'don't leave.'

'We must go,' she continued and they struggled to their feet.

They shuffled and stumbled out of Koh Krabei, still heading south, but this time the numbers in the group had dramatically fallen. Koh Krabei had been a filtering station and people were being sent in all directions except towards Phnom Penh. As they moved south they came across the Bassac River, a main tributary of the Mekong; here they rested during the midday sun. Sokunthea and Piseth used the time to bathe and clean their wounds and Sokunthea tried to use her particular ailment as a source of humour, trying to cheer up Piseth who appeared to be falling into some kind of depression.

They reached the crossing point at Prek Tauch only to find no boats available for crossing, and previous groups had cut down most of the trees so no raft building was possible. As the river was low the soldiers decided that a human chain across the river was the only way across; people would join hands all the way across the river so that others could cross. Swimmers were identified and thrust out into the front; these would fringe the deepest sections and would have greater survival chances if swept away. The river bottom was made of clay, which clung to any would-be wader, it was uneven with high shallows accompanied by deep troughs, and with no rope to bind people together slippery hands were the only means of contact. If anyone was washed away they had to fend for themselves.

Sokunthea stood at the back of the group and began to watch the results of Ankor's destruction of society; instead of the weakest members linking up in the shallows and the strongest in the more turbulent areas people opted for where it was safe. The line began to form and to disintegrate, older people and young children were washed away in areas of the river where they should have been safe. Sokunthea and Piseth stepped out into this chaos clinging to whatever and whoever they could; several times they sank below the water only to reappear coughing and spluttering, clinging to the next support. They arrived over halfway across on a large sandbank, beyond which was what appeared to be the deepest part of the river. Several had attempted to cross and been washed away; the human chain theory had stopped here as the sandbank became more crowded and the first soldier arrived demanding to know why they had stopped.

'Move on... get across,' he said and began pushing and striking people on the sandbank. This just added panic to an already anxious situation; with the ever-increasing mass looking for leadership, it arrived Khmer Rouge style.

The soldier fired in the air first but as this just caused people to drop to the floor he changed tactic and started shooting people. The human chain feeding the sandbank disintegrated leaving people to fend for themselves. Those on the sandbank, Sokunthea and Piseth included, dived into the water. Sokunthea had learnt to swim while at university – access to the university swimming pool was a perk for tutorial staff and she had taken full advantage of it, while her husband had preferred drinking beer and nightclubs as his university entertainment. After diving into the river with her husband to avoid the bullets, Sokunthea regained the surface and looked around for Piseth. He came to the surface slowly, and she swam over and grabbed around his shoulders. Like any non-swimmer contemplating death, when help appears to arrive he attempted to kill them as well, or that's how it seemed to Sokunthea. She dived down and pulled away from him and climbed back to the surface again. 'Lie flat... on your back,' she gasped.

Piseth just continued to panic, so she looked around and noticed they were drifting towards a crop of sandbanks; all she had to do was to manoeuvre him at the right time and he would run aground. Timing was critical, and as the first sandbank appeared she grabbed him by the hair with one hand and under the chin with the other and swung him around. He crashed into the steep side of the first bank as Sokunthea was swept past him and down the river; she was getting very tired but managed to half-swim, half-clamber onto a bank covered with shallow water about one hundred yards further downstream. She looked back at her husband, who appeared to be unconscious laying on the edge of his sandbank: she became concerned that he might slip off and be drowned. As she was kneeling, trying to gain some strength, she began to notice the bodies floating past her. There was no point in attempting to see if any of them were still alive, as she didn't have the strength to help anyway, so she just continued to watch Piseth. After a short rest she swam to where Piseth lay, he was conscious and, like her, just lying still in order to gain strength.

'What a mess,' she said, while pulling him further out of the water. They sat together, looking across the river counting the bodies drifting past or beaching on various sandbanks. Their thoughts were shaken by gunfire behind them; as they turned they saw the inevitable soldier standing on the bank behind them.

'Come!' he shouted and waved his rifle. They managed to wade to him via several sandbanks and once ashore he led them to the remnants of the group scattered across a rice field. 'Check for your bags,' he said, pointing to a pile of clothing and baggage that had been saved. As Sokunthea looked through it for her personal bag she noticed others containing rice and some water; while the soldier wasn't looking she collected together what she could and quickly stuffed it into her own bag, then joined the group.

They waited until it began to get dark, and when it was obvious no other survivors could be found they were marched into the local village of Prek Tauch, where they rested. Sokunthea shared the extra rice and water she had obtained with Piseth and swallowed another bactrum, then fell asleep.

The day began early. Sokunthea and Piseth shared a small meal of rice and fish and half a bottle of water, then the group continued south and Sokunthea noticed Thai. She pulled on Piseth's arm and nodded towards him.

'He must have arrived during the night,' she said, but Piseth just continued walking. The trek to the next village of Prek Ambel was five kilometres and to the group's surprise they were allowed a midday stop; many of them had noticed that the leader who ordered the chain across the Bassac and the gun crazy soldier from the sandbanks were missing. Even the Rouge has some rules, thought Sokunthea.

The village of Prek Ambel appeared not to have been exposed to the events that were devastating the rest of the country; the villagers watched the new arrivals enter their village and then carried on working the fields. There appeared to be no urgency in their labours and the arrival of several hundred people appeared to be a normal event. The group were led into an old school, which consisted of a long, low building divided into four classrooms each capable of holding forty schoolchildren; now they were packed with one hundred and sixty travellers. After they had been closed in for several hours the doors were opened and the inmates encouraged to form a line. At the end of the line was situated a large table on which stood three large metal bowls. As the line approached a large spoonful of rice soup was deposited onto a piece of banana leaf; Ankor had decided to provide. The travellers sat anywhere they could within the school compound, a luxury after being confined to the classrooms.

Sokunthea and Piseth sat against the side of the building and began drinking their food. Sokunthea looked across the scene and mused on how it was that people forget the harshness of the past if their empty bellies are unexpectedly filled. People began to talk again, children ran to find friends and then explore, even the soldiers appeared more relaxed, walking amongst the group repeating the same line: 'We said Ankor would provide.' While Piseth and Sokunthea were watching this they failed to notice Thai's approach.

'You'll be able to bathe at Ang Chang pagoda tomorrow night,' he said.

They both looked up at him. 'Ang Chang is far,' said Sokunthea.

'That's why we are building up your strength... your group has lost too many people.'

'So you are feeding us up.'

'You will need your strength, there's lots to do.'

'Then why kill us?'

'Ankor only kills those against Ankor.'

'Like us,' said Sokunthea.

'No... no, you can only get yourselves killed.' He walked past them towards a group of soldiers.

'That man has plans for us,' said Sokunthea.

'Rubbish,' said Piseth.

'Then why has he not had us shot for killing that soldier?' continued Sokunthea. She stood up looked at Piseth, 'He has plans.' She turned and went back into the classroom.

Sokunthea's sleep was spasmodic with thoughts about Sinarth, Piseth and now Thai; she became convinced that she had met him before but could not remember where. She remembered the bathing incident but couldn't accept that his only plan was to rape her and kill Piseth; if he had wanted to do that he'd had plenty of opportunity. There was something else, something.

The day began with some unusual order; each of the classrooms were emptied at separate times and the occupants were marched off in different directions. Sokunthea's group was now down to one hundred and fifty-five; as they began to walk south-west at a high pace, Sokunthea sensed a growing urgency in the soldiers to get to the next destination quickly, as though a clock had been set and they were behind. The group had lost its old and young and was able to maintain the increased pace set by the soldiers and, as midday approached, they were over half-way to their destination. They were allowed to rest along the way; Sokunthea and Piseth finished their food and water and tried to stay cool. As she sat under a small tree Sokunthea looked out across the countryside and was struck by the absence of cattle. Normally at this time of year the cattle would be used to eat up the remaining rice stubble and, along with their dung, help fertilise and prepare the fields for the next crop. If the Rouge were out to increase rice yields they were certainly going the wrong way about it! Her thoughts were disturbed by the call to move on; Piseth pulled her to her feet and the journey to Ang Chang continued. It was early evening when they arrived and the sight of the pagoda pond seemed to cheer everyone. This contrasted sharply with the destruction that had been unleashed on the temple; where previously a fine old Cambodian Buddhist temple had stood now only rubble greeted them. The need to cool down overrode the sight of destruction and within a short time most of the group were either bathing or just cooling down next to the water. The group were congregated in and around the monks' teaching house within the pagoda's compound; food was not non-existent and the drinking water had to come from the pond which, to this band of ex-city dwellers, was unthinkable.

'I'm thirsty,' said Piseth.

'Well, it's pond water or nothing.'

'Have we nothing left?'

'Nothing... except this empty bottle which I'd better fill while I can.'

'I'll never drink that stuff, I can't.'

'Look,' said Sokunthea, beginning to get annoyed, 'do you think where we're going there's going to be fresh, clean water waiting... I think not, so get used to this or die.'

She stood and marched off to the pond carrying her plastic bottle; she walked to the opposite bank from the bathers and looked around for a safe place to fill her bottle. With the aid of a tree branch she was able to slide down to the water's edge, where she leaned out and began to collect the water. As she looked around she saw a piece of orange-coloured cloth partly twisted under the base of a fallen tree and partly floating. It was a monk's robe, she thought, and she reached across to retrieve it. As she pulled, first a hand appeared and then the shaven head of its dead owner; she released the robe and the bottle and began clambering up the bank. As she did, a firm hand grabbed her.

'And what has frightened you?' Thai said.

'A monk.' She pointed to the water. 'He's dead.'

'They're all dead,' said Thai, 'they're parasites, they deserve to be dead.'

'All?' She looked at Thai's face.

'Come,' he spun her around and, grabbing her arm, began to march her towards the temple ruins.

'Where are we...'

'You want to see dead monks.'

She looked to where he was taking her. 'No... oh, God, no.'

As they reached the ruins Thai threw her to the floor, as she looked ahead she could see the charred bodies of monks, many monks.

'When our men arrived they said they would pray for us and went inside, so we blew everything up, the temple, the monks and the prayers.'

'Why?'

'There's no room for parasites in Ankor... monk, bourgeois or criminal, we'll kill them all.'

She saw in his face a cold hatred and knew that debate was of no use. 'Let me get back,' she said.

'Not a word of this... you understand.' She nodded and ran back to the schoolhouse.

'No water?' said Piseth on her return. 'You gone off it, too?' Sokunthea just lay down with her back to him and didn't speak.

The following day could not come too soon for Sokunthea; she was up early and ready for the call to depart. As the group headed south-west the talk was about three men who had gone missing in the night, no doubt never to be seen again, thought Sokunthea. The day was as long and arduous as the others, with short stops at noon and early afternoon to avoid the blistering sun. The group, without food and water, was beginning to look bedraggled and the pace began to fall. Once again the soldiers appeared more interested in preserving the group so the beatings and bullying of the past had been replaced by encouragement and support. They crossed the county border of Takeo and entered Kampot. Sokunthea realised that Takeo would not be her final destination and as early evening fell the group was urged to keep going; it was clear that once again they were behind their allotted timetable so it was very late when they entered the village of Tani. They were led to the village centre and there they collapsed with exhaustion. As Sokunthea lay on the ground gulping in air she heard a developing argument from the village chief's house.

'We have none to give,' appeared to be the words of the village head.

She listened more intently.

'We've got to get them to Tuk Meas by the day after tomorrow, they need water at least,' the voice appeared to be

Thai's.

'They can drink canal water.'

'Where's the canal?'

'Your direction… about five klicks.'

'They won't make five klicks.'

'Who cares… that's sixty less mouths to feed.'

'You know the order. Tuk Meas needs people, desperately, for the coming rice season.'

'And so do I… I've my quota to fill, if I miss the quota I'm dead.'

'A little rice won't bust your quota.'

'How do you know? You field commanders just have to watch the border. I've got to get these city people to work like rice workers and get the rice out by the end of the year, and many of them are useless… if they don't work they die, if I don't meet my quota I die… there's no rice here to spare.'

'What about the ones remaining here – will you feed them?'

'Of course; I need them in the fields tomorrow.'

'Okay, give me the rice and I'll distribute it.' The two men then went beyond Sokunthea's hearing range.

After what seemed half the night the group were called to eat; this consisted of very watery rice soup and a small bamboo cupful of dark water, but nobody complained.

In the morning the group was divided, half staying, half heading further south. When Sokunthea realised that she and Piseth would go on with Thai she was surprisingly happy; at least he tried to get us some food, she thought. As mentioned the previous night, five kilometres out of town was an old irrigation canal, surprisingly still holding water. The group passed the midday sun here, in or near the water. Sokunthea was no exception; the warm water was the only release from the grinding heat of the sun and she was determined to spend as long as possible in the water. As she finally exited she noticed Piseth talking with Thai and it clearly wasn't one way, so she decided to detour around them in order to get closer without them noticing.

'Then you'll have to take us all the way,' Piseth said.

'Impossible… I've got you this far.'

'But the deal was to keep me safe.'

'You are not Rouge... they know you are not Rouge, and, anyway, I can't take a woman on to the border... people will be suspicious.'

'Take her as your whore.'

'I can't have a whore... or any woman, the educators watch me too you know.'

'Leave her then... just take me... if you still want the money and the contacts you'll think of a way to keep me alive.'

'You sure they'll never find the radio?'

'Never.'

'And you'll be in with them when this is all over.'

'That's what the American attaché said before he left.'

Thai turned and walked away, and Sokunthea left her hiding place and approached Piseth.

'What did he want?' she said.

'Wanted to make sure I had no money.'

'And have you?'

'None... I haven't even got a change of clothes.'

'Isn't it strange that we always seem to be taken along by him?'

'He's after you, that's why.'

'No... I keep telling you there's something else... something, are you sure you don't know him?'

'Yes, but he may know me, of course, I mixed with some shady characters prior to all of this.'

'I've seen him somewhere... if only I could remember.'

'The nightclub, maybe.' Piseth knew this would irritate and take Sokunthea's mind off the conversation.

'Maybe,' she said.

The journey to Tuk Meas was completed in relative silence between Sokunthea and Piseth; she kept going over in her mind what she had heard. Why was Piseth denying the relationship between him and Thai, what was that about the radio, the Americans, the spy... the guard? Thai was the secretive guard at Piseth's house, always there, always in the shadows, always in the know. The guard who had disappeared before the Rouge arrived had now reappeared and was caring for them on this long exodus, this exodus to Tuk Meas.

Tuk Meas

Tuk Meas from a distance looked like the typical Cambodian village; houses on stilts and made of wood and leaves. It was situated at a crossroads, which extended in the four main directions, the major route heading south-east to the Vietnamese border only twelve kilometres away. In the fields surrounding the village Sokunthea began to notice people, hundreds of people, some working in the paddy-fields, others on what appeared to be a re-routing of a canal and a third group on a new canal construction. The next thing she noticed was that everything was being done by hand; there were no oxen to pull the carts of earth or drag the plough through the paddy-fields, people appeared to be tied to them and they had to drag their burden along. As they got closer she saw people working on their knees in the paddy-fields preparing the ground for planting and strutting amongst them were children, young children of about twelve, Sokunthea judged. They all carried a fine cane whip, which they used regularly on the people; they would scream at them and whip them, and if they observed any others watching them they would become the next victims.

They staggered on down the narrow sandy track into the village, yet nobody in the fields dared to lift their heads. Sokunthea had passed through the hunger barrier but still needed water desperately and remembered the previous stop, where new arrivals were fed and watered, people moving on were not. 'Well, I'm not moving,' she said quietly. They staggered into the village square, half stumbling, half being pushed along.

'Line up,' shouted Thai and the group formed a bedraggled line.

'You took your time,' said the man approaching Thai.

'The longer the walk, the tireder...'

'Don't give me that shit.' He turned to begin his inspection of the group and immediately Sokunthea knew the facial burn... the soldier on the river bank. He walked down the line. 'City folk,' he said, 'Seventeen of April scum.'

'I need to take some on,' cut in Thai.

Scarface turned and looked at him. 'Why?'

'Building defences, carrying munitions.' He shrugged his shoulders.

'No, I need them here.'

'But we must have defences.'

'And I must have rice… get your soldiers to build the defences, I can't spare anyone.'

'If you didn't kill so many…'

Scarface cut him off in mid-sentence with a stare of pure hatred. He turned to his aides. 'Get them out of the sun and give them water; I want them in the fields tonight.' With this he marched back to his quarters.

After consuming a small glass of rice-field water the group were dispersed into the fields. As they entered the field a young girl approached them.

'In a line over there,' she said and pointed to a row of rice planters already heavily at work. Sokunthea and Piseth moved towards the line, slowly moving forward with their elbows deep in mud. They crouched down behind them.

'What do I do?' whispered Piseth.

'Feel the mud and pull out anything that could damage the rice.' As Sokunthea turned back to her chore the pain of the whip crashed across her back.

'What were you talking about?' screamed the young educator.

'I was…' Whack! Another blow hit her across the chest and neck.

'Shut up… who asked you to speak?' Another whack was administered, then another. Sokunthea's rage began to grow as another blow came then another.

'Stop that…'came a voice from the edge of the rice field. It was Thai. 'I've not brought these people here for you to kill on the first day!' he screamed.

The educator stopped and looked at him. 'Who are you to tell…'

'What's happening here?' came the voice of Scarface as he

headed towards the rice field.

'This woman was conspiring with this man to slow the rice production,' said the educator.

Scarface walked up to her and looked down at Sokunthea who began, 'I was just...' Her words ended abruptly as Scarface's fist struck her firmly in the mouth. He then grabbed her hair and dragged her to the side of the rice field.

'You have brought me trouble,' said Scarface to Thai, 'and I don't like trouble.'

'She was helping her husband, getting him to work... these city people know nothing about rice, they need training not beating.'

'These Seventeen of April scum need to learn who are the masters now.' Scarface looked across the rice field towards Piseth, who was busily working and ignoring his wife's situation. He looked at Sokunthea. 'So you can teach rice planting.' She nodded and he grabbed her hair again, pulling her head back. 'Well, how did a Seventeen of April woman like you learn that skill?' He stared threateningly into her face.

'I worked in the rice fields before I went to Phnom Penh.'

'Hum... good.' He let her go. He turned to the educator. 'Place her at the end of the line; she can show the others and they can keep pace with her... if they fall behind you know what to do.' He grinned and turned to Thai. 'Come, let's celebrate before you depart tomorrow.' Thai nodded and they left.

It was after dark when the group were allowed out of the field and showed their living quarters. They were separated into gender and marshalled into groups of four for washing and eating purposes; the food consisted of rice soup, which filled the stomach but did little else for the body. The progressive dehydration was beginning to take its toll also, Sokunthea's periods had been stopped for some time and although she didn't mind that the lack of general body moisture was becoming uncomfortable.

As she began to settle someone asked, 'Are you all right daughter?'

Sokunthea's eyes slowly adjusted to the dark and she saw an old lady sitting up with her back resting against a wooden pillar of the house. 'Fine, I'm fine,' she said.

'That husband of yours wasn't much help was he?'

'He couldn't do anything.'

'Well, it was all his fault… anyway, listen, around here are lots of mines, you know the ones they put to kill you.'

'Mines?' said Sokunthea sharply.

'Shush… the educators will hear us talking and then… creeck.' She made a cutting gesture across her throat. 'Mines,' she continued, 'in the ground everywhere, if you find one you're supposed to bring it to the attention of the educators or the guards.'

'I should think you are,' said Sokunthea, still startled.

'But they get you to carry it out; you see they need these mines down on the border. They can't afford to buy everything from the Chinese, so at the end of the month these things are put on a cart and taken down to the military on the Vietnamese border, but unfortunately they don't always arrive.'

'Why not?'

'Boom!' said the woman. 'They're unstable; they go up, along with the poor buggers tied to the cart.'

'You mean…' Sokunthea stopped.

'Whoever finds the mines has the honour of transporting them… the honour!' She began to chuckle. 'Don't pull out the mines, push them along to the end of the line, let the educators find them, they can have the honour.' She laughed again. 'Shush, educator.' She slid down onto her mat and began to sleep. As Sokunthea stared up at the roof she heard her name softly called out from outside.

'Sokunthea, come… come out, sister.' It was the educators. 'Come out.'

She rolled onto her knees and made for the doorway; outside, in the half moonlight, she could see the dark shapes of four teenagers, educators. As she stepped down the ladder she was grabbed by both arms and led away from the buildings down towards the canal.

'You got me into trouble, sister,' said one of the figures whom she quickly recognised as her assailant from earlier that day. As she turned to speak a foot struck her in the lower abdomen knocking all the air out of her; she buckled to the floor, coughing and gasping for air. Then more blows from hands and feet began to rain down on her, and she was pulled to her feet and pushed down the canal bank and fell into the water. More blows struck her and her head was forced below the water on several occasions; each time the period underwater was longer and longer. She could feel her strength leaving her and had begun to wonder if she would die in this canal when the man's voice hit her.

'Out… get her out and bring her to my hut.' As she was being half dragged, half carried across the village square her head began to clear, her four assailants them dropped her onto the wooden floor of a village hut. 'Out,' the man's voice said above her.

'But we…' A female voice tried to interject.

'Out!' the command came again.

Sokunthea could hear the sound of disappearing feet. She lay still on the floor for a while listening for any other sign of activity.

'Are you injured?' came the voice. 'Come over here and sit… those women are very proud, they tell me you are a threat… ha, ha… a threat to what I asked… to them they said, to them and me… ha, ha, women – I'll never understand them.'

Sokunthea stirred, coughed a couple of times and rolled onto her side to see who was her saviour… it was Scarface.

'Ha, you are alive… good, come over here, we can talk.'

She slowly struggled to her feet and sat on the edge of a large wooden bed; Scarface was commanding its centre.

'Better, that's better… here have a drink, water, I'm afraid, but at least it's the clean stuff… my educators are pretty loyal and they stick together; upset one, upset them all.'

'They're sick,' replied Sokunthea.

'No, you cannot say that, they are the new Kampuchea, the Ankor, the salvation of the nation.'

'They're sick.'

'I think you're right… but don't quote me.'

'Why am I here?'

'Oh, come on; I saved your life.'

'Why… you have this reputation of taking so many!'

'Well, Thai was right; to kill someone on their first day wouldn't look good, there's plenty of time to kill.' Sokunthea glanced at the floor and the room fell silent.

'How's your dancing these days?' Sokunthea and Scarface's eyes met.

'I don't dance, I'm a married woman.'

'How's Sinarth? He killed two of my men that night... well, you know that.'

'Your men tried to...' She stopped.

'Well, it was the dance, you see, everybody was tense and then you two... wow, it blew everybody's mind.'

'It cost Thea her life. When did you recognise me?' said Sokunthea after a pause.

'I watched you bathing in the canal... beautiful. Then I knew.'

'And do I need to fear?'

'We all need to fear.'

'And will I have more attacks... more night chats?'

He looked at the floor. 'Take care, there are things even I can't protect you from.'

'The educators.'

'They report everything and everybody... cross them too many times and...' He shrugged his shoulders.

'I'd like to go now.'

'Sure. Chandra!' he called out. 'There's a price,' he said, smiling at Sokunthea.

An educator entered the room.

'Six lashes then back to her room.'

'Good,' came the reply. The educators returned and dragged Sokunthea outside, they pushed and dragged her along the dusty road to a small copse just outside of the village. The educators stood in a circle around her.

'What do you think you're...' she began to speak until a hard blow struck her across the face. A hand grabbed her *kroma* and pulled it from her body; as Sokunthea tried to hold it up the first whip struck her across her naked back, then another, and she dropped to her knees as more blows fell on her. After the punishment had been administered she was deposited outside her hut. She staggered onto her mat and lay still; the whipping hadn't really hurt and she felt some of the girls hadn't put their hearts into it, so no skin was broken.

'His wives got you,' came the old lady's voice.

'What?'

'His wives... his wives got you.'

'I'm not sure I...'

'He has a group of educators, they look after him... they'll be watching you, last woman he had they killed her.'

'Last... I'm married, my husband is in the other hut.'

'Makes no difference; if he wants you, he'll take you and then they'll get rid of the evidence, I thought he'd have had you tonight.'

'Well, he didn't and if he'd tried I'd...'

'Gone along with it... because you want to live.'

The morning came all too soon and Sokunthea was once again a member of the rice line with her arms covered in mud, slowly moving forward beneath the burning sun. Piseth was again alongside Sokunthea and they both watched with some regret the departure of Thai and his small band of soldiers. Sokunthea's back was her major concern as she groped her hands through the mud in front of her; although the beating had only been a warning she knew her every action was being watched by the wives and she was determined not to repeat the previous day's actions.

'Hurry, you're falling behind,' came the young voice behind her.

Sokunthea looked up and then down the line. 'Keep pace with me!' she called and began to move forward more quickly. The educator seemed satisfied and moved off.

'Slow down,' said Piseth, 'this is killing me.'

'It's better than being a human bullock. If we don't keep up a good pace they'll find other work for idle hands.'

'I'm not idle.'

'Where's the radio?' Sokunthea had spoken the words without thinking.

'What?'

'The radio... your salvation, and don't lie, we haven't time.'

'How did you...'

'I recognised Thai... and overheard your conversation.'

'He wants it... he thinks it's his meal ticket when all this is over.'

'And is it?'

Piseth just shrugged.

'Where is it?'

'In the water tank on the roof… if you want it you'll have to feel around for it like this and if you're lucky you'll feel… Christ, what's this?'

Both looked down as Piseth pulled to the surface a large anti-personnel mine.

'Don't show it,' Sokunthea whispered but it was too late; Piseth was already climbing to his feet and a guard had spotted him. He was motioned to carry the mine to the sandy road and Sokunthea saw him carrying it like a baby and disappearing down the road.

'Find more… Ankor will reward anyone who finds mines!' came the call from the educators and Sokunthea thought of what the old lady had said.

As the noon sun came overhead Sokunthea was tapped on the shoulder. An educator nodded and Sokunthea stood up and followed her. They walked towards the village and by the time they reached the village square the rice field mud had dried on her skin and clothing.

'Sit,' said the educator. Sokunthea was placed under a tree and the educator walked towards a small hut; compared to the fields all around was quiet and still. A small number of Rouge appeared to be carrying out some form of administration while others sat in small groups talking.

'Here, over here.' Sokunthea looked across the square and noticed the educator calling her, so she stood and walked towards her. She followed the educator into the small hut where two men were sitting talking.

They did not look up then one asked, 'What is your name?'

'Sokunthea Sen.'

'Where are you from?'

'Phnom Penh.'

'And your village?'

'Rhor Kar.'

'You were a teacher, were you not?'

'Yes.'

'A teacher from Rhor Kar.'

'Yes.'

'You were a member of the army of Lon Nol,' stated the second man.

'No.'

'You were stationed in Neak Loung.' Sokunthea knew where this information had come from and she knew an honest answer would cost her husband his life.

'I was not.'

'The penalty for lying to Ankor is death,' said the first questioner.

'I have not lied.'

'Was your husband a soldier for Lon Nol?'

'No, he is a doctor.'

'We have records that he worked for Lon Nol,' interjected the second questioner.

'He did not, he avoided the call up, Lon Nol was after him.'

'How do you know this?' came back the first questioner.

'They came to our house looking for him.'

'You claim to have experience of the rice.'

'I worked for many years with my father in the fields around Rhor Kar.'

'Why did you marry a Seventeen of April?'

'I am not familiar with this term.'

'A city dweller, a parasite,' came the angry voice of the second questioner.

'Arranged.'

The first questioner stood and walked around Sokunthea, he touched her back. 'I see you have had trouble with my workers already.'

Sokunthea looked straight at the young educator. 'Just a misunderstanding.'

'I hope you do not repeat it. You will attend the education classes at five o'clock.'

'With my husband?'

The man turned. 'No... no, this class is not for him.'

Sokunthea was led outside and back to the shade of the tree by the young educator.

'Wait here, I'll get you some food.' Sokunthea sat back and was determined to rest her aching back. The educator returned with yet more rice soup and Sokunthea began to eat.

'So you're not one of them, then,' said the educator.

'One of who?'

'Them… the Seventeen of April people.'

Sokunthea was silent then she said, 'Did you ever go to the city?'

'Never.'

'You ever want to go?'

'Sure.'

'If you had you'd be a Seventeen of April by now.'

She sat down. 'I don't really know what that means, but Phally says we are better than them and we should keep them in order.'

'And who's Phally?'

'She's the one who beat…'

Sokunthea looked at her. 'Never mind. Where are your parents?'

'I don't know… but Ankor is taking care of them.'

'I'm sure it is, not like here though, yeah?'

'Oh, no, much better.'

Sokunthea just nodded and finished her food. What have they done to our young? she thought. 'We'd better get back,' she said to her young friend.

'Oh, yeah… sure.' They walked together back to the rice field.

When Sokunthea got back her husband had already returned to the rice field and the human line was moving slowly across its surface. Standing on the edge of the field was Scarface and he gestured to Sokunthea to come to him.

'So you have been interviewed by the educators.'

'So that's who they were.'

'Don't be fooled by them; they are not fools.'

'Are they the ones you can't protect anyone from'

'Hummmh,' he nodded.

Sokunthea paused and then said, 'They mentioned Neak Loung; I think you were there.'

He turned and looked at her. 'The baby story was a lie and your husband didn't deserve it, he should have taken his punishment and not hidden behind you.'

'If you punished every man who hides behind his wife when the chips are down you'd punish the entire gender,' she smiled.

'He's a fool and he'll get you killed, the educators know about him.'

'And do they know about you?'

He glared at her. 'No, and they never will.' He walked away. 'Work... to work!' he called over his shoulder.

'Where have you been?' was Piseth's first question, as she rejoined the line.

'Educated.'

'Where?'

'Educated... I was taken to the educators, my education begins at five.'

'Well, I've seen the biggest pile of mines ever... they've got hundreds of them back there.'

'And how many will die moving them?'

'What? I saved your life finding that thing, it could have exploded...'

'You've put your life in jeopardy, you mean.'

'Well, that's gratitude.'

'Stop talking there!' Sokunthea and Piseth looked across to a guard observing them. They continued in silence for a while, then Sokunthea spoke.

'They'll want volunteers to take the mines to the border.'

'Great, that'll get us away from Scarface for a while.'

'That'll get us killed, if those things explode.'

'And if we stay here?' He glared at her.

'Did you recognise Scarface from the boat?'

'Nah, I did some business with him later in Phnom Penh, he was there at your night out.'

'I know. Will he help us like Thai?'

'No... he's unstable, dangerous, my medical teacher would call him a psychopath but he's just plain bad.'

'Has he recognised you?'

'Of course.'

'And he knows your contacts... the Americans, I mean.'

'I don't think so, he just thinks I ran medical supplies.'

'When the educators saw me they asked about Neak Loung and if you were in the army.'

'What did you say?'

'You were a doctor and had never been in the army.'

'Will they want to see me?'

'They see everybody.'

'That trip to the border sounds more appealing.'

For the rest of the afternoon the line moved slowly forwards beneath the hot sun. The Rouge had changed the size of the average Cambodian rice field, making them six or eight times bigger. By removing the traditional water-holding banks they hoped to increase the yield. Sokunthea knew that this would only lead to uneven water levels across such large fields and would reduce the crop, and that therefore the lines of levellers were more important and shouldn't be rushed.

Just before five she was called from the fields and told to wash and then go to the classroom, a large square wooden building standing on small stilts on the edge of the village square. She arrived with several other women and sat on the floor; small bowls of rice soup were passed around with what smelt like fish. As the group began to eat a young woman stood up and began to inform the gathering that she had attempted to visit her husband in another compound. Immediately several young female educators began to yell at her.

'You are a whore, you are against Ankor!' They grabbed at her and tore her clothes from her body, so she stood naked, shaking and crying in the middle of the room. Then one of the two men who had questioned Sokunthea tapped his cane on the floor, and the tirade stopped.

'Why do you need the love of your husband, when Ankor has all the love you need?' He spoke softly but clearly.

'I just needed his comfort,' she replied, then burst into tears again.

'Do not the women in your compound give you comfort?' She shook her head. 'Point to a woman from your compound.'

She looked at the man then turned her attention to the gathering, looked around slowly then pointed straight at Sokunthea. Everyone in the room looked at her choice.

'Come forward,' said the man, 'come forward.'

Sokunthea stood up slowly and walked towards the naked woman.

'Why do you not give your sister comfort?' said the man.

'I'm new... I don't really...'

'But she needs comfort and she feels she knows you.' Sokunthea looked at the girl, who tried to force a smile. 'Will you give this girl comfort?' continued the man.

'Yes... yes,' said Sokunthea quickly.

The man banged his stick on the floor and said to the gathering, 'This woman' – pointing at Sokunthea – 'will be responsible for this woman' – pointing at the naked girl. Sokunthea picked up the torn clothes of the girl and wrapped them around her and they both went to the edge of the group and sat down.

'Thank you,' whispered the girl, 'I'll try not to be too much trouble.'

Sokunthea smiled at her. 'What is your name?'

'Tiny,' she said.

'How long have you been here?'

'I don't know, time passes, I don't know,' and she began to cry silently.

'Why did you try to visit your husband?'

'They moved us out of Phnom Penh on our wedding day and we never... anyway, he's ordered to take the mines tomorrow and I may not...' She began to cry again.

'Do people come back from taking the mines?'

'I don't know... they say not.'

'Well, I'm sure he will,' she said, trying to cheer Tiny up. 'My husband found one, he says the pile is only small.'

'Well, if he found one, he'll go too.' She engaged Sokunthea in eye contact then began crying again. They walked back to the hut together and sat on Sokunthea's mat.

'Who's your friend?' said the old woman.

Sokunthea introduced Tiny and explained the circumstances of their meeting.

'So you've got to take care of her then,' continued the old woman.

'Is that a problem?' Sokunthea looked from Tiny to her questioner.

'If she tries to see her husband again it is.'

'Why?'

'Well, you are responsible. If she gets the call from her husband and they catch her you both get it. Right?' the old lady looked at Tiny.

'Yes,' said Tiny in a quiet mumbled reply.

'But I can't be held responsible for everything you do,' said Sokunthea looking at Tiny, 'that's stupid.'

'That's Ankor,' said the old woman, who then rolled over and went to sleep.

'You won't try to visit him again will you?' Sokunthea asked Tiny.

'No, not if you stay with me. I'll be all right.'

Sokunthea picked up her bundle and walked over to where Tiny had been sleeping. 'Let's settle here tonight,' she said, 'away from the door.' Sokunthea and Tiny lay down together in the hot hut; Sokunthea could hear the faint crying of Tiny and put her arm around her and held her close.

'What will happen to us?' Tiny began.

'Nothing. We'll be okay.'

'Aren't you afraid?'

'Sometimes… but they like to see that so I don't show it.'

'I wish I was brave like you. That's why I picked you.'

'What?'

'You look so strong, brave, that's why I picked you in the group.'

Sokunthea gave her a squeeze. 'Well, we'll be brave together.'

'What will we do if our husbands die on the road with the mines?'

'Survive.'

'You don't think much of men do you?'

'I think if it's their survival or yours, they'll choose theirs.'

'Even husbands?'

'Even husbands.'

The hut fell silent then Tiny said, 'Have you ever had sex?' and Sokunthea thought of Sinarth.

'Yes.'

'Is it good?'

'To a prostitute it's money, to an abused woman it's a way to avoid another beating, to most women it's their duty, but yeah, it can be good with the right man.'

'But how do you know who is the right man with an arranged marriage?'

'The Cambodian woman's dilemma.'

'What?'

'Let's go to sleep.' As they held each other closer Sokunthea felt Tiny's mouth on hers and they both kissed.

'You won't leave me?' whispered Tiny.

'No,' said Sokunthea, and they both fell asleep.

Sokunthea and Tiny woke as they had fallen asleep – wrapped in each other's arms. Outside they could hear many voices calling, 'Parade, parade.' As they stumbled outside they were pushed into a line stretching around the four sides of the village square; around them were educators shouting, 'Stand up straight, keep still, hurry up there.'

In the centre of the square stood the two senior male educators and Scarface; Scarface nodded and a man was pushed out into the middle of the square.

'That's my husband,' whispered Tiny.

'This man,' began the educator, 'has transgressed; he was caught several nights ago attempting to enter the quarters of the females, so to prove his faith to Ankor he has volunteered to transport the much needed mines to the border in order to keep out our enemies, the Vietnamese. Ankor in its wisdom and forgiveness has granted this wish and asks for more such volunteers in this essential journey.'

There was no movement in the line, then Tiny ran forward and stood by her husband's side; as Sokunthea looked on she noticed many eyes turning towards her.

'You have to go,' said the old woman, 'you are responsible.'

Sokunthea stood her ground until a strong push in her back sent her sprawling onto her face and out of line; she looked back and saw Phally smiling. Sokunthea stood up and walked forward to join Tiny and her husband.

'No.' Sokunthea looked up; it was Scarface speaking. 'I need all the experienced rice planters I can get.' He was looking at the senior educators.

'One makes no difference, and she agreed to be responsible.'

Scarface stared at Sokunthea who cast her eyes down. The next entrant to the centre was her husband, praised as a finder of mines, followed by two other men and three women. The senior educator thanked them for their patriotism and wished them a good journey. The parade was dismissed and the nine were led to a large tree where they sat and ate rice soup.

Tiny turned to Sokunthea and said, 'I'm sorry to do this but we have had such little time together.' Sokunthea just smiled.

'This way!' came an order from a young soldier and he led them out of the village and into a small scrub area. In the centre stood a wooden ox cart, to its left a large pile of rice straw and to its right, scattered on the floor, some fifty mines of all different shapes and sizes. 'Load,' came the order.

Sokunthea walked forward and began laying straw in the base of the ox cart, and two other women came and assisted.

Piseth and two men had approached the mines and were carrying them over when Sokunthea shouted, 'Not yet! We have to pack them properly first or we'll all die,' and the men stopped. The building up of the cart with a layer of straw, then a scattering of mines, then more straw took two hours and all were tired when it was complete. As Sokunthea sat in the shade of the cart a cup of water was pushed towards her face; It was Scarface offering her a drink.

'You've done a good job for a Seventeen of April.'

'I plan to stay alive.'

'Well, you're going the wrong way about it.'

She glared at him. 'I didn't volunteer for this, your wives gave me a helping hand.'

'You're a threat.'

'Tell them I'm not.'

He bent and took her arm, helping her to her feet. 'You do that on your return,' and he turned to walk away, 'because I think you'll return, Seventeen of April. Get them moving,' he shouted to the guard, then he paused. 'Put her,' nodding towards

Sokunthea, 'in charge of the food and drink.' He turned to Sokunthea. 'Don't waste it,' and walked away.

The group looked at each other and then at the cart. 'What... how...' said Piseth.

'Come on, hurry,' said the guard. Again they looked at each other until all eyes fell on Sokunthea.

'Okay, we want five at the front pulling, two at the back pushing and two out in front walking the ox cart tracks making sure it's smooth and getting rid of loose stones. Let's go.' The group seemed to react automatically and the cart began to move smoothly. Sokunthea had taken up a position at the back, pushing the cart; this was partly for some shade and partly to keep a running check on the state of the packing. For she knew loose packing meant doom for them all. Alongside her was Tiny.

'How long will it take to get there?'

'About four days.'

'Four days... four days from that hell back there.'

'Longer if it blows up.'

They both laughed then stopped, then realised there were no educators and began to laugh again, only louder.

'That man was right; you'll get us back,' said Tiny.

'How old are you?' asked Sokunthea.

'Eighteen.'

'And your husband... I couldn't help but notice he was older.'

'About forty, I think.'

'Doesn't it worry you that he was trying to get into several female huts?'

'He says it's because I wouldn't come to him.'

'Why did you marry him?'

Tiny looked at Sokunthea. 'He had something on my mother...' She stopped.

'Men.'

'I can control him.'

'That's what they all say.'

'He's been okay to me.'

'Just be careful; he seems a little desperate to me and now's not the time to loose your virginity and become pregnant.'

'Oh, he agrees; the night I was caught he said he wanted to talk to me. I wouldn't want children; not here, not now.'

As they moved south-east they approached a small group of trees lining the road. 'Stop!' shouted Sokunthea and the cart ground to a halt. 'Let's rest,' and she pointed to the trees. Nobody objected, including the single guard who was walking several yards behind them, and they all sheltered under the trees.

Piseth came over to Sokunthea. 'How far have we come?'

'Maybe half a klick,' she replied.

'And how's the packing holding up?'

'Oh, I'm fine,' she said, glaring at him.

'I'm sorry.' He paused. 'I still worry about you, you know,' he continued.

'Sure.'

'Sure; we've been through a lot.'

'What do you want?'

'Nothing… I'm just trying to make sure we're okay.'

'Well, we are okay and we'll be even more okay when we deliver this stuff.' She nodded to the cart.

'When do we get the food and drink ration?'

'I see,' Sokunthea glared at him. 'Not until noon.'

'What if we can't wait that long?'

'Then you fall out and the guard shoots you.'

'Some of us have bigger thirsts than others.'

'Control it.'

'How, when you're pulling that bloody thing?'

'We have enough food and water to get us to the rendezvous. If we drink it now we're as good as dead, so control it.'

He glared at her then said, 'You should have been a man.'

'Thank God I'm not.' She looked at him in disgust. She stood. 'Let's go; come on, next stop food and water.'

Sokunthea and Tiny were now out in front checking the wheel lines and moving rocks and other hindrances from the path of the cart. The sun was getting ever hotter as they approached midday.

'I told my husband about us being careful,' began Tiny.

'And?'

'He seemed a little annoyed, he said maybe I shouldn't talk to you.'

'And what do you think about that?'

'He says we've never done... he thinks you've done it lots of times.'

'But he doesn't have to do it in nine months' time out in the rice field.'

'I know, I told him.'

'And?'

'He asked me if I loved him.'

'Blackmail.'

They walked on in silence, watching for debris that could jolt the cart. As noon approached it became clear that no shelter would appear next to the road. The landscape was flat and barren, and everyone was waiting for the rains. Sokunthea stopped the cart and they all sought shelter in its shade, the food and water ration was distributed and everyone ate and drank in silence.

The heat and the humidity began to build during the early afternoon and Sokunthea could see that the heavy rains would begin soon. She didn't want to be exposed to a severe rain storm, not with that cargo, and she began to urge everyone on to greater efforts. The sky became darker and darker and sporadic raindrops could be felt; the need for some shelter and rest grew more urgent, as Sokunthea tried to urge the group to even greater speed.

'Stop... stop!' yelled Tiny. 'There's a hole in the road!'

The cart slowly came to a halt and Sokunthea climbed back onto the road and, looking back, observed an open water drain cut at an angle of forty-five degrees across the road. The drain was deep enough to take half the depth of the wheel, while wide enough to take its width; a further problem was the angle which meant that if the cart was rolled into it, it would surely topple over.

'Damn,' said Sokunthea, and she looked up into the sky for inspiration.

The group huddled around her, each one looking at the obstacle and shaking their heads. Sokunthea walked away from this growing group anxiously back down the track. She knew that if the heavy rains and wind came and the cart was left exposed it would explode and they were good as dead. If they found shelter and the cart survived the rains the drain would fill and they could not continue their journey. As she looked around Sokunthea could feel the raindrops getting bigger and becoming more frequent; suddenly she walked up to the guard.

'Bayonet,' she said and held out her hand.

The guard took one step back and levelled his AK-47 at her.

'Bayonet – to dig up the road,' she pointed down.

He didn't move, then slowly reached behind his back and pulled out the bayonet and handed it over to her. Sokunthea dropped to her knees and began furiously to dig at the road behind the cart.

'Come, get this soil and pack the cart lines in front of the wheels.'

The group looked at her at first then exploded into action as they realised the plan. As Sokunthea frantically dug, hands appeared and carried away the earth and clay boulders as they were prised loose.

'Check the fields for wood, straw, anything that will pack the drain. Hurry!'

As with many Cambodian rain storms, following the first few drops there was a pause before the main downpour. How long this would last Sokunthea did not know but she was determined that there would be no rest until the tracks were constructed. The rains had begun to fall more heavily when Tiny came running up to her.

'I think we're ready.'

Sokunthea looked up; she scrambled to her feet and ran to the front of the cart. Two lines had been built across the drain which, although uneven, looked secure. She turned to the soldier again and pointed to his rifle.

'Beat it down,' she said. 'Flatten it.'

The soldier nodded and, using the butt, packed the soil down further. The rain became intense and there were already signs of water accumulation building up in the higher rice field; they had to get the cart across now. With five pulling and two on each wheel they moved forward slowly; as the first wheel reached the drain bridge they progressed spoke by spoke and the cart moved on slowly without rocking. The rain was now in full flood and the wind was beginning to gain strength as it swept across the open landscape. The cart was rolled forward slowly but as its right wheel began to cross the small traverse the rain water broke through into the drain and rushed up against the wheel. The soil began to wash away and the cart started to rock, then topple towards the rice field below; the track line was not holding.

Three of the men refused to allow their fate to be decided in the drain and abandoned the cart and began to run up the road; through the pouring rain running down her face Sokunthea saw the disappearing shape of her husband. The soil trackline began to give way but Sokunthea grabbed the wheel and with all her strength tried to hold it up. It was no good; it slipped again and Sokunthea knew this was it – then a wedge appeared and was rammed under the wheel, which gave the trackline and the wheel the support it needed. Sokunthea screamed, 'Push!' and the cart moved forward; as it did a shot rang out.

As the cart reached the safety of solid ground Sokunthea looked back and saw the young soldier lying in the rice field holding his abdomen; she realised he had forced his rifle under the cart wheel and held it up just long enough for them to push it to safety, but in doing so the rifle had fired. She ran back to him.

'Here, over here, give me some help!' she shouted to the dark night sky. The remaining group appeared around her. 'You two help me carry him, the rest move the cart to a safer place.'

As the group moved ahead with their burdens they noticed a Chinese burial ground next to the road appearing from the darkness ahead, so they moved in there for shelter.

'Lay him here,' Sokunthea called to the group carrying the soldier and they laid him on a small slab inside some family's mausoleum. She began to undo his clothing in order to see the extent of his wounds; the soldier lay still, quietly crying. The bullet wound had entered his abdomen and there was no sign of exit. Sokunthea knew from her Neak Loung days that abdominal wounds almost certainly led to death.

'I will die,' he whispered, then grabbed her arm. 'Don't let me die.'

Sokunthea smiled at him and began to pack the wound to stop the bleeding. 'You won't die; the bullet's out, if we pack it you'll be okay.' She was lying. She made the soldier as comfortable as possible, made one final check on his dressing and then went outside. It was still raining heavily and the group was scattered across the burial ground under what ever shelter they could find.

'Where's Tiny?' said Sokunthea to one of the women.

'She went over there with her husband,' came the reply.

Sokunthea set off in the direction that the woman had indicated; she came to the edge of the burial ground and looked out across the dark fields and not being able to see anything, she had turned to go when she heard a choking and thrashing sound coming from her right. She slid down the burial mound and crept along the edge of the rice field, the rain was incessant and the dark of night hugged the ground. Then she saw legs kicking in the air and quickly realised a woman was being held down in a water drain with a man on top of her. Sokunthea's rage surfaced and she pulled a short iron rod from the surroundings of an old grave, and rushed at the man who, because of the torrential rain, did not hear her. He was indeed sitting across a woman, holding her head down below the water drain and pulling at her clothing with his other hand; Sokunthea hit him hard between the shoulders. He arched backwards and screamed, although the night took away the sound; as he turned to see his attacker she hit him again, this time across the head. As he crashed to the floor the head and upper body of Tiny appeared from the drain, coughing and trying to gain breath. Sokunthea grabbed Tiny by the elbow and pulled her clear of the onrushing water; the man lay still next to her.

'You all right?' she asked of Tiny.

Tiny began to cough then said, 'Fine, I'm fine now.'

'Let's get back to the group.' Tiny nodded. They headed back to the burial ground and on to the mausoleum.

'Keep an eye on him,' said Sokunthea, pointing towards the soldier, 'I'll organise the rations.' She went outside.

As she approached the cart she realised something was missing... the rations were gone. She stopped, then immediately began to search for her husband. She found him sheltering under a small tree.

'Where's the food? And don't play stupid.' He pointed to his right; Sokunthea could see two bags of food and the water bottles. She checked them and found one bag empty and only three bottles full.

'You bastard!'

'It wasn't just me, we've all had some.'

Sokunthea looked at another group huddled under the cart, who looked away.

'Okay,' she said, 'this lot is mine,' and she walked back to Tiny and the soldier.

As she entered the mausoleum Tiny said, 'He's dead.' Sokunthea ran over and tried to find a pulse... nothing. She turned to look outside and the rain stopped. Tiny and Sokunthea sat at the entrance of the mausoleum, eating and drinking.

'What do you think has happened to my husband?' said Tiny.

'I don't know and I don't care,' came the reply.

'He nearly killed me... just to get what he wanted.'

'Why did you go with him?'

'He said there was good shelter.'

'I think he's dangerous, not just for you but all women.'

'I think so too. When I said I wouldn't let him he just went berserk... I'm afraid of him.'

'Well, when he wakes up he may have gained some sense.'

They both laughed, then Tiny said, 'You really hit him.'

'He deserved it.'

Sokunthea stood up and shouted across the burial ground for help to dispose of the soldier. They slid open the mausoleum casket and dropped him in with his host, then the group dispersed to find somewhere to sleep. The morning came quickly and the group gathered around the cart.

'So what do we do now without the guard. Escape?' Piseth was looking at Sokunthea.

'We go on,' she said.

'Why? There's no one to force us.'

'So where do we go, doctor? Make a run for it? Where; we have little food and water, there are Rouge soldiers all around... how do we survive?' The group went quiet, 'We go on,' said Sokunthea, 'that's the only way to show we have nothing to hide.'

'Tiny, Tiny, come quick! Your husband is dead.'

The group followed the woman and Tiny to the edge of the burial ground; her husband was lying where he had fallen the night before. Only in daylight could you see the extent of the head injury he had received.

'Leave him,' said Sokunthea, 'We have to get going before the rains come again.'

'But somebody must have done this,' said Piseth and he looked at Sokunthea.

'Whoever did it is needed to pull the cart; there's only eight of us now so let's avoid a lynch mob. Move!' she screamed at the group.

'But shouldn't we at least bury him?' said Tiny.

Sokunthea looked at her and nodded, so Tiny's husband became the third occupant of the host's mausoleum.

The rains had kept away until the early afternoon and the journey along the road had been relatively trouble-free. The midday break had seen the last of the water but a little rice soup remained. The group had decided to keep pressing ahead and were therefore pleased to reach the Kampong Trach crossing late in the evening. Before the war and the Rouge this small crossing had small stalls selling many rural products; now only the shells of the stalls remained. These dark skeleton shapes gave it a ghostly feeling as the group began to camp in them; the stalls were cannibalised in order to make two secure shelters as it was clear that the rains were not far away.

Sokunthea passed around the last of the rice soup and laid out the water bottles in order to catch the rain when it fell. The group ate in silence as the sky danced with light and sound. As the rains began to fall the women made their way to the rear of their stall and began to wash themselves in the pouring water; they stripped to their *kromas* and washed out their other clothing in the pouring rain. This ritual of bathing with one's clothes on is handed down through generations of female Cambodians enabling them to get clean and maintain some dignity; unfortunately the cleanliness it provides is not universal and care has to be taken to avoid developing sore areas and rashes. For this reason, and to satisfy her own need to be thoroughly clean, Sokunthea decided to abandon her dignity and stripped naked; she was quickly followed by Tiny. The two women washed their bodies clean then helped wash each other.

'It's good to be alive!' shouted Tiny and she began to jump up and down in the rain.

'We're alive... we're alive!' shouted Sokunthea as the emotions of the previous day were released and the two women danced around together.

Although the rains were heavy that night the shelters had been well constructed and the occupants spent a comfortable night. In the morning they set off due east towards the Vietnamese border; the rains had come early but as they set out they stopped. The group was still fresh and confident that their journey would end in success and the road appeared flat and wide. Time was on their side and the rendezvous with the border military at the Ba Chuc river would be ahead of schedule. This air of confidence was soon shattered as the first shell hit the road; the group abandoned the cart and headed for cover. Soon a second, then a third shell smashed into the road getting closer and closer to its target.

Sokunthea looked on helplessly but she knew if the group was to receive favour for its journey it had to deliver the mines and no Vietnamese gunner was going to rob them of that. She stood.

'We've got to shift it!' she shouted and ran to the cart; she arrived at the same time as a shell exploded some twenty yards away. She looked back at the group, which was still hiding in a ditch. It was Tiny who came next followed by most of the women; the men begrudgingly followed later.

'What shall we do?' said Tiny on her arrival.

'Push it behind those trees.' Sokunthea pointed to her right.

The cart arrived at its new home as a shell landed slap in the middle of the road; the group ran for cover. Two more shells fell but it was obvious that the Vietnamese gunners were shooting blind and getting bored; as the group lay in the ditch, enjoying the silence, two soldiers dropped in beside them.

'Who are you?'

Sokunthea spoke. 'We have the mines from Tuk Meas.'

The soldier looked at her in disbelief then said, 'Let's roll it forward,' looking at the cart. The group pushed the cart down the road for another kilometre then were ordered to turn left; they went down a small track and entered a small military camp well camouflaged into the forest. The group collapsed on the floor while the soldiers went to one of the small buildings. Sokunthea looked across a small open square to what appeared to be some kind of military bunker, she stood and walked across to it and noticed that it looked out from the trees across a small river, the Ba Chuc river; on the other side was Vietnam and possible safety.

'So you made it to the front after all.' Sokunthea turned around to see Thai. 'How is your husband?'

'He's over there.' Sokunthea pointed to the cart.

'Is he?' Thai turned and walked towards the group; Sokunthea followed. Thai stopped at a group of soldiers. 'Get them to unload the mines and bring that one to the office.' He pointed at Piseth. Sokunthea went back to the group and slowly they unloaded the straw and the mines from the cart, then a soldier came towards her.

'You, the office,' he said. She walked across the square and into an open entrance area; it almost looked like a small school, Sokunthea thought.

'Sit down,' said Thai and she sat next to her husband. 'How did the soldier die?' Sokunthea looked at him and began to describe the incident. 'Hmmmh – sounds reasonable, but then Scarface is not reasonable.'

'Will we have to go back?' asked Piseth.

'With two dead people, yes… especially when one is a soldier.'

'Damn.'

Thai turned to Sokunthea. 'You know who I am.'

'Yes.'

'And about your husband.'

'Yes.'

'Do you believe his radio story?'

'Yes, I've seen it.'

'Where is it?'

'I don't know, I'm not interested.'

'See, I told you,' cut in Piseth.

'When this war ends…'

'I know,' said Sokunthea, 'you'll need connections.'

Thai smiled, then turned to Piseth. 'You can stay here one day, maybe two, then you'll have to go back. This place is not safe; we already exchange fire with the Vietnamese and it won't be long before it's all-out war.'

'Why do you need all these mines?' asked Sokunthea.

'That's simple; the government can only buy so much from the Chinese with rice, so what we can find we use.'

'The Vietnamese are not going to be stopped by a few mines,' said Sokunthea.

'That's why you need connections,' replied Thai.

The Tuk Meas group were allowed to rest for a couple of days, then it was time to return with the empty cart. The three men with the party wanted to volunteer for military service and stay, but Thai realised that with two dead there would be some kind of investigation when they returned. The journey back was completed in less than a third of the time out and two days after setting off the group was camping on the edge of Tuk Meas.

'What will they do to us tomorrow?' asked Tiny of Sokunthea.

'Give us medals.' They laughed.

'Seriously.'

'Two are dead; one they don't care about.'

'My husband.'

'Your husband... the other was a soldier, so someone's to blame.'

'You... you think they'll blame you?'

'No... I don't know.'

'My husband was a rat and the soldier was an accident.'

'But there are no accidents in Ankor... someone will pay.'

'Why don't we run away?'

'Where to? We have no food, no water, where do we go? If we run they'll suspect wrongdoing and find us. No, we have to face this out.'

'And die.'

'Maybe.'

'I'm glad I lost my husband... you were right, he was no good.'

Sokunthea put her arm around Tiny and they settled back to sleep.

The following morning they entered the village, dragging the empty ox cart with them and by seven they were all back in the fields planting the rice. As Sokunthea pushed a handful of rice stalks into the mud the whack of an educator's cane struck her across the back.

'You are wanted,' said Phally. Sokunthea stood and followed the young educator and was led to the hut of Scarface; she entered and was told to sit.

'How did he die?' said Scarface as he entered the room. Sokunthea described the events. 'And the other man?'

'I killed him,' said Sokunthea and explained why.

'You are a very dangerous woman,' said Scarface. 'The educators want to see you; tell the truth and you may be okay.'

'The soldier was an accident, the man a rapist; isn't anyone going to recognise that I got the mines through?'

'If it's praise you want, you are in the wrong place.' He nodded to Phally, 'Take her to the educators.'

She walked behind her guard towards the educators' building and as they reached the square Phally turned. 'You are a very tough woman. Sen Li told me you're not Seventeen of April.'

'No, I'm not.'

'What did you see out there?'

'Where?'

'Towards the border… out there.'

'Have you ever left this village?'

She looked down. 'No, never.'

'So where did you get this idea about city people?'

'Thalin.'

'Thalin? Who's…'

'You people call him Scarface. I know it doesn't look good, but he's a very brave man.'

Sokunthea considered this then said, 'How do you know him?'

'He comes from this village; when he was younger he was the joker around here, always having fun, always chasing the girls.'

'Was he successful?' Sokunthea looked at Phally.

'No, his face always frightened them away.'

'I thought he got his face in the war.'

'No. No, he was burnt as a child, some say deliberately by his father.'

'And now the girls can't run. People say you and some of the other female educators are his wives.'

'He likes to think that, but we know what he wants; one or

two of the other women have...' she stopped. 'He wouldn't touch an educator, he knows the penalty.'

'So why the nickname?'

'He's unstable; we keep a close eye on him. Rou, our leader, asks us to keep an eye on him.' Phally looked towards the educators' building. 'They want you,' she said. Sokunthea nodded and they continued their walk.

'Look... what you did, the mines, the pervert and all... well, you're okay.'

Sokunthea smiled and entered the building; she was still smiling when she came face to face with her husband. 'What are you...?'

'I'll ask the questions,' said Rou. Sokunthea looked across the room at the tall elderly educator. 'Sit down,' he said.

Sokunthea looked around; Rou and his assistant were sitting behind a long, low table, to her right stood Phally, near the door, and her husband had positioned himself opposite her, leaning against the wall. The room had two windows along the wall beside her, both closed to keep out the sun, and a concrete floor; it was hot, very hot.

'Your husband has been helping us in our investigations; he claims that you are not new to creating trouble for Ankor.' She stared at Piseth as Rou continued. 'He claims that you were once a teacher and are on, shall we say, friendly terms with Thalin and Thai.'

'How long have you known Thalin?' asked his assistant.

'I first met him when I arrived here.'

'And Thai?' he continued.

'He escorted us here.'

'When did you become their mistress?'

'I am not...'

'Why would your husband lie?' cut in Rou.

Sokunthea's mind filled with a multitude of answers but she offered none. 'I don't know.'

'Did you tell your group not to disclose any mines that they may find?' chimed in the assistant.

'Yes.'

'Even though that is against Ankor?' His anger was showing.

'Finding mines means transporting them; everybody was scared of having to take them to the front.'

'Why did Thai want to take you to the border with him if you are not his mistress?' asked Rou calmly.

'I don't know.'

'Your memory is poor; I suggest that you need to think more clearly. Put her in the cage.' He looked at Phally.

'Up,' said Phally and she walked Sokunthea out of the room.

'Where are we going?' asked Sokunthea.

'There.' Phally pointed to the edge of the square where four small bamboo cages stood in the hot sun. She stooped and opened the door on the top of the first one.

'Do people die…?'

'Sometimes,' cut in Phally. 'Your husband is a fool.'

'Why?'

Phally looked around as she locked the cage door. 'He's implicating Thalin with you. Under Ankor rules he could be shot; Thalin won't let him get away with it.'

'And what about me?'

'It depends on how long they keep you in here. I'll try to get some water to you tonight… I'm sorry,' and with that she was gone.

Sokunthea looked up; she guessed it was about noon and the sun was beating down. The cage she was in measured two by one by two foot, just enough for a small curled-up body in a sitting position. She let down her hair in an attempt to block the sun's rays from the back of her neck, and her *kroma* was pulled over her feet but there was no cover for the back of her arms and shoulders; they would burn and badly.

She began to think about Piseth's plan; it was simple, get rid of all his previous contacts by joining forces with the new élite. Why not? He'd done it before. She began to think back to all that had happened to her, to Sinarth, to Neak Loung, to her mother. What a husband she had ended up with, an arranged husband, a husband she was brought up to please, never question, obey; now he was trying to kill her because she was in the way.

She began to doze under the weight of the sun and only woke when the late afternoon rains began to beat down on her; it was torrential but soothing. She realised that she was fixed in an almost foetal position and was unable to feel parts of her body. As the rain fell the water level around her began to rise and she realised that her cage and the other three were built in a small hollow. Her mind began to race again, to the times she saved Piseth's life, the soldier at the water hole, the sandbank; all flashed in and out. She began to massage her legs and neck hoping to keep at least some circulation going and the rain kept falling.

Later that night she woke; the rain had stopped and she was sat in one foot of water, and Phally was at the cage.

'Drink if you can, I can't stay long.' She passed a small canister of water through the bars; Sokunthea sipped as much as possible. 'How are you?' she asked.

Sokunthea just nodded and began a soft laugh; Phally poured the rest of the water over her burnt shoulders and arms.

'You must check for leeches,' she said, 'try and get them off.'

Sokunthea's laugh began to develop a hysterical note and grew in volume.

'I must go,' and Phally left.

Sokunthea drifted in and out of consciousness; in her more lucid moments she would attempt to massage herself and find leeches, often pulling them away but leaving their teeth still in her. By morning the water level had fallen and the extent of the leech invasion could be seen; Sokunthea began to develop a mild fever with convulsions. She thought she heard the voice of Rou, then blacked out again. When she woke she was lying in her hut with Tiny looking over her.

'You look like death,' she said, 'I thought those leeches had eaten the life out of you.'

Sokunthea rolled over and grabbed her bag; she felt into the lining and removed her last few bactrum tablets.

'Where'd you get...?' Tiny stopped.

Sokunthea swallowed her last tablet. 'It's a long story.' She curled up and closed her eyes.

'Your husband is causing a lot of problems, you know.'

'He's no husband of mine.'

'He's got those educators after Scarface.'

'Thalin.'

'What?'

'His name is Thalin.'

'Well, him... the old one is going to see some soldier at the border, get his story.'

'Is that why they let me out?'

'Maybe, I don't know.'

Sokunthea opened her eyes and looked at Tiny. 'Get me a drink.'

'Oh, sure, sorry.' She passed her a bamboo cup full of water. 'That Scarface – Thalin – he's really angry.'

'That makes two.'

'I mean *really* angry; he's taking it out on everybody, driving people to the edge, which makes your husband even more unpopular.'

'When will he get back?'

'Who?'

'Rou.'

'Oh, he's only just set off; maybe a couple of days.'

'So I've time to sleep then.'

'Yes, well... Oh, sorry, I have to report to Phally. Anyway, see you tonight.'

Sokunthea tried to sleep but her stiff joints and skin burns made lying on the floor mat difficult. In a rush of panic she sat up and checked herself over for leeches, but found none. Her mind drifted again to the foolish game that Piseth was playing; Thai wanted the radio but Thalin was dangerous and unstable. She imagined Piseth repeating his behaviour from Phnom Penh, always looking for the advantage, unconcerned about its effects on others, always trying to find an opening. Thalin had referred to his men when talking about Sinarth; he had clearly been in the bar that night, but how was he connected to Piseth? She was tired of trying to work out all these connections: Sinarth, Thai, Thalin and her husband. Sinarth was dead, killed while trying to escape Phnom Penh; now Piseth was after the rest. She tried to sleep.

She heard the voice of Phally and woke; it was dark and the rains were falling.

'You've slept a long time,' said Phally.

'I needed it.'

'Rou has gone…'

'I know, to the border.'

'His assistant Yan is in charge.'

'I thought Thalin was in charge.'

'He is, for rice and control, but for Ankor it's Rou.'

'Can he overrule Rou?'

'Thalin is capable of anything; here, sit up and take a drink.' Phally helped Sokunthea into a sitting position.

'Pass me my bag.'

Phally pulled it across the room to her and Sokunthea retrieved another bactrum.

'What are those?'

'Medicine.'

'Don't let Yan see them, otherwise it's certain death.'

'That's crazy; why stop people having things that will save their lives?'

'It's the rules of Ankor.'

Sokunthea swallowed her tablets. 'Why is Ankor against medicines?'

'Yan says it's because they were cheated in the war.'

'Cheated? How?'

'Oh, I don't know, really. Yan said that Ankor bought its drugs from some criminals in Phnom Penh but because it had no real doctors they were cheated, bought drugs that were no good, didn't work. Now all drugs are banned and anyone carrying them… greeek…' She drew a line across her neck with her hand.

'Where did Ankor get its money?'

'Oh, from the Chinese; they supplied everything, that's what Yan said, anyway.' She leaned forwards. 'They don't like the Vietnamese, either.'

'Why didn't the Chinese supply the drugs?'

'Oh, Chinese drugs are no good. Someone will be back later with some food; you'd better eat it, tomorrow you're back in the fields.' Phally leaned over and kissed Sokunthea on the forehead then stood and left. The show of affection brought tears to Sokunthea's eyes and she began to think of Sinarth's kindness and gentle touch. 'Don't be silly,' she said to herself, wiped her eyes and tried to sleep.

She woke with the sound of people entering the hut; they were returning from the fields, late, very late.

'I've some food for you,' said Tiny as she sat down beside Sokunthea.

Sokunthea sat up and began to eat. 'Why is everyone so late?' she asked.

'Thalin… he's making life hell.' She began to cry.

Sokunthea held her close. 'Never mind, I'll be out there tomorrow, I'll get him sorted.'

Tiny laughed, quietly. 'Your husband sits with the educator all day; he does nothing and Thalin just stares at them. There's trouble coming and soon.'

Sokunthea tried to change the subject. 'How's the rice coming on?'

'Stuff the rice. Nobody knows what they are doing. We're city people, what do we know about rice growing?'

Sokunthea looked at Tiny's small body and the tears in her eyes. 'We'll be okay.'

Tiny wiped the tears from her face. 'Thalin is cutting back on everything, food, water, he's rushing the work. It's your husband, it's the pressure he's putting on.'

'I'm surprised he hasn't killed anyone.'

'That's what worries everybody, even the young educators. I'm afraid.'

Sokunthea and Tiny settled down for the night. It was a typical hot and humid rainy season night, generally sleepless, and an assortment of insects took their turn at biting body after body just adding to the overall discomfort. Sokunthea's short sleep was broken by Phally.

'He wants you.'

Sokunthea got up and followed her out of the hut. They walked down the edge of the village square trying to keep to the shadows; as they approached Thalin's house they could see that all the lights were out but the side door was open. Sokunthea went inside.

'You look well,' came Thalin's voice from the shadows. Sokunthea stood silently in the dark. 'Leave us,' Thalin said to Phally and the door closed. 'Your husband seems out to cause trouble… what's he after?'

'Security.'

'Then he's playing with fire.'

'What did you and my husband get up to in Phnom Penh?'

'It's best you don't know.'

'Well, whatever it was he wants you out of the way.'

'He's a fool if he thinks he can play with me like this.'

'You said you couldn't save anyone from the educators; he's decided to join their team.'

'Their team – an old man and a fanatic.'

'Some say you're the fanatic.'

'I'm crazy, all right, crazy enough to know how to survive.'

'And if Rou comes back with Thai?'

'He won't.'

Sokunthea decided not to pursue the issue. 'How do Thai and Sinarth fit into this?'

'They don't… not really. Sinarth killed two of ours, and when your husband told us when and how he was getting out we were waiting. He was just a muscle man, a mover.'

'You're saying my husband set him up.'

'Sure, he used him then got rid of him, screwing you didn't help his case.'

'And Thai, how do you know him?'

'He was sent into the city to sort out the medicines; it wasn't long before he joined the racket.'

'And you?'

'I just circulated the medicines; took some from Lon Nol, some from the Rouge. Half the time they were buying medicines they'd previously paid for.'

'Where did all the money go?'

'Thailand. The Thais bankrolled the entire war, every crook in Cambodia has an account there. Cambodia suffers, Thailand makes money – ha!'

'And Piseth?'

'He had the Americans, wouldn't share them… smart really, some say he still has.'

'Does that make a difference?'

'Not to me, the Americans are going to be away from here for a long time, everybody is.'

'Can I go now?'

'What will you tell Yan?'

'I've nothing to tell, its not me they're really after. Will Thai talk?'

'No chance.'

'Then it's my husband's word against mine; if he says I'm a whore, your whore, then we're dead. Goodnight.'

Sokunthea found Phally waiting outside. 'He's nervous, I've never seen him so nervous.' They began to walk back to Sokunthea's hut. 'How are things organised around here? I mean, who is the real boss?'

'The educators operate for Ankor; they re-educate – sometimes that means killings. Thalin is responsible for getting the rice quota that's been set; he can use any means and that means killings too.'

'And Thai?'

'He's a border commander; the army stays out of rice production and education, he only has authority at times of war.'

'If Thalin starts killing who can stop him?'

'The educators can stop any killing unless it is a clear breach of the rules.'

'If the educators order a killing can Thalin refuse?'

'No.'

They reached her hut and Phally went on her way. Sokunthea looked up at the stars as a cool breeze came off the rice fields; she looked across to the cages and wondered if she would be visiting them again.

By six they were all in the fields planting the rice; there was no time for rest as hectare after hectare was brought into production. The hard physical work coupled with little food and drink, began to take their toll and the educator's whips were active. As Sokunthea came back to the seed rice station for more plants she met Piseth; their eyes met briefly and then parted. She collected her plants and was guided to another field by Chandra. As she entered the field she noticed Thalin and Phally in deep conversation; she crouched down to begin planting and realised that Piseth was just ahead of her and to her right. As she planted her first row there was a splash in front of her; she looked at the object ahead of her then looked up to see Piseth staring too.

'What is that... what is that?' Chandra screamed, and struck Piseth and Sokunthea with her whip. As a guard came over Chandra shouted, 'They have concealed food!'

Sokunthea stared at Piseth; the guards soon bound Piseth's hands behind him and forced him onto his knees. Sokunthea was dragged to her feet by Chandra and Phally, both shouting, 'Educate, educate!' To Sokunthea's horror a plastic bag was produced and placed over Piseth's head and to cries of, 'Educate, educate!' Sokunthea was manoeuvred to the back of Piseth and her hands placed on the bottom of the bag. She could feel Piseth begin to move and twist his head in an attempt to gain air, but she held the bag tightly pushing down hard. 'Educate, educate!' was being shouted and the whips were striking her from all angles. Piseth began to twist more and she realised he would die if she did not release the bag but as she did so stronger hands came on top of hers and tightened the bag further. Sokunthea began to cry; her husband was dying and she was killing him. She tried to pull away but Thalin's firm hands held her rigid; Piseth began to twist more, then fall to his side but Thalin still held Sokunthea's hands in place. She began to wish he were dead, why should she have to suffer this, he didn't mean anything to her, why couldn't he die? She cried more and more and tried to free herself but Thalin held firm. Piseth sank lower and lower; first his legs then his whole body appeared to go into convulsions as the bag was held firm. Sokunthea's thoughts began to become verbal.

'Die, please die, I can't do this... I can't do this!' she screamed for Thalin's ears but he continued to hold firm. 'Let me go, let me go!' she screamed.

Piseth was now laid flat in the rice field and Sokunthea with Thalin behind her had sunk to their knees. The whole rice field was silent, work had stopped as a man lost his life through asphyxiation. After Piseth's final kicks his body fell still and Thalin released his grip on Sokunthea's hands and stood up.

He looked around. 'Get them to work!' he shouted, then looked down at Sokunthea. 'Put her in the cage,' he said to Phally.

Chandra and Phally helped Sokunthea to her feet and

supported her as they led her to the cage; when out of sight of Thalin they all began to cry. As Sokunthea was helped into the cage she looked at Phally. 'Let me die,' she said and the cage was closed.

Sokunthea sat in the cage trying to forget what she had done but like those of all who desire amnesia, her thoughts continued. The picture of Piseth's blue face appeared to her as it twisted, almost screaming for air, then came the flashbacks: the house, the nightclub and, of course, the wedding. Then the demon appeared with its words of counterbalance: yes, he did deserve to die, yes, he had tried to leave her and fly out with her father's money, yes, he stole medicines and he killed Sinarth, but…

The rain began to fall early; it was light and wouldn't encourage the leeches to come rushing for their next feast, but Sokunthea really didn't care. She sat in a daze, just staring ahead of her. Trying to block the thoughts of Piseth meant closing her mind to everything. She re-focused when she heard the lock of the cage being opened and looked up to see Phally.

'Rou's back and you're wanted.'

Sokunthea pulled herself up and out of the cage; Phally tried to help but she pushed her away.

'It had to be done,' said Phally, 'others were suffering.' She linked arms with Sokunthea, who didn't resist.

'You planned it,' she said to Phally.

'No… not that way, that was Thalin, he changed the plan.'

'But you wanted to kill him.'

'And so did you.'

'No. No, he was bad but… not kill him.' She began to cry.

'Listen, he'd started to tell Yan… well, stories, stories about Thalin.'

'Maybe I should tell some stories.'

Phally looked at her. 'You knew Thalin?'

'Only briefly… and not as lovers.' She glared at Phally.

They reached the educators' building and entered. Rou was studying some papers on the desk. He slowly raised his head and looked at Sokunthea. 'Sit down,' he said.

Sokunthea sat on a chair at the corner of the desk and near the door. As she looked around for Yan, Rou began to talk.

'Many things have happened while I've been away.' He was looking at Phally.

'Your husband and accuser is dead and I have lost an assistant.' Sokunthea stared at the floor as the room began to fill with uncomfortable silence. 'Have they found Yan yet?' he said to Phally.

She shook her head and Rou shrugged his shoulders.

'Well, you will be pleased to know that the original charges from your husband are false. In fact, if he was still alive he would be in serious trouble. Do you know anything about his death?'

'No,' interrupted Phally, 'she was taken to the cage.' She looked at Sokunthea.

'The policy is that the thief is choked in front of the accomplice; where is Yan?' He stared out of the door. 'What was the food you decided to steal and where did you get it from?'

Sokunthea began to speak but her mouth was dry and she cleared her throat. 'I didn't see any food.'

'Your bad memory has returned again.'

This finally released all of Sokunthea's anger and pain, she stood.

'Look, you bastard, have me killed, you're going to do that anyway, but my mind is fine, I'm not the whore of anyone, I'm not a smuggler or a murderer,' she glanced at Phally, 'I'm just a woman who is trying to survive this crazy fucking world of yours.'

She reached forward, trying to grab him but he was too quick; he pushed her arms away then grabbed her hair and brought her head down onto the table hard. She fell backwards onto the floor knocking her chair over; the blow had dazed her and opened a small cut. Phally bent down and helped her back to her seat, and she sat and leaned forward onto the desk, her head throbbing.

'You are a dangerous woman,' continued Rou, 'but a brave one. Thalin has reported the incident that led to your husband's death. I'm satisfied that all procedures were followed. Normally you would be killed too but you did get the mines through and the rice needs planting.' He looked at Phally. 'Take her back to Thalin – and keep a special eye on her.' Phally nodded.

Sokunthea was taken to Thalin who dispatched her immediately to the rice fields where she put everything from her mind and just planted and planted and planted the rice. It was dark when Tiny found her; she was still in the fields.

'It's food time, Sokunthea, it's food time.'

She looked at Tiny, 'Okay,' she said and straightened up slowly.

They began to walk back to the huts; the moon was full and Sokunthea looked across the rice fields that seemed to stretch forever into the distance. Everything was peaceful, no city life noise, no lights. They entered the edge of the village, which was still and silent; what a contrast to what happens here in the day, she thought. Sokunthea began to feel tired, as the day's physical and mental exertions caught up with her, and as she climbed into her hut a small voice entered her mind and it said, 'I'm alive.'

She sat with Tiny and they ate the rice soup; there was no supplement now and the soup was more water than rice. Food stocks were obviously low and with the rice crop several months away the situation would deteriorate.

'Why did Rou let you off?' began Tiny.

'Let me off?' Sokunthea turned and looked at Tiny. 'I was involved in the act of killing my husband and I can't get the thought out of my mind. Let me off?'

'I'm sorry, I just thought you... thought they would kill you.'

Sokunthea put her arm around Tiny. 'No, they've just left me to my nightmares.'

Over the following months the rice planting spread from the village like ripples in a pond; often planters would remain near the fields away from the watchful eyes of Thalin and the educators. They would try to fish in the growing rivers and canals or catch land crabs; everything that walked, crawled, crept and flew was taken and eaten, often raw.

Sokunthea, Tiny and a small group of rice planters had been given the job of fillers; this entailed going out to the rice fields and finding areas of field where the first planting had not taken. This group then removed the non-growing rice and filled the area in with new. It was a job that Sokunthea liked; they moved from field to field and were therefore allowed to stay out all night.

Following the filling-in of one area the group settled down beside an old canal. The men moved into the dark waters trailing a large piece of cloth behind them hoping to catch fish and crabs; some of the women began to collect small pieces of wood in order to make a fire while others began to bathe. Sokunthea just sat on the canal bank and looked around. She was pleased with herself; this group of city dwellers had become a good team of rice field scavengers under her tuition, they worked well together and shared what they found. As Sokunthea decided to get undressed and bathe one of the men approached her.

'Come look at this.' He pointed to the canal.

Sokunthea followed him; he led her to the canal edge and pointed down into an old crab hole. She stared, and then realised what she was looking at; the half-eaten head of someone.

'What shall we do?' said the man.

'Nothing until morning – and don't catch any crabs.' She looked down again and felt sick.

In the morning Sokunthea went back to inspect the body.

'Shall we get it out?' said Tiny.

'No… no, leave it,' replied Sokunthea.

'Who is it? Do you know?'

'I'm not sure,' said Sokunthea, 'but I think it's Yan.'

'God!' and Tiny turned away from the appalling smell.

'Shall we get it out?' asked one of the men.

'No. The part below the water line will be eaten away already and most of the above has gone; no, leave it.'

'Shall we tell anyone?' asked the man.

'Leave that to me, I'll tell someone,' said Sokunthea and she knew who she had in mind.

The news that Sokunthea's fillers had found a body spread quickly through the village after their return. Sokunthea had decided to try and forget the discovery then realised she may be implicated if she did not report it. When she told Thalin she knew it was old news; she was ordered to lead a group back to the place where the body was and bring it to the village. The job was gruesome and by the time they had returned only bones and small pieces of flesh remained; the crabs had fed well. Rou and Thalin concluded that he had stepped on a landmine and fallen into the hole, but how they made this judgement only they knew.

As the rice planting had ended Sokunthea and the others were ordered to collect food, anything, so once again she went out scavenging. While returning from one of these expeditions she discovered the first bodies of that season, all in a dry ditch with their hands tied and their heads bashed in; no precious ammunition could be wasted.

On arrival back at the village they passed several more bodies. The village had been struck first by cholera then by dysentery; many people were ill and with no medicines many would die. Sokunthea went back to her hut and found Tiny who was trying to give water to the old woman.

'What happened?'

'Oh, thank God you are back – someone made prohok... either there was something wrong with the fish or the water they stored it in. Anyway, we've had many deaths.'

'What's been done?'

'Nothing, except killing – Rou became ill and some of the villagers wanted to get away, so Thalin killed them. It's awful, what shall we do?'

'Okay, okay...' Sokunthea began to think. 'All water has to be boiled, twice if possible.'

'Don't tell me, tell Thalin.'

'Fine, I will.'

Sokunthea left her hut and headed for Thalin's house; when she arrived she found him lying on his bed with Phally fanning him, trying to keep his temperature down.

'You ill too?' she said.

Phally came over to her. 'He'll be okay, but this outbreak has really hit us.'

'Well, what are you doing about it?'

'Well, Rou and Thalin are ill.'

'So?'

'They are our leaders, they decide.'

'God...' She looked at Thalin, then said, 'Leave him, he'll sleep; come with me.'

She led Phally outside and they went from hut to hut getting everyone out. She ordered all the sick to be moved to one hut; water was to be double-boiled and all food was to be brought to one kitchen and cooked under inspection. The sick would be nursed in teams and cleanliness would be enforced.

Over the following weeks the number of deaths declined although Rou and the old lady didn't survive. Thalin, like all unwell men, played the role of invalid and enjoyed being nursed by Sokunthea and his remaining wives. On his return to duty he announced that the measures introduced by Sokunthea would remain until the crop was in and that she would be responsible for maintaining cleanliness and inspecting the food.

Sokunthea began her new duties with vigour; debris was swept into piles and burnt, water containers were covered to deny the dreaded mosquito its breeding ground, all drinking water was double-boiled. Yet while undertaking this work Sokunthea became aware of the lack of food within the village, a shortage that without proper planning could result in a shortfall before the next crop could be harvested. She decided to see Thalin.

'You won't make it to the next crop, your food stocks are too low.'

'So what do you plan to do?'

'I?' she coughed. 'I didn't know I had the authority.'

'Well, you have and here's the fun: we have two hundred and forty-six people but enough food for eighty-six. I may add that if all those people hadn't died we would only have had enough food for thirty. My guards and educators must be fed; what' left, not much, is yours.'

'Well, if the Seventeen of April scum –' she smiled at Thalin – 'don't get fed, you don't get rice, if you don't get rice you miss your quota… then you're in deep shit.' She glared at him.

'Organise the rice – and make it last as long as possible.'

'Equal shares.'

He glared back. 'Equal shares.' Sokunthea left, smiling.

Over the coming months the rice soup became weaker and weaker as did the personnel; even with the occasional scavenge the food supplies were just not enough. One evening, after a long day of checking and reducing supplies, Sokunthea was met at her hut by Phally, who looked thin and pale.

'You all right?' she said.

'I'm fine,' said Phally.

'What's up?'

'He's setting you up.'

'What?'

'Thalin, he's setting you up.'

'How… why?'

'People are saying you're in charge… it's you that's cutting the food, you've become a Rouge.'

'But I'm trying to save them, get them more food.'

'I know, I'm just telling you to be careful; if things get worse with this food situation then they will blame you, not Thalin.'

'You sure you're okay?'

'I just ate something.'

'What? I'm supposed to be supervising the food.'

'Well, even we have developed a black market – we learned from your husband.'

Both began to cry. 'Come inside; I have some fresh water, we'll wash it out.'

'No, I have to go… but remember, watch Thalin. He's still dangerous and with no Rou to control him…' She turned and left.

That night Phally and three other young educators paid the price for eating raw food: their bodies were found the following morning. Sokunthea decided to double her efforts, asking people to stop hiding and eating raw food. She even offered a reward for information on people hiding food; to the group she was becoming more and more Rouge.

The rice crop, when it was harvested, came just in time. All food had run out several days before the harvesting began; enough time, thought Sokunthea, to stimulate work but not leave the people too malnourished to do the work. Thalin decided that Sokunthea was too valuable a scapegoat to allow her back to her group and allocated to her the duty of recording quotas from each field. This comprised of checking and weighing the harvested rice as it was brought into the village for threshing. Thalin kept the pressure on her by insisting that a tight timetable existed and the rice had to be delivered on a certain date to Takeo. Sokunthea soon began to transfer this pressure on to the people, insisting that they work harder and quicker; she had convinced herself that to do this would keep Thalin away from the fields and reduce the chances of someone else being suffocated.

The rice crop was almost in when Thalin was visited by Thai and a small group of his soldiers; they had arrived with early palm and rice wine, and their aim was to celebrate and bargain. Sokunthea lay in her hut and listened to the noise coming from Thalin's house; she knew that the rice yield had passed Thalin's required quota, which meant he was secure for another season. Yet as they celebrated the people who had produced the success were sitting in the dark eating brown rice soup. The new order, she thought, looks a lot like the old one. As her thoughts again began to travel back to the past Chandra disturbed them. 'They want you,' she said, looking at Sokunthea.

She stood and went outside. 'What are they doing?'

'Getting drunk,' said a disgusted Chandra.

'Why is Thai here?'

'I don't know. Let's go, he said to get you quick.'

'Who?'

'Thalin.'

They walked quietly towards his house. 'I'm sorry about Phally.' Sokunthea tried to continue the conversation.

'She was stupid, saving and eating those crabs.'

'How long did they save them for?'

'Too long...' She stopped. 'If it wasn't for you they'd be alive.'

'How'd you come...?

'Under the old system we came first, we're educators; after you got to Thalin we were all the same.'

Sokunthea could see that Chandra was shaking; this was not the time to argue. 'I can go the rest of the way myself if you like.'

Chandra nodded and headed off to her hut. As Sokunthea crossed the entrance to Thalin's house the noise fell, then Thai stood and greeted her.

'Welcome.' He approached her and offered her a chair to sit on.

She looked across at Thalin, who was sat back in a large cushioned armchair, smiling. The wines were obviously making their mark on the men; all seemed over the limit. In the room were ten men with Sokunthea, the only woman. Thai came back to her with a cup of rice wine, but she shook her head.

'Oh come on – celebrate,' he said.

'No,' she said.

'Well, try this then.' He offered her the palm wine.

'I don't – just give me water.'

'Never mind,' said Thalin, 'you're not here to drink, you're here to strip,' and they all began to laugh.

'Oh, no,' replied Sokunthea, 'not this time,' looking at Thalin.

Thalin began to get to his feet. 'If I say strip you strip.' He swayed forwards.

Sokunthea stood. 'It's time I went,' She turned towards the door as Thalin lunged at her. She sidestepped and deflected his body away and he fell head first into a coffee table and hatstand before crashing to the floor. The room fell silent and then the slowly building laughter of Thalin could be heard. Sokunthea stepped over him, shouted goodnight and left. She quickly walked back to her hut without looking back, and on arrival she headed straight to her sleeping place and lay down next to Tiny.

The following day she was summoned to Thalin's house. 'Thai and his men will be leaving today and he needs twenty bags of rice, see to it.'

'But that will take us below the quota.'

'No,' replied Thalin, 'the quota will be delivered as planned.'

'If it doesn't come out of the quota it will come out of the surplus and we'll go hungry again.'

Thalin just stared at her. 'Prepare the rice for Thai, he goes in one hour.'

Sokunthea knew it was pointless to argue. She went outside and found Tiny. 'I need your help.' She nodded towards the guard who let Tiny go.

'You seem more in charge than Thalin,' said Tiny as they walked away.

'Well I'm not; he's just ordered me to take almost fifty per cent of our stocks and give them to Thai.'

'So what does that mean for us?'

'Rationed food again or we run out two months short.'

'But we need the food! Following the food poisoning and such we're in a bad way, even now people are hungry…'

'I know, I know,' cut in Sokunthea. 'I'm trying my best.'

Tiny remained silent as they walked towards the rice store. As they got to the outer gate Thai and some of his men were waiting.

'Has Thalin instructed you?' said Thai.

She nodded. 'It's not right you taking this food, we've worked hard for it.'

'And we are defending your country and we need rice,' Thai snapped.

'We'll be on rations again.'

'And so will we.'

They passed the guard and entered the store. Sokunthea collected her records and checked out the twenty bags. She knew Thai had some justification for his point of view; the soldiers had no opportunity to grow their rice and taking it from the local village made common sense. Unfortunately, common sense was in short supply in Cambodia.

As he left the store Thai asked, 'Did Piseth tell you?'

'No,' said Sokunthea.

'I thought he may have told you.'

'Exactly what should he have told me?' Sokunthea was annoyed to be forced to think about her dead husband.

'The radio will be worth its weight in gold when this is all over.'

'Well, I'm not interested in it.'

'Things are going to change in this country; the Vietnamese are getting itchy, they'll be coming soon.'

'Well, they can have it.'

'The radio is important; the Americans will pay a lot of money for information.'

'I'm not interested.'

Thai spun around. 'If you know where it is, it just might keep you alive.'

'Like Piseth.'

They stared at each other in silence, then Thai said, 'Watch out for Thalin…'

'You don't need to tell me,' cut in Sokunthea.

'If the Vietnamese come we'll fall back on to Bokor, if you get forced out, head there.'

Sokunthea just slammed shut the doors of the rice stocks and walked towards Thalin's house.

'Twenty bags delivered as ordered,' she said.

'Have they left?'

'They're loading now.'

'Good, right I want you to organise the journey to Takeo with the quota. You leave in three days.'

'You want me to go?'

'You're the hero of the mines, of course I want you to go,' he smiled at her.

Sokunthea turned towards the door then said, 'Thai thought the Vietnamese would come soon.'

Thalin laughed. 'Then we must hurry with the quota.' As she left she could hear his maniacal laugh and realised that he was more of a threat to the Cambodian people than the Vietnamese.

Over the following two days Sokunthea developed her plans for transferring the quota to the provincial capital of Takeo. This would take eight ox carts and sixty-four people. When she presented her plan to Thalin he insisted that only forty-eight people were needed and that the round trip should be completed in four days. This was two days less than Sokunthea had planned; he wanted everyone back in order to begin a new project.

The trip to Takeo proved uneventful although exhausting; many of the villages they passed were at differing stages of rice collecting, yet all the people they met appeared to have the same drawn appearance as if in a state of shock, the most common feature being thin through lack of food. As they neared Takeo the road began to fill with other groups taking their quotas. As the road filled the pace slowed; the hot season was with them again and the sun was merciless on the open road. The only shade available was beneath the cart.

On the approach to Takeo, Sokunthea began to notice an increase in the number of people resting beside the road; these were not travellers bringing the rice quotas, they were covered in dust and wore clothing from head to toe in order to block out the sun, the dress of labourers. As the rice train stopped again Sokunthea went and sat with a small group of the labourers.

'May I sit?'

They did not reply so she sat next to a small group of women.

'Do you work here in Takeo?'

An older woman spoke. 'We cannot talk to you, you may be a spy.'

'No, I'm not a spy, I'm from the fields at Teuk Meas.'

'What's it like down there?' asked another woman.

'Tough.' Everyone nodded.

'We're building canals, in every direction.'

'Is there enough water in the dry season?'

'They say so.' She nodded towards a small group of Rouge soldiers.

'How long have you been building?'

'A year, maybe two... who knows any more? Tell us about the rice, have you brought all?'

'We've brought what we were told.'

'Good, we need all the rice we can get,' they all agreed.

'So our rice is for you?' Sokunthea continued.

'Some of it, they promised.'

'Is no one growing rice round here?'

'A little, but with all the mines and such it's dangerous.'

'Why don't you clear them?'

They all laughed quietly. 'We do,' said the older woman, 'and many die.'

The line of ox carts began to move and Sokunthea rejoined the road. By late evening they had travelled one kilometre and were stopped outside a small hut. A middle-aged man in a blue Chinese suit held out his hand. 'Papers.' Sokunthea handed them over and he disappeared inside; he returned shortly, smiling.

'Go ahead, there is a compound on your right. Rest there for the night.' Sokunthea moved her group onwards, when they arrived at the compound she noticed only a small number of ox carts waiting. With her group settled down for the night she went to get more information from the other travellers.

'Where are you from?' she asked the members of a small group sat around a campfire.

'Kampong Chrey,' came the reply.

'Why are there so few of us here in this compound while the road was packed with ox carts?'

'They didn't meet the quota,' said a young man.

'What? All those carts, they didn't make... I can't believe it.'

'It's true, I got it from a guard. All those who don't make the quota go to another compound and some say they don't come back... they're re-educated.'

'I can't believe that, they'd have to kill hundreds.'

'Why not? They haven't the food to feed them.' The young man appeared irritated at having his word challenged.

Sokunthea decided to change the subject. 'How long do we stay here?'

'Until they tell us to go.'

'But there's no shade or water.' Everyone stared into the fire and silence spread over the group.

'I'm in no hurry to go back,' said an old man sitting just outside the group, 'what's there to go back for?'

Sokunthea said her farewells and returned to her group where nourishment had been prepared.

'Where are they from?' asked Mai, a young girl travelling with Sokunthea's group.

'Kampong Chrey.'

'Is that far?'

'A fair way, yes.'

'How long have they been here?'

'I don't know.'

'Will they travel back with us?'

'Part of the way. Why?'

'I think some of my family may be there, it's their village.'

'Well, go over and see, ask them.'

'I will.' She stood and walked off.

Sokunthea watched her and wondered what a young girl must be thinking about all this, what a mess, people killed for not making a rice quota, starved and beaten, split from their families, choking each other – shit, she began to cry.

Tiny appeared with some water. 'Here, drink this.'

She looked at her and took the water.

'Now we don't want you falling apart,' continued Tiny, and she sat down beside her.

'I'm okay, just the occasional nightmare, you know the one.'

'Have we done something bad or good to be in this compound?'

'Oh, good, I think… who knows with the Rouge?' The tears turned to laughter.

'Will we get back in time? – to meet Thalin's deadline, I mean.'

'Who cares? No, really, I don't care any more, I've seen so many die I've become immune. If Thalin wants to kill me I'm ready.'

'Don't speak like that, I need you.' Tiny put her arm around Sokunthea. 'We all need you.'

'Some people think I'm one of the Rouge anyway, they'd be happy to see me get it.'

'Rubbish, what do they know?'

'They know enough to get me killed; if the Vietnamese come they only have to point at me and say Rouge and I'm dead.'

'Nobody will do that.'

'Tiny, I have enemies and I don't just mean Thalin; I'm in the middle, neither Rouge nor Seventeen of April, so when trouble comes I'm nobody's friend.'

'Well you're my friend, so let's stop talking about this.' Sokunthea finished drinking her water while Tiny laid out the sleeping mats under the ox cart.

The next morning three official-looking men entered the compound; they checked the papers again and smiled at each other. Then a cameraman appeared and, with the officials stood in front, the rice-filled ox carts were photographed. By late afternoon Sokunthea and her group were headed back south; progress was good and by starting early and finishing late they hoped to meet Thalin's deadline. They had passed through Tani and were heading due south when Tiny told her Mai was missing.

'I think she's gone to Kampong Chrey,' she said.

'Damn, I'll go after her.'

'No, it's her problem.'

'If we don't all get back Thalin will make it our problem. Slow down and I'll meet you at the crab hole where we found Yan tomorrow night.' Tiny nodded.

Sokunthea left the group and headed back to Tani; she knew that if stopped by the Rouge she was dead. Nobody was allowed to travel alone across the countryside in the new Cambodia. Travel passes didn't exist, if you were out of your village and not with a group on the road you were against Ankor; be against Ankor and you were dead. The first night she pushed herself until late, she had bypassed Tani knowing that to enter would attract unwanted attention. She came across a small Chinese burial site, which was a perfect place to rest, so she decided to sleep there. The sounds around the burial site only heightened her senses and she quickly found sleeping impossible, when she did sleep the nightmare of her husband's death appeared. The following day she was up early and made rapid progress down the Kampong Chrey road. After travelling for three hours she noticed the distant cloud of an ox cart train ahead, so she increased her speed.

She caught and stopped the train by mid-morning but could not see Mai.

'Who's in charge here?' An older man came forward. 'We are missing a girl from our train, I think she is here.'

'No,' said the old man, 'we have no one.'

'Listen, I don't know the game you are playing but if she does not return with me many people will die – you understand.' She looked straight at the head man.

The man disappeared behind a cart and returned with Mai and a young man. 'This is Raz; he is Mai's cousin.'

'She's going with us,' said Raz, 'all her family is in Kampong Chrey.'

'And all her family will die in Kampong Chrey if she goes; she is allocated to Tuk Meas and if she goes missing they will find her and all who are sheltering her. They are not stupid, they know her family is in Kampong Chrey, that's the first place they will go.'

She turned to the old man. 'Look, this is not the time to think of the love of a family, it's the time to think of its life, its survival. She has to come with me.'

'No!' shouted Raz. 'You're just Rouge anyway, go before we kill you.'

Sokunthea stepped forward and punched Raz hard in the face; he collapsed to the floor with blood coming from his nose, then she looked at Mai. 'Move!' she shouted and the stunned girl began to walk back down the road. She turned to the head man. 'If he –' pointing at Raz – 'comes after me, I'll kill him.' The headman nodded and the two women set off back down the road.

They walked for the rest of the day and most of the night and arrived at the crab hole in the early hours of the morning. Tiny was waiting.

'I thought you weren't coming.'

'Sorry, it took longer than I thought.'

Tiny looked at a tired and sullen Mai. 'What's wrong with her?'

'She didn't want to come, so I had to persuade her.' Sokunthea brandished her fist. 'Oh, right.'

Just after daybreak the group headed into Tuk Meas half a day late. Thalin summoned Sokunthea to his house again.

'Papers,' he said. Sokunthea placed them on his table, and he sat and read through them. 'Good,' he said. 'Anybody not make the quota?'

'Lots,' said Sokunthea.

'Good… good.' He stood and came around the table. 'Well now, there's been some changes while you've been away. The remaining rice will be divided into staff rice and worker rice, no more equal shares. You will manage it – as staff, of course.' He sat in his lounge chair. 'You have quite a reputation around here, did you know that? More important then me, they say,' he smiled. 'No longer the poor, vulnerable rice girl but the Rouge in charge of the rice, heady stuff.' His tone changed. 'You will report to me every day. I want workers fit enough to work and sleep. Feed them too much and they get soft, understand?' He was staring straight at her, and she nodded.

She walked back to her hut and told Tiny, 'That means less rice.'

'I don't know until I see the stocks but I suspect so.'

'Can't you refuse?'

'Yes, and he does it and we get even less food.'

'Well, we have to go to his meeting and find out what the plan is.'

'What plan?'

'I don't know but Chandra says it's big.'

They left the hut and joined others collecting in the village square. Thalin arrived and announced that the local pagoda pond would extend, and the work would begin immediately.

Tuk Meas' pagoda had been blown up as part of the Rouge campaign to eradicate Buddhism from the country. To the people it was a sacred site to sneak to and pray when things became difficult. Thalin had ignored such actions but now he appeared determined to use the water on the site to increase rice production. This meant destroying what was left and digging up the burial areas, a task that he knew would increase tension.

'That's why he's given in to the educators,' Sokunthea said to Tiny.

The group were marched away to the pagoda and Sokunthea headed for the rice store. She spent the morning weighing and calculating the rice stocks; the prospects looked grim. Even with one bowl of rice soup per two days there would still be a shortfall of fifteen days before the next rice came. That evening, before retiring, she informed Thalin.

'Have you built in a loss factor?'

'What, from mice, theft? Who's going to…' and then she realised what he meant. 'How many do you expect to die?' She glared at him.

'Maybe ten per cent.'

'Around twenty people.'

'Something like that.'

'Natural or enforced?'

'Both, if necessary.'

'One day these people will rise up…'

'Rubbish, they're fools, they'll do what they are told. If they don't they die, these people like being shat on, it's in their history, their blood.'

'Then it's in your blood too, you're one of them.'

'But I'm on top, that gun says so.' He pointed to an AK-47 leaning against the wall.

She looked back at him. 'When do we start rationing?'

'Now.' She turned to go then he called out, 'You're one of us now, ask your people; you're one of us.'

She walked hurriedly back to her hut and Tiny. The hut was the scene of sheer exhaustion with bodies lying everywhere, unclean, uncovered, many not even bothering to lie out sleeping mats. She found Tiny in her corner. 'How are you?' she asked, but Tiny just groaned. 'Are you sick?'

'No, just let me sleep.'

'What was it like?'

'Hard work – just let me rest.'

The morning arrived too soon for Tiny and the other labourers, but Sokunthea had risen before them to prepare some kind of breakfast.

'Only rice soup again, I'm afraid,' she said to Tiny, who just grinned.

'This second pond will kill us,' she said after a short pause.

'No chance; you're too strong, and anyway, they need you to plant rice next.' Sokunthea smiled trying to cheer up her friend.

'How are the rice stocks?' Tiny responded.

'Low… but with me in charge we'll get by.'

'Huh.'

'Move, move, come on!' A young guard began to round them up.

Tiny threw her banana leaf to the floor. 'Same for lunch or will we have chicken?' She smiled, turned and left.

Sokunthea went straight to the rice store where Thalin was already waiting. 'A saving already,' he said, smiling. Sokunthea looked at him. 'The old woman in hut three –' he nodded towards the door – 'died in the night, so more rice for you.'

'Firstly, she was only forty; secondly, she is not outside my ten per cent calculations, which means I've lost a young woman for no gain.'

'Hm. You gave them food this morning – don't run out.'

'They needed it, the body can take only so much…'

'I'll decide what the body can take, you make sure the rice lasts.' With that he left.

Sokunthea ran through her calculations again; she began to total how much rice she would save following the death of Thalin's old woman, then she stopped abruptly. 'What am I doing?' she said to herself. The thought that she was working out rice savings per death appalled her. 'This is what I'm reduced to.'

She stood, left the store and found herself walking towards the old pagoda. As she approached the sound of activity seemed to be everywhere; groups were clearing away rubble and stones from the surface while others were appearing with large baskets of earth. As she reached the lip of the hole that was being dug she looked down on what seemed to be a sea of people digging and pulling at the earth with their bare hands. Simple digging tools were absent or held by a selected few. These few would walk around the bottom of the hole and loosen the earth, then a hoard of labourers would begin removing the earth into waiting baskets. Unless tools were found this was not going to be a simple dry season job and the casualty rate would be high. 'That's why he's doing it, the bastard, he's given away too much rice to appease his masters and he can't just kill us so he works us to death.'

She turned and stormed back to the village; she passed Chandra leading another group of villagers up to the pagoda but her mind was set on confronting him, so she walked straight to his door and marched in. The entrance and meeting room were empty so she carried on walking through to the back of the house. She heard his voice curse as she entered the kitchen.

He looked up at her. 'I need a doctor.' He held up his hand that was bleeding from a small cut. 'Now my housekeeper is dead I can't get a good cook,' he laughed. As he turned Sokunthea's temper snapped and she threw herself at him, striking him around the head several times. Thalin responded by punching her hard in the abdomen, Sokunthea doubled up from this blow and Thalin pushed her hard backwards. She fell into a narrow corner with a wall and steel cabinet on each side, hitting her head; after a pause Thalin dropped on top of her and began ripping at her clothes. She tried to strike him but he punched her several times in the face and began to force her head back into an empty water trough, which lay behind her. She tried to kick and struggle but he forced her legs upwards then towards her, curling her into a ball. Her next pain came as Thalin entered her; her vagina was dry and sore due to months of dehydration and poor diet, and as his penis entered her it tore and seemed to burn within her. She tried to speak but he just pushed her head further and further back. To struggle was impossible; as his body fell onto hers she was forced further down into the corner, and every rise and fall of his body forced her deeper and deeper into the corner. The sensation of a man once again inside her was a mixture of excitement, pain and disgust, and then it was over. Thalin stood and began to rearrange his clothes; Sokunthea lay still for a while then began to get up. Her body had been wedged into the small space and rising was difficult; only with Thalin's help could she get out. She got to her feet and glared at him then, realising her nakedness, began to cover her body with her torn clothes.

'Here, put this on,' and he threw a tunic at her.

She grabbed it and pulled it around her shoulders, her eyes on Thalin all the time. She felt incredibly dirty and disgusted and ran out of the kitchen and through the house, out towards the water barrels. She began to wash herself all over but was unable to cover her entire body, so she turned and ran up the rise to the old pagoda pond and threw herself in. The water was cold and refreshing; she wanted to dive beneath its surface and never return. As she dove the thoughts running through her mind were of how stupid she had been to attack him, go to him, challenge him; had she learned nothing about men? she asked herself. She surfaced and looked around. She was still alone; she lay flat on the surface of the water and stared up into the sky. The thought of him entering her, his breath on her cheek, caused her to give a loud scream. As she came to a horizontal position she noticed a small group of labourers had appeared by the pond's edge; they were looking at her. She felt like a peep show, her body becoming unclean again, as she looked at the group all covered in dust with ragged clothes. She began to wade towards the bank yet as she did she noticed how some of the group began to point at her. As she rose from the water she looked down and realised the cause; the black Rouge tunic that she was wearing must be the final confirmation to all that she was one of them.

She spent the rest of the day walking, thinking of what had happened and how she would deal with it. Again her mind resorted to thinking it was all her fault, the what ifs came and went. She was startled by Tiny's intervention.

'Don't go in there.' She looked at Tiny and realised she had found her way back to her hut. 'Please don't go in there, it will cause problems,' Tiny said again.

Sokunthea looked at her. 'Why?'

'They say you are one of them, you wear their uniform.' She

looked up and down Sokunthea.

'I wear it because…' She stopped.

'I know you help them to help us but to wear the uniform… people don't trust you any more.'

'Do they trust Thalin?'

'No, but many thought you different…'

'And now?'

'I try to defend you, I do, but they need a scapegoat, someone to direct their anger towards.'

'So what about Thalin?'

'He's too high, too strong.'

'Well, fuck them; let's see how they cope with Thalin's approach to rice sharing.'

'We're not all like them.' Tiny put her arm around Sokunthea's shoulder. 'What happened.'

'Nothing, I needed new clothes and this is all that is available,' she laughed and looked up to the night sky.

'I've brought your things out,' said Tiny after a short pause, 'although there's not much.'

Sokunthea looked at the almost empty bundle at her feet.

'Where will you go?' asked Tiny.

'To hell,' and with that Sokunthea turned and headed for Thalin's house.

'I still love you,' shouted Tiny after her but Sokunthea just headed on.

She walked into Thalin's house and sat in the entrance area. He was sitting behind his desk looking at a paper. 'I've been thrown out,' she said, 'by your little people.'

He stood and walked towards her. 'A challenge,' he said. He walked to a side window and shouted, loudly; a soldier soon arrived. 'Get hut three out in the square now!' The soldier disappeared.

'No, stop,' said Sokunthea.

Thalin turned to her. 'Nobody challenges me.'

'I didn't mean…'

Thalin walked to the door. 'You're one of us now,' he smiled and walked outside.

Sokunthea stood in the doorway and watched as the members

of hut three were lined up. She could hear Thalin's voice informing them that only he had the authority to remove someone from a hut, and ordering that they stay there all night. Sokunthea watched them from the doorway for most of the night; they stood in a single row and several of them fell to the floor and were beaten back to their feet by the guards. She counted three that were dragged away.

The following morning she woke to find she had slept in a small chair and someone had covered her. Thalin was standing over her. 'Feed them,' he said. She stood and walked out to the rice store, not daring to look at the group of hut three still standing in the early morning rain. With her helpers Sokunthea was able to prepare the rice soup; she added extra rice in order to give it more substance and, she hoped, give the labourers more strength. When she returned to the square to serve the food the group from hut three had gone.

'I've sent them to work early,' said Thalin, who was standing in the middle of the square. He bent over and looked at the food. 'Hmmm, not bad... I've just found my new cook,' he said looking at Sokunthea.

'I'm busy,' she said.

'You cook,' he said and returned to his house.

Sokunthea's contacts with Tiny diminished over the following months. When they did briefly meet Sokunthea noticed the increasing physical wastage of her friend. When she asked about the new pond all she received was a blank look, the look of someone without hope.

'Hang in there, he's got to switch to rice preparation and planting soon,' she would tell Tiny. Tiny just looked back in sheer exhaustion.

Sokunthea had decided to become Thalin's cook for the same reasons she had become his food controller – influence. She would badger him to switch to rice preparation, telling him he would not meet his quota, but the pond had become an obsession, a symbol of his control over the village. Sokunthea realised Thalin was racing against the coming rains; if the pond was not complete in time it would be washed away and the food problem would remain for a third year. If he left repair and preparation of his rice fields too late, he wouldn't get the same yield. The damage it was doing to his workers appeared to be of little interest to him and he had failed to notice the increasing tension in his educators and soldiers.

Sokunthea's contact with Thalin grew; the rape was never mentioned and Sokunthea was determined not to get herself into such an exposed position again. She gave her advice freely and although not always appreciated, it appeared to be listened to by Thalin. The rice stocks appeared to be higher than Sokunthea had calculated; not only had the death rate kept them up but the almost exhausting work rate had appeared to cut appetite. Thalin had appeared pleased when she informed him, then responded that the rice was her responsibility. This laying down of boundaries between them improved their confidence together and following another of Thalin's orders Sokunthea moved into his house.

She justified this move in her mind by reflecting on the growing hostility towards her. 'If they say I'm one of them, maybe I should be,' she rationalised. Thalin appeared to be the perfect host and clearly enjoyed her company. To her this murderer of her husband, this rapist, had to be watched from close up and if along the way she could help the workers then that was okay.

After a typical evening where she had cooked a late meal and cleaned away Sokunthea retired but her sleep was soon disturbed when she realised Thalin was in her room.

'Get up,' he said, 'I need your help.'

Sokunthea stirred slowly as Thalin headed for the door then, hearing voices from below, she dressed quickly and followed him. On arriving outside she noticed a small group of soldiers, not from the village; these were border soldiers. Three were lying on stretchers while two others were sat resting against the village square tree. Standing was a group of about ten, all gathering around Thalin; Sokunthea approached them.

'You must have a doctor amongst you,' she heard one of the soldiers say.

'No, we have no doctors,' replied Thalin.

'I know medicine,' cut in Sokunthea, 'my husband was a doctor.' She walked past the group and went to the first stretcher.

'He's dead,' she shouted over her shoulder. After further examination she declared one dead, two severely wounded who would die and the rest with flesh wounds. 'What happened?' she asked the soldiers.

'The Vietnamese, they're getting ready to move against us.'

Thank God, thought Sokunthea.

'Can't we stop them?' asked Thalin.

'We'll try, just have your men ready to move with us tomorrow.'

'Impossible,' said Thalin, nodding his head, 'without my soldiers nothing will get done around here.'

'If the Vietnamese come they'll be nothing around here,' responded the soldier, 'and anyway I have the authority.'

Thalin nodded to Sokunthea and she followed him back to his house. 'How long will the other two last?'

'Dead by morning, I'd say.'

'Right… get to the rice store and hide as much as you can.'

Sokunthea looked at him then headed for the door.

'Don't,' he shouted after her, 'let them see you.'

She left the rear of the house and crossed to the rice store using as much cover as possible. The entrance to the rice store was guarded twenty-four hours a day and to Sokunthea's surprise Chandra was stood there.

'New duty?' Sokunthea said.

'God, you frightened me. What's going on? Thalin told me to come and replace the guard, some meeting.'

'Good. Listen, the soldiers will depart tomorrow taking some of ours with them; Thalin thinks they'll take the rice so we've got to move some.'

'Where and how, what can the two of us do?'

'We can get a few bags out; we'll go through the back, there's a hole in the wire. We'll take them to the pagoda.'

Under a half moon and at times hearing Thalin's voice bellowing out, keeping the soldiers occupied, they stashed twelve bags. The work was exhausting and Sokunthea's back ached when she finally reached her bed.

The following morning the soldiers returned to the front leaving Thalin just four of his original men, their two wounded and three bodies. They took half the rice in the store and promised to defend their country. Thalin and Sokunthea were glad to see them go.

The loss of more than half his guards forced Thalin to change plans; the pagoda pond was stopped and the preparation of the rice fields began. With the loss of the soldiers and the pilfering of Sokunthea and Chandra a period of full rice rations began. Even the partly finished pond had benefits, for as the rains came so did the frogs. Throughout the planting season Sokunthea was able to provide rice with fish or frog and the strength of the workers improved, yet Sokunthea was still worried. Why, she asked herself, is Thalin being so generous? She decided to ask Chandra.

'That's easy,' she replied, 'he's worried about stories from the front. If the Vietnamese come he's had it.'

'Where does that leave us?'

'They won't be interested in the little fish.'

'I'm not so sure; over one hundred people have died in this village, many of them murdered.'

'Nearer three hundred.'

'God... Thalin can't clear that away with an extra bowl of rice.'

The planting season went smoothly and old tensions within the village eased. Even Thalin made a token gesture of working in the rice fields, cutting the first stems. As the reaping season came to an end the signs of potential problems at the border increased with the arrival of several hundred villagers from the border area. These villagers increased tensions again within Tuk Meas, as they needed feeding and housing. Thalin began to think of his quota and Sokunthea her rationing. The new workers brought stories of Vietnamese encroachment of the border, the lack of rice and, of course, deaths. They were accompanied by several educators and one in particular had a reputation for immense cruelty; her name was Sak. Immediately she began to take on the role of Rou, organising education lessons and openly disagreeing with Thalin's more relaxed approach. Thalin became more aware of the potential threat from her and began to allow old practices to return, which included beatings and caging. Sokunthea concentrated on her role of rice rationing and offering independent advice to Thalin.

As 1978 rolled on Thalin, with Sak's encouragement, completed the pond and decided on a new project which involved the digging of a large well to the south of Tuk Meas, which would enable him to produce dry-season rice. The project, like the pond, became an obsession; Thalin insisted that the newcomers built it. This was his way of reducing their numbers according to Chandra and the role of overseeing its completion was given to Sak.

Each night Sokunthea would hear of the number of deaths and other mishaps around the project and, to her surprise, she didn't care. The well proved to be a disaster, as it produced salty water which when channelled onto the fields, killed the rice; this basic lack of insight cost more lives, but unfortunately not Sak's.

As the harvesting season was coming to an end the village was once again crowded with soldiers; this time their orders were to move back. All systems, which would help the enemy, were to be destroyed, and dykes, ponds and wells were high on the list. The villagers toiled hard to destroy what they had sacrificed to build.

Thai had returned to the village and was now in charge; he arrived, basing himself at Thalin's house and reacquainted himself with Sokunthea.

'You're still alive, I see,' he said.

'Just,' she replied.

'I see from your uniform that you have joined us.'

'Not really – a case of necessity,' and she looked at Thalin.

'Thalin tells me you are in charge of the rice.'

'Yes.'

'How much do we have?'

'To feed all, enough for about two weeks.'

'Hmm… the food will come with us.' Thai looked at Thalin, who nodded.

'What about the villagers?' said Sokunthea.

'Anyone who doesn't volunteer to fight goes to Takeo,' said Thai, 'and we,' looking at Thalin, 'go to Bokor.'

'Bokor,' said Sokunthea, 'that's near Kampot.'

'We fight there,' cut in Thalin.

'But you leave all of the country open to them!' exclaimed Sokunthea.

Thai laughed. 'We stop them getting to Kompong Som, our

only port.'

'Listen,' said Thalin, 'leave the military things to the men, okay.'

Thai turned and headed for the door. 'By the way,' he turned and said, 'you're coming with us.'

Sokunthea looked at Thalin. 'Is this real… I mean, are the Vietnamese coming?'

'According to Thai, yes and soon.'

The following morning the village was like a military camp with people shouting orders and large groups of men and women moving into columns. The largest group, consisting of most of the workers and Seventeen of April people, moved north to Takeo, whilst the military group with a handful of volunteers moved west. Sokunthea had mixed emotions as she saw friends moving with the other group, especially Chandra, yet Tiny had volunteered to move west with her, a decision that Sokunthea hoped she would not regret.

Bokor

The journey to Bokor began and the first night's rest was at Kampong Trach, a small Cambodian village twenty kilometres south-west of Tuk Meas. The village was empty; the only sign that people may have lived here was the destruction of dykes and ponds in an attempt to deny the enemy anything. That night Sokunthea was invited to a meeting with Thai, Thalin and other military personnel.

'We are ordered to Bokor,' Thai began. 'Our aim is to deny the enemy entry to Kompong Som; we do not know when the enemy will come but we suspect it will be after the rainy season, therefore we must be ready in three months.'

'How many men will there be?' asked Thalin.

'At Bokor?'

'Yes.'

'About one thousand.'

'You expect the Vietnamese to attack?' asked a young officer.

'They have to; Bokor gives us complete command of the eastern approaches and the coastal road to Kompong Som. The safety of the harbour at Kompong Som is paramount, it's our only port and we must keep it open.'

'Where will our supplies come from?' asked Sokunthea quietly from the back of the group. Everyone turned and looked at her.

'Ankor has promised supplies,' said Thai, and the group laughed.

'But what if Ankor can't reach us?' continued Sokunthea.

The room went quiet.

'Supplies will come from Kompong Som and scavenging in the hills. We are also taking some with us; in fact, that's why you are here, your job is to manage what we have.'

'What we have will not feed this group for a month, let alone one thousand.' She stared around the faces in the room.

'Others will have food,' cut in Thalin. 'Ankor knows how

important Bokor is; they'll supply us.'

'Like they did the villages?'

Thai glared at her. 'The meeting's over. We leave at daybreak tomorrow; we have to join up with a small artillery unit outside Kampot in two days. That's all.' The group dispersed. As Sokunthea left the meeting Thai came after her.

'I need to talk to you.' He put his hand on her shoulder to interrupt her walking. 'I need to know if Piseth told you where the radio was.'

'I don't...' began Sokunthea.

'I'm prepared to protect you if you trust me; there are many men who think you should be put back with the Seventeen of April group, and that would be bad for you.'

Sokunthea turned. 'What are you going to do with an American radio on the top of Bokor?'

'That radio is my future; in a land of no money it's a goldmine.'

'I don't understand you men; you've killed half the country for your greed and now, when it looks like you're finished you're planning the next million. Well, I hope the Vietnamese blow the hell out of you.'

Thai struck her across the face instinctively; Sokunthea fell to the floor holding her face. The blow had resulted in a large cut along her upper lip, and she dabbed at it with her hand and arm. Thai helped her to her feet. 'I'm sorry,' he said, 'whatever we have become we will not let the Vietnamese take us over, never.'

Sokunthea began to walk away, then turned. 'You'll be doing business with them in six months, another lovely war to enrich yourself.'

Thai turned and walked back to his quarters.

True too his word, Thai had the group heading for Kampot by five o'clock; Sokunthea had prepared no food, deciding that one meal a day would have to suffice. Her lip had swollen during the night and she had lost a tooth but with Tiny's help the inflammation was kept to a minimum. The rains had begun during the night and the road to Kampot was beginning to break up; before Pol Pot this very same road was tarmacked but he had ordered all such roads to be dug up as good communication and transportation was not needed by Ankor. This slowed the group down as the hand-pulled ox carts began to sink in the mud; late that night they reached the crossroads of Kampot and the coastal town of Krong Keo.

The group began to settle by the side of the road, sheltering under trees and bushes; no fires were allowed in case enemy infiltrators were about. Sokunthea served cold rice soup and chicken to the soldiers and just rice soup to the rest. Everyone ate quickly and in silence and retired to whatever shelter they had prepared. The rains began again, pouring down as only monsoon rains can, and within ten minutes all were wet. As Sokunthea and Tiny tried to take shelter beneath one of the ox carts, Thalin took Sokunthea's arm.

'You are wanted,' he said.

Thalin walked towards a large thorn tree where Thai had taken up shelter and led her beneath a large plastic sheet which was keeping the majority of the rain out. Sokunthea looked around at the regular faces then spotted the new arrival who was speaking.

'So you have to help.' He was looking at Thai, who turned and stared out at the rain.

'How many men are there with the guns?' he asked.

'About forty,' came the reply.

'Any shell wagons, supplies?'

'Four.'

'Oxen?'

'None.'

There was an audible groan around the room.

'Thalin.' said Thai, 'you will lead this group on to Kampot with a minimum of personnel; the rest will leave with me in one hour to get these bloody guns. Sokunthea,' he continued, 'is everything packed and ready?'

'Well, yes.'

'Good. You will come with me, I'll need someone to assess the food down there; in the meantime help Thalin. Remember,' he said, looking at the both of them, 'keep only the minimum.'

As they got outside Sokunthea asked Thalin, 'What was that all about?'

Thalin laughed. 'The artillery guns we were supposed to meet outside of Kampot are stuck in the mud of Krong Keo and the Vietnamese are crawling all over the place.'

'What? How?'

'Thai and you are going to save them,' chuckled Thalin. They walked quietly on. 'What has Thai got on you?'

'I don't know...'

'Ah, come on, don't treat me like a fool, it was the same when you and that creep of a husband of yours came to Tuk Meas, Thai wanted to protect you then... why?' Thalin continued, 'Something is happening with you and him, something important... I could help you.'

'I still have no idea what you are talking about. Now let's work out some figures.'

Thalin's group had to move the four ox carts carrying rice and small arms ammunition on to Kampot. It was decided that thirty, including Thalin and Sak as guards, would be needed; the rest, about sixty, would go south with Thai. By midnight Sokunthea found herself with Thai's group heading south to Krong Keo. The rain had stopped and the group, keeping to single file, followed their guide along the track. Nobody talked as they kept the required length away from the person in front, yet followed them step for step. The Rouge were the experts in booby traps and mine planting and this road had already been prepared for any unexpected traveller. Without stopping the group reached the outskirts of Krong Keo just as the day broke; they moved forwards slowly, less afraid of the mines, more afraid of a sleepy guard reacting too quickly. As they approached a group of shacks a soldier appeared and challenged them; a verbal exchange occurred and the group was passed on.

Thai turned to one of his assistants. 'At least they have some guards out.'

They pressed on towards the town centre and as they did Sokunthea noticed the many beautiful houses that had been blown up and burned; what a waste, she thought. As the road entered a small dip and turned she saw the pile of human skulls next to the road; the whole group slowed to stare at these grotesque objects and wondered what had happened. Around the bend they discovered what they had come for: in a line along the road stood three large artillery guns interspersed with four ox carts. As Thai approached, a small group of soldiers came from the roadside.

'What's the problem?' he asked.

'Not enough muscle to move them,' came the reply.

Thai looked around. 'Who is in charge?'

'Commander Chhunly.'

'And where is he?'

The soldiers looked at each other, then finally one replied, 'He's drunk, over near the tree.'

'Show me.'

The soldiers led him to their commander; the rest of Thai's group began to rest while Sokunthea walked up the line of equipment assessing its situation. She was startled by the sound of a gunshot and walked back to the group. When she returned Thai was already back and called all the group together.

'The local commander has just handed command over to me.' He looked around; no one spoke. 'I've instructed the local officer to bring in all the sentries, we'll need all the help we can get.'

'You won't move them,' shouted Sokunthea from the back, 'not unless you have tyre repair.'

'Explain,' said Thai.

Sokunthea came to the front. 'Each gun has two wheels with two tyres; that's six tyres in all. The front gun has a wheel missing, the second gun is okay but the third gun has a tyre shot out and a missing wheel, and there's no spares.'

'Shit.' He turned to his assistant: 'Search the village for tyres or tyre repair equipment,' then back to Sokunthea: 'Come with me, let's have another look.'

As they walked back to the guns Sokunthea said, 'Did you really shoot him?'

'Yes.'

'For being drunk?'

'For putting the guns at risk, for failing to take command, for selling his oxen and for the skulls.' He walked ahead of her.

'How did all those skulls…' she stopped.

Thai turned back to her. 'Because this one didn't just like killing, he also liked to remind himself that he liked killing by piling them up.' They walked the line of the equipment and Thai agreed with Sokunthea. 'How are we for food?' he finally said.

'There's not a lot on the carts, not for a hundred people, anyway.'

'Never mind, feed them; with a good meal inside them they'll push harder.'

Sokunthea organised the meal preparation and began to remove the rice from the carts. In doing so she noticed one of the artillery shell boxes was open; when she looked inside it was empty. She summoned Thai, who ordered all the shell boxes to be opened; all were empty.

'Why the hell have guns but no bullets?' Sokunthea said to herself.

The food was served and everyone sat along the roadside and around the guns eating, Thai's assistant had reported that no spare tyres or repair equipment could be found; the situation appeared hopeless.

'We'll have to destroy them,' said Thai finally, 'we can't stay here much longer.'

Sokunthea began to stand slowly, then said, 'Do they need tyred wheels to fire?'

'No,' said Thai.

'Then put the cart wheels on them and leave the carts for the enemy.'

Thai jumped to his feet and hugged her. 'I knew I needed you along!'

He ran off to find his assistant and soon everyone appeared busy in changing wheels. The spare cart wheels were strapped to the guns and they were suddenly being propelled forwards. With around one hundred men and women to push, Thai was able to set a fast pace and as the nightly rains began again they made camp just ten kilometres from Kampot. With no food to fill them and no fires allowed to keep them warm, the group huddled around the guns talking quietly, hoping for morning and the end of the rains.

Thai sat with Sokunthea. 'We did well today,' he said.

'I could say we were lucky,' replied Sokunthea.

'How... why?'

'Well, the cart wheels could have cracked under the weight of the guns or they may not have fitted and who knows? Without the original wheels the guns still may not work.'

'Nah. We're okay, and anyway without shells they won't work.'

'That's crazy, why provide guns and no shells?'

'Oh, he got shells all right, he just sold them. Even under Ankor there's corruption.'

'You're sounding a little disillusioned.'

'When you see those skulls you have to be.'

'Who were those people?'

'Servants to the big houses along the coast. Ankor hates the rich and the people who work for them... they couldn't work in the fields, there was no use for them.'

'They were people, Cambodian people.' Sokunthea looked down the dark road ahead of her. 'Sometimes, Thai, I think you are almost human and then the hatred comes out, the need for revenge. What's wrong with you Rouge – do you want to kill all Cambodians?'

'Look at yourself, just look at yourself, dressed in Rouge combat gear, attached to a Rouge combat unit; you are Rouge too.' He stopped, looked up to the night sky, then back at her. 'I just want to stop the Vietnamese stealing my country.' He stood and walked away.

The night's sleep was disturbed by the sound of small arms fire coming from ahead. Thai quickly dispatched a small group of soldiers forward to assess the situation and placed the rest of his men on alert. As daylight came, the group returned, informing Thai of a firefight with a platoon of Vietnamese soldiers.

'What were they attacking?' he asked.

'A convoy of ox carts ahead; they have food,' the soldier said with enthusiasm.

'That must be Thalin,' said Sokunthea. 'Are they all right?'

Thai looked at her. 'Send some of your men ahead to the carts; tell them to wait.' He turned. 'Come on let's move.'

Within half an hour they had reached Thalin and the food carts; along the way they had passed the bodies of two Vietnamese soldiers, and a third was discovered close to Thalin's column. He had his hands tied behind his back and had been shot through the head.

'Why?' asked Sokunthea of Thai.

'He was a spy, everyone shoots spies.'

When the two columns joined, Sokunthea went to find Tiny and greeted her with a hug. They sat beneath a small bush, so pleased to see each other.

'I'm glad you're back, you and Thai, Thalin was becoming a little strange.'

'Anyone missing?'

'Yes, that cow Sak shot Li, an old lady, said she was stealing rice.'

'And?'

'It fell from the cart, she was scooping it up from the road.'

'And what did Thalin do?'

'Laughed and warned us that he was in charge.'

'Any other losses?'

'Two were killed by the Vietnamese last night, I was really scared.'

'It's a good job we were not far away.'

'Yeah. Thalin was useless, he just lay under a cart and started to fire his gun anywhere.'

'And Sak?'

'She was enjoying every minute, running up and down shooting at shadows.'

'Who killed the Vietnamese soldier?'

'The captured one?'

'Yeah.'

'Sak.'

'We have to watch that woman.'

'She hates you.'

'How do you know?'

'She told me; said you were not one of them, didn't know how you got the favours that you did, and said she'd put a stop to them.'

Sokunthea and Tiny's conversation was stopped by the call to move by Thai, and the column headed on to Kampot. As they reached the outskirts of the town Sokunthea began to hear a screeching sound building up behind her, then she heard the cry of Thai: 'Down!'

The first bomb smashed into the rice field to Sokunthea's left, the displaced water and mud falling onto the column. The second fell ahead, obliterating one ox cart completely and sending a second into the air. Sokunthea lay where she was, not daring to move, then she thought of Tiny and reached out for her. Tiny's hand grabbed hers and they looked at each other, both covered in mud and both alive.

'Off the road... off the road!' came the cry, and everyone who could obeyed. As the group took shelter behind earth banks and in drains the noise of the fighter could be heard again. It swooped in low across the rice fields; to the pilot the guns must have been sitting ducks but no bombs came, and as quickly as it came the plane disappeared.

'No bombs, no bombs!' Sokunthea could hear Thai shouting. 'We're secondary; come on, let's move!' he screamed.

The non-Rouge members of the group were directed forward to clear away the debris and the dead while the Rouge began to push the guns. There developed a growing satisfaction amongst the whole group that the guns were safe; the Vietnamese would not have them. This elation continued as they entered Kampot, a seaside town much favoured by the French during their colonial days. Kampot stands on the mouth of the Prek Teak Chhu river, a wide, shallow, tidal river with dangerous undercurrents. Before the Seventeen of April it was the home for twenty thousand people with an important seafood industry and popular with Phnom Penh tourists; now it stood empty except for several hundred soldiers. The soldiers were there to protect the bridge, the only crossing point on the river and of vital military importance should the Vietnamese invade. This was the real target of the fighter; take out the bridge and the entire Cambodian border and plains troops were trapped. The Cambodians were already withdrawing many of their forces and equipment and the road leading to the bridge was beginning to be congested with troops and civilians.

As the guns approached the bridge the local commander began to order all other traffic off the road. He informed Thai that he wanted the guns across the river immediately, suggesting that the fighter may return. As Sokunthea walked along with the group she looked at the retreating people and thought of the lines of despair she had first encountered at the Red Cross. A nation on retreat is not a pretty sight, she thought, but this was a nation retreating from no external enemy.

A light rain again began to fall as they entered the first section of the bridge; this was made of concrete and had recently been hit in an attack. The second section extended a third of the way across the river in one piece. It was made of iron girders and, although appearing undamaged from a distance, once they were on the bridge it was clear that the original floor had been destroyed. The floor was now made up of wooden slats, which rocked and moved out of position as the weight of the guns moved on. Instead of moving smoothly the wheels of the guns would roll into and out of the grooves between the wooden boards, banging and clattering as they went; it was clear this river crossing would be slow.

Thai had ordered that the guns were not to be exposed all at once on the bridge; as the first gun reached the third section the second would begin its journey along the second. The third section of the bridge was of the original French concrete; this spanned the centre of the river and was the most exposed. It also contained the main bridge defences, with a large automatic gun and troops sheltering behind piles of sand bags. Although tired the group were urged to keep going by the soldiers, many of them staring up to the sky; ahead lay the fourth section, similar to the second but, to Sokunthea's horror, the floor had to be transported also. This was achieved by moving the gun forward twenty wooden boards then bringing the boards from behind to the front and repeating the action. As the first boards were laid into position Sokunthea looked down the river and out to sea. She turned to Tiny.

'What a farce,' she grinned at her friend.

'It will take us ages to get across; why can't they cut more trees, make more boards?'

'Maybe the Vietnamese keep blowing them away.'

'Get moving.' The voice of Thai broke their conversation.

Sokunthea looked at him; he had arrived from the rear with

Sak.

'What's holding everything up?' he asked Sokunthea when he got closer.

'The bridge has no floor,' said Sokunthea sarcastically.

Thai looked past her. 'Shit.' He turned to Sak. 'I'm going back to hold the other groups; get this thing across and make it fast, okay?'

She nodded and as Thai left she turned to Sokunthea and Tiny. 'Don't just stand there, get the boards in place!' she screamed.

Sokunthea just stared at her, then said, 'The bridge is overcrowded already; only so many boards can be moved at any one time, otherwise we're all in the river.'

Sak stared at her in almost disbelief then, after a pause, began to pull her pistol from her belt. Sokunthea slammed her fist down hard onto Sak's wrist and the gun fell to the floor. Then, as Sak tried to retrieve it, Sokunthea's knee came up and crashed into her face, sending her sprawling backwards. Then the cry of, 'Move!' was heard and she and Tiny turned to the gun and began to push.

'She'll get you for that,' said Tiny.

'I know – but it was great.' The two women laughed as they pushed.

The journey across the fourth section was long, taking over one hour; as they reached the concrete of the fifth section and then solid ground the group were exhausted. Sokunthea and Tiny decided to go down to the river to wash and relax; they had not washed since Tuk Meas and as they entered the cool fresh water their bodies almost cheered for the opportunity to be clean again. Sokunthea first observed something was wrong on the bridge when she noticed soldiers running on to section four, then she realised the second gun was leaning at a precarious angle.

'That's going to topple into the river,' she said aloud.

Tiny looked up to the bridge as the first person fell through the floor, then another and another.

'What the hell?' said Sokunthea. 'Come on, let's get them out.'

Sokunthea and Tiny made their way up the bank, picking up long pieces of wood and other things that might float. As they approached the base of the bridge several more people fell through, hit the water and disappeared. They waded out to the bridge support and looked up; above them was the second gun with its wheels through the bridge. It was being held up by its barrel and carriage; many hands appeared to be holding it but it was clear that in the end its weight would win. As she looked up Thai's face appeared between the boards and looked down at her.

'What are you doing?' he asked.

'Washing,' she smiled.

'Get up here!' he shouted.

Sokunthea and Tiny scrambled up the riverbank and headed back across the bridge. Thai met them halfway.

'Ideas,' he said harshly.

'Who the hell caused this?' asked Sokunthea.

'Sak; to speed things up she laid only every second, then every third board.'

'Prat.'

'Well, never mind, how do we get it out?'

'How the hell do…' she stopped and looked up; the noise of the fighter engine increased as it got closer. In a rush it had passed over them and continued up the valley.

'We have to shift it now!' shouted Thai.

Sokunthea's eyes were following the fighter trail up the valley. 'Let it fall through,' she finally said.

'What, you're…'

'Let it fall through; we can drag it out of the mud later and in the meantime move the other gun off the bridge.'

Thai nodded and ran back to the group around the second gun. As Sokunthea approached the sound of the gun hitting the water could be heard, as could Thai's voice ordering the group to relay the boards and begin moving the third gun. Sokunthea, Tiny and Thai retreated to below the bridge to check on the semi-submerged gun.

As they did the fighter returned and opened fire on the bridge, from where the soldiers began to return the fire. Sokunthea, Tiny and Thai took shelter behind the bridge's supports as a second fighter appeared and launched two rockets at the central section.

'They're after the gun!' shouted Thai, trying to make his voice heard above the noise.

'Is it moving?' screamed Sokunthea.

'Yes, I think so.'

The first rocket flew below the bridge and hit the river higher up, the second hit the second section blowing away part of the support and sending wooden boards scattering into the sky.

'Get the boards from that section,' Sokunthea was pointing, 'we can move the gun quicker.'

Thai ran from his hiding place up onto the bridge and gave the orders; the transfer of boards from the second section to the fourth helped to speed up the progress of the gun. The fighters had other ideas; they came in again low, below the level of the bridge, which made the automatic gun obsolete as it could only point upwards, not downwards. With only small arms fire directed at them they targeted section four and the gun; Sokunthea and Tiny watched as they came screaming in. The first fighter launched his rockets too far away; both fell short of the bridge and he passed under the second section and on up the valley. The second fighter delayed his rocket delivery and came closer and closer to the fourth section; as he did the fighter pilot became startled to see the gun on the bridge turn towards him. He launched his rockets hurriedly; one passed below the bridge while the other struck the underside of the bridge, bringing wooden boards and iron crashing down into the river. This cascade of material ruled out the pilot's chance of passing below the bridge and he pulled his plane up in order to pass over it. As the plane, now very close to the bridge, climbed upwards, the gun on the bridge fired.

The explosion was deafening as the resultant fireball and debris from the disintegrating fighter hit the bridge and the gun. The bridge held but the gun was blown backwards off the bridge and into the water. Sokunthea and Tiny, who were still below the bridge taking cover, felt the bridge shiver, then settle. When silence returned, they both ran up to the bridge to look for survivors. The scene was chaos; bodies and debris were everywhere. Sokunthea worked her way from body to body assisting where she could. Finally she reached the body of Thai enmeshed against the side of the bridge, his search for radios over.

The first fighter did not return and the surviving members of the group collected on the river bank; the river crossing had reduced their numbers by half. Thalin appeared with the local commander and began to take charge: the second gun would be dragged from the river immediately and the party would continue to Bokor with just the two pieces. By evening the gun was out of the mud and the party five kilometres out of Kampot; they rested in an old pagoda.

'What happened back there?' Tiny asked of Sokunthea.

'I don't know.'

'I thought the guns had no shells?'

'So did I.'

'You realise there's no Thai to protect us; Sak will – we're in trouble.'

'I can't stop thinking of poor Thai.' Sokunthea began to cry. 'He was a good man, oh, I know he was a Rouge, but a good man.'

Tiny put her arm around her friend. 'Come on, let's sleep.'

As Sokunthea and Tiny settled down Sak approached. 'You,' she pointed at Sokunthea, 'he wants to see you.' She nodded in the direction from which she had come; Sokunthea got up and followed her.

'You think you're so clever, don't you?' Sak began to speak. 'Well, I'll soon be in charge of people like you; this war won't stop us from getting our revenge.'

'Revenge for what?' asked Sokunthea.

'The killings, the corruption; you city people bled this country and now it's payback time.'

'By killing us all? The Vietnamese are about to invade and you want to kill Cambodians? You're crazy.'

They reached Thalin's fire without further comment; Thalin indicated for Sokunthea to sit by his side.

'How's the food?' he asked.

'There's no food; you left it in Kampot, remember?'

'I had no choice, the local commander claimed it as payment for passage.'

'Christ, we're supposed to be fighting the Vietnamese not stealing from each other.'

Thalin leaned forward and whispered, 'We're beaten already.'

Sokunthea stared into the fire and thought of the patriotism of Thai.

'You've got to find us food,' Thalin continued.

'From where?'

'Anywhere, scavenge it, you're good at that.'

Sokunthea thought. 'Okay, but I choose my team.'

'That's okay, but Sak goes; I've got to make sure you come back.'

'When do we start?'

'Tomorrow; we should make the base of the hill station at Bokor by mid afternoon. Meet us there – with food.'

Sokunthea walked back to Tiny; at least they wouldn't have to push the gun, she thought.

By first light Sokunthea had chosen her team of scavengers, all the remaining women attached to the group, and, with Sak, the thirteen of them set out. The sky was grey and the rain would soon he falling; Sokunthea had first thought of going straight down to the coast in the hope of catching sea food but a rainy, choppy sea would make that difficult. The narrow strip of coastal plain that they were entering had few rice fields and hence drainage canals but this area might produce more food. As the land began to climb there might be edible leaves and wild potatoes. Sokunthea divided her group into three: one to search the canals for frogs and fish, the second to search the rice fields for abandoned rice still on the stem and the final group to check the upland for wild foods. Sak followed Sokunthea as she and Tiny chose to check the rice stems.

'Return here with your finds at midday,' said Sokunthea as the groups departed.

'Why did you choose only women?' asked Sak as they entered their first rice field.

'They work harder and are more diligent.'

'Not as strong, though.'

'Oh, no. Strength is inside you; after all they've gone through – they're strong.'

It was then that Sokunthea heard her name called out; she turned and saw two members of the upland group running after her.

'What's wrong?' she asked.

The women were breathing heavily. 'A cow... a cow on the hill!'

All the women began to run back and others joined them as they passed. Eventually they reached the upland area and there, eating its full, was a large water buffalo.

'How do we catch it?' asked Tiny.

'It's got a ring,' said Sokunthea. She turned to Sak. 'Give me your gun belt.' Sak stared at her. 'I need your belt for the buffalo's ring,' Sokunthea said, pointing to the animal and the ring in its nose. Sak released it slowly. Sokunthea then stepped forward confidently and slid the belt through the ring as the animal looked up. The watching group cheered and clapped their hands excitedly; as Sokunthea took a firm grip on the belt the animal bolted for higher ground. Sokunthea held on and was dragged over bushes and rocks until the animal had settled and finally stopped.

As the group ran after her and the animal, Sokunthea looked up from the ground. 'Thank you very much,' she said, and they all laughed, except Sak. The animal was tethered to a tree and the group went about their chores. By midday, when they congregated together, they had amassed a large and variable collection of foodstuffs which they loaded onto the buffalo and headed for their rendezvous with Thalin.

As they travelled back along the coastal road they heard the familiar sound of jet engines. 'Off the road!' shouted Sokunthea and everyone headed for the bushes. Sak and Sokunthea found themselves side by side in the mud.

'What does he want?' asked Sak, nodding to the sky.

'The guns I think... I hope Thalin's awake otherwise our rendezvous will be interesting.'

'Thalin's a fool,' said Sak. 'When the Bokor commander takes charge then you will see a real soldier and defender of Cambodia.'

Sokunthea just looked up to the sky. 'It's gone,' she shouted to the group. 'Come on, let's go.'

Thalin had reached the base of the hill station and had camouflaged the guns well, so well that Sokunthea's group almost walked straight past.

'Where's the food?' asked Thalin as he appeared from some hidden position.

'God, you scared me,' answered Sokunthea, then she turned. 'What about that?' she said, pointing to the buffalo.

'How do we cook it?'

'We don't, it pulls a gun up that bloody hill.'

'We'll need more than one for that job; we'll eat it.'

'Are you crazy?'

'No, I'm hungry, very hungry and so are my men.' He looked around.

'Listen, with that animal's help we'll get the guns up; without...' she shrugged her shoulders.

Thalin stared at Sokunthea, pulled his revolver from his belt and shot the buffalo through the head. It crashed to the floor instantly. 'We eat.' Thalin turned and re-entered his camouflaged hide.

That evening the group enjoyed their best meal for many years. Someone found a Cambodian violin and began to play nationalistic and local tunes and many sang and clapped and celebrated into the night.

Thalin sat with Sokunthea. 'You did very well today.' He paused and stared into a nearby fire. 'Thai's not here to protect your secret; if you want me to help then I've got to know it's worthwhile.'

'And I've got to know that if I tell you I'm not dead.'

'So there is something.'

'An American radio and contact number, plus a million dollars.'

'Wheww... worth protecting.'

'Sak tells me you're finished when we get above.' She nodded upwards.

'I'm not in charge, that's for certain, but I've had interfering bastards around me before and I'm still here.'

They both stared ahead. 'I'm sorry for what I did.'

'I don't want to talk about it.'

'You were... strong, powerful, everybody liked you; you were strong when I was weak. I'm sorry.'

Sokunthea looked at him. 'And the others, the wives?'

'They were nothing... a crush on the local commander, but you are different – a woman.'

'Well, this woman says if you try it again I'll kill you.'

The silence between them continued against a backdrop of singing and laughter.

'Do you know that half the people here were being tortured and starved by the other half just a month ago?' said Sokunthea.

'It's amazing what the threat of invasion does to a country, old times are forgotten.'

'What a nation! What a nation, we are starved and killed by our own people, the Vietnamese come to save us and we all join together to fight them.'

'So why don't you make a run for it?'

'Because your friend Sak is watching me like a hawk.'

'Hm, she watches me, too.'

'What is waiting for us up there?' Sokunthea nodded upwards.

'The houses of the élite, the Cambodian superrich, only now they've been turned into a garrison – progress.'

'But who lived up there?'

'The rich, the king and all his cronies, when you'd got bored with stealing the money from the country you'd R & R at Bokor; magnificent views, magnificent houses.' Thalin shrugged.

'And we're going to fight amongst it.'

'Why not? If we're going to die, let's do it in splendid surroundings,' he laughed.

'What will you do if the Vietnamese win?'

'That depends on your million.'

'If they catch you they'll kill you.'

'You too.'

'I'm not Rouge, I'm Seventeen of April scum, remember.'

'People have short memories; you're with us so to them you're Rouge.'

'I'm trapped and you know it.'

'Then we need each other; I keep you alive, you help me when this thing is over.'

'Be careful; two men have tried a similar agreement with me and both are dead.'

Thalin stared at the people singing and dancing. 'That's how it should be,' he mumbled.

'Not any more,' replied Sokunthea, 'the world won't forget what we did.'

She stood and began to look for Tiny who was talking to a young soldier. 'I'm going to get some sleep,' she said.

'Okay, I'll join you later,' said Tiny and their eyes met. Sokunthea bedded down at the edge of the road under an old mango tree; the rain didn't fall that night and Sokunthea knew the dry season was about to begin and with the dry season would come the Vietnamese.

Sokunthea woke at daybreak and realised that Tiny had not returned. She realised that Tiny's relationship with the soldier was deeper than first thought. Within an hour Thalin had the column moving up the mountain. The road to Bokor had once been in pristine condition but again Pol Pot's ideology had put a stop to that; the road had been blown apart, and to reach the top would be hard work. With around sixty men and women to push and pull, the guns began well on their journey up until they reached a section where the road had been dynamited. No wheeled object would get past and with fighters expected, no wheeled object could be left exposed on the hillside. Thalin called a council in search for advice.

'We can't move,' he began, 'and we can't leave these guns here; I want ideas.'

'Let's get more help from above,' said a young soldier.

'Let's rebuild the road,' said Sak, looking at Sokunthea.

'Let's spike the guns and leave them; we have no shells anyway,' said Thalin's aide.

Thalin looked around and then at Sokunthea. 'Any ideas?' he asked.

'Take them apart and carry them up.' She looked at him.

Thalin turned to his aide. 'Can we do that?'

'Maybe,' came the reply.

The guns were parted into five components with each one allocated a team to carry it upwards; by late evening the advanced groups had reached the top of Bokor. As the groups arrived they headed towards one of the large houses situated on the plateau; the house had belonged to the king but now was just a shell blown apart by the new ideology. The sections of the gun were laid down and the group began to finish the remaining meat of the buffalo. A small fire was lit and people sat around it reheating their buffalo pieces. The night was dark, very dark and as Sokunthea looked out across the land below she wondered when they would come. Thalin came and stood beside her.

'You frightened me,' she said with a strut.

'Sorry. It looks as if we're alone,' he said after a pause.

'Where's the thousand men?'

'You know Cambodians, they love to exaggerate.'

'So what happens when the Vietnamese come?'

Thalin shrugged his shoulders. 'That won't be for several weeks, they'll wait for the dry season.'

'And in the meantime we sit here and starve.'

'It's scavenging for you again tomorrow.'

'Well, if you want animal meat I'll need a gun.'

'Sak will go.'

'I thought you didn't trust her... she could shoot me and you'll lose your radio.'

'She's one hundred per cent Rouge and she's also related to the Bokor commander; I can't show favour to a Seventeen of April... well, not when it comes to guns.'

'You afraid of this commander?'

'I don't know until I meet him.'

As they looked ahead Sak approached from the darkness. 'A group of local soldiers is here, they want to speak to you.'

Thalin looked at Sokunthea then spoke to Sak. 'The commander with them?'

'No, he's at a small supply village at the base of the hill organising equipment.'

Thalin walked back with Sak to meet the men while Sokunthea headed for the fire and some food.

The local soldiers consisted of six men; they had been left on the plateau on guard and were camped inside a church. They'd seen the group emerge from the road but thought them to be Vietnamese so stayed hidden, but the smell of the roasting buffalo had forced them to venture out and they realised they were amongst fellow Cambodians. They reported to Thalin that the plateau was quiet and that the main body of men would arrive over the next few days from Kompong Som. During the report they kept glancing at the buffalo meat, so were relieved when Thalin cut the report short and told them to eat. The night passed without incident or rain; Thalin had posted guards around the camp's perimeter and it was one such post that woke the camp with news of troop movements at the rear of the plateau. Thalin, his aide and Sak headed towards the advancing troops and eventually met up with the commander, the brother of Sak.

The commander's name was Van Serun; he was a professional soldier who had fought against Lon Nol's forces at Chenla, inflicting huge losses on the Royal Cambodian Army. He had fought alongside the Vietnamese in that battle and understood their tactics better than any other officer; he was proud, nationalistic, firm but fair and his men were loyal to him.

He quickly had his engineers reconstruct the guns and positioned them so that they commanded the entire coast road from Kampot to Kompong Som. The Cambodians were expert in booby traps and mine laying and he put their skills to good use laying these deadly weapons across the escarpment rising to the plateau. Next he fortified the main buildings and took the church, built for visiting ambassadors of Christian countries, as his command post. With the soldiers was a group of Seventeen of April workers; their job was to bring up the hill all the supplies and ammunition which were presently being unloaded at a base camp. The following day Sokunthea and the few remaining Seventeen of April workers who had brought the guns were added to this group.

The work was hard: ammunition boxes had to be carried and dragged up the side of a small stream which drained the plateau; it was narrow but offered good cover against prowling fighters and helicopters. Its disadvantage was that it was steep and the path was narrow resembling a goat track. Carrying the heavy ammunition boxes up was fraught with obstacles, including the people coming down and more soldiers going up. The task was even harder for Sokunthea and Tiny as Sak was put in charge and she delegated them to bring up the ammunition boxes. As night fell Sokunthea and Tiny were stranded halfway up the gully; Sak had wanted one more run, no doubt hoping they would miss their footing in the dark.

'There's a small opening in the rock over there,' she nodded past Tiny, 'we'll camp there.'

They left the box and headed for the cave; it had a small entrance but appeared quite large, as they looked further inside. They sat either side of the entrance, stretched out their legs and looked back down the trail to the base camp.

'When will they come?' asked Tiny.

'Soon,' replied Sokunthea.

'What's it like?'

Sokunthea looked at her friend. 'A battle, you've been in one – I haven't,' Tiny continued.

'Hectic,' replied Sokunthea, 'often you don't know who's winning and how.'

'Were you afraid at Neak Loung?'

'Of course.'

'Many people will die here, won't they?'

Sokunthea nodded. 'Yes,' then paused. 'You've just got to keep your head down, no heroics.'

'Don't worry!' and the two women laughed.

'I know it doesn't help to talk about it, but I'm hungry,' said Tiny.

'We'll breakfast tomorrow at base camp.'

'But we're going up.'

'If we go up they'll be no food, the food's down.'

'What about the…?' asked Tiny, looking towards the box on the trail.

'In the cave,' said Sokunthea.

'Sak will kill us if she finds out.'

Sokunthea shrugged her shoulders. 'We'd better get some sleep. I'll do first watch.'

Tiny went further into the cave and Sokunthea continued to stare down the trail. Everything around was black; the lighting of fires was prohibited and the exposure of light was punishable by death, but the breeze was warm and collected at the base of the gully from the sea and blew upwards. As her eyes adjusted more and more to the dark she could make out the small trees bending, then two dark shapes appeared, coming down the path slowly. She glanced at her sleeping friend, remembered her words about heroics and decided to stay where she was. The figures were getting closer, then the front one struck his foot on the ammunition box and tumbled headfirst down the hill. The second crouched down; Sokunthea thought this strange for a Vietnamese patrol, and the shapes clearly had no guns.

'Who are you?' she whispered. The figures looked towards the cave. 'Don't be afraid, it's Sokunthea and Tiny.'

They began to walk towards the cave; Tiny had woken and the two women watched them crouch before them.

'Is that you, Ro?' asked Tiny, and the figure nodded.

'What the hell are you doing?'

'Getting out,' came the reply.

'Where to?' cut in Sokunthea.

'Anywhere – if we stay here we'll die.'

'And if they catch you?' asked Tiny.

'We'll take that chance; the Vietnamese are coming, they're on our side. Come with us.'

Tiny turned to Sokunthea. 'It's too early,' said her friend.

'What's that got to do with it?' jumped in Ro. 'Come with us, don't listen to her; she's Rouge, anyway.'

Sokunthea felt the urge to knock Ro down the hill but just said, 'You go now and they'll miss you and come looking; go when the fighting starts and they don't know if you're dead, up the hill, down the hill – no search.'

'Is that your plan?' said Ro. 'Well, we overheard Sak and that murderer Thalin planning what they would do to us when the Vietnamese came; we're witnesses.'

The group fell into silence, then Tiny said, 'I'll stay. Good luck!'

'Wait,' said Sokunthea, 'help me with the box.' Sokunthea and Ro carried the box into the cave and Sokunthea broke the lid. Inside they could make out a dozen handguns with bullets hanging from a rack; they lifted it out and below were three small boxes of hand grenades. Ro and his friend took two handguns each and a box of grenades.

'If there's a firefight below, we have a chance,' he said. They departed into the night; Sokunthea and Tiny remained awake all night, expecting to hear the sound of gunshots and explosions from below, but by morning none had been heard.

'I think they got away.' Sokunthea turned to Tiny.

'Will they go after them?'

'That Sak is crazy enough, but it's not them she wants, it's me.'

'So that's why you wouldn't go; if you went Sak would have a whole brigade after you.' She smiled at her friend and took her hand in order to get on her feet.

Sokunthea smiled. 'Down for breakfast?' Tiny nodded and they set off for base camp.

The base camp had been situated in a small valley about a kilometre from the gully; trucks brought the ammunition in from Kompong Som. It was mainly Chinese-made and already Van Serun, the area commander, had complained about its quality. To Sokunthea this was just another aspect of this crazy organisation called the Rouge; here they were dragging ammunition boxes up a hill, ammunition that may not work.

'The Chinese are really stuffing us,' she said to herself.

The commander of the base camp was a bureaucrat and scared, very scared; he'd seen some of the atrocities carried out by the Rouge and knew that if the Vietnamese won it could be payback time. He wanted friendship from all, especially the Seventeen of April group, to whom he provided breakfast if they were in the camp at early morning. Sak had tried to stop this practise but her brother had not supported her on this occasion.

Sokunthea and Tiny joined a small queue collecting a bowl of rice soup and chicken; the food seemed surprisingly plentiful and both went back for seconds. In the queue a small group of solders had gathered, returning from night duty.

'Quiet night?' Sokunthea asked.

One turned and looked at her. 'No problem,' he said eventually. Sokunthea smiled at Tiny.

After the food they walked to the ammunition depot where they were allocated another box of Chinese weapons.

Sokunthea felt cocky. 'These any good?' she asked of the quartermaster.

He looked at her, then said, 'Bloody useless; the Chinese

know we're in trouble and they're dumping all their rubbish onto us at full price.'

'I thought they were on our side,' Sokunthea pursued.

'They're on their side; be very careful, firing caps.' He tapped the box, smiled at them and then said, 'Move it.'

The two women started down the sandy track towards the water gully. This was the easy part; the track was flat and wide enough for two to pass. Unfortunately Sak had placed specially-chosen helpers to stand along the track and move people on. As they reached the water gully a five-minute rest was allowed; this wasn't Rouge charity, it allowed more important travellers to climb the hill first and, of course, welcomed the new descenders, coming to collect another cargo.

Sokunthea and Tiny were signalled to begin their climb; they entered the gully through a narrow break in the rock face – here the path was the stream bed. The hill then went up steeply with one member of the team climbing higher, holding the box, and the second joining her before they could pull it up together. They then entered a zigzag path climbing up an incline of about forty-five degrees; the path was uneven with stones and tree-roots sticking up. This lasted until another steep incline where positioning and strength were necessary. Then came a gentle slope, where a small pond of stream-water collected and the cave of the previous night was situated. Sokunthea and Tiny always stopped here, took refreshment and rested as long as they could. The final section was another forty-five degree challenge with its accompanying stones and roots. Sokunthea and Tiny had reached the pond safely, where they began to wash and rest.

'It's not that heavy,' said Tiny, as she looked towards the box.

'Dangerous though,' was Sokunthea's response.

'Will they find the box in the cave?'

'Maybe, but they've got to hurry, the Vietnamese won't be long now.'

'Do you think Ro made it?'

'Yes…'

Sokunthea's voice was cut out by a loud explosion coming from below; she looked up expecting to see a fighter pass over, but it did not happen. Sokunthea and Tiny ran to the rim of the pond area and looked down. Several soldiers and Seventeen of April workers were scattered across the hillside.

'Shall we help them?' asked Tiny.

'I'm not going back down there, let Sak sort it.'

The two turned, picked up the box and headed upwards. As they had almost reached the summit they began to hear the explosions and the sound of automatic weapons being fired. As their headline came above the summit they saw the Vietnamese fighter halfway through its run, dropping bombs and strafing the ground. People were running in all directions; some were returning fire, but Sokunthea grabbed Tiny's arm and pulled her down.

'No heroics.' She smiled and they both sat with their backs against the summit and kept their heads down. When silence returned they heard the voice of Sak.

'Up, get up, you cowards.' Sokunthea just looked at Sak with disgust.

Sak shouted to a guard and they began to escort Sokunthea and Tiny towards the command headquarters. Sak bypassed the officer in the entrance hall and marched straight into her brother's room where a meeting was being held.

'These two should be shot for cowardice,' she blurted out.

Van Serun looked at her, then at Sokunthea. 'Well?' he said.

'We were protecting the firing mechanisms; one box has already blown up on the hillside, and this is the only one until tomorrow. Of course if you want the Vietnamese fighter to blow it up…' she shrugged her shoulders.

'Don't play with me,' said Van Serun. He looked at Sak. 'What's this about losing the other firing mechanisms?'

She looked at the floor.

'Find out,' he said and banged the table hard with his hand. As the group turned to leave, Van Serun called after Sokunthea. 'You!' She turned. He pointed to a side door and she walked towards it. 'The meeting is over,' he said and he followed her.

'Thalin has been telling me all about you,' he said as he entered the room.

'All?'

'You were the saviour of the guns.'

'I think a few people were involved in that.'

'Hmmm. You don't like my sister-in-law do you?'

'She's a fool.'

'Be careful, she's still family.'

'And she's still a fool.'

'Why, feel free, say what you wish.'

Sokunthea stared at him. 'She gets women to carry the heavy ammunition boxes up the hill and she objects to feeding the carriers; through exhaustion and lack of food they drop your precious firing pins and you can't fire the guns. She's a fool.'

'And you could organise it better?'

Sokunthea looked at him. 'I'm not one of you.'

'You don't want to defeat the Vietnamese?'

'Sure; they're invading my country, but I don't want to return to the killings, the skulls.'

Van Serun looked out of the window, then said, 'Organise the supply route.'

'And Sak?'

'I'll find something else for her.'

'I'll need soldiers to help.'

He nodded. 'They'll be available.'

Over the next week the amount of supplies reaching the summit increased, Sokunthea had instructed base camp to feed all supply carriers. Ropes were provided down the steepest parts of the gully so boxes could be pulled up and the midway pond was a rest area. Van Serun was pleased with the increase in supplies, for he knew the attack would come soon and the base camp would have to be abandoned. The air attacks continued but were sporadic, a sign that the enemy was more interested in reconnaissance than bombing; that would come later.

When the invasion came it arrived on Bokor's doorstep quickly. On the night of December the eighth an amphibious unit from the Vietnamese island of Phu Quoc worked its way up the tidal river at Kampot. By morning they had secured the western end of the bridge over the Prek Teak Chhu. The land units had crossed the border and were racing to join their amphibious colleagues, hoping to trap as many troops as possible. The small Rouge garrison left to guard the bridge and to destroy it if necessary fought bravely and it was the sound of this fighting that greeted the garrison on Bokor the following morning. Van Serun called a meeting and invited Sokunthea.

'Gentlemen, the war has come. We must hold this hill for as long as possible; by doing so we enable Kompong Som to continue supplying the army and we give time for the army to regroup.' He looked at Sokunthea. 'How is the food situation?' he asked.

'We have enough for two months.'

'And the ammunition?'

'We emptied the base camp yesterday.'

'Right. The enemy must take this garrison quickly; I expect a full frontal attack.' He looked around the room. 'They always underestimate we Cambodians and that will be their failing.' He paused. 'Kampot will fall soon; I expect an attack tonight or early morning. Let your men rest now but be prepared tonight. Any questions?'

'What about the Seventeen of April workers?' asked Sak.

'Hmm, they will be given the opportunity to fight with us.'

'And if not?' she continued.

'We will lock them in the church cellars; if more supplies come during the fighting we may need them.' He looked at Sokunthea. 'If that's all, to your positions.' As the meeting ended Van Serun took Sokunthea's arm and led her into another room.

'You have done very well in bringing up all the supplies. I would hate to lock you in the cellars.'

'Sak wanted you to shoot us.'

He nodded. 'I know, so what are you going to do?'

'If I go in the cellars I may die, if I stay out, the same; do I have a choice?'

'Try to convince the others, if they all fight we can get rid of this Seventeen of April rubbish.'

'Try telling Sak.'

'Talk to your people.'

Sokunthea turned to leave and as she did Van Serun's arm came around her waist gently turning her to him. His other hand raised her chin and he gently kissed her. Sokunthea did not resist; the tenderness of the experience was something that she had not experienced before.

'Talk to your people,' he whispered.

She stepped back from him, regaining her control. 'I'll try.' She turned and left. Outside the building she met Thalin. 'You're back in with the élite I see.'

Sokunthea walked past him but he followed.

'You're looking for greater protection than me, is that it?'

She stopped. 'If greater protection means I don't trust you, then yes.'

'Sak won't like you getting in with her brother.'

'In-law, brother in-law.'

'So that's why he doesn't always back her up. Anyway, when the fighting starts he'll be too busy to keep an eye on you.'

'And you?'

'I'm in charge of the medical unit, some fool thinks I know something about helping people.' He shook his head. 'Come to think of it, that's you, you do know something about medicine. I'll see Van Serun – great,' and he turned and ran back to the command headquarters. Sokunthea watched him disappear inside then headed for the Seventeen of April group, only to be met by Sak.

'So you have my brother too,' she said.

'I'm too busy to talk to you,' and Sokunthea brushed past her.

'You may think that you can get any man to do your bidding but I'm a woman. I'll see you'll get what is due.'

Sokunthea walked on with a broad smile on her face.

Only about thirty Seventeen of April carriers were still alive. Sokunthea asked Tiny to collect them together and she related Van Serun's words. Many of the men decided it was better to fight with the Rouge than die in a cellar; the women chose the other way.

'What will you do?' asked Tiny.

'Join the medical team, help the wounded, but I won't fight,' she replied.

After further protracted discussion the men had decided to join the army and all but six women wanted to volunteer for the medical group; the remaining six chose the cellars. Sokunthea began to walk back to the command headquarters to inform Van

Serun when the Vietnamese fighters decided to return again. They came in low, sweeping across the hill station. Sokunthea dived to the floor and waited for the first explosion, but it did not come. As she looked up she noticed a second group coming in low over the neighbouring hills; they split, then fired their missiles. The first fighter was targeting the guns; both his rockets hit the large rock, which shielded the guns from a rear attack. The second fighter went for the supplies area with devastating effect: the rockets hit home followed by a huge explosion as ammunition boxes blew up. Sokunthea lay flat on the ground, then realised that the group were still in that area.

'Tiny,' she said to herself. She stood and began to run back; as she reached the supplies area she saw a few bodies and these were mainly soldiers. She wandered around in the debris and smoke, calling out Tiny's name, and eventually getting a reply.

'Over here!' Sokunthea ran to where the voice was; Tiny and almost all the group were sheltering behind a garden wall.

'Is everyone all right?' Sokunthea asked.

'Sure, they're okay,' said Tiny. 'Will they come back?' she nodded towards the sky.

'Who knows,' said Sokunthea, then she heard Thalin's voice.

'Sokunthea, Sokunthea!'

'Who's that?' asked Tiny.

'My protector,' said Sokunthea sarcastically. 'Over here!' she shouted.

Thalin emerged from the clearing smoke. 'How many have we lost?'

'I've no idea,' replied Sokunthea.

'Come on, let's check for wounded.'

'Let's make sure the fighters aren't coming back first.' As she spoke the reconnaissance fighter made another pass over the hill. 'They're coming again, down!' she shouted to the group.

On the second run the first fighter attacked a large mansion house where water was being stored; its rockets were again on target, smashing into the building and spilling much of the precious liquid. The second fighter went again for the guns, this time using napalm. Sokunthea had heard of this substance when in Neak Loung but the sight of it frightened her. As it hit the ground and rocks sheltering the guns its fireball rushed into the sky with a gushing sound which appeared to be sucking all the air from the scorched area. Then she began to hear the screams of the burning soldiers.

'Come on,' she shouted at Thalin. 'Now's the time to be a hero.' She looked at Tiny. Tiny, Thalin and Sokunthea were the first to reach the scorched area; many bodies were lying on the floor burning, some soldiers were sitting holding badly burned arms or tearing their clothes away from badly burned skin. The smell was a mixture of gasoline and pork fat; Sokunthea watched Tiny turn and begin to vomit.

'Leave the burning ones,' she shouted to her companions and she began to direct them to the soldiers who would benefit from help. Other Seventeen of April people arrived and began to give help, quickly followed by other soldiers wanting to support their comrades. Van Serun arrived to see the extent of the damage but just stood and watched Sokunthea treating individual wounded and organising the treatment of many others. By mid-afternoon the dead had been burned and their ashes spread over the hill, and Sokunthea had ordered the wounded to be moved to the now partially destroyed mansion house, which she began to turn into a hospital. By early evening she was ordered to attend a meeting at headquarters; she and Thalin were the last to arrive.

'I believe they will attack early tomorrow; their jets have not softened us up enough yet and they're still worried about the guns. What's our situation with regards supplies?' He looked at Sokunthea.

'The food and ammo is the same as yesterday; our problem could be the water.'

'Explain.' he said.

'Instead of burying it or camouflaging it, you left it exposed around the mansion house. That's what the fighter was after, not the building.'

'So how much water is left?'

'I've no idea, I've been busy.'

Van Serun turned to Sak. 'You were in charge of the water, what's left?'

'About ten barrels.'

'How long will that last?'

'A month.'

'Two weeks,' cut in Sokunthea.

Sak glared at her.

'Damn,' said Van Serun. 'What about the men?' He pointed towards his adjutant.

'We have four hundred and thirty, all ready to die for their country, sir.'

Van Serun nodded. 'The wounded?' He looked at Thalin.

'We have eight, all being cared for in the mansion house,' replied Thalin.

'We need medical equipment and drugs; there are none,' cut in Sokunthea.

'I will radio Kompong Som for our last delivery; I'll include your request.'

'When will the delivery come?' asked Sokunthea.

'Who knows,' came Van Serun's reply. 'Be ready for guerrilla attacks tonight, be alert and good luck.'

The meeting ended and Sokunthea and Thalin walked back to the mansion house.

'We're rats in a trap,' said Thalin, 'if they don't shoot us they'll starve us out.'

'I'm more worried about that crazy Sak than the Vietnamese.'

'Well, you do rile her.'

'She's incompetent in everything she does; if she was one of us she'd be dead in a rice field somewhere by now or a skull next to the road.'

As they entered the mansion house Tiny greeted them. 'Another soldier has died and two others have returned to their positions on the hill.'

Thalin nodded. 'Two more to fight the enemy; what happened to the thousand they promised?'

'Ankor lies,' said Sokunthea and walked ahead.

The mansion house was a large, two-storey, fifteen-room building, which in its heyday must have been magnificent. After Pol Pot's soldiers had attacked it with grenades and the two rockets from the fighter had done their damage most of the upper floor had collapsed downwards. Only one third of the roof was intact and all of the doors and windows had disappeared long ago. On her return there Sokunthea called her group together; they consisted of all the female Seventeen of April workers and three men.

'I want Tiny and three of you to find a large sheet or piece of cloth, paint, anything; we must make a large red cross and attach it to the roof, The rest of you try to find any mats, covers, beds from the other old houses, anything that we can use.'

'And me?' asked Thalin.

'Get us some food,' she smiled at him.

As the group dispersed Sokunthea went to check the remaining patients. Two had severe body burns from which Sokunthea knew they would not recover, and a third had almost lost his arm to the napalm and if he was to live it would have to come off. The others would be back fighting when needed. She walked out of the patient area and met Van Serun.

'So this is your new hospital?'

She smiled. 'With a bit of organisation.'

'Where did you learn your medicine?' he continued.

'Neak Loung.'

He stared at her. 'I had friends there, on both sides.'

'It seemed to me that everyone was on both sides.'

'We're all Cambodians.'

'Then stop killing us,' she snapped. 'I'm sorry, I didn't...'

'We have made mistakes but if the truth of this time ever comes out there will be many nations in shame, many people having to ask questions.' He turned to leave and she reached out and touched his arm.

'I need your permission to remove a soldier's arm.'

'Show me,' he said.

Sokunthea led him back into the makeshift ward and to the soldier with the now rotting arm. As she took away the dressing the gangrenous smell of the flesh filled the air.

'Leave us,' said Van Serun and Sokunthea walked away and sat in the entrance hall. Van Serun joined her after a short time. 'He will let you remove the arm,' he said. 'Do you know how?'

'I've seen.'

He met her eyes. 'He's a good soldier, don't let him die.'

Tiny's scavenging group returned with several Rouge *kromas*, they looked at Van Serun who stood and then departed.

'What did he want?' asked Tiny.

'Check his men,' came Sokunthea's reply.

'And?'

'Nothing. Oh, he gave permission for us to remove the soldier's arm.'

Tiny stared at her friend. 'Well, it's better he's with us than against us.'

'Okay,' said Sokunthea, keen to change the subject. 'What you got?'

'Rouge *kromas*, we can tie them together, make a cross.' Tiny was pleased with her idea.

'Great,' said Sokunthea, 'let's get it on the roof as quickly as possible.' Sokunthea returned to the ward area to re-dress the soldier's arm. He was crying.

'I will die, won't I?' he asked when she arrived.

'Of course not,' replied Sokunthea, 'you're too strong.'

He fell silent and looked at her. 'I'm not one of them, I'm just a soldier.'

'Don't worry soldier, to me you're a patient and one that I intend to live.' She gave him a reassuring smile.

Sokunthea finished the dressing and left the ward to check on her other scavengers. Thalin had arrived back with two bags of rice and some dried fish. Members of the other team were trailing in with material, old beds and the odd instrument like pairs of scissors and tweezers.

Around midnight, when eyes and ears were straining for the sound of the enemy, Sokunthea began to prepare for the removal of an arm. With no anaesthetic available the young soldier had consumed the right amount of rice wine. He was laid on a low bed and held there by several colleagues; light was provided by four candles, which cast long shadows from the participants against the walls. A small wooden block was placed between the soldier's teeth and his arm was strapped at a ninety degree angle from his body.

Sokunthea looked at the rotting arm and nodded to Thalin, who tightened a tourniquet around the join where the humerus meets the shoulder. She waited for the tourniquet to take effect, then looking into Thalin's sweating face she took a razor blade in one hand and a piece of linen in the other and began to cut. The tissue fell away smoothly and Thalin's tight grip on the tourniquet was perfect to reduce the blood loss, and she was soon to the bone. She swabbed away a little more venous blood then picked up the handsaw and, focussing totally on the bone, began to saw. As she did a soldier entered the room.

'Dowse the candles, there's Vietnamese outside.'

They all looked at Sokunthea; she carried on sawing then said, 'Place the fire bowl under the bed with a candle and dowse the rest.'

In this strange, almost dark subterranean world Sokunthea felt and heard the bone crack and part from the shoulder. She felt with her fingers; the cut was clean. She handed the saw to Tiny, who passed her the red hot iron from the small fire bowl now under the bed.

'Release now, Thalin, slowly.'

Thalin, who had been holding the tourniquet tight, began to slacken it and as the blood began to flow Sokunthea began to cauterise the main vessels. Tiny brought up the remaining candle from the floor and the three of them glared at a shoulder with no arm.

'Release more,' said Sokunthea and Thalin duly obliged.

The fire bowl below the bed began to hiss as blood fell from the shoulder through the slats of wood, only to burn on the fire. The smell of burning blood, candles, alcohol and human sweat permeated the room. The silence was broken by the sound of automatic gunfire from outside.

'Release again,' came Sokunthea's steady voice, and Thalin followed her instruction.

'All the way,' she added.

Concerned faces were still looking at the shoulder stump when Sokunthea announced it was finished. Tiny washed the stump and wrapped it tightly as the others left the room. Sokunthea went to the entrance hall and sat in a corner on the floor.

Thalin approached her with a drink of water. 'It's still not safe out here.'

'Sit down and shut up then,' came her reply.

Thalin sat. 'You did a good job.'

'That's premature.' They both looked out into the darkness.

'Will he live?' he continued.

Sokunthea drank her water. 'That's what it's all about.'

The night appeared to race by and as dawn broke the sound of the first booby trap explosion came from the hillside. This was quickly followed by others; the Vietnamese had already advanced halfway up the hill without detection, mainly due to the work of their engineers the previous night. Now the frontal attackers had to take their chances. Automatic fire burst from all around the perimeter of the hill and troops could be seen moving from one position to another. Sokunthea and her medical group took shelter in the lowest part of the mansion along with their patients.

Soon the sound of mortar fire could be heard as the Vietnamese gunners got into position. Sokunthea decided that she needed a small team to be ready to collect the injured from the fighting, so Tiny and two men prepared to join her. They took position near the entrance hall and looked out across the battleground. The Vietnamese mortars were becoming increasingly accurate as they rained down on foxholes and trenches. The Cambodian response was just as fierce as Van Serun moved his troops cleverly around the hill rim.

Although the sound of the enemy was everywhere and his destruction easy to see, Sokunthea could see that no Vietnamese soldiers had succeeded in reaching the top of the hill. As the fighting on the hill appeared to subside the two large guns opened up, firing at some distant target on the flat lands below. Their sound appeared to galvanise the efforts of both sides and once again the intensity of mortar and automatic fire increased. Sokunthea realised that the mortar line was advancing towards the mansion as the Vietnamese gunners set up new advanced positions.

Then, as if a truce had been called, the explosions stopped; Sokunthea and her team looked out across the scene of destruction and decided it was time to help the wounded. All in a line they darted towards the first line of trenches just as the first fighter began to drop its deadly load. The medical team dived for cover as the napalm burst into life on their left-hand side. A second canister appeared to bounce and rise before it burst into flames and descended across the defenders' forward trenches. This was no time to be a hero, thought Sokunthea, as she knew a second fighter would be arriving soon. She sat in the trench looking into the sky and spotted it coming over the jungle then levelling off to seek its target. From being a spot in the distance its grey and green fuselage appeared to race directly towards her, then she saw the bombs fall from its wings and, as if in slow motion, glide accurately and destructively onto the church.

Without thinking Sokunthea jumped to her feet and began to run to where the bombs had exploded. As she approached the building it was still covered in smoke and debris was still falling; soldiers were trying to make their way out, some obviously injured, but Sokunthea rushed past them. She entered and fell into the entrance area, sidestepping debris and bodies, her mind set on finding one person: Van Serun. The door to the meeting room had been blown away and she rushed in. Scattered across the floor were maps and other papers; she saw two bodies lying near a window but instinctively knew they were not him. She began to call his name, 'Serun, Serun!' but there was no reply. She looked to the door, which led to the small room where they had had many meetings, and she tried to open it, but it was stuck. She put her mouth close to the door and called again, 'Serun, Serun!' She felt a hand on her shoulder and turned quickly; it was Tiny and the team.

'What's wrong?' Tiny asked.

'The commander, I think he's in there,' replied Sokunthea.

'I'll get the door open,' said one of the men and with help began to force a space large enough for someone to get through. Sokunthea, followed by Tiny, squeezed through the gap and found Van Serun unconscious and trapped by the legs.

'We'll need help,' Sokunthea said to her friend.

'Why the hell wasn't he in the cellars?' she replied.

Sokunthea went back to the door and began to pull it wider; the two men slipped in. They cleared the debris and concrete weight that was pinning Van Serun down and, using a desk top as a stretcher, began to carry him out. As they did the sound of the external world hit them with great ferocity; the battle appeared concentrated on two fronts and for the first time Sokunthea saw Vietnamese troops on the summit. They carried Van Serun quickly across to the mansion house and down to the lower level where the other patients were sited. Sokunthea began to check him for any sign of trauma and as she did so he regained consciousness.

'Get me up,' he said.

'No, I think you've broken a leg,' said Sokunthea.

'Then strap it, I've got to get outside.' He tried to rise.

'Lay still!' She called to Tiny, 'Get some short boards, two or three, and some rope.' Tiny disappeared, then Sokunthea called to the two men, 'Hold him.' They came over and looked at Van Serun. 'Hold him,' she repeated and they placed their weight on the commander. Sokunthea removed the shoe from the broken limb and, holding the ankle, pulled down on the lower section of the leg. Van Serun cried out.

'You have an overriding fracture; I have to straighten it if it is to heal.'

Van Serun's body went tense and he began to sweat as the pain increased.

Tiny reappeared, carrying several pieces of wood and a ball of string. 'This is all I could get.'

Sokunthea nodded. 'How's the fighting?'

'I don't know,' came Tiny's reply.

Sokunthea looked at Van Serun who had passed out again. 'Here, hold this and don't let it slacken.'

Tiny took hold of the ankle as Sokunthea began to place the wood around the leg and strap it with the string. 'Will it hold?' asked Tiny.

'Sure.'

As she was finishing, several soldiers came running into the ward and began to take cover. A young officer approached Sokunthea.

'How is he?' and he nodded towards Van Serun.

'He'll live,' said Sokunthea.

'We have to move, move you all.'

'Why?'

'The Vietnamese have taken part of the perimeter; when night comes they'll attack here. You have to get out.'

She nodded and looked around the makeshift ward.

'We'll retreat to the church and the garden house; you can have the cellar for a hospital.' He smiled. 'Get your people going then we'll booby trap the place.'

Sokunthea called the group together and began to delegate patients; she had decided that she and Tiny would move the commander.

With the sun slowly falling over the western ridge Sokunthea's makeshift hospital made a slow transfer to the church. The last out were Tiny, Sokunthea and the commander with two soldiers for protection. Van Serun had entered a delirious state with a high temperature and what appeared to be convulsions; he also spoke out loudly as if giving orders. Once in the church cellar Sokunthea began to reduce his temperature with the help of cold, wet cloths and he began to regain consciousness.

'Sit me up,' he said. Sokunthea was surprised at his control. 'Where's my adjutant?'

'Dead,' came Sokunthea's reply.

'Get me a soldier.'

The sound of the commander's voice attracted the young officer who had been waiting for this moment; he sat next to Van Serun.

'What's the situation?' Van Serun asked.

'The enemy is on the hill, opposite the mansion house.'

'Where are we?' Van Serun began to look around.

'The church,' came the reply.

'We must counterattack, tonight.'

'We can't, we've less than two hundred men.'

'We must; they'll be regrouping. We have to get them off the hill or they'll finish us tomorrow.'

'But with two hundred men?'

'Take everyone, military and non-military, men and women; we must get them off the hill if we are to survive tomorrow.'

The young officer looked around and his eyes finally landed on Sokunthea. 'You've got to convince them to fight,' he said nodding towards the Seventeen of April group.

'Why should they?'

'Because the Vietnamese will kill them.'

'The Vietnamese will save them.'

'No, no; it's past that now, the Vietnamese have lost many men coming up that hill. They see you as Rouge, all of you, all of them,' and he pointed to the Seventeen of April group.

'If they won't fight we can always use them as shields.' Sokunthea recognised the voice of Sak.

She looked at Van Serun. 'I'll talk to them, but don't let that animal near them.'

'Don't take long, we attack at first dark.'

The Seventeen of April group were sitting in the corner of the cellar as Sokunthea approached. 'We heard and we won't fight,' said Tiny.

'They say the Vietnamese will kill you anyway.'

'We'll take our chance,' continued Tiny.

Sokunthea smiled at her friend, reached over and touched her shoulder, she turned and went back to the Rouge. 'They won't fight,' she said to Van Serun.

'Then we shoot them,' cut in Sak.

'No, no, we won't do that. Bring them over here, I want to talk to them,' said Van Serun. 'Sokunthea find me some paper and a pen.'

As Sokunthea set off upstairs in search of the stationery, the group were brought to his mat and he spoke to them. On her return all but two of the group had decided to join the counterattack and Van Serun began to outline his plan. After they had received their orders, arms and ammunition, flak jackets and other military equipment was distributed. Sokunthea and Tiny found themselves together in a mixed platoon of men and women, Rouge and non-Rouge.

The night was very dark with only a quarter moon; the silence was broken by the cries of the many wounded and dying still lying unattended in no-man's-land.

Van Serun's plan involved a small unit re-entering the booby-trapped mansion house and setting off a large explosion. One of the large guns would be wheeled out of its sheltered place to fire directly onto the Vietnamese positions, while the army would counterattack along the opposite rim. Sokunthea's group had to advance to a central trench and hold it against any counterattacking Vietnamese forces. As Sokunthea waited she looked at her friend Tiny.

'Why did you change your mind?'

Tiny stared into the darkness.

'Why?' Sokunthea persisted.

'To kill the enemy.'

'You don't sound very convincing.'

Tiny moved further down the wall.

'He said he'd shoot you.' Sokunthea turned to meet the face of Thalin.

'What?'

'Serun said if they didn't fight he'd shoot you.'

'The bas…'

'Forward, move forward, quietly,' the soldier in charge said.

As they did the mansion house exploded with a huge bang which lit up the entire battleground ahead of them. When the fireball subsided the group moved forward quickly, then the sky lit up as the Vietnamese fired flares into the night. Small arms fire began to come in their direction and Sokunthea saw one then two fall ahead of her, then she heard the field gun open up with an ear piercing Wham. Mortars then began and the trace of bullets could be seen flashing across the dark sky; Sokunthea tripped over a soldier's body and stumbled headfirst into the trench they were to hold. Others dropped in beside her, scared, relieved, determined and wondering why the hell they were there. With Tiny on one side and Thalin on the other Sokunthea quickly checked their weapons as instructed and waited. Fire was coming from the Vietnamese in all directions, as they tried to second-guess where the next attack would come from but not expecting an attack from the side.

When the battle did start its ferocity was similar to that of the morning with hand-to-hand fighting and no quarter given. The big gun fired again and in the light of its explosion a line of troops could be seen advancing towards the trench where Sokunthea and her platoon were waiting. The order to wait had been given as

Sokunthea's anxiety rose. She looked along the sight of her gun but could see nothing as sweat began to fall down her face. She could feel her heart thumping in her chest and a growing nausea; she knew she was scared. She was thinking of what Thalin had said and how she would deal with Serun when the scream 'Fire!' brought her back to the present.

All around her automatic weapons opened up with deafening noise; her own weapon appeared to have jammed until she realised she still had the safety on. Return fire began to trace towards the trench, biting great lumps out of the soil in front of her, then she heard a chilling cry, as a group of the enemy rushed forward; none reached the trench line. Then, as she turned to look down the trench line to her colleagues, a bright flash erupted beside her and she collapsed into the bottom of the trench.

When Sokunthea woke her eyes were covered and she could hear the sound of a radio.

'We need them now, I expect the enemy to attack again tonight.' It was the voice of Van Serun. Sokunthea began to remove the covers from her eyes. 'Wait, wait,' came Van Serun's voice, 'you'll need time for your eyes to adjust.'

Sokunthea stopped. 'Am I blind?' she asked.

'No, just scorched; many soldiers suffer it, you'll be fine.'

'How long?'

'Later today, maybe tomorrow.'

'Where's Tiny?'

'She's fine, was a hero last night, fought well. Here let's take it off slowly.' Van Serun removed the eye covers and Sokunthea opened her eyes. 'Okay?' he said.

Sokunthea could see normally from her left eye but her vision from the right was blurred. 'I'm fine.'

'Sure?'

'Sure.' She looked at Van Serun through watery eyes. 'Did we hold them?' she asked.

'Held them and pushed them back off the hill, but they'll be back tomorrow.'

'Did we lose many?'

Van Serun looked at her. 'It's no good counting in war; we held the ridge, that's what counts.'

'And tomorrow?'

'We'll have replacements by then, they're coming up the hill now. Will the Vietnamese be surprised,' he laughed.

'How's the leg?'

'Painful, I have a staff meeting, you up for it?'

She nodded and handed him his crutches. As she helped him arrange them she looked into his eyes. 'Would you really have shot me?' she asked.

'I'd shoot anybody to keep this hill for one more day.' He looked straight ahead.

The meeting occurred in what remained of the old church. In the room were Van Serun, Thalin, two young officers and Sak. Thalin greeted Sokunthea as she entered.

'It's good to see you up and about,' he smiled.

'I'm just happy still to be here.'

'Report,' said Van Serun to the group.

The young officers reported that less than one hundred soldiers remained on the hill.

'Never mind,' cut in Van Serun, 'the reserves are on their way up.'

'How many?' asked Thalin.

'Six hundred.' There was a sense of relief in the room. 'Get them into position as soon as they arrive,' Van Serun told his men. 'How are we for supplies?' He looked at Sak.

'We must start to empty the new base camp before the enemy fighters get at it.'

'Organise it,' said Van Serun. 'The enemy will attack with everything tomorrow so we need all the supplies we can get up the hill.' He looked at Sokunthea. 'The new soldiers have some Seventeen of April workers with them; get them onto the supplies, work them, we need all the ammunition we can get.'

'Thalin,' Van Serun continued, 'how many wounded can still fight?'

'Twelve, maybe fifteen.'

'Get the rest down the hill; when your eyes are improved,' he turned to Sokunthea, 'you can help.'

She glared at him.

'Meeting over,' he declared.

Thalin took Sokunthea's hand and began to lead her out of the church.

'I'm not an invalid,' she said.

'You've upset him,' countered Thalin.

'Good,' and she headed off to find Tiny.

'Hey, wait for me, we've got to get the wounded down, remember?'

'Tonight. You're crazy and so is he.'

'Well, let's prepare them at least; then we can move them in the early hours.'

Sokunthea looked at him. 'How many men will his majesty allow to carry the wounded down?'

'None, it's up to…'

'To Seventeen of April scum… so what happened to, "We're all a team…"?'

'More of you arrived. I mean, not you but them.'

'Get away from me, Thalin, or I'll swear I'll bust your head open.'

Thalin realised she was not fooling. 'Okay, okay, but if he wants his men down you'll take them down, better for you to organise it than Sak.' He began to walk back to the church. 'Oh, if you want Tiny she's at the garden house.'

Sokunthea located her setting up a field hospital next to the garden wall. 'You never rest?' she greeted her friend.

'Sokunthea!' Tiny walked over and hugged her friend. 'We thought you'd be out for some time, eyes are tricky things.'

'I'm fine; this one hurts like hell but at least I can see out of it. How many have we?' she asked, nodding towards the wounded.

'Now about forty-five; some are being taken back to fight. I don't know what they will do with the others; they can't stay here in the open, not if the Vietnamese start shelling again.'

'They're going down the hill.'

'When?'

'Now.'

'We can't, unless we get some soldiers and then it's dark.'

'I know, but this is Rouge logic.' They both stared at each other in disbelief then began to laugh.

'Can I join the joke?' Thalin said as he approached.

'You are the joke,' said Sokunthea.

'Come over here.' Thalin led the two women towards the garden house. 'Sak wants you to take the wounded down and bring supplies up.'

'Logical,' said Sokunthea.

'There's about forty of you with the reserves; Sak's bringing them over. We should start to get the wounded ready.'

'So Sak is taking over; I don't like this,' said Tiny.

'Van Serun has agreed, he's determined to get all the supplies he can at any cost.'

'So Miss Rouge is in charge and when she's blown up half of us and destroyed the ammunition what's Van Serun going to do then?'

'Attack with everything I've got.' They turned and looked at Van Serun with Sak at his side.

'Get these soldiers ready,' he said to Thalin. 'You,' looking at Sokunthea, 'will take the first down and set up a field hospital down there.'

'Let's get moving,' cut in Sak.

'I want to speak to you,' Van Serun said to Sokunthea. She could see he was in great pain from standing to long on his injured leg.

'My feelings for you will not stop me holding this hill as long as possible; every day gives the army time to regroup and I intend to give them all the time I can.'

'I had no idea you had feelings for a Seventeen of April scum, that's against Ankor.'

'Forget Ankor, we fight for Cambodia.'

'And die?'

'And die.'

'Well, I don't want to die for your Cambodia.'

His brow became smothered with sweat drops as the pain in his leg grew. 'You will take the first of the wounded down and stay down there, organising the hospital.' He turned to leave. 'Goodbye, Sokunthea,' he called back and headed for the church.

Sokunthea realised his plan, a plan for her safety: she would remain at the bottom of the hill away from all the fighting and, if things went wrong, an easier place to escape from. Sokunthea rejoined the wounded and listened to Sak talking to a new group of workers.

'When you get to the bottom of the hill there will be a field hospital waiting to take the wounded. You are then required to collect supplies and bring them up the hill.'

Sokunthea looked round the group; they were thin, and some were leaning against each other while others just stared ahead.

'Let's get moving!' came Sak's usual cry.'

Sokunthea thought of making a challenge then decided against it. She grabbed Tiny. 'We take the first one down and stay there.'

'Escape?' came Tiny's startled reply.

'No, not yet, but we have to set up the base camp hospital so…'

'We don't come up again,' cut in Tiny with delight.

'What are you two hatching?' asked Thalin.

'Who to take down,' said Sokunthea, 'we're the first, remember?'

'Well, I have the perfect case for you.' He pointed to a soldier lying on a straw mat with multiple dressings over his body. 'He's immobile… oh, and blind, you'd better get him ready.'

Tiny looked at Sokunthea. 'How the hell do we…'

'Get some floorboard wood from the mansion and I'll find some rope.'

Sokunthea headed for the remaining ox carts and removed the rope from the old bridles; she arrived back at the garden house as Tiny appeared with two long, thick planks of wood.

'Great,' said Sokunthea.

'There's lots of soldiers over there,' said Tiny, 'I think we're in for trouble tomorrow.'

'We will be if we don't get off this hill soon.' Sokunthea began to place the planks below the wounded soldier and wrap the rope around him tightly. 'Come on,' she said to Tiny, 'hold this down.'

Soon the soldier was wrapped tight and was ready for transportation. 'Get Thalin to give us a hand,' Sokunthea said to Tiny. 'He obviously wants to get off this hill as well.'

So, as the first light began to rise, Sokunthea, Tiny and Thalin began their descent of the gully. As they passed the pond and cave area they could hear the mortars begin their deadly work above. It took the three of them over thirty minutes to reach the bottom and begin the trek to the base camp; when they arrived the camp appeared to be in chaos. Boxes of supplies were being unloaded from three trucks and dumped in piles as the truck crews rushed to get away. The organisation of the previous camp was non-existent now; only haste to drop and leave prevailed. The previous camp commander had not returned, deserted was the rumour. Boxes broke open and spilled their contents across the ground and no one appeared to care that six hundred comrades were waiting for supplies.

'This is crazy,' Sokunthea said to Thalin, 'can't you do something?'

'What? I'm a village commander, this is military; they wouldn't listen to me.'

Sokunthea thought of Van Serun's patriotism and then of Thai. 'This Cambodia of yours is rotten.'

'Stop arguing,' said Tiny, 'our patient is dead.' She sat on the ground and quietly began to cry. Sokunthea looked at her friend and then up at the sound of the final truck pulling away.

'Bastards!' she yelled.

'What shall we do?' asked Tiny.

'We'll still set up a camp, over there near the stream. Where's Thalin?'

'He jumped on the last truck.'

'What?'

'Maybe we should have joined him.'

'Never mind, let's check some of these boxes, see if they are medical supplies or food.'

'Why don't we just run for it, like Ro?'

'To where... what do you think the advancing Vietnamese are going to do to two women, alone, one dressed in a Rouge uniform? I can't believe Thalin did that.'

'It's Serun isn't it?' continued Tiny. 'You and him have something going.'

'It's not Serun it's, it's Cambodia, it's wanting to know why, it's wanting to stop the Vietnamese, it's wanting to stay alive.'

Sokunthea looked around only to see Sak coming towards her. 'What's happening here?' she asked.

'It's called dump the supplies and run,' Sokunthea responded.

'Where's the commander and Thalin?'

'Gone,' said Tiny angrily.

Sak looked at Tiny's patient. 'He still alive?'

'No,' came Sokunthea's response and as she did they heard the jet fighters pass over and head towards the hill. Sak looked back at Sokunthea.

'You two organise these boxes; I'm going to stop the transfer of the wounded and get the workers down here.' She began to run up the track towards the gully, and Sokunthea looked at Tiny.

'Let's start with this load,' she said and they walked towards the pile of boxes unloaded by the first truck.

'Do we still look for medical supplies?' asked Tiny.

'No, there'll be no wounded coming down from up there. Let's sort out the ammunition, weapons, anything to kill with.'

They began to stack boxes in categories, ammunition first, then weapons, followed by explosives. The boxes were heavy and needed two people to lift them. They stopped to watch a further attack launched by the Vietnamese fighters onto the hill.

'I'm glad I'm not up there,' said Tiny.

'Me too,' came the reply.

'What did you mean by stop the Vietnamese; I thought they were our saviours.'

'In many ways they are, but like the Cambodian saying, if you invite a tiger into your home he may never leave. Right from school I was taught not to trust the Vietnamese, that they want Cambodia.'

'Me too.' Tiny walked over to another pile of boxes. 'Isn't it strange, Cambodians kill Cambodians and our enemy comes to stop it, then all Cambodians unite and fight them; it defies logic.'

'There's no logic in Cambodia, only survival but now it's the survival of the country. I think if Vietnam takes us, Cambodia will disappear.'

'This box is empty,' cut in Tiny, 'and this one.'

Sokunthea looked at the empty boxes. 'How many more?'

'One here and here; this last truck just dumped empty boxes, no wonder they were quick.'

'Leave them; we've done enough.'

They sat on the empty boxes to rest. 'That little stream looks refreshing.' Sokunthea looked at her friend. 'Come on,' and they wandered over and began to wash. Sokunthea began to laugh. 'Just look at us, there's a war all around and we bathe.'

'Just what I was thinking,' came Sak's voice, 'get out.' Tiny and Sokunthea looked up to see Sak and six soldiers looking at them. 'Get over there with the others.'

Sokunthea and Tiny grabbed their things and walked over to a group of twenty workers brought down by Sak.

'What's in the boxes?' Sak pointed to the piles

Sokunthea began pointing. 'Ammunition in those, weapons there and explosives there.'

'And those?' Sak pointed to the empty boxes.

'Empty,' said Tiny.

'Where's Thalin?' she continued.

'Gone,' replied Sokunthea.

'Gone where?' asked Sak.

'Just gone,' repeated Sokunthea.

'Okay, let's get started, two per box,' Sak shouted at the group, then she turned to Sokunthea and Tiny, 'and that means you.'

They walked quietly over to an ammunition box and grabbed the handles on each side. As they did, Sak slammed a pair of handcuffs on each of their wrists with the other clasp around the box handle.

'What the...' Sokunthea began to say.

'So you won't run away,' cut in Sak.

'How the hell do we get these off?' continued Sokunthea.

'When they are all up you get released,' and she waved the key in front of them. 'Now get moving.'

Sokunthea and Tiny began a journey that they knew of old: along the track and up the gully. The ammunition box was heavy but not as dangerous as the explosives. As they reached the gully they heard the sound of shots from behind them, so they took cover in the gully's entrance. It was Sak who entered.

'Come on, move, they need that stuff up there.'

'What's the shooting?' asked Sokunthea.

'Some people never learn,' and she looked over her shoulder as another two handcuffed workers entered the gully.

Sokunthea and Tiny began to climb; they knew the routine and even handcuffed to the box their methodology didn't change. As they reached the pond area Sak was waiting.

'No rest, not this time, get this stuff straight up to the top.' Sokunthea and Tiny followed Sak up and reached the edge of the plateau. 'Keep your heads down,' said Sak, 'the Vietnamese are on the hill.'

The three sat below the edge. 'The Vietnamese have the mansion house and the east side of the hill, we hold the rest; when we go over head for the garden house and then the church.'

They crawled up and on to the hill top and headed for the garden house wall. As they arrived automatic gunfire from their right burst along the ground and smashed into the wall.

'That way,' said Sak and they crawled along the wall and turned towards the back of the house. There they found several soldiers sheltering from the enemy's fire. 'Distribute these,' Sak told them and they opened the box and began to hand out its contents. 'You two, back down the hill.'

'What about the cuffs?' asked Sokunthea.

'Go fill the box, bring up another load.'

'Why, you...' and Sokunthea lunged at her but this time Sak was prepared. She swung Sokunthea around and hit her on the back of the head with her pistol; Sokunthea collapsed to the floor. She lay there dazed for several minutes and when she finally recovered Sak had gone.

'Where's the bitch...'

'Helping the next group over the edge,' came Tiny's reply. 'We'd better start down.'

'No, we stay here,' came Sokunthea's angry reply.

'Don't be crazy, she'll kill us.'

'Then who will bring up the supplies?' Sokunthea said as she sat on the box.

'Look around,' said Tiny, 'look at these men, they have no hope without ammunition.'

'Who cares?'

'You do, remember, tiger in the house and all that; let's go.'

Sokunthea looked her friend, who had tears in her eyes. 'Let's go,' she said.

They began the descent down the hill, passing struggling colleagues on their way up. They could hear the sound of war increasing in their ears and realised the Vietnamese must be making another attack. They reached the bottom and began to run along the track to the base camp; as they did they passed four bodies lying by the road. They arrived at the base camp out of breath and two soldiers began to load their box.

'There's bodies down there.' Tiny pointed back down the track.

The two soldiers continued loading the box.

'Aren't you interested?' cut in Sokunthea.

'Educated,' came the reply and the work continued.

'We need water, do you have water?' asked Tiny and a soldier passed his water canister to her.

'Ready, you can go,' the other said and they began the repeat journey.

As daylight began to fade more than half of the supplies had been transferred up the hill; the workers settled down beside the garden house wall, still handcuffed to their boxes. Three middle-aged workers appeared handing out rice soup to the tired group, followed by Sak. She walked up to Sokunthea and unlocked her handcuffs.

'He wants to see you,' and she nodded towards the church. Sokunthea and Sak, both in a crouched posture, headed for Van Serun.

The church was a pile of rubble, having been the main target for the fighters, but its cellar was deep and could still house tired soldiers and their commander. As Sokunthea entered the building she looked up and in the dark night her eyes picked out a large wooden cross standing upright amongst the rubble. Sak led her down steep steps into the cellar where soldiers were resting. They stepped over sleeping bodies and card players and through an atmosphere of choking smoke to reach the rear of the cellar where Van Serun was lying on a wooden bed. He motioned for her to come and sit next to him.

'You have brought us valuable material,' he began.

'We had little choice.'

He looked at Sak. 'What happened to commander Thalin?'

'He ran.'

'So why didn't you?'

'Thalin's a brave Rouge commander, I'm just a stupid Seventeen of April.'

'Your sarcasm is still at work.'

'Why do you want to see me?'

'My leg, I need your professional opinion.'

'Let's look.' Sokunthea began to remove the dressing and restraints from his leg and as she did so the familiar smell of gangrene began to spread. 'It's badly infected and needs to come off.' She stared at him.

'Not possible,' he replied.

'Then you will die.'

'Is there no medication, creams… anything that you can give him?' cut in Sak.

Sokunthea stared at the floor, then up at Sak. 'Your Ankor doesn't allow such things, and anyway the supplies only contain munitions.'

'How long have I got if we do nothing?' Van Serun looked at Sokunthea.

'A week, and most of that you'll be delirious.'

'And if you take the leg off?'

'Don't you listen; Ankor doesn't allow doctors to take a leg – I can't.'

'You took an arm,' cut in Sak.

'An arm's different and I was lucky.'

The three fell silent.

'The Vietnamese will change tactics tomorrow; I need to be awake for that. Their frontal attacks will stop and they'll try to contain us. Tomorrow night, you'll operate tomorrow night.' Van Serun stared at Sokunthea, who began to shake her head.

'Sak,' continued Van Serun, 'get her what she wants, we'll operate here.'

Sak nodded. 'No supplies run for you, I want you here,' he continued, looking at Sokunthea.

'What if you die under the knife?' Sokunthea cut in.

'My men know what to do.' The sound of gunfire could be heard outside but nobody in the cellar moved. 'Take her back,' said Van Serun to Sak. As Sokunthea started to leave Van Serun called out, 'They say you're lucky; let's hope for my sake it's true.' He laughed.

Sak escorted Sokunthea back to the garden house wall where Tiny was waiting.

'Problem?' asked Tiny.

'Van Serun's leg has to come off and guess who has the honour?'

'Phewww, I hope it doesn't end up like your one-armed soldier,' said Tiny.

'Why? He lived.'

'Yeah, went back to fight and was killed this morning.'

'Well, Van Serun says I can have anything I need, so you're in too.'

'Well, it must be better than being handcuffed to this damn thing.'

Sokunthea and Tiny lay down sandwiched between the garden wall and the ammunition box; all around them in the dark they could hear sporadic gunfire and voices. Sokunthea stared up at the stars and began to think of the coming event, the removal of Van Serun's leg, then she thought of Thalin and his rapid escape. 'No more protection from him,' she whispered to herself.

Before dawn Sak had returned, despatching the workers down the hill for the rest of the munitions and reluctantly releasing Tiny from her bonds.

'You two get to the church; head towards the garden house, then the stables, from there to the ruined pagoda and approach the church from the rear, got it?'

'Why?' asked Tiny.

'Because while you two babes were asleep the army relocated. All that central area is booby trapped, now move.'

Sokunthea and Tiny followed Sak's instruction exactly; they passed foxholes and short trench lines where well sheltered troops were preparing for the coming events. As they approached the church Sokunthea saw in the daylight the large wooden cross standing high amongst the rubble and thought it was not out of place in the land of Buddha. They entered the church through a small side door, still strangely in use, then down narrow winding steps and into the rear of the cellar. The cellar was strangely empty; the sleeping bodies of the previous evening had gone. Sokunthea looked around.

'We'll have that bed and the small table; help me move them to the middle of the room,' she said to Tiny.

'What else?' asked Tiny.

'I need a small wood saw, shaving blades, a knife or bayonet… ah, a stove, needle and thread – I can't do it!' Sokunthea sat on the bed.

Tiny sat next to her friend. 'You can; he'll die if you don't.'

'He'll die if I do.'

'Think of the arm you took off…'

'The arm was different; it was instant, not planned like this, I had no time to think about it. My first panic attack was when the arm came away from his body.' She stood up and walked over to the table. 'He was a simple soldier,' she turned to Tiny, 'and he didn't have a crazy sister-in-law who may kill if something goes wrong.'

'He's just a man, forget the rest; he's just a man, like the soldier…'

'I care for him, okay. He's not like the soldier, I care.' Tiny sat quietly and watched Sokunthea wipe the tears from her face. She turned to look at her friend and began to laugh. 'I must be crazy, eh? Loving a man who threatened to shoot me.'

'Does he know?'

'I think so.'

'And does he feel the same?'

'I think so.'

'Wow… is this the reason why you wouldn't run away?'

'I think so.'

Tiny stood and walked towards her friend. 'Well, I think we're going to do a great job. Now, let's get on with our scavenging.' They hugged each other and set off to find what they needed.

They searched the church for any items that would assist the operation: a flag was taken to be torn into bandages, wood was collected for the stove, which had to heat the knife to red-hot temperatures. Tiny took a bayonet from a dead soldier's equipment, while Sokunthea searched Van Serun's personal belongings for razor blades or a sharp knife. The sound of the fighting outside failed to break their concentration; alcohol was needed for an anaesthetic and steriliser and a strong rope for a tourniquet. A soldier's helmet would be used as a surgical bowl, an ice saw to cut through the bone.

'This will not work... this will not work!' Sokunthea shouted at the roof.

Tiny came to her. 'There is no other choice; now, what do we need?'

'He'll die, I know he'll...'

'Look, I once said that I chose you because you were brave, remember?' Sokunthea nodded. 'Well don't lose it now, you can do it, you must do it.'

Sokunthea exhaled. 'Okay, we must find a needle and thread, strong thread, and some wood for a gum-shield, now what else?' She began to look around the room. 'We need more cloth to soak up the blood and pack the stump; get some uniforms, there must be some spare.'

Tiny smiled and set off in search of the requirements; Sokunthea began to check the resources she had already and didn't hear Van Serun enter.

'Preparing for my doom?' he asked.

Sokunthea turned and looked at him. 'This could kill you.'

'My leg is killing me, with pain,' he grimaced as he sat on the edge of the bed.

'What's the situation outside?'

'We're holding them and the guns are still keeping their armoured column from getting to Kompong Som.'

'For how long?'

'Another day, then another.'

'I don't want to do this,' Sokunthea cut in.

'I know, but there's only you that I trust.'

'And if you die?'

'And if I live?'

Sokunthea turned away from his gaze and stared at the wall. 'If you live we'll have to get you off this hill and away before morning.'

'If I live I stay.'

She turned back to face him. 'With one leg you'll be holed up here until the Vietnamese burst in; it'll take at least a week before you can get up and around, and the Vietnamese won't wait.'

'You fail to understand if I go my men will follow; they fight for me, I have to stay.'

'Alive or dead?'

'Alive or dead.'

Sokunthea walked across the cellar and sat beside him on the bed. They looked at each other then kissed. 'You said I was lucky; well, here's another piece of information for you: every man I've loved is dead and that's why I can't operate on you.'

'And every woman I have known has betrayed me; it's time we both had a change of fortune.'

A young soldier entered the room.

'Well?' asked Van Serun.

'The line is intact, the enemy have gone strangely quiet.'

'Withdraw every third man from the front lines; keep them in a reserve near the stables, they may try to outflank us.'

'Sir,' the soldier saluted and departed.

'Will we keep them away?' asked Sokunthea.

'For another day or two, then it's hit and run.'

'Except you won't be able to run.'

'But my men can.'

Sokunthea placed her head on his shoulder. 'Did you kill Cambodians?'

'In the war, yes.'

'No, after the war, the exodus people, the Seventeen of April scum?'

'I'm a soldier, not an executioner.'

'But you're Rouge.'

'I fought to free Cambodia of Lon Nol and his corruption; the city people were seen as beyond hope. They had to suffer like the farmers suffered.'

'But not to die.'

'They would have died anyway; who had food to support the cities? We, the army, were starving; my unit fought for six months on only the rice that we could capture. In 1974 there was no food in Cambodia and very little since.'

'Commander,' Van Serun's adjutant cut in, 'there's a message from Central.'

Van Serun waved his hand for the message to be brought forward. 'Like hell; ask Captain Hok to report.' The adjutant nodded and left.

'Problem?' asked Sokunthea.

'Central want us to fight to the last man; well, I'm putting into operation our withdrawal plan.'

Hok appeared. 'Sir,' he saluted.

'Hok, I want you to begin our withdrawal plan at twenty-two hundred tonight.'

'But you...'

'Don't think of me, I'll be fine; just start getting the men off the hill as ordered, understand?'

'Sir,' he saluted again and left.

'You said you weren't leaving; what's changed?'

'Central; they were supposed to cover a strategic withdrawal and now they've decided to let us die.'

'Was this worth it? We're stuck at the top of this hill, hundreds dead, for what?'

'We held them back.'

'So why doesn't this Central of yours come and help?'

'I don't know, but it's time for my men to leave.' Van Serun began to lay back on the bed.

'Let me look at your leg again; I have to decide how high to cut,' said Sokunthea. She unwrapped his leg and looked at the infected site; the tentacles of the gangrene appeared to be spreading along the blood vessel tracks.

'Can you feel anything in your toes?'

'No.'

'In your ankle, around the wound site?'

'No.'

'Around the knee?'

'A little.'

'But up here okay?' Sokunthea grabbed his thigh.

'Fine.'

'So where's the pain coming from?'

'Inside.'

'Inside all the leg or just the bottom part?'

'Up to the knee, inside.'

'Rest, get some rest. Oh, how long does it take you to get drunk?'

'What? Ah, yes, a couple of hours.'

Sokunthea saw Tiny enter the cellar with more material and she walked over to her. 'So what we got?'

'Almost everything, including a needle and cat gut.'

'Tiny, where did you get that?'

'They killed a Vietnamese medic; he had a bag full of stuff: here, look.' Tiny opened the bag to reveal an assortment of dressings, creams, bandages, syringes and drugs.

'What are these?' Sokunthea picked up the drugs and began to read.

'I don't know,' said Tiny, 'I can't read Vietnamese.'

'They're American and by the expiry dates they're from the last war.'

'No good, then.'

'Anything is better than nothing; come on, you lay out the table and soak some instruments in the helmet and I'll work out what we can do with these.'

The two women busied themselves with the task at hand while Van Serun slept on the bed. As the afternoon wore on the sound of mortar fire resumed. Van Serun woke and called for his adjutant who helped him out of the cellar.

'He'll kill himself before you get the chance.' Tiny nodded towards the departing Van Serun.

'Well, I feel happier with these,' said Sokunthea, holding up some injection vials.

'What are they?'

'Morphine.'

'Any good?'

'Good? If they work, fantastic; we won't need to get him drunk.'

'Tiny saves the day again,' she laughed and began to place the instruments and the alcohol in the helmet. 'How long do they have to soak?'

'Leave them until we need them.' As Sokunthea spoke a loud

explosion occurred outside the church bringing debris and dust down from the roof.

'That was close,' said Tiny.

'I hope they hold them otherwise our plans are useless.'

'Van Serun will hold them even if he has to beat them back with his crutches.' They both laughed.

'What attracted you to him?' Tiny asked after a short silence.

'I don't... power I suppose, I feel safe with him.'

'You know he threatened to kill you?'

'Yes, Thalin told me.'

Another loud explosion occurred.

'They're getting the range,' said Sokunthea.

'Do we pull back?'

'To where?'

'The stables.'

'No, he'll hold.'

The women sat together tearing up material for swabs and bandages, then Tiny asked, 'What if he does die?'

Sokunthea lifted her head and stared at the ceiling. 'Run, I suppose, because if he dies his men will withdraw.'

'And Sak?'

'Unknown... she wants an excuse to shoot us, we know too much.'

The noise of fighting outside appeared to fade and men began to enter the cellar, sitting on the floor against the walls. Sokunthea noticed how tired they looked and wondered when they last ate.

'Have we no food anywhere?' she asked Tiny.

'No, nothing, although I did see some sweet potatoes in the stables; how long they've been there I don't know.'

'How much?'

'A couple of sacks, just dumped.'

'Let's get them.' They stood and exited through the rear door.

As they crept towards the stables they looked back, towards the battle area; the line had held and the main battle area was littered with the dead and dying.

They reached the stables and rested against its wall.

'Did you see all those bodies?' Sokunthea asked her friend.

'No, I don't want to look.'

'Let's get inside.' The women entered the stables and Tiny directed Sokunthea to the two bags of sweet potatoes.

'They smell a little, but they'll be okay!'

'What do you want to do?' asked Tiny.

'We'll boil them in the cellar; at least they'll have something to eat.'

Tiny nodded and the two women began to drag the bags outside and to the church. As they passed foxholes and trenches they distributed the contents of one of the bags to eager soldiers. Once in the cellar they lit up the fire bowl and, using an old baby's bath found by Tiny, they began to boil the potatoes. Van Serun had returned in their absence and was lying on the bed watching them.

'Any of that for me?' he asked jokingly.

'No,' came Sokunthea's reply. 'How do you feel?'

'How should I feel?'

'Don't worry, I can do it.'

'Well, that's more positive.'

'Yeah, you'll be okay.'

'Shouldn't I start drinking soon?'

'No need, I've got a surprise for you.'

'Good, I like surprises.'

As they spoke the adjutant approached. 'Captain Hok has pulled the men back as ordered; we can begin to abandon the hill when you are ready.'

Van Serun nodded.

The adjutant then turned to Sokunthea. Captain Hok or myself would be happy to assist you in any way.'

Sokunthea looked at Van Serun then back at the adjutant. 'Thank you, I will need someone to hold the tourniquet, someone with strong hands.'

The adjutant looked at her. 'I'll ask Hok.' He turned and left.

'You really going to abandon this hill?' Sokunthea asked Van Serun.

'We fight best in the forest, hit and run; losing my command here is playing into the Vietnamese hands.'

'So why stand and fight in the first place?'

'So why all the questions, you want my job?'

Sokunthea realised how tired he looked. 'I'm sorry. Rest; I'll tell you when we're ready.'

'Oh, what's the surprise?'

'I have morphine, so no pain.'

Van Serun turned onto his side and began to sleep.

When he woke Sokunthea was sitting beside him on the bed.

'Let's take this off,' she said as she unbuttoned his tunic and began to slide it over his shoulders.

Van Serun looked round the bed and his eyes fell onto a soldier standing beside the bed.

'Good luck, sir,' said the young soldier and shook his hand; he was followed by another then another. While Van Serun concentrated on the line of men, Sokunthea injected the morphine into his veins. Within minutes he was unconscious; Sokunthea, with the help of Sak, removed his trousers and she examined the leg for the last time. She looked at Sak.

'Wish me luck,'

Sak stared back at her. 'Make sure he lives.'

Sokunthea nodded to Hok, who tightened the rope around the top of the leg.

The razor blades cut through the leg tissue smoothly; Tiny, using the red hot bayonet, cauterised the blood vessels as they progressed. Sokunthea quickly reached the bone and began to fold the leg tissue back.

'The saw,' she said to Sak, who picked it up slowly and handed it to her. 'How is he?' Sokunthea asked.

'Still asleep,' came Sak's sharp reply.

Sokunthea began to saw the bone and as she did a high-pitched whining sound began to develop outside; this was soon accompanied by automatic gunfire and the soldiers in the cellar began to head for the exit. Sokunthea continued to saw as the noise grew louder and louder.

'What the…' said Sak and she left the bed to find out what was happening.

Sokunthea continued to saw. 'Hok, concentrate, hold it tight.' He nodded.

The familiar noise of a helicopter grew louder, but this one was clearly in trouble; then a loud crash followed by an explosion occurred. The operating team were sent sprawling onto the floor as part of the roof fell in. Sokunthea looked up to the unconscious Van Serun; the ice saw was still in his bone and blood was spraying everywhere from an artery.

'Hok, Hok, stop the bleeding!' Sokunthea shouted at the prostrate form of Hok, but there was no response.

'He's dead,' shouted Tiny. 'We've got to get out.'

'No, Van Serun!' Sokunthea stood up and reached for the tourniquet.

'He's dead too; nobody can survive that amount of blood loss.' She spun Sokunthea around sharply. 'We have to get out.'

'No, we can save him,' she glared at Tiny, 'we can save him.'

Tiny slapped Sokunthea hard across the face. 'He's dead, we have to get out.' She pulled her friend towards the back stairs and began to push her up the steps.

'What about Hok?' Sokunthea looked back at him and noticed a piece of shrapnel had removed half of his head. As they reached the exit a second explosion occurred hurling them to the floor; as Sokunthea got to her feet she looked for the cross but in its place was the burning tail section of the helicopter pointing to the stars.

'This way,' said Tiny and directed her friend towards the garden house.

They ran in a crouching position as men and explosions surrounded them; some of the voices they heard were Vietnamese but they kept going. When they reached the garden house wall two bullets ricocheted off the wall beside them, and they looked across to see Sak coming towards them.

'Keep running,' said Sokunthea and the two women reached the edge of the hill and jumped down into the gully. Sak appeared behind them and fired again; both women lost their footing and began to roll down to the pond area. Sokunthea was the first up.

'Come on!' she shouted but Tiny did not move; she ran over to her friend and turned her onto her back. 'Tiny!' she shouted but there was no response.

'You're next,' came Sak's voice.

Sokunthea looked up to see her coming down the hill; she stood and looked behind her, the hill turned into a rock-fall area, too far to jump down and to begin to climb down would leave Sak standing over her. Then she remembered the cave; she ran through the pond and scrambled up the short hill to its entrance.

'You can't escape,' shouted Sak, 'you're mine, finally mine.'

Sokunthea ran into the cave and straight to the ammunition box they had abandoned previously; she threw off its lid and pulled out a pistol and magazine. The gun was familiar to her: a standard military weapon, the type provided to her husband when he served Lon Nol. She released the safety and inserted a bullet into the chamber, then, crouching behind the box, she waited for her unsuspecting guest. Sak walked slowly and confidently up to the cave entrance.

'You're trapped now, no more running.' As she walked into the cave Sokunthea fired twice and Sak slumped to the floor. Sokunthea stared at Sak's body for several minutes, then remembered Tiny. She stood and walked to the entrance; as she did, she heard deep breathing and a choking sound coming from Sak. She raised the pistol to her head and fired again.

'That's for Tiny,' she said, and she walked outside.

When Sokunthea reached Tiny her friend was clearly dead, Sokunthea took her head and shoulders onto her lap and cradled her. She began to cry, 'You were right, we should have left with Ro or Thalin or on a thousand and one occasions, we should have left.' She bent over and kissed her friend. 'Goodbye.'

As she lay Tiny's head back onto the grass a Vietnamese voice called out, 'Stop!' Sokunthea looked up to see three soldiers beginning their descent of the hill; she ran to the rock-fall and began to clamber down. She reached the bottom and began to run; the soldiers began to fire but their aim was based on guess work, not a clear target. Sokunthea reached the final rockfall and climbed down, only to be grabbed from behind around the neck.

'And who are you?' the Cambodian voice asked, and he pushed her out of the gully and onto the track. 'That way,' he pointed with his gun. She was directed to a small clearing next to the track where a small group of Seventeen of April workers and three soldiers squatted.

'Who are you?' a new voice asked.

'A soldier, like you,' she replied.

'You come from the top?'

'Yes.'

'What's it like up there?'

'The Vietnamese are on the hill.'

'What about Van Serun, Hok and Sal?'

'Dead, I think.'

'Come here, let me get a closer look – you're that doctor, you took off Yogi's arm.'

'That's right.'

'You were always with Van Serun. Hmmm, where are you going?'

'Away, before the ones coming down the hill get me.'

The soldier nodded to his colleagues and they headed back to the gully.

'Why they after you?'

'They're after anybody in this uniform.' She tugged her tunic.

His men returned. 'Soldiers coming down the gully.'

'How many?'

'Too many.'

'Let's go.' He stood and looked at Sokunthea. 'You can come with us or stay.'

'I'll find my own way.'

'Okay, but stay off the main road to Kompong Som; it's crawling with the enemy.'

'Thanks.'

The soldiers left and she looked at the workers. 'Stay where you are, as you are, and you'll be fine.' She then stood and began her own retreat.

Retreat

Sokunthea moved quickly along the track then cut into the bushes to find higher ground. She paused several times in order to listen for following footsteps but none were to be heard. The sun had slowly begun to climb as she moved onwards and upwards, she could see the red clay track below her winding its way to the main road to Kompong Som like a river to the sea. She thought of Kompong Som and wondered if it was the place to head for then quickly rejected it; that was one place the Vietnamese would definitely be. She carried on upwards with no clear idea of where she was going; she just wanted to get away, be alone. She came across a small stream, which ran down to the base camp area, the stream where she and Tiny bathed, and she began to cry.

She stooped and splashed water onto her face then heard the first scream; she looked around quickly but no one was in sight, the scream then came again; it was a woman. Sokunthea crossed the stream and walked further up the hill; there lying on her back with her legs in the air, was a young woman.

'What's the problem?' she asked. The woman was startled and drew back. 'Don't be afraid; what's the problem?' she repeated, then noticed the size of the young woman; she was about to give birth. 'Where's your husband?' asked Sokunthea.

'He left me, said I was slowing him down.'

Sokunthea just stared at her. 'Bastard,' she finally said.

'Help me, please,' said the young woman, 'I've never had a baby, please help.'

'Sure,' said Sokunthea, 'now let's look at you.' She quickly examined the woman and realised the birth was imminent. 'Give me your blouse; I need it to wrap the baby in.'

The woman removed it and Sokunthea placed it between her parted legs.

'Now relax, the baby is in good condition and the right way up.' She smiled at the perspiring young woman. 'What's your name?'

'Ti Tiny,' she said.

Sokunthea looked at her and tears began to well up in her eyes.

'You okay?'

'Fine, I just had a dear friend with that name, that's all.'

'Had, do you mean?'

'Yes.'

'I'm sorry.'

'Never… now I think the baby's ready; I want you to push only when I ask and try and breath in a rhythm, like this,' and she mimicked shallow regular breath. Ti Tiny nodded and began to force. 'No, stop; don't force, breathe steadily and push from above. If you force you just squash the baby and we don't want that.'

Ti Tiny nodded.

'Now push!' said Sokunthea. 'Push, push not force.'

'I can't, aaaggh.'

'Good, good, now stop; the head is out, I must feel for the cord and make sure that it's not in the way. Now push slowly, again.'

As Sokunthea spoke the baby seemed to take over and launched itself into her arms; Sokunthea held it upside down for a short while to drain any fluid from its lungs, then gave it the first slap of life. Within a short while mother and baby were united and Sokunthea walked back to the stream to wash. She looked over her shoulder and back to the scene and realised it was an incident that she would never experience. She walked back to the mother.

'We have to find some shade, you can't sit out here all day.' She helped the mother move to the shade of a small tree then took the baby to the stream to wash it; she looked at the new miracle of life before her then remembered the death and destruction of the night before. She returned the baby to her mother for feeding.

'Where will you go?' she asked Ti Tiny.

'With you, I hope,' came her reply.

'No, no; I've lost too many people who travel with me, no.'

'But what shall I do?'

'Go down to the main road, there're many people there, they'll help.'

'But the Vietnamese – my husband said they'll kill me.'

'If you stay here alone you'll die; the Vietnamese won't hurt you.'

'But my husband said…'

'Your husband isn't here, he left you; go down to the road, everything will be fine.'

Sokunthea stayed with Ti Tiny until the morning and watched her begin her descent down the hill, then turned and continued her climb upwards. As the foliage began to clear she recognised the tubers of root potatoes and dug them up with her hands; as she sat peeling the skin away with her fingernails the barrel of a rifle prodded her side.

'Who are you?' came the Cambodian voice.

'A soldier,' she answered.

'Get up and come with me.' She obeyed.

He took her into a small camp with shelters made from wood and leaves; there were many soldiers sitting around cleaning weapons, talking and playing cards. She was directed towards a tree where several men appeared to be in discussion.

'Sit there,' said her captor.

She looked around this tranquil, almost unreal, scene and then she heard a familiar voice and turned.

'Welcome back to the army.' She looked to see the adjutant, Sall, standing before her.

'How did you manage to get out?'

'Van Serun always had an escape plan.'

'He died, you know.'

'Yes, I know.'

'What happened?'

'The Vietnamese attacked us with two helicopters; we just didn't expect it.' He turned and leaned against the tree. 'Helicopters, at night; only the Vietnamese could do that.'

'Didn't you have any warning?'

'Sure, we heard them, we hit one of them, that's the one that hit you.' He turned to face her.

'He didn't deserve to die that way.'

Sokunthea began to quietly cry.

'Have you eaten?'

She shook her head. 'I started some root potatoes but your guard put a stop to that.'

'Root potatoes, where did you find them?'

Sokunthea gestured with her hand.

'I'll get some of the men over there; we need all the food we can get.'

She stood and they both walked over to a small kitchen where she was handed a bowl of noodles.

'Aren't you afraid the Vietnamese will find you here?'

'They're mopping up on Bokor and racing to get to Kompong Som; we'll hit and run for a while then move north.'

'To where?'

'The Elephant mountains, Pursat.'

'Pursat.'

'We have to regroup, be re-supplied.'

Sokunthea squatted on the floor. 'If they take Kompong Som and Phnom Penh how will you get re-supplied?'

'The Thais, they'll sell us anything.'

'Is nobody clean in this war? How many other nations have prospered from the killings in this land?'

Sall looked across the camp. 'You can stay with us if you wish,' he eventually said, 'there's several roaming bands in the mountains, all kinds; dressed in that tunic you could have all sides after you.'

'Well, I've nothing else and anyway I'm proud of the uniform of my country.'

'I thought you'd be ashamed.'

Sokunthea was silent.

'We move north tomorrow; if you decide to stay I'd appreciate you showing us where the root potatoes are and anything else that we might eat.'

Sokunthea looked down at her hands and smiled. 'Okay captain, bring a knife or something and follow me.'

The captain and a small group of soldiers accompanied Sokunthea out of the camp and to the potato area where they spent several hours digging up their evening food. Sokunthea helped prepare the food and spent time explaining to the men the leaves and roots that they could eat while living on the mountain. As night came she met again with Sall.

'Noodles and hot potatoes; better than the Royale in Phnom Penh,' he smiled.

'You been to the Royale?' asked Sokunthea.

'Yes, a long time ago; it's blown up now, of course, Ankor couldn't stand what it stood for.'

'And yet you fight for them.'

'Like you, I fight for my country.'

'How long did you know Van Serun?'

'Several years, he was a great soldier.'

'Did he ever marry?'

Sall looked at her. 'Yes, but she couldn't leave the luxuries of Phnom Penh for the Rouge.'

'She still alive?'

'Maybe; she left the country before we took over with some rich guy, Van Serun didn't care.'

'Children?'

'Nah… why?'

'Oh, I just wanted to know if there were any relatives… to tell – of his death.' She felt Sall's eyes burning into her. 'Well, I think I'll get some sleep.'

'Sure; corporal, show this lady to her tent. Goodnight.'

Sokunthea nodded and followed her guide.

The next morning the soldiers began to prepare to move north; as Sokunthea was finishing dressing Sall entered her tent. 'Are you coming with us?'

'No, I've decided I'm better alone.'

'Well, here,' and he threw down military camouflage clothing and a bayonet. 'It's better than the Rouge uniform and that'll help you dig up your dinner.'

'Thanks.'

'Where will you go?'

'Back down to Kompong Som, join the prisoners.'

'Take your time, there'll be heavy fighting down there.'

She picked up the camouflage tunic and looked at Sall.

'Ah, sure, I'll see you when you've dressed,' and he left.

The uniform fitted quite well; with a few turn-ups and tucks and with the bayonet tied around her waist she walked out into the camp to say her farewell to Sall.

'Wow...' said Sall on meeting her, 'we should have more women in uniform.'

Sokunthea looked up and down her attire. 'Well, it's baggy enough to take all the different bulges.'

'Bulges... sure,' he stared at Sokunthea.

'Would there be any food?' Sokunthea asked, staring into Sall's delighted face.

'Oh sure – some rice soup and potatoes. Come, I'll take you over.'

The two of them walked to the kitchen. 'Will you be safe surrendering? I mean looking like that.'

Sokunthea stopped. 'Like what?'

'Like some... army girl,' he looked away embarrassed.

'You mean an easy girl.'

'Well, you do look a vision for a lonely soldier.'

'Don't worry, I'll deal with any problems.'

'Okay, if you run into problems, we'll be heading due north for Kirirom.'

She nodded and began to eat.

Before the heat of midday set in, Sokunthea headed southwest towards Kompong Som; she had decided that surrender to the Vietnamese would bring her war to a rapid end. She kept to the high ground, working her way towards the crossroads village of Veal Renh. She had decided to enter the town from the north, reasoning that any captured Cambodian forces would be held in that area. She stopped only to look for food and water, living mainly on berries and leaves. The hill overlooking the Svey estuary was heavily wooded and although she repeatedly saw small deer and hog she was not equipped to kill them. The first night she partially slept in a tree, unsure of what other animals may be prowling after dark.

As morning approached she could hear the sound of heavy artillery and thought of the guns she had helped drag to the Bokor; the wood seemed a little less cluttered and she made good speed, still travelling south-west then turning westward at midday. That night she slept in a tree overlooking the Svey river and knew she would reach Veal Renh by early afternoon. As she tried to find some comfortable position she saw dark shadows moving below her; they moved quickly and quietly over the ground and disappeared as fast as they had arrived. Sokunthea stayed awake for the rest of the night in case they returned and when morning came she began her circle around the village. As she approached the crest of a small hill she could hear explosions and gunfire; she lay on her stomach and crawled forward. When she looked down the narrow valley and road leading into Veal Renh it was littered with burning tanks; she looked further on to the village and saw smoke billowing up. Then she heard the shots, she looked down to the scene of the tank battle and watched as the Vietnamese dragged a group of Cambodian soldiers together and shot them. She stared down with a mixture of disbelief and fear, then a voice came from behind in Vietnamese.

'What do we have here?'

Sokunthea froze and her mind began to race.

'Turn round,' came the voice again, 'turn round,' and a hand grabbed her right shoulder and pulled her about.

Almost without thinking she had released the bayonet and as she spun round she slashed the soldier across the face; he screamed and fell to one side. It was then she saw the other about to release his rifle from his shoulder; she sat up and threw her bayonet in one consecutive movement. The second soldier fell backwards – the bayonet had obviously hit home. She looked to her right as the first soldier, bleeding heavily from his face, began to manipulate his pistol in her direction. She swivelled on her hip and kicked him; he fell backwards and dropped his weapon. Sokunthea pounced; she got to her feet and reached the pistol before the soldier could recover. The soldier looked up at her and the blood spreading out across his face reminded her of Van Serun's leg. She glanced at the second soldier with the bayonet sticking out of his throat and realised her chance for surrender was over.

Sokunthea and the first soldier looked at each other; he thinking of shouting for help, she of shooting and running. They stared at each other, then, as if in slow motion, the shout began to form in the soldier's lips and Sokunthea fired. She didn't look back to see if she'd killed him, although she thought she probably had, she just ran over to his accomplice, removed the bayonet and headed back into the woods. She ran and ran, climbing high above the main road from Phnom Penh to Kompong Som; as she looked down she could see the slow moving Vietnamese military machine working its way north to Phnom Penh. She stopped to catch her breath and squatted on the ground.

'How did I get in this mess?' she asked herself, 'they're supposed to be here to rescue me.' She stared across the valley: ahead of her the mountain range fell to the road and the advancing Vietnamese, and she realised she would have to turn back, cross the Svey to the east side and try to catch Sall.

That night she slept on a ledge of a small rock-face facing the Elephant mountains; her sleep was regularly disturbed by the Vietnamese soldier's face and the blood draining out of Van Serun. She woke suddenly and sat up, her body covered in sweat; she sensed someone close, and as her eyes adjusted to the dark she noticed more dark shapes moving north in parallel to the road.

'Why are the Vietnamese walking in the mountains at night?' She realised they must be Cambodian and took a risk.

'Don't shoot!' she called out. The shapes disappeared. 'Don't shoot, I'm Cambodian, I was at Bokor.'

'Who commandeered at Bokor?' came the reply.

'Van Serun.'

'Show yourself on the hillside.'

Sokunthea dropped down from her ledge and walked on to the hill; two soldiers quickly appeared and removed her gun and bayonet, and they gestured for her to follow. She walked to a bush crouching behind which appeared to be the group leader of a Rouge detachment.

'Who are you?' he asked.

'My name is Sokunthea, I was with Van Serun on Bokor.'

'How did you get here?'

'I got lost, I'm just wandering.'

'Where did you get the Viet gun?'

'Two of them jumped me down there; I managed to kill them.'

'So it was you that drew them away.' He looked around at his men. 'Give her her gun back,' he said to a soldier behind her. 'You're coming with us,' he said to Sokunthea.

The soldiers moved quickly and quietly and Sokunthea had trouble keeping up but by daylight they had crossed the road to the east side and were making camouflage hides to rest in. Sokunthea was shown where to rest; the hide was a slit trench just long enough for her body with a foliage cover. Sokunthea climbed in and fell asleep. She woke to someone shaking her.

'Get up!' She obeyed and followed the soldier to his commander. It was mid-afternoon and beginning to cool.

'Here, take some food,' said the commander and handed Sokunthea root potatoes.

'Thanks.'

'Which command were you in?' he asked.

'I don't understand.'

'Command, zone.'

Sokunthea began to look at the soldiers around her; she noticed they were all young, very young and all dressed in Rouge uniforms. Their manner was brisk, almost hostile, and Sokunthea realised these were the real thing; she scrambled for an answer.

'Tuk Meas, I served with Thalin.'

He nodded. 'Good man, he always got the quota out, no matter what the cost.' He chewed on his potato. 'How did you get to Bokor?'

'We retreated there with commander Thai.'

He stared at her. 'We never retreated.'

They fell silent, then he looked at her. 'I have a job for you; we have rounded up some Seventeen of April scum, they need convincing to go north,' he laughed.

'What's north?' Sokunthea inquired.

'North, that's Central's order: all Cambodians to move north.'

'But to where?'

'They'll tell us when… why do you ask, Ankor will provide.' He glared at her and Sokunthea had time to look into his young face, a face of no more than eighteen, a face that had been removed from its parents at thirteen and told to believe absolutely – and did.

'Yes, Ankor will provide,' she replied.

'We will move high into the Elephant mountains and join the migration north through Kirirom. You will lead the Seventeen of April workers; they are lazy so make them walk.'

'Where are they?'

'Up there on the hillside. Come, I'll show you.'

Sokunthea followed the commander up the hill and, crowded together, she saw a group of around twenty adults and a dozen children. They all looked tired, dirty and thin.

'We move in one hour, get them ready.'

Sokunthea walked over to an elderly woman. 'What's your name?' she asked.

'Kiry,' came the subdued reply.

'How did you get here?'

She looked up at Sokunthea. 'They took us from the road, said the Vietnamese would shoot us, said we had to go north with them.'

'When did you last have food?'

'Three days ago, in Kompong Som.'

She looked across the group trying to catch their eyes, all were tired and distant, the look of despair. Sokunthea looked back at Kiry. 'Are there pregnant women in the group, any injured?'

'Not that I know.'

'All city people or some villagers?'

'We're Seventeen of April, the corrupt, the idle; they wouldn't mix us with villagers,' she said angrily.

'Okay, okay,' said Sokunthea. She paused, then said, 'What was your job… in Phnom Penh?'

'Pharmacist.'

'I was a teacher.'

The woman stared at her. 'You mean…'

'If we work together we can outthink these teenagers, they're not smart.'

'But they have guns and they're prepared to shoot us.'

'Have they shot some of you?'

She nodded.

'I want you to identify the weakest members in the group, I have a plan to leave them behind. I'm going to see the commander and will meet you again in ten minutes.'

Kiry nodded.

Sokunthea went to find the commander who was talking to a small group of his men. He turned to Sokunthea as she approached, and said something to his men who all laughed.

'I need to speak to you, commander.'

'Speak.'

'The workers need food; I can't beat them all the way to Kirirom otherwise none will arrive.'

'Who cares?'

'Ankor cares, otherwise they would not ask you to move them north.'

'What do you plan to do?'

'You and your men have been eating root potatoes, they are growing all around here. Give me six workers and half an hour and we'll collect them for the journey north.'

He thought over what Sokunthea had said. 'Good idea, I'll get some of my soldiers to join in.'

'What, and let Seventeen of April scum see Ankor grovel in the dirt?'

The commander was clearly taken aback by Sokunthea's response. 'No, no, of course you are right. Take who you like but be ready by eighteen twenty.'

'Yes, sir,' said Sokunthea.

When she returned to the group Kiry was waiting; beside her sat an elderly couple. 'These just won't make it,' said Kiry.

'Have they been in trouble with the soldiers?'

'No.'

'So they won't be missed?'

'No, I don't think so.'

'Okay, get me about ten people then follow me.'

Kiry rounded up the required number and the group moved out onto the semi-open hillside. Sokunthea sat them in a circle and told them what to look for and they dispersed into small groups and began their search. Sokunthea moved into the edge of the forest line with Kiry and the elderly couple and they squatted to dig for the potatoes. Sokunthea carefully looked around then removed the cover from her hide of the previous night and the elderly couple slipped inside. When the potato-collecting group returned the soldiers were ready.

'Move them on, Sokunthea,' said the commander. 'Keep to this track and remember we will be watching you from up there,' he pointed to a higher ridge. 'Keep them all together; we don't want stragglers, understand?'

'Yes.'

'Let's go,' and the two parties moved out.

By morning the group had reached the source of the Svey river and Sokunthea had ordered them all to bathe. When the commander arrived he stared at the group frolicking in the water and ordered Sokunthea to report to him.

'Who gave you authority to allow that?' he pointed to the workers still in the water.

Sokunthea placed her hands on her hips. 'They stink,' she countered, 'you try walking behind them all night; they stink.'

The commander stood silent for a while then burst out laughing. 'Okay, but get them out and into the tree line; the Viets have helicopters and they're looking for us.' He walked away, still laughing.

Sokunthea spotted Kiry and walked to her. 'We did it,' said Kiry.

'Well, that's two down, who were that couple, anyway?'

'He was a doctor, I don't know about her.'

'Well, let's hope they make Kompong Som... I'm ordered to get everyone out of the water and into the tree line, can you do it?'

'Sure,' said Kiry.

Sokunthea looked up the valley to the mountain top and then across the blue sky. She took in a deep breath and exhaled. 'I hope they made it,' she said to herself.

'Looking for inspiration?'

She turned to see the commander watching her. 'Just wondering where we are.'

'The Elephant mountains, of course.'

'I mean in terms of the war, are we winning?'

'We are directing the enemy into a position where their defeat is inevitable.'

'What happened to the tanks back there?'

'They inflicted a defeat onto the enemy.'

'And the men?'

'We will rise again. Why all the questions?'

She began to follow her group to the tree line and shade; the commander walked with her.

'Your group co-operated well, we should make up for lost time.'

Not another schedule, thought Sokunthea. 'It's amazing what a little food can do,' she said.

'When we get into the higher ground we will have plenty of food.'

'I hope so.'

They walked to a large tree and squatted below its branches. 'Was it true what they said about Thalin?' Sokunthea looked at him.

'That he had many... many wives,' he smiled.

'No,' came Sokunthea's cold response.

'I heard he had women who protected him and did it with him.'

'Did it?' Sokunthea looked at him and noticed his teenage embarrassment.

'I mean they had fun together.' His voice became nervous.

'Fun,' replied Sokunthea, trying to sound superior while keeping back the laughter, 'there was no fun at Tuk Meas and certainly not with me. Now I must check my group.' She stood and walked off to find Kiry. As she left the shade voices began to rise and she looked behind her to see two soldiers coming up the track, pulling the elderly couple with them. Other soldiers ran to give assistance and the commander began to talk to his men; he looked at Sokunthea then signalled for her to approach him. She walked slowly towards him and heard him order the couple to be placed next to the tree.

'They escaped you,' he said, 'good job I have a rear guard. Bring them over here!' he shouted to his men who collected the Seventeen of April group and brought them in front of the tree. 'This is what happens if you try to escape Ankor.' Two soldiers raised their guns and fired several rounds into the couple; they sank to the floor.

'No!' shouted Sokunthea and tried to run forward but was

grabbed by the commander.

'Back under cover!' he shouted and held Sokunthea tightly around the waist.

She broke free and ran to the elderly woman, wrapping her arms around her and crying hysterically. As the tears began to subside she looked up, around her she saw the faces of the soldiers staring at her in disbelief and as her eyes fell on the commander his expression was one of horror.

'Get up,' and he reached for her and pulled her to her feet. 'Ankor doesn't grovel for the likes of these.'

She regained her feet and looked at him. He was eighteen years old, she thought, taken from his parents at thirteen and educated the Rouge way. Now he and his fellow juveniles were all that Ankor had left; Thai, Thalin and even Serun had seen it and had enough. Even if the Vietnamese didn't win the war they would have stopped this madness, they would have changed, but not these, these youths of Ankor; the ideology had been driven home hard.

The commander stared into Sokunthea's tear-soaked eyes. 'Get your charges organised; I want to be in position to raid Svay village by dark.' He pushed her to one side. She walked over to Kiry and the rest of the group.

'Knew they wouldn't get away,' said Kiry, 'nobody can escape.'

'We can, we can, because there's no other choice.'

Kiry began to walk away.

'Listen,' said Sokunthea, grabbing her by the arm, 'where are they taking us? You don't know,' she continued, 'they may want to march us to the other side of the country; can you do that?' and she spun Kiry around. 'This lot are collecting us for some reason, yet they show no concern as to whether we live or die, why?' asked Sokunthea.

'Because they want the children.' Kiry stared hard at Sokunthea. 'Look around, why are they so few men here?' She fell silent, then, 'They shot those two because they have no value, but the women and those kids,' she pointed at a group of children squatting in the ground, 'they want them.' For a moment Sokunthea was stunned, the words of Kiry were running through her mind. 'Fight on, we never retreat, hold the hill to give the

Rouge time.' Her thoughts were interrupted by the commander.

'Let's get moving,' he said.

Sokunthea obeyed, corralling her group and with Kiry leading they returned to the rocky path and continued up the mountain. The Rouge unit divided into two, one staying, the other descending the mountain and disappearing into the tree line. Sokunthea decided she wanted more information and slowed down, enabling the commander to catch up.

'I'm sorry about what happened back there,' she opened.

'Don't do it again.'

'I think I got a flashback to my mother.'

He looked across at her.

'She was shot in front of me, by Lon Nol's men,' she lied. 'Sometimes, well I can't forget it, I'm sorry.'

He took her hand. 'That traitor killed my family too, but the educators helped me overcome it. Did you not have educators at Tuk Meas?'

Yes, yes,' said Sokunthea, 'but they were busy with that trash,' and she nodded towards the group in front.

'Hmmm, my educators taught me not to remember, that it was a weakness; if you remember you can have emotions and that's the greatest weakness of all.'

'Don't you miss your family?'

'To miss is an emotion; they were there, now they are gone. I only need Ankor.'

'Where are we going?' asked Sokunthea after a short pause.

'North.'

'North's a big area, how far?'

'As far as Ankor says.'

'I'm not sure these will make it,' she nodded towards the group ahead.

'The tough ones will, the weak, well, we don't need them.'

'And the children?'

'They go north.'

'With or without their mothers.'

'With or without.' They walked on in silence for a while. 'They get in the way, don't they,' said the commander.

'What?' replied Sokunthea.

'Emotions, emotions, of course; you think of mothers and children, I think of the needs of Ankor. What's that?' He looked up and scanned the sky. 'Off the track!' he shouted and the group dispersed. Sokunthea and the commander squatted down under a tree as the helicopter passed overhead.

'Are they looking for us?' asked Sokunthea.

'I don't know.'

They sat in silence staring out across the lower hills and the dividing valley.

'Will it come back?' Sokunthea broke the silence.

'Who knows.'

Sokunthea laughed. 'That was a dumb thing to say.'

The commander nodded.

'What's your name?' asked Sokunthea.

'Brother 1120.'

'What?'

'Sy, just call me Sy.'

'Are you from this area, Sy?'

'Prey Veng.'

'That place saw a lot of fighting.'

'It did.'

'Are any members of your family still alive?'

'You're on about remembering again.'

'I'm sorry, shall we…'

'We have to go.' He stood and entered the open. 'Come on, let's move,' and the journey continued.

As darkness fell the group camped just north of the village of Svay; they had descended from a higher level down to the roadside and while doing so Sokunthea had noticed a large row of unharvested rice along a ridge where the road plain met the hill. She approached Sy and explained her observation.

'No, you must stay here and quietly.'

'But we need the food,' she insisted.

'If our raid is successful we'll get food.'

'And if not?'

He turned and looked at her. 'No,' he said.

As Sokunthea left she could see Sy's men preparing for an assault; she went back to her group and found Kiry.

'You're right about them wanting the children,' she said.

Kiry shrugged her shoulders. 'I want food,' she answered.

'There's rice down there.'

Kiry looked at her. 'Where?'

'Along the edge of the rice fields, nobody has bothered to harvest it.'

'Well, I will.'

'Good; we'll need a small group of skilled rice cutters, maybe six.'

'And where will we get the knives from?'

'Well, I've got my bayonet and I stole a couple more from them,' she gestured towards the preparing soldiers.

'So what's the plan?'

'Well, it looks as if Sy is planning to use all his troops; when they depart we should be ready to leave and while they're killing each other we'll harvest.'

Sy approached Sokunthea. 'You have your pistol; only use it in an emergency. We'll be back before daybreak.' He turned to leave. 'Oh, can you manage alone or do you…?'

'No, no, I'll be fine; look at them, they're exhausted.'

'Good, I'll need all the help I can get down there.'

'Good luck.'

He disappeared into the darkness.

'You seem to be getting on with him,' cut in Kiry.

'Men, I've learnt they are big children; play to their egos and you've got them.'

'I wish I was that confident around them, they always seem ready to pounce to me.'

'Pounce?' Sokunthea shook her head.

'Pounce, for sex.'

They both laughed.

'When sex is on their mind that's when they're the most vulnerable,' mused Sokunthea.

'What's our plan?'

'Wait for them to go, then follow me.'

'Why don't we just escape?'

'Good question. Do you think this lot would get far?' She nodded towards the group.

'No.'

'And if they're recaptured?'

'Okay, so I tell them to wait.'

'For now, yes; here, take one of these bayonets and give the other to someone who knows how to cut rice quickly.'

'Sure,' said Kiry and she walked to the group.

Sokunthea and her group left the camp fifteen minutes after the soldiers. They walked rapidly and silently in single file with Sokunthea in front. As they reached the first rice field they began to hear small arms fire coming from down the valley; Sokunthea turned to Kiry.

'Split into pairs, one cuts one collects; you know the routine by now.'

Kiry nodded and passed the instruction down the line. Sokunthea paired off with a young girl called Li and they both began work in the ankle-deep water. They worked quickly and silently, all Sokunthea's rice-cutting experience enabling her to move methodically through the rice, not missing a stalk. Li was surprisingly quick in tying the rice stalks into bundles, which enabled them to move ahead of the others. The sound of fighting down the valley increased and the rice gatherers ducked down as flares were fired into the night sky.

Sokunthea told Li to rest and went in search of Kiry. 'How's it going?' she asked.

'Slowly,' came the reply.

'Okay, I'm going into the next field with Li, you clear this one out.'

Sokunthea led Li into a higher rice field where the water level was much lower. As they crossed over a dividing mound of soil between the fields a flare went up exposing them in its light. They slid down into the rice field and waited but no gunfire followed their movement.

'That was close,' said Sokunthea to her assistant. 'Come on, let's get cutting.'

They continued at the speed which they had achieved in the previous field and Sokunthea was soon tired and sweating heavily. She turned to Li.

'Let's rest,' she said, and they both squatted, trying to rest aching limbs and breathing heavily.

Then Li said, 'Why do you help us?'

Sokunthea looked at her assistant; she guessed her to be around sixteen. She was very beautiful but thin, very thin. 'Where are you from?' she asked.

'Phnom Penh, of course, genuine Seventeen of April.'

'And your parents?'

'Dead.'

'Natural or…'

'Murdered.'

'In the fields?'

'Yes.'

They stared into the darkness. 'You bundle rice well,' continued Sokunthea.

'I learnt to survive.'

'I'm on your side,' said Sokunthea, sensing slight hostility from Li.

'But you work with them.'

'I learnt to survive.' She stared at Li who then smiled.

'Are you from Phnom Penh?'

'Yes, but don't tell them.'

'Will they kill us?'

'Not if I can help it.'

'You were not very successful with the doctor.'

Sokunthea fell silent.

'I'm sorry, I shouldn't have said that.'

'No, no, you are right, that's why I gather information from the commander. If I know his plan I can develop my own.'

'Like getting this rice.'

'Yeah.'

'The other teams are coming,' said Li.

Sokunthea watched them cross the rice field mound and slide alongside them.

'The firing is coming this way,' whispered Kiry, 'we should get out.'

'Okay, let's collect the bundles and follow me.'

Sokunthea led the team along the edge of the rice fields collecting the bundles and then began to climb to higher ground.

Kiry had been right; the automatic gunfire was getting closer and further down the valley mortars could be heard.

'Quickly, come on let's move quickly,' Sokunthea urged them on.

The group moved higher up the slope of the hill, regaining more and more cover as they climbed.

'Are we safe yet?' gasped Kiry.

'I'm not sure, those mortars are getting very close... Down!' shouted Sokunthea and everyone hit the ground as a mortar shell exploded just below them.

'That was close!' yelled Kiry.

'Too close,' came Sokunthea's reply. 'We have to keep climbing.'

The group moved off in a close bunch and climbed as quickly as they could; soon they regained the narrow path that would lead them back to the waiting area. Sokunthea dropped back to walk alongside Kiry.

'You okay?'

'Sure,' said Kiry, 'a bit shaken up by that mortar, but okay.'

'I hope the rest of the group haven't run off.'

'I hope they have,' responded Kiry.

They continued to climb the path together.

'The soldiers must have taken a beating; what were they after?' inquired Kiry.

'Beats me.'

'Well, let's hope they don't return, then we can be off.'

'I think this lot will return, we've just got to stay alive and plan our escape.'

'Well, I'll leave the planning to you.'

As they walked on they heard Li's voice calling to a friend.

'They're still here,' said Kiry.

'Good,' came Sokunthea's reply.

The remaining group emerged from the hiding places to talk and check the success of the rice-cutting group. As they did so Sokunthea became aware of dark shadows moving around their periphery. Almost immediately Sy appeared.

'Come, let's go.' He took Sokunthea by the elbow and began to lead her further up the path.

'What's the hurry?' she asked.

'Just keep moving, we need to create some distance between us and them by daybreak,' he motioned back down the path.

They moved ahead, climbing higher and higher with dark figures joining the column as they progressed.

Sy stayed by Sokunthea's side, then eventually said, 'I see you have disobeyed my order.'

Sokunthea continued to walk in silence.

'You are proving to be a security risk and I don't like that.'

'We needed food,' responded Sokunthea; 'you ordered me to get these people north. Well, they will only walk if fed occasionally.'

'I told you I would bring food back from the raid.'

'Did you?'

He looked away. 'No, there were too many of them.'

'Well, be glad that I have enough for everyone.'

'If you were one of them I'd…' he pointed at the Seventeen of April group.

'What, shoot me?'

The group moved wearily on, not making a sound; even the young children seemed to sense the urgency in their progress up the hill and into the Elephant mountains. By daybreak they had crossed the Svay peak and sought rest in the northern part of the Bokor valley. Sy ordered a halt and the group camped for the day; Sokunthea collected together the rice stalks and began to shred the rice from them. A small fire was built, with Sy's permission, and soldiers and Seventeen of April people sat around the bubbling rice pot watching it cook. Sokunthea organised the collection of water from a nearby stream then watched as the younger children splashed and played along its bank. As she collected a bucket of water she looked around and thought how good it was to be alive. The early morning was warm with a cool breeze coming across the Elephant mountains, the sky was blue with no clouds in sight. Sokunthea stared down the valley towards the Bokor hill station and thought of Tiny. Her thoughts were then disturbed by a developing argument; she turned and saw that around the boiling rice two men had begun to shout at each other. Sokunthea headed towards the fracas and arrived on the scene at the same time as Sy.

'What's the problem?' Sy asked.

The two men immediately stopped and looked at the young commander; one of the men, a soldier, spoke first.

'The food is for us, right, commander?'

Sy looked across at Sokunthea then back at his man. 'Of course.'

The second man involved in the argument then angrily spoke. 'The women and children need the food; they haven't eaten for days.'

Sokunthea watched the horror sweep across Sy's face; he had been challenged by a Seventeen of April scum. His hand began to move towards his revolver as Sokunthea stepped forward. She threw the water in her bucket over the man, then hit him across the side of the head. He fell to the floor; she had saved his life.

'How dare you say that!' She looked at the other startled members of the group. 'Get him away, there's food for all.' She stared at Sy, whose expression of horror had been replaced with a smile. 'Now get back,' she continued and everyone moved away except Sy.

'I was getting worried about you,' he said, 'but I realise you're still one of us.' He smiled.

'I'm just following your orders and trying to get those people north as Ankor wishes.' She stirred the boiling rice, 'but he was right: no food and these people won't move, and if you shoot them all Ankor will shoot you.'

'What do you know about what Ankor will do?'

'I know they want people to be moved north, no doubt to fight some long-term jungle war. That's why you are here, isn't it, collect the people and move them north?'

'How do you know the order?'

'It's obvious, it's Ankor; have a problem, move the people, just like the cities.'

'The cities were cleared to end corruption, to make the idle work.'

'And now, moving everyone north, emptying the south?'

'The Vietnamese will hide behind the people, use them as shields.'

'The Vietnamese are after you, not the people.' She glanced at

Sy.

Sy walked back to his hide thinking over what Sokunthea had said.

By early morning Sokunthea, with Kiry's help, had served rice to everyone and still had enough left to enable her to plan an evening feed before the group moved on. As the group finished their rice and began to retire to their various hides across the hillside and in the trees, the sound of helicopters moving up the valley could be heard. Sy gave the order for everyone to take cover and Sokunthea climbed into a slit trench, which she then covered with leaves. The sound of the helicopter grew louder; Sokunthea believed it was hovering over her and as it moved away the sound of machinegun fire could be heard. Sokunthea placed her hands over her ears and closed her eyes tightly as the helicopter appeared to return, then wham! Sokunthea jumped up out of her hide thinking the helicopter was dropping bombs; as she did she saw it crash to the ground in flames, and she ran back further into the forest for cover. A second helicopter appeared and began to fire into the forest; this was followed by two rockets, which chased off into the thick woodland before exploding. A rocket, which appeared to come from the ground, traced up to it and blew off its tail; it spiralled to the ground with a great explosion. Sokunthea saw Sy through the smoke that a multitude of fires was creating.

'We have to get out!' he shouted; he turned and ran towards her.

'Move the group on, we're heading for Koh Sla,' he said as more explosions and helicopters arrived.

Sokunthea nodded and ran off in search of Kiry, who she found leading a small party through the forest to higher ground. 'Head to the source of the Demrei river, I'll see you there.'

'Where's that?' Kiry replied.

'Straight ahead of you,' Sokunthea shouted as she went in search of others. As Sokunthea skirted the fighting area the sound of gunfire stopped to be replaced by a loudspeaker message.

'People of Kampochia, we are your friends. Stop fighting, we have come to save you.' The message repeated itself and drifted away with the wind as the helicopter turned away. Sokunthea continued with her searching, moving quickly through the forest, then she paused, thinking she had heard something ahead. As she crept forward slowly a large wooden branch hit her across the head and she fell to the floor. When she awoke a woman was attempting to dress the wound that the wooden branch had caused on the back of her head.

'Where are we?' she grumbled.

'Shush,' said the woman, who Sokunthea recognised as a member of the Seventeen of April group. She tried to elevate herself onto one elbow but was held down. 'Don't move.' Sokunthea glanced to her right and saw two Vietnamese soldiers talking to the man she had struck with the rice bucket.

'What is happening?' she whispered to her nurse.

'Vanterin brought you here, he's bargaining with them.'

'Bargaining, over what?'

'You.'

Sokunthea stared at the woman. 'How did they get here?' she continued.

'From the helicopters, they came by rope.'

'Helicopters, rope... what the?' Sokunthea decided she would not lie down any more, she rolled onto her side and began to stand. As she did the two Vietnamese soldiers came towards her. She stretched and looked at them; they looked tough, tough and angry, she thought. As the first one approached her, he struck her hard across the face; she gave a slight scream and turned away. The second seemed to restrain his colleague and engaged her in eye contact.

'Are you a soldier of the Khmer Rouge?' he asked in clear Cambodian.

'I am a soldier of Cambodia.'

'I have no time for lies, my colleague here has lost many men today and he is very angry. In fact he wants to shoot you; now, are you a soldier of the Rouge?'

She looked past the two men at the man whose life she had saved, then turned and looked at the small group of Cambodians squatting on the ground. She realised that to deny would be futile. 'Yes, I'm a Rouge fighter.'

Her questioner smiled and began to walk around her, looking at her. 'You're the first one I've met,' he finally said, then he spoke over her shoulder, 'you don't look very frightening to me,' and laughed. He looked at his colleague. 'Bring her to my tent, we need more information from her.' As they walked towards the encampment he looked at the Cambodian who was bargaining with Sokunthea and said in Vietnamese, 'Shoot him and take that lot,' pointing at the squatting group, 'to Svay.'

'I thought you were here to save them,' said Sokunthea and the party stopped.

'So you speak Vietnamese; we'll have to be careful what we say,' said her questioner who began to laugh. While walking to the tent Sokunthea began to count how many soldiers were present, what equipment they had and whether they were supplied for a long stay or just for reconnaissance. Her questioner seemed to sense what she was doing.

'Checking us out, hey?' he said as he lifted the flap of the tent and entered.

'It's habit,' said Sokunthea.

'Don't worry, your friends won't return.'

'That's good news, they might shoot me for being captured.'

Her questioner burst out laughing. 'And we'll definitely shoot you if you don't talk.'

He sat on a small camp-bed and gestured for her to sit on a similar bed opposite to him.

'How long have you been fighting?' he asked.

'I'm Cambodian, we always fight.'

He began to laugh again. 'Oh, I like you; I like you but I was told all you Rouge had no sense of humour, men… and women,' he looked up and down her body, 'of steel.'

'Maybe I'm trying to convince you that I'm not Rouge.'

'Oh, good, you are very good,' his tone changed, 'now where are your men heading?'

'North.'

'Where north?'

'The Elephant mountains.'

'We're in the bloody Elephant mountains.'

'Further north.'

'Okay, why?'

'To escape you.'

'Oh, I see, it's the around the houses answer time.' He stood and began to pace up and down the tent. 'How many do you have?'

'What?'

'Men, of course, how many men?'

'Maybe a hundred.'

He stopped and looked at her. 'Now we were doing so well, don't spoil it; how many men?' he towered above her.

As she spoke a single gunshot rang out. 'About thirty,' she answered.

Her questioner lifted the flap of the tent and looked outside. 'Your accuser is dead.' he returned to his seat.

'Your men are well armed, they shot down two of our helicopters with their B-40 rockets – how many more do they have?'

'Maybe ten or twelve.'

'You are lying.'

'No, along with landmines the B-40 is the preferred weapon of the Rouge.'

He stared at the floor. 'You have been very helpful, except for their destination.'

'Because I don't know.'

'Come now, don't spoil it.'

'Does everyone in your army know where they are going? I didn't have a high enough rank to know.'

'You have been very helpful; don't stop now.'

'If I knew I would say.'

He looked at her, then down to his hands. 'They want to kill you,' he nodded to the tent entrance, 'are you ready to die?'

'No, but I've seen a lot of it – it has no meaning any more.'

'Then goodbye, Rouge soldier, and know this: your country is no more, it belongs to us.' He went outside; Sokunthea sat staring into the corner of the tent then began to reflect on her future.

'Is this it, killed by the people who I thought would save me, betrayed by a Cambodian whose life I saved?' She began to silently cry.

Two soldiers entered the tent and dragged her out just as her questioner was taking off in a helicopter; she was dragged to a tree where her hands were tied together and a rope thrown over a branch above her head; she was hoisted up and left to dangle. She watched as several more helicopters came in to pick up their human cargos and depart. As she watched the ever-decreasing number of military personnel collect around the departure zone a soldier walked towards her and removed his pistol from its holster. He looked up at her and began to raise the gun; as he did a second soldier approached him and whispered something, he nodded. Several soldiers ran forward and Sokunthea was lowered to the ground; the soldiers then began to remove her clothes and she lay there naked, knowing what would happen next. The soldiers then rolled her onto her abdomen and, bending her legs back, began to intricately tie her up. The fine rope that they used went around her ankles, up her back to her wrists then through a complicated knot to around her neck. She lay there, still expecting the first man to enter her and the beating but they began to leave and head for the last helicopter.

As the final soldier stood and looked down at her he said, 'Die slowly and painfully, just like my comrades,' and they left.

All around her was silent; she was still alive, they hadn't raped her. It was only when she started to move that she understood why. Every movement of her wrists or feet tightened the fine rope around her throat and once tightened it would not release; she would strangle herself slowly as she tried to escape. She lay on the ground, trying to stop her head and shoulders falling forwards as this would bring on her death more rapidly. She tried to arch her back more in order to ease the tension in the rope but this only tired her more quickly. It began to go dark and her strength was beginning to wane; she knew she would not see morning and began to wish they had just shot her. Night settled in and her battle against fatigue had begun; sleep meant death yet sleep would inevitably come. Her head began to feel as if it were made of gold as it slowly rolled forward; every jerk meant the rope tightened. As the pressure to sleep grew and her oxygen supply reduced she thought she heard the voice of Tiny and she answered, 'Yes, I'm here, I'm coming, we'll be together... I'm coming.'

When she woke she lay under a tree covered with Sy's tunic;

he was kneeling next to her gently tapping her face.

'She's alive… she's okay,' she heard him call out.

Sokunthea began to cough and sit up; she felt her neck, gently touching the abrasions around her throat.

'They nearly got you,' said Sy.

'Give me some water.'

Sy called out for water and some appeared.

'Why did you come back?' she asked.

'For you.'

'Rubbish.'

'Okay, we left too much stuff behind, I just hope the Viets haven't found it.'

'They were here in force.'

'I know.'

'They want to find your rocket launchers.'

'So do I.'

She tried to laugh, then fell silent. 'Who found me?' she asked eventually.

'Me.'

'So I've nothing to hide from you.'

'No.' They both laughed. 'Are you able to travel?' he said finally.

'Sure.'

'This is a landing site for them now so I think they will be back tomorrow.'

'Where are we headed?'

'We have a camp over the next ridge, we'll be there in a couple of hours.'

She stood and put on the tunic, which fell to mid-thigh.

'I'm sorry but we have no spare trousers,' said Sy and they laughed again.

'Tell me,' said Sokunthea, 'how did you find me in the dark?'

'Yeah, that was strange.'

'Why so?'

'You were talking to someone but whoever it was they'd gone by the time we got to you.'

They walked on in silence.

The journey to the camp seemed to take hours with Sy often

supporting Sokunthea and at times even carrying her. On reaching the camp Sokunthea was found a place to sleep which she did immediately. While sleeping she dreamed of Tiny, a vivid dream in which she could feel Tiny's hand as they sat talking. Tiny encouraged Sokunthea to remain with the group and repeatedly said, 'Watch out for the children.' The dream ended with Tiny hugging Sokunthea and repeating, 'Look after them.' When she woke her throat was sore and her neck stiff; she met Kiry who offered her rice soup and she sat with her eating slowly.

'How many got away?' she said in a croaky voice.

'Us or them?' she referred to the soldiers.

'Anybody.'

'Half the group are missing, either in the forests or the Vietnamese have them. The Rouge... most got away.'

'I was captured with a group of them, the Viets took them back to the road.'

'They made a mess of you,' Kiry inspected Sokunthea's neck.

'It could have been worse.'

Kiry stood as Sy approached. 'I'll be off, talk later.'

'Sure.'

Sy reached Sokunthea and threw a pair of battle trousers at her. 'They're camouflaged, they won't see you next time.'

She chuckled, 'They didn't see me last time, I was betrayed,' as she rubbed the wound on the back of her head.

'I was going to ask how you got that.'

'Well, another scar of war.'

'Well, we have to move, are you still able to move them?' He looked at Kiry and her group.

'Yes.'

The day was spent heading towards the southern Mount Aoral peak through thick forest. As the day progressed hunger again became the major problem and although the Seventeen of April group was now small it consisted of many children.

Sokunthea approached Sy. 'Can't we stop and find food?'

'There'll be food at Koh Sla.'

'And how far to there?'

'Four, five kilometres.'

'What's at Koh Sla, it's not exactly north is it?'

'No.'

'So why detour south-east when we are supposed to go north?'

'It's a holding centre.'

'Of what?'

'People.'

Sokunthea stopped as the column moved on, and Kiry came alongside her.

'You look as if you've seen a ghost.'

'We're doubling back to collect more people and we can't even feed the ones we have.'

The group entered Koh Sla just before dark; it consisted of a narrow dusty track and on each side large penned-in areas made of barbed wire. In the pens were people, many people; Sokunthea looked at it all in horror. Higher up the track several small leaf-made huts stood on each side, and here the group divided. Kiry and her group were led away while Sokunthea and the rest of the soldiers were taken further on then delegated a house of their own. Sokunthea knew that to protest would be futile; she was considered Rouge and would have to take the privileges that meant.

Sokunthea was allocated a small room at the back of one of the leaf huts; she was shown where to wash and told an evening meal would be served at ten. Her guide reminded her of the educators from Tuk Meas, softly spoken and kind but not to be trusted. She looked around her room, just big enough for a small bed; there were no windows and the door was covered by a large dirty curtain. Her guide returned with a small candle and told her to use it only if she had to, then left without leaving a method to light it. Sokunthea climbed onto her bed and lay staring at the roof. 'What is this place?' she said to herself and tried to imagine what had been happening in Koh Sla for the past four years. She decided she needed a bath and some fresh air and went in search of the water barrels. These were situated at the rear of the hut in a cluster; she desperately wanted to wash her hair and her dried up head wound, which still periodically gave her pain. The area was quiet so she decided to undress and slip into the centre barrel; as she lowered herself in the cool water embraced her and its ability to refresh engulfed her mind and body. She sat there in sheer delight with this ecstasy up to her neck, and it was then she heard the first voice.

'He has to, he has no choice.'

'But as he says he's a fighter, not a sheep herder.'

Sokunthea lowered herself further down into the barrel as the two men stopped and began to urinate up the side of the barrels.

'We must keep the re-education process going, and that means children – all the children we can get.'

'I know, Narum, I know; he was one of our first students, one of the best, but he can't understand why he can't fight.'

'Because we've bloody lost, that's why.'

The second man gave a great sigh and stopped urinating. 'Look, Narum, I know we have to clear these Seventeen of April scum out of here; if anybody knows what we have been doing here... well.'

'Listen, nobody will find out; he will lead the remaining group out to Kirirom and we will burn this place to the ground then disappear, but he has to take them.'

The two men turned and walked back to the house, still talking; Sokunthea sat still for a short while then washed rapidly. She climbed out of the barrel, dressed and headed for her room. When she arrived her educator guide was sitting on her bed and had lit the candle.

'I thought they were for just emergencies,' said Sokunthea.

'Well after tonight we won't need them.'

'Why not?'

'Well, tomorrow we're off and this place will disappear.'

Sokunthea saw a chance to gain information. 'Disappear?' she said naively.

'Yes, they won't leave this for them to see.'

'Why?'

'The cages, the bodies.'

'What bodies, I haven't...'

'Of course not, they're all burnt; well, some are still in the forest.'

'How many?'

'Hundreds.'

Sokunthea decided to sit down. 'Why?'

'Who knows anymore; you kill one, you kill a hundred. Haven't you killed any of them?'

'Of who?'

'Them… the Seventeen of April scum; you're one of us, aren't you?'

'Sure.'

'And you haven't killed any?'

Sokunthea thought of her husband, then Tiny. 'Sure, one or two.'

'One or two?'

'Well, I've been with a fighting unit.'

The educator moved further up the bed to allow Sokunthea more space. 'Wish I had been,' she said eventually.

'How long have you been here?' continued Sokunthea.

'Four years.'

'And a lot of people have been killed here.'

'Sure.'

'What were you doing here?'

'Someone had the idea that instead of killing people we should get them to work; crazy. Asking city people to clear the forest to grow rice where it's never grown before is the same as killing them.'

'Is that what happened, they died of hard work?'

'Hard work, malaria, starvation and the quotas.'

'So who's left?'

'A mixture.'

'Of what?'

'Seventeen of April scum and others.'

'Others?'

'Everybody, we're collecting everybody and taking them north.'

'Do they have a choice?'

'Hah hah hah, a choice!' Sokunthea noticed the girl was crying and she fell silent.

'What will you do?' she asked eventually.

'Go with you.'

'Well,' said Sokunthea wearily then she smiled, 'let's be friends then,' and she held the girl's hand. 'What's your name?'

'Sun Sony.'

'I'm…'

'I know, everyone is talking about you.'

'Oh.'

'They say how you fought the Vietnamese and that you were at Bokor.'

'Well…'

'Weren't you ever afraid? I mean, many soldiers died at Bokor.'

'That they did and yes, I'm afraid all the time.'

'But brave,' cut in Sy. 'Come on, there's a meeting and you're needed.'

Sokunthea climbed off the bed to follow Sy; she looked back at Sun Sony. 'See you later.'

'Oh yes, this is my room, too.'

She rushed to catch up Sy.

'What meeting and what is this place?'

'To plan our departure and it's a holding centre.'

'Death camp, according to my roommate.'

'Don't listen to her, she's crazy. Right, the two commanders are Narum and Seopeap.'

They entered a small room with a low sloping ceiling; inside were the two men sitting on the floor, who motioned for Sy and Sokunthea to sit. The room was lit by a single candle and the air was full of smoke coming from the two men who were smoking traditional cigarettes: tobacco rolled in banana leaf.

'Sy,' said Seopeap, 'it's good to see you.'

'Thank you, sir.'

'This is the area commander Narum.'

'Yes, and this is my assistant Sokunthea.'

'Hmm, a woman,' said Narum.

'But a fighter,' said Sy.

'Good, good,' said Seopeap. 'Sy, I know you are a fighter too but the only way to help Ankor now is to move the people north as far away from the Vietnamese as possible.'

'How will that stop the invasion?' cut in Sy.

'We can't stop it, we have to absorb it,' said Narum.

'How?' Sy replied.

'Remember your teaching? The revolution is not won with

one battle; if the enemy is greater you absorb him, fight him from within,' responded Narum.

'Don't forget your teaching,' cut in Seopeap.

'So we go north, we empty the land and flee,' continued Sy.

'We deny him the people to use against us, we leave him a barren land, and then we take it back piece by piece.' Narum stared at Sy.

'I'll move them out tomorrow.'

Narum smiled, 'Good.'

'How many are there?' cut in Sokunthea.

Narum glared at Sokunthea.

'About one hundred,' said Seopeap, 'mainly women and children so they won't be a problem,' he smiled at Sy.

'Have they any food?' continued Sokunthea.

Seopeap laughed. 'No one has food.'

'Then how will they march north?'

'You will make them,' said Narum finally and he stood and left the room.

Seopeap followed and Sokunthea turned to Sy. 'How are we going to get over one hundred women and children north without food in their stomachs?'

'You heard Narum.'

'Narum's a fool.'

Sy turned and looked at her. 'He could have you killed.'

'By who, you? He's murdered hundreds of people here and now he's clearing his tracks and you are the means to his salvation.'

'You don't...'

'No, women never know what they are talking about,' she stood, 'but listen to me; he's dumped a hundred people on you that Ankor expects to be delivered north. You can't shoot them so how do you expect them to go if there is no food?'

She left the room and walked back to find Sun Sony asleep and the candle almost burnt out.

Sokunthea woke early after a troubled night where sleep was hard to find; she wanted to see Kiry and hoped she'd had a better night than her. As she left her hut she noticed that the educators and soldiers had been busy already and the inmates of the compounds were being lined up. Sokunthea walked down the dusty track looking through the wire at their faces; as she turned to walk back up the hill towards the huts the educators began the process of moving the people out and onto the track. She could see Sy, Narum and Seopeap smiling and shaking hands; whatever agreement had been reached had been concluded. Sokunthea looked up to the sky, thinking, I wish the Vietnamese would come and get this lot. She walked back to her hut, past the sad, drawn faces of the people and the smiling faces of Narum and his murderers. Sy watched her as she entered the hut and she made her way out to the water barrels at the rear. She splashed some water on her face and realised Sy was stood next to her.

'If they stayed here they would die,' he said.

'If they stayed here the Viets would find them and we would escape.'

'We're leaving now, we don't need to escape.'

'And the road to Kirirom – how far will we get before the Viet's helicopters are on to us?'

'It's forest almost all the way, we'll be hidden.'

'And the food?'

'Scavenge, hunt, whatever it takes – those are my orders.'

'From murderers like Narum.'

'I've warned you not to say that. We're moving out and I expect you to be with us.'

He went back into the hut then out onto the track to join the column moving north.

Sokunthea stared into the water. Where's the bloody Viets and their helicopters, she wondered. She walked back to her room, then noticed the candle and the lighter Sun Sony had used the night before. She placed the candle under the edge of the leaf wall and lit it; she paused to watch it take hold then she left the hut and joined the migration. As the last of the refugees left Koh Sla the hut was well ablaze and the smoke was billowing high into the sky. Sy had seen the smoke and was urging the refugees on for he knew the helicopters would be arriving soon. As the refugee party moved higher and higher into the mountain the sound of gunfire could be heard in the vale below. Sokunthea looked back.

'I hope the bastards didn't escape,' she mumbled.

Sy and his men urged the group to move more quickly, while always keeping to cover; several times the sound of helicopters could be heard but they were always a hill or valley away. By nightfall the group stopped on the edge of the Aoral mountain range and Sokunthea, with the help of Kiry, began to count how many had survived such a rapid climb.

'I make it that we have lost about thirty,' said Kiry as she sat next to Sokunthea beneath a large tree.

'Sy won't be pleased.'

'He shouldn't have pushed them so hard.'

'He has to learn how to look after people he was taught to hate.'

'Your sympathy's with him.'

'No, but I think that our salvation does not lie with the Vietnamese.'

'You've changed your story.'

'I've been captured by them, remember.' They both looked ahead into the darkness.

'We need food,' said Kiry.

'I know; I've done nothing else over the past four years but hunt for food.'

'Then you need to start hunting now.'

'I'm sorry, I'm just a little…' Sokunthea began to cry.

Kiry placed her arm around her. 'I'm sorry too; it's tiredness, I suppose.'

Sokunthea wiped the tears from her face. 'Do you think the missing thirty will be okay?'

'Who knows? We're so high up.'

'We'll look for them tomorrow and I'll ask Sy to organise some scavenging groups. Now that's something I know a lot about.' She smiled and they both began to settle down for sleep.

Sokunthea was woken in the middle of the night and taken to Sy; as she arrived she noticed Sun Sony squatting on the ground.

'Sorry to wake you,' said Sy as he walked towards her, 'but I thought you should hear this.' He turned to Sun Sony. 'Repeat what you said.'

Sokunthea squatted down beside the young woman and, seeing she was nervous, took her hand in hers.

'Well, somehow a fire broke out.' She looked up at Sy. 'Do you want me to say it all?'

'Yes, yes.'

She looked back at Sokunthea. 'Well, a fire broke out, we don't know how, so we rushed to put it out, then we heard the sound of them, their helicopters, I mean. Before we really knew what was happening they were on top of us. They killed Narum and took away Seopeap…'

'What else did they do?' asked Sy.

'They took photographs, they photographed the cages and then when they learned about the bodies in the woods they photographed them, that's how I managed to escape. They were so busy photographing that I sneaked away easily…'

'Yes, yes, tell us what you were told,' cut in Sy impatiently.

'Well, it was about you.' She looked directly at Sokunthea. 'They showed us a drawing of you and asked us if you had been in the camp. We said yes then this officer began to scream and shout. He said there was a reward for you and that you were a senior Rouge commander, a number one target, he was angry.'

'Go on,' encouraged Sy.

'Well, they said they had captured you but you had escaped, that you had killed many of their men and made fools of others and they were going to get you.'

'Would any of the people captured know where we are headed?' asked Sokunthea.

'Seopeap,' cut in Sy, 'and he'll talk.'

Sokunthea got to her feet and looked at Sy. 'What do you plan to do now?'

'If they want you that badly… we'll have to avoid Kirirom.'

'So where will we go?'

'I don't know, I'll have to check my maps.'

'How about splitting into two groups?'

'No, never divide your forces.'

Sokunthea began to walk back to her sleeping place next to Kiry. 'So, I finally made Rouge commander,' she laughed and lay down.

The group was up early and moving north as dawn broke; Sy had informed Sokunthea that their destination was Stung Kliech, which was situated some three days' walking north-west of Kirirom. Sokunthea had told Kiry of the events of the night before and both agreed that the news about Narum was good. To avoid the Vietnamese they had agreed to cross over the southern Aoral range and enter the western Kirirom valley. This would give them greater cover from preying helicopters and enable scavenging for food to occur. Food had now become the number one priority for everyone in the group and as they camped for the second day without eating Sy called a meeting to discuss how to get food. Sokunthea was asked to attend and she took along Kiry and Sun Sony.

'We need ideas as to how to gain food,' said Sy. His audience consisted of the three women and two military men.

'We can divide the women into scavenging teams collecting leaves and root plants,' suggested Sokunthea.

'Okay, but what if they wander off?' asked one of the soldiers.

'To where?' said Kiry.

'Look,' said Sokunthea, 'you military have to accept that the priority is food, not losing some people.'

'I agree,' said Sy, 'I want to send some of my men out to hunt, there's game in these forests and we should get something.'

All nodded.

'How do we cook the stuff that we find?' asked Sun Sony.

'Good question,' said Sy.

'Easy; some of your men still have their helmets, they make good cooking pots.'

All laughed.

The group made good progress, spurred on by a new optimism caused by being out of the camp and the effort to get food. Sy's team of hunters had begun successfully killing wild boar and deer and with Sokunthea's and Sun Sony's knowledge of wild foods a nightly meal became a usual event. Sy's assessment of the environment was right also, with forest providing almost constant cover and with it a selection of small streams offering fresh water. The usual pattern of travelling by night and resting during the day had stopped, much to the relief of the mothers with small children; it also enabled the meals to be cooked fully, as there was no rushing to dowse smoke that could be seen from above. Relations within the group also improved with several of the young soldiers playing with, carrying and feeding the children.

As evening fell on the third day the group had left the main trail that headed for Kirirom and entered the Prek Tnoat valley. Almost immediately they encountered a number of Cambodians who joined the group. Sy decided to make camp in order to rest and reassess the situation; he called a meeting of his men and Sokunthea. They gathered below a large tree where a fire was burning. Sy spoke.

'We are encountering a number of Cambodians fleeing Kirirom.' He looked at Sokunthea. 'They say the Vietnamese are there and there has been much fighting. I have asked one of them, a village chief, to talk to us.'

Sy squatted down and a tall, thin man stood and spoke in a quiet voice. 'The Vietnamese arrived and fought the soldiers guarding us. Many were killed. We…' he looked around, 'the village folk just ran.'

'How many are scattered across the mountain?' asked Sokunthea.

'I don't know; many were being taken by the Vietnamese down the mountain to Route Four.'

'And the soldiers, what about the soldiers?' cut in Sy.

'Many died, others just ran.'

'Were there soldiers from Bokor there?' asked Sokunthea.

'No, I don't think so. I don't know, the soldiers were from many places.'

'Think, it's important,' she continued.

'No, no… some soldiers had moved on, the ones left were from Kompong Som, many were wounded,' he began to cry then stopped and looked around the group. 'They shot them, even the wounded, they shot them.'

The soldiers in the group began to whisper to each other as Sy asked, 'Where did the Bokor soldiers go?'

'North, everyone is headed north.'

'But where?'

'Mount Aoral, the northern Mount Aoral, I think.'

'And where are the Vietnamese now?'

'Still in Kirirom, waiting for the next group, I suppose.'

'Us,' cut in Sokunthea.

A silence fell over the meeting and the tall thin man sat down slowly. Sy looked around at his men.

'We attack tonight.'

The sound of agreement could be heard all around.

'Disperse and prepare your weapons; I'll need a small recon team to go ahead of us, volunteers only.'

The meeting began to disperse and Sokunthea headed for Sy. 'I want to go too,' she said.

'This is not the time for heroes.'

'That's what I once said on Bokor. I'm not a hero, I'm Cambodian and you are short of men.'

'We have enough; hit and run, that's all I plan.'

'Hit and run and they'll follow us, they're waiting for us.'

'You don't know that.'

'I feel it.'

He stopped. 'You will have to move these on,' he glanced at the group.

'The new head man can do that better than me and with Vietnamese around shooting people they won't need motivation.'

He let out a big sigh. 'Okay, but you follow orders, right.'

'I'll get prepared.' She turned and began to leave. Sy called after her.

'Remember I'm the real commander.'

Sokunthea found Kiry then introduced her to the village chief. 'You two will have to move them on for at least another kilometre then rest in the trees.'

'But the food I've already prepared…'

'Okay, okay, eat then move, find shelter.'

'How will the soldiers find us?' asked the village chief.

'Don't worry,' said Sokunthea, 'this lot can find anything.'

The small band of heavily-armed soldiers moved out towards Kirirom moving through the dark forest as if they knew every tree, stream and hazard. Sokunthea had been supplied with a second handgun and told to keep close to Sy. The pace of the men was becoming exhausting to Sokunthea but she was determined not to slow them down.

They're good, she thought, very good.

After two hours of a rapid pace the group met with the forward recon unit and they all came into a circle for report.

'They have become lax, sir,' said the young soldier reporting.

'Explain,' responded Sy.

'There are two helicopters still on the ground parked in the centre of the hill station; around them are three buildings, only the south is open. The eastern building appears to be a holding centre, we saw several Cambodian civilians looking from the windows, and the building is guarded but only lightly.'

'How many?' cut in Sy.

'Three men.'

'Go on.'

'The northern building is the barracks; I estimate about forty men.'

'And the western?'

'A store, food and equipment, again guarded by two men.'

'You said they were lax.'

'Yes, sir, they're having some kind of party; a large fire is burning in front of the barracks and they are celebrating something.'

'Right, five men each will secure the eastern and western buildings then give crossfire as they come out of the barracks, four will disable the helicopters then concentrate fire onto the barracks. I will attack the barracks from the rear as they leave; they'll be in full exposure of the fire, sitting ducks, as the English say. Any questions?' The group remained silent. 'You will give me and my men ten minutes to get in position, then we will attack. That should give you enough time to achieve your objectives. Good luck.'

As the men departed Sokunthea realised just how many men were left with Sy. 'You've only twelve men here.'

'And a woman.'

'But is it enough?'

'It's all we have.'

'But how are you going to get forty or so out of their building?'

'It's amazing what a couple of B-40 rockets can do.'

Sokunthea heard several soldiers laugh.

Sy's team moved into position and as they entered the perimeter of the clearing around the hill station it was clear even to Sokunthea that the Vietnamese were not expecting an attack. The group moved forwards towards the barracks; the flames and the sparks of the large fire in front could be seen shooting higher than the roof. They moved quietly and efficiently, the nearer they got to the rear the louder the singing became from the front. Sy looked at his watch and his men prepared for action.

Sokunthea had heard the noise of the B-40 before but at such close range it was different: the click to engage, then the whoosh! of the launch then wham! as it hit the building. Several B-40 rockets found their target, as the entire back of the barracks building seemed to disintegrate. As the smoke and flames began to grow Sy's group poured automatic gunfire into the building; the air was full of shouts and screams but that didn't stop the assault. The group moved forward in order to take up more accurate positions and as they did so two large explosions occurred at the front of the barracks.

'That's the helicopters!' shouted Sy and he began to move forward with Sokunthea closely following. More and more explosions were occurring in and around the barracks as the Rouge soldiers fired their B-40s. Sokunthea thought no one could survive such an onslaught, then Sy grabbed her arm and nodded to his left. Sokunthea stared into the darkness, then noticed several figures sneaking away; she followed Sy.

He moved like a cat over the ground and had quickly outmanoeuvred them; they turned and Sokunthea counted three with a fourth being supported. They realised that Sy had cut them off and two turned to face their enemy; Sy killed them quickly with one burst of his automatic weapon. The third headed for the perimeter and Sy followed, while Sokunthea approached the injured one carefully; he was by now lying on the ground. As she moved slowly and steadily towards him she heard Sy's gun remove the life of the third soldier. Sokunthea looked at the back of her enemy.

'Turn around slowly,' she said in Vietnamese.

The body on the ground began to turn, then said, 'Well, if it isn't the little Cambodian commander.'

Sokunthea realised it was her interrogator. 'Circumstances have changed,' she replied.

'That they have.' He looked at her, then past her as Sy approached.

'Who is this?' asked Sy.

'My interrogator.'

'The one who left you to die?'

'Yes.' Sy raised his gun.

'No, no, don't shoot him, he may be helpful.'

'How?'

'Information.'

'You have learnt nothing,' Sy said and shot the interrogator through the head.

'Why...'

'Let's move,' and he began to pull Sokunthea along by her arm.

'Okay, okay, I'm coming, but I don't understand you Rouge.'

'Then one day I'll teach you.'

They entered the rear of the barracks and quickly passed through to the front; the original fire had begun to burn down while the flames from the helicopters were still strong. They headed towards the store building and joined the rest of the men; inside they had found canned and dried food along with ammunition.

'Collect all we can carry and I want us out of here in ten minutes,' ordered Sy.

'What about them, sir?' a soldier pointed to a group of Cambodians.

'Get them loaded up with as much as they can carry and they come with us. Now move!' Sy turned and ran towards the third building with Sokunthea in chase, as they approached two of his men stepped forward.

'She didn't...'

Sy burst past them and entered into the large room, followed by Sokunthea. The first thing that struck her was the smell, then some of the faces and the shapes. The flickering light from the burning helicopters exposed a room about twenty feet by ten; the floor was covered in debris. Around the room, sitting with their backs against the walls like broken mannequins, were several young women, their naked, bruised and battered bodies the discarded remnants of violent rape, the playthings of the powerful, the toys of the victor. Sokunthea stepped forward and looked up at the dangling body of a young girl, not able to take the shame any more.

'We should bury them,' she finally said.

'We haven't time,' came Sy's reply.

'Then I'll bury them.'

'We leave in three minutes.'

'Don't you understand?' Sokunthea turned on him, full of rage and with tears streaming down her face, 'they're women, my sisters and you bastards…'

'Get her out of here,' Sy ordered to one of his men.

He picked Sokunthea up around the waist and carried her outside; Sy followed then turned and released two hand grenades inside the room. As they moved away the explosion brought down the roof.

'They're buried, now let's go.' He began to signal to his men and they started to melt back into the forest. Sokunthea remained with Sy and strangely felt secure when she was with him; as they progressed through the forest she came alongside him.

'I'm ready for the lesson.'

'What… oh, the soldier.'

'He was an officer in the Vietnamese army, he had information.'

'About what, where his troops are? I'm more aware of where my troops are.'

'He may know that, too.'

'And I'm supposed to spend hours beating it out of him until he doesn't know what he is saying and I don't know what I've asked? No, the enemy only gives you fifty per cent of the truth under torture and even that has changed within twenty-four hours. Shoot them and let them worry about what we will do.'

'The Rouge teach you that?'

He looked at her. 'Don't take prisoners, travel light and fast, strike hard, that's what the Rouge taught me.'

The party stopped as a soldier from the forward group came back to report. 'The civilians are camped up ahead, sir, do you want us to move them on?'

'No,' said Sy, 'we'll all rest here.'

The soldiers, of course, could not rest; their adrenaline was up and the thought of sleep was alien to them. They had lost two comrades in the fighting with two others slightly injured and one missing. Tales had to be boasted of bravery and daring and of memories of the dead; inside they were simply saying, God, I'm alive.

Sokunthea found Kiry, who was trying to rest beside a group of small children. 'Has everyone eaten?' she asked.

'God, you've just come back from a war and all you want to know is whether everyone has eaten.'

'It's the woman in me, I suppose.'

'And I think it's the need to be wanted, to be relied upon; still, you were a teacher.' Kiry turned over to try to sleep.

'Aren't you interested in the fighting?' asked Sokunthea.

'No.'

'Good, because I'm too tired to tell you.'

The group was up early and had begun their journey north as daylight began to show through. The enthusiasm and relief of the soldiers was still palpable and appeared to rub off on the group, which moved quickly and silently on through the forest. Kiry had reported to Sokunthea that there was enough food for one more day, which pleased Sy when he was told; he wanted more speed and less hunting on this post-fighting day. As they reached noon the sound of helicopters could be heard further down the valley, but the group, now in thick forest, just kept going, almost motivated by their noise. The second night they camped next to a tributary to the Prek Tnoat where people washed, relaxed and ate the remainder of the food. Sokunthea bathed too with Kiry and then began to walk between the families and soldiers as they gathered together. Small fires were allowed and the glow of clean bodies sitting together talking, laughing, brought up the same old questions in Sokunthea: why had Cambodians done what they had to each other? As she walked it became clear that the group had grown – many were new faces that she could not recognise. It was difficult to determine who was Seventeen of April and who was farmer; the war against Vietnam had brought different people together in a way that no enforced Ankor plan could. As she passed by individuals would want to shake her hand or even just touch the bottom of her *kroma*, such attention began to overwhelm her and she sought privacy and peace. She walked to the forest and leaned against a tree taking in deep breaths in an attempt to clear her head. This couldn't be that period in a woman's life could it? she thought.

'God, I'm only in my thirties!' she said aloud.

'And still beautiful.'

Sokunthea turned to find the owner of the words. It was Sy, standing close by. 'I've been looking for you,' he said.

Sokunthea just stared at him, then reached out and pulled him towards her; she kissed him quickly, then again, more slowly, prising his mouth open with her tongue. He held her close just kissing and following her every move. Ankor has not taught him about this, she thought. She pulled him to the ground and began to loosen his trousers, then, putting her hand down, she felt his hard penis and pulled it free from his clothing. Sy had opened her tunic and was stroking her breasts as she undid her trousers and pushed them down. She guided his penis into her and put her hands up against his hard, strong chest; for a teenager he soon realised what to do and the rhythm of their bodies began to co-ordinate.

Sokunthea couldn't remember for how long they made love; her mind had wondered to other places and times, pleasant places, places of valuable memories, places of pleasure. When her concentration returned Sy was lying next to her and her body was warm and sweaty; she looked at his firm young body and for a glancing moment felt ashamed that she had taken advantage of him, of this boy. He saw her watching him and rolled over to her and kissed her again.

'You are beautiful,' he repeated. Sokunthea began to dress. 'Don't go, we've only just started.'

She sat up with her back against the tree. 'We will not do it again.'

'Why, was I no good?'

'No, no,' she looked down his young muscular body; 'I was weak.'

'Weak?' he sat up and began to dress.

'Weak, I needed sex, I needed someone to care. We women get like that sometimes; now I need to get on with my life.'

'And us?'

'Hah... there's no us, you're a commander, I'm – I don't know what I am – and we're in the middle of a war. I needed someone tonight, I needed you, now let's get back to reality.'

'But I think I love you.'

'Hah! The old male trap, make me feel invaluable, treat me like a queen, then a rag doll, then a punch bag, then find someone else. No, thank you. This is what I mean by being weak – what has happened has happened, I needed it to happen, but it doesn't mean love and it doesn't mean it will happen again.' She stood and made her way back to the groups.

For the next two days the group continued north; the food they had obtained from Kirirom meant that hunting and scavenging was not necessary. Sokunthea had managed to avoid Sy and his attempt to repeat their actions of the past. Sy tried all he could to attract Sokunthea's attention even being friendly to Kiry, and his approaches to her were a mix between the hurt little boy to the all-conquering war hero. Sokunthea kept her distance. As evening fell on the third day it began to rain, heavily; the group of around thirty soldiers and, with growing additions, over a hundred civilians, were stretched out along a red muddy path slowly winding their way down to Stung Kliech.

Sy approached Sokunthea. 'I'm sending a recon team ahead, they may be waiting for us again.' Sokunthea just nodded.

As night settled in the rain seemed to increase and Sokunthea looked back down the bowed heads of the people following her. Rain was running down the path like a river and the children hugged their mothers, trying to get as much shelter from the downpour as possible. At the head of the column Sy stopped and began to raise his gun, and Sokunthea could see soldiers disappear into the forest on both sides. The rain continued and the sky suddenly filled with thunder then a sharp flash of lightening which lit up the group.

'What is it?' asked Sokunthea as she approached Sy.

'I don't know, something ahead.' They stared into the darkness ahead, then left and right into the jungle. Sokunthea began to step forward. 'No, don't,' said Sy and he reached out to take her arm.

But Sokunthea kept going; slowly she advanced down the path with the wind blasting the rain into her face and body, she inched forward looking into the forest from side to side. Then the thunder cracked again and as the lightening struck Sokunthea saw it; a bull elephant came charging out of the forest towards her screaming its defiance. She dived to her left as it charged past her and on to the group; she heard Sy's gunfire before the trumpeting sound of the elephant regained ascendancy. Sokunthea got to her feet and regained the path; as she looked along it the lightening struck again, just enough to give her a short picture of people scattered everywhere. She began to run up to the group; the first person she met was Sy trying to get to his feet.

'Are you all right?' she asked.

'Yes.' They both moved on together; the elephant had ploughed through the forward members of the group before turning into the forest.

'Is everyone all right?' shouted Sokunthea.

Only groans and faint calls responded; as she walked forward a mother began to cry and Sokunthea followed the noise. When she reached its source a woman was sat cradling her child, by the blood discharge from its mouth Sokunthea guessed it had been trampled.

'Sokunthea, Sokunthea!' Sokunthea turned as Sun Sony approached. 'It's Kiry.'

Sokunthea grabbed Sun Sony's hand as she led her to where Kiry was lying under a tree. She knelt beside her. 'What's the problem?' Kiry didn't respond.

'The elephant hit her, went over her,' Sun Sony continued.

'Kiry, Kiry, can you hear me?' asked Sokunthea. Sokunthea began to check for a pulse then loosened Kiry's clothes to inspect her body; as she did Kiry coughed and blood spilled out down her chin and onto her chest.

'Kiry!' shouted Sokunthea again.

Kiry opened her eyes and looked at Sokunthea then pulled her towards her. 'They want the children.'

As Sokunthea sat back Kiry gave out one last cough of blood and died. Sokunthea looked up at the unforgiving rain and as the lightening struck, Sy's face flashed into view.

'This one we bury,' she said to him and with the help of Sun Sony began to pick Kiry up and carry her further into the forest. In silence, Sokunthea and Sun Sony dug a shallow grave to lay their friend to rest.

'She should be burnt,' said Sun Sony.

'It's not the night for it.'

'But some wild animal might have her.'

'Well, at least the Rouge didn't.'

Sokunthea began to look for rocks and stones to cover Kiry's resting place as the rain continued; she worked all night and as dawn began to break she found Sun Sony asleep under a tree and sat quietly beside her. The rain had stopped several hours earlier but Sokunthea hadn't really noticed. She had begun to think of what Kiry had said and her dream of Tiny: 'Save the children.'

She looked at the sleeping Sun Sony, a girl of maybe twenty, tall for a Cambodian, plump, just as the Cambodian males liked. She patted her thigh. 'Come on, let's go,' and as Sun Sony began to stir she added, 'we have to catch the others up.' They started walking down the path, which even at this early hour had begun to dry.

'Where are we going?'

'Stung Kliech.'

'Where's everybody else?'

'Up ahead I hope,' responded Sokunthea, 'we should catch them before they reach our destination.'

'We could get a ride there.'

'What?'

'Stung Kliech, there's a road and it goes north.'

'I don't know, not my country.'

'Yeah, we helped put it in; well, the city scum… I'm sorry.'

'The city scum may find themselves in charge again soon so I would lose that approach if I were you.'

'I know, but they trained us, you see, they trained us,' tears began to roll down her face.

'Okay, I understand.'

Sun Sony kicked out at a stone. 'Well, you are one of us anyway.'

'Sure.' Sokunthea stared ahead and noticed the rear of the group ahead. 'We got them already,' she said to Sun Sony, trying to cheer her.

Sun Sony looked up. 'Sometimes it's better without them.'

'What do you mean?'

'They'll remember me from the camp; if the Vietnamese ever get us, I'm finished.' The tears continued.

'What did you actually do in the camp?'

'The children,' she blurted out, 'I organised the children to go north.'

'North for the children, but what about the parents?'

'They'd been killed and anyway Ankor wanted them.'

'So you took children from parents and sent them to Ankor.'

'Some of the time, yes.' They walked on quietly.

'Don't hate me,' said Sun Sony, 'I did what I was told.'

'How many did you send north?' asked Sokunthea after a pause.

'Many, too many.'

Sokunthea and Sun Sony joined the group as it entered Stung Kliech; as they walked along the main track Sokunthea was surprised at the number of soldiers encamped in the forest. As she made her way to the front of the group she could see trucks parked amongst the trees to hide them from prying eyes. Sy was coming towards her.

'We can camp here tonight but the Vietnamese have entered Phnom Penh so we must move by morning.'

'Have we...?'

'I know, any food; yes, a little but it's for the women and children. See, Ankor does care.'

'Where is it?'

'Go towards the trucks and they're serving it out.' Sokunthea and Sun Sony set off without another word.

'So the enemy has taken our capital,' said Sun Sony.

'Well, maybe they'll give it back if we ask,' replied Sokunthea.

'Can we beat them?'

'No.'

'Hey!' Sun Sony stopped and spun Sokunthea around, 'Whose side are you on?'

'Theirs.' Sokunthea pointed to the long line of civilians queuing for the food and walked on.

Sy had been right; the women and children were fed and fed well with rice soup and pork and even roast chicken, the smell of which floated over the entire camp sending the non-eaters, the men, crazy. After eating and drinking her fill Sokunthea went in search of Sy who was playing cards with a group of his soldiers.

'Have you any news of the Bokor brigade?' she asked.

'Yes, they've been sent to the north of Phnom Penh, Odong; they'll stop the Vietnamese from moving up Route Five and cover our flank.'

'So they'll see action again.'

'Yes, the lucky devils.'

'How long do we stay here?' she continued.

'A couple of days.'

'Then where?'

'Amleang.'

'What's there?'

'Don't know, it's just another relay station.'

'Relay?'

'Relay, another stop on the way north, but we'll get there pretty quick, I think.'

'We will if they feed us like they did tonight.'

'I think that's the last of the food for a long time.'

'Then don't expect them to walk.'

'Oh, they'll walk, okay, they'll walk.'

'So no early start tomorrow.'

'Depends.'

'On what?'

'How soon they –' he nodded towards the trucks – 'have to leave?'

'Will they take us north?'

'I don't think so.'

'Well, I'll catch some extra sleep then.'

'Sure, oh I'm sorry about Kiry even though she was one of… well I'm sorry.'

Sokunthea turned away and realised that there was no Kiry to go and find, no Kiry to sleep with. She felt a kind of loneliness engulf her; she became uncertain of what to do and where to go and began to feel faint. As she swayed and began to fall Sy caught her.

'Are you all right?' She didn't reply and he lowered her to the ground. 'Stay there while I get some water.' Sokunthea was going nowhere, her head was buzzing and her temperature was rising. Sy returned. 'Here, drink this,' he said and he poured the cool water into her mouth. Sokunthea sat up and took the cup of water from him, drinking it all.

'Anymore?' she asked.

'Yes, I'll get it.'

She watched Sy walk to the water barrel to obtain a refill, a cool breeze came across the ground and washed over her. In front of her was the track and on the other side she could see the outline of one of the trucks; she began to wonder why they were there.

Sy reappeared. 'Here, I got a canister full.'

'Thanks.'

'You going down with something?' Then, startled, he said, 'You're not pregnant?'

Sokunthea spat out the water in her mouth and began to cough, then laugh. 'You think you, the other night… ha ha ha!'

'Okay, I don't know about these things.'

'You sure don't.' She took another mouthful of water. 'Anyway, I can't be pregnant.'

'Why?'

'Because I can't.' They both stared towards the truck.

'Do you want us to…'

'What?'

'Well…'

'Have sex? Why don't you say what you mean,' she said

harshly. 'When attacking the enemy you're clear and precise – stop blubbering and say what you want.'

He turned and forced her to the ground, kissing her as he did.

'Not here,' said Sokunthea, 'not here.'

Sy sat up. 'Where?' Sokunthea stood and led him by the hand to the truck.

Sokunthea was woken by the sound of women wailing and screaming; she looked over at Sy's naked body then began to dress quickly. As she climbed out of the truck Sy woke and began to follow her; she dropped to the ground and headed towards the sounds. Dawn was just creeping over the horizon as she reached the trucks where the food had been served the previous night. There she saw children, lots of children, all being taken from their mothers and loaded onto the trucks. Sy approached her from the rear still arranging his attire.

'What are they doing?' asked Sokunthea.

'Taking them north, that's what the trucks are for.'

'What – and the mothers?'

'They'll walk now.' He turned to go.

'Hold it,' she turned to face him. 'You knew those trucks were for this and yet you let me… you bastard.' She turned back and headed for the trucks being loaded.

'Don't!' shouted Sy and ran to stop her. 'They'll shoot you if they have to, Rouge soldier or not, now obey orders and let them get on with their job.'

'Job? They're stealing children.'

'The children are our future.'

'And the mothers?'

'They'll walk faster and longer.'

'Bastards.' She turned and looked at the trucks. 'Bastards!' she shouted out loud. Sy grabbed her around the waist and began to drag her away as she kicked out and screamed further abuse.

Sun Sony came forward to help; 'Get her over to those trees,' Sy nodded ahead. They got her to the tree and pinned her to the trunk. 'Stay still!' Sy shouted at her.

She glared at him. 'You have to stop them.'

'They have orders and they won't stop.' She tried to move but Sun Sony and Sy held her back.

The loading of the children onto the trucks took about one hour; Sokunthea spent the time squatting on the ground at the base of the tree where Sun Sony and some of Sy's men guarded her. She was full of controlled rage; the tears had dried to her face and she just stared at the last truck as it disappeared down the dusty track. The wailing and screaming of the women had still not fully subsided as they were scattered across the ground or in small groups attempting to console each other. Sy had given his men the order to mobilise and they were preparing themselves for the continued journey north. She thought of Sy and how he had known what would happen, how they had made love in one of the trucks that would remove the children – who had used whom.

'Damn!' she shouted out loud and began to stand.

'Stay calm,' said Sun Sony, 'there's nothing you can do.'

Sokunthea glanced at her. 'Don't worry,' she said in a croaky voice, then after a pause, 'we'd better get them organised for the chase,' and she nodded towards the women.

'Okay.'

Sokunthea slowly left her tree prison and with Sun Sony by her side she walked up to the women. 'Listen to me!' she shouted. 'Listen to me!' the women stopped and stared. 'Your children are safe and they are waiting for you in the next camp, so let's move.' She turned and began to walk down the track slowly.

'They're following,' Sun Sony said.

'Of course they're following; Ankor knew they would follow, for their children they'll crawl all the way to Thailand if necessary.'

'Will they be in the next village?'

'What do you think?'

They walked on in silence.

The journey to Amleang would take them on to the mountain ridge of the northern Aoral peak. The terrain, although still heavily wooded, was difficult underfoot with steep hillsides consisting of small rocks and shale. The path leading to Amleang appeared to travel down the backbone of the range and, due to rain, had been washed away in places. This did not reduce the pace of the column as the women who had lost their children were out in front generating the speed; Ankor's assessment had again been correct. The friendliness, support and camaraderie of the last leg of the journey had gone; there was no more chatting between the soldiers and the civilians, no more support or help, the column just walked on in silence. Sy was keeping his distance from Sokunthea, making sure his men were not relaxing, as the Vietnamese could be anywhere. Sun Sony had filled the role of Kiry, always by Sokunthea's side and in her own, sometimes cumbersome, way trying to help. On the first night the column simply rested where it stopped, exhausted bodies just lay down next to the path, many huddled together to keep warm. The temperature had fallen as they climbed higher but due to their efforts they had not felt it until now. Sun Sony sat close to Sokunthea.

'I wish we had a lighter we could start a fire.'

'He'd tell you to put it out.' Sokunthea threw a glance towards the soldiers' encampment.

'No, he's cold too.'

'Ah, well,' Sokunthea rummaged in her combat trouser pockets and produced the lighter from Koh Sla.

'Where'd you get that?'

'Don't you recognise it?'

'Yes, but how...' she stood up. 'You started the fire, you gave us away to the Vietnamese.'

'And if I did, what are you going to do?'

'You could have got me killed, all of us killed.' She looked around.

'Or I could have saved our lives.'

'How do you work that...'

'By keeping the helicopters off our backs, by keeping Narum from killing you and to keep us warm on a bloody cold night in the Elephant mountains.'

'What do you mean about Narum?'

'Oh, wake up; after we left who remained who knew what had really taken place in Koh Sla?'

'Narum, Seopeap and me.'

'And what did they plan to do?'

'Destroy it, cover it up.'

'And then?'

'I don't know, get away, I suppose.'

'And after it was destroyed who would know about it?'

'Narum, Seopeap and… no, they wouldn't have, no, I worked for them. Seopeap was like a father… no.'

'Narum would kill anyone to save himself, to stop people talking.'

'No, I can't…'

'Me, this lighter and the Vietnamese saved your life.'

Sun Sony shivered. 'I'll start a fire,' and wandered off to collect twigs; soon a small fire was burning. The light attracted a number of women who came over to warm themselves and take a light to begin their own fires. Sokunthea looked into the eyes of all that came; they were cold and distant, unable to respond even when the light struck them. Behind them were minds that were thinking about someone else, somewhere else and a failing hope of seeing them again. Several soldiers came over and as they approached the women moved away; with the soldiers was Sy.

'Are you calm now?' Sokunthea looked up at him then into the fire. 'They had to go, they were slowing us down; they're better off on the trucks, it's quicker.' Sokunthea remained silent. 'I didn't tell you because you would have got yourself killed.'

'How?' she responded.

'By doing something stupid.'

'Like having sex with you,' she glared at him.

'At least it stopped you asking questions all night.'

'Questions?'

'Yes, I could see your mind ticking over as you looked at that truck. You were asking yourself, why are they here? And you'd have worked it out.'

'So you screwed me instead.'

'I think it was you who took me there, remember.'

'Bastard.'

'Okay, but as a soldier in my command I expect you to get these people north. There should be no problems with regards to motivation.'

'You're so sure, aren't you, you and your Ankor. Well, if these women begin to believe that they'll never see their children again they'll become desperate and then dangerous, so watch out, commander.'

Sy bent down and took a light from the fire then walked back to his men.

Sun Sony, who had been listening to the conversation from a distance, glanced at Sokunthea. 'Could they... kill us?'

'When a woman reaches desperation anything's possible.'

'He's handsome, isn't he?' said Sun Sony, changing the subject and watching Sy depart.

'What?'

'Sy, he's very handsome.'

'And becoming very arrogant.'

'Did you really?'

'What?'

'In the truck.'

'You need to learn to close your ears.'

'I know, but...'

'We did and we won't any more.' Sokunthea began to lie down, trying to find a comfortable place to sleep.

'What's it like?' came Sun Sony's voice.

'I've been through this conversation before.'

'What?'

Sokunthea sat up and looked at her new inquisitor. 'You're a good Cambodian girl and you know nothing about sex, right?'

'Yes.'

'But you want to know.'

'Oh, yes.'

Sokunthea looked briefly up to the stars. 'Think I've been here myself,' she said to the sky.

'What?'

'Never mind. Sex is something that one cannot explain, you have to find out for yourself, but there are many problems. First, if you're not careful you're pregnant; second, if you get a lousy lover and stay with him you have lousy sex; third, if, after giving up your body to a man you think he owns you and will care for you for ever and ever, you have a lousy life.'

'But everyone has to have a husband.'

'Why?'

'Well, because without a husband what are you?'

'Free!'

'Well, if you have sex with a man that you don't marry then you're...'

'What?'

'You know.'

'A prostitute?'

Sun Sony stared into the fire. ' I don't think you are... well...'

'Listen, prostitutes were created by men to keep women in their place; if men don't like prostitutes why do they keep using them?'

'I'm tired, I think I'll go to sleep.'

'Fine.' Both women settled down next to the diminishing fire.

'You aren't angry with me, are you?' asked Sun Sony over her shoulder.

'No.'

Sokunthea lay awake remembering her own questions about sex before her marriage and her mother's response. The sex with her husband, then Sinarth, her rape and now her encounters with Sy; all were different. From being a naïve pleasure thing, to being abused to now dominating her partner, her sex life had seen it all but for the first time with Sy she was in control and she liked it.

'What is sex like?' she mumbled to herself then slept.

At dawn the column began its journey again, climbing still higher into the mountains and although the sun was hot the temperature was decidedly cool. The season is quickly changing, thought Sokunthea as she looked down the valley to the developing grey clouds. She looked at Sun Sony. 'It will rain tonight,' she said.

'Yes.'

'We can do without that.'

'There's nothing we can do.'

'I'll see what Sy's plans are,' said Sokunthea and she hurried ahead to find him.

Sy was up at the front of the column still monitoring his men and trying to generate the pace.

'We need to stop earlier,' said Sokunthea as she reached his side.

Sy looked at her. 'Talking to me, eh?'

'I'm telling you that we'll need to stop earlier.'

'Why?'

'It will rain later, we won't be able to make fires like last night.'

'The low cloud keeps their planes and helicopters at home; we have to push on.'

'Look, they have no food and if you tire them out then leave them soaking wet and cold they'll start to become disheartened.'

'They'll walk for their children.'

'Not if they become disheartened.'

'When do you want us to stop?'

'Sometime before the rain so that we can collect some firewood.'

'The forest is thinning ahead; we'll have little cover soon. We have to get to the other side of this ridge, then we'll have plenty of cover, plenty of wood.'

'The rain won't wait that long.'

'Then we should stop now? No, it's too soon.'

'Okay, let's collect some wood as we go, then when we do rest if the rain comes we'll still have heat.'

'All right, but I don't want the civilians wandering everywhere. Small groups, all right, with a guard.'

Sokunthea dropped back to Sun Sony and informed her of the decision, so the column was picking up sticks and fallen branches from trees as they walked. This activity began to distract the women from their thoughts of their children and for some became a game. By mid-afternoon, with the column exposed in more open scrubland at the ridge, the rain began to fall gently. Individuals gathered under what shelter was available and several fires were lit. With no children around making noise, playing games or requiring washing or feeding the campsite was strangely quiet. The column had taken on three clear characteristics: the soldiers, the women who had lost children and the others, mainly elderly men. Sokunthea visited the women's group to listen and talk with them, many had seen Sokunthea's attempt to stop the removal of their children and they welcomed her but made it clear that Sun Sony was not welcome. The night was cold and with the rain falling in a fine drizzle everyone was huddled close together.

'Will our children be at Amleang?' asked one mother.

'I don't know, I hope so.'

'But why did they take them?' asked another.

'To get them away from the fighting.'

'To make us walk faster, you mean,' suggested another.

'That too.'

'I was thinking of leaving, of giving myself up to the Vietnamese but not now, not now that they have my child.' The mother began to weep and was immediately consoled by another.

'Have other mothers suffered this?' asked a fresh face.

'I don't know but I guess so.'

'How can you fight for people who are so evil?' The questions continued.

'I fight for Cambodia and Cambodians, not them.'

'Will you get our children back for us?' asked the weeping woman.

'I will try.' The rain mercifully stopped but the cold wet ground was not very inviting to Sokunthea. She set off to find Sun Sony who was sitting all alone. Crying.

'You all right?' asked Sokunthea.

Sun Sony nodded and began wiping her eyes and nose. 'They hate me.'

'Who?'

'All of them.'

'They'll come round.'

'I only did my job, you know what it was like: if you refused they killed you.' She began to cry again.

'Look, if they really hated you they would have killed you by now, they're confused by you and by what's happening.'

She continued to cry.

'Listen, how many of that group even know you now? Most of the camp members have run off and our new recruits are villagers.'

'They know me, they've talked.'

'Okay, then do something for them, something they'll respect you for.'

'What?'

'I don't know; come on let's visit the military.'

'No, they ignored me earlier.'

'Well, if you're with me they won't, come on.' The two women walked over to the group of soldiers congregated around their fire.

Sy met them. 'Out for a stroll?'

He's trying to be smart, thought Sokunthea. 'No, we wanted to hear your plans for tomorrow.'

'Well, up ahead the cover stops and we have to cross some open ground over the ridge and down into the next valley.'

'That shouldn't be a problem,' cut in Sun Sony.

'Providing we're not spotted,' replied Sy.

'How much open ground is there?' continued Sokunthea.

'A lot.'

'How much is a lot?'

'About a half-day march for that lot.' He nodded towards the civilians.

'What about the food situation?'

'Again? That's all you think about. We have none and I hope there will be some in Amleang.'

'If not?'

'Let's wait and see.'

Sokunthea walked over to the fire and squatted down; Sun Sony followed her. 'Can't we scavenge?' she eventually said.

'I think he wants speed, not scavenging.'

'But there's no Vietnamese up here, is there?'

'Who knows.'

'I could get the people some food; they might accept me then.'

'Don't do anything stupid.'

'Like what?'

'Like expose our position.'

Sun Sony began to sulk. 'I'm only trying to help.'

'I know, but help, don't cause further problems, all right?'

'Sure, I'll follow you.' They began to leave.

'No more questions?' asked Sy as they departed. Sokunthea looked at him then continued her exit. 'We start early tomorrow,' he shouted after them.

The column had started slowly; the earlier rush to catch the children had begun to wane due to lack of food and fatigue. Sokunthea had not seen Sun Sony and had concentrated on motivating the group as much as possible. After one hour of walking the path finally began to enter a more open area: short grass and bushes were to be their only cover. Sy called a halt to the column as it stood on the edge of this partial cover; ahead was just open ground which consisted of a steep rise with many small stones and rocks underfoot.

'It will be the same for the descent on the other side,' Sy told Sokunthea.

'Let's cross in small groups, the Viets would have to be pretty keen-eyed to spot those.'

'Okay.' He turned to one of his soldiers. 'Split the group into four then start moving them across one at a time.' The soldier nodded and left. 'Come sit over here for a while,' he said to Sokunthea and they both crouched down beneath a small bush.

'We seem alienated these days,' he began.

'Stealing children does something to me.'

'I didn't steal any children.'

'But you knew about it and didn't tell me.'

'I've explained all that.' They both watched as the first party set off. 'I take it that we won't be having sex any more.' He glanced at her.

'Right.'

'I thought we could get away from this, drop south-west; no one will find us in Koh Kong.'

'Well, and I thought you the do-or-die Rouge soldier.'

'Everyone changes.'

'I promised someone I'd look after the children.'

'You're right, you know.'

'What?'

'Some of the things you've said, you're right.'

'If you really think that and also want to pack it in, why don't you let these people go?'

'I'm not stopping them, not any more.'

'No, you don't have to, you stole their children.'

The second party moved out onto the open ground.

'Would you come south-west with me?'

'When?'

'After we reach Amleang; we can leave these people there, it's close enough to Phnom Penh for the Viets to find them.'

'And they find their children?'

'Ah, forget the children.' He stood and walked out into the sun. 'The children have their own future now and we have ours.'

As the third group set out across the open ground Sun Sony came rushing forward out of breath.

'Hurry, hurry!'

'What's the problem?' asked Sokunthea.

'Soldiers, lots of soldiers coming up behind us.'

Sy signalled to two men to investigate then ordered the rest of the groups out onto the open ground. 'How do you know?'

'I was scavenging.' She looked at Sy, 'I know I wasn't supposed to, but anyway I saw these soldiers in green, coming up the path.' As she spoke Sy's men returned.

'Vietnamese, several companies, we have to disperse,' he said. 'You two get out there and move those people on, I'll try to delay their arrival.' He nodded to his men and they began to take up ambush positions.

Sokunthea walked over to Sy. 'They'll kill you, there's too many.'

'Get going, and remember the children.' She turned and taking Sun Sony by the arm ran into the open ground.

As she urged the group on to more speed the sound of automatic gunfire began to develop from behind her. The forward groups stopped, trying to work out what was happening behind, while the rear groups rushed to catch them up; as the groups came closer together the first mortar shell exploded. The groups scattered in all directions; Sokunthea and Sun Sony dived to the ground as a second and third mortar exploded. Sokunthea began to slide and roll down the hill towards the valley, hoping Sun Sony was following; as she began to enter more ground cover again she came to rest in a shallow ditch. The sound of gunfire seemed far away and Sun Sony was nowhere to be seen.

She stayed in the ditch until sunset and then began to make her way back up the hill, hugging the tree line and moving quickly but smoothly across the ground; Sy's men had been good role models. As she climbed higher she became more responsive to every rustle of the trees and rush of wind. Her first contact with the Vietnamese was the light at the end of the cigarette being smoked by the sentry. The wind was taking the smoke the other way but as she worked her way around him she smelt that too. She realised that a sentry meant a camp was nearby, and shortly she could see the light from the fires.

'Sloppy, these Vietnamese; they beat the Americans so they don't have to worry about anything, sloppy,' she mumbled to herself. She crouched down in order to regain her breath and assess the situation; as she did a soldier walked straight past her in the dark, then, as he approached a tree, he stepped over something. A tripwire, thought Sokunthea instantly, an inner tripwire. She moved forward slowly. It was a simple device: a wire attached to a hand grenade, designed to injure someone but warn the camp.

'Maybe they're not that stupid,' she mused. She crossed the wire and headed to the fringe of the camp; the Viets had erected a series of small combat tents and men were sat out in the cool mountain air cleaning weapons and talking. To her left she could see a fenced area guarded by several sentries with soldiers coming back and forth, which she decided she should investigate.

She worked her way around the perimeter of the camp slowly and approached the secure compound from the forested side. Inside she could see Sun Sony tied to a pole; in front of her were a women and a Vietnamese officer.

The woman was shouting at Sun Sony, 'Murderer, you murdered people, you murdered children.' Sun Sony, head bent down, did not respond. The woman then struck Sun Sony, again and again.

'Good, good,' she could hear the interrogator call.

It was clear that Sun Sony had taken a beating and was unconscious to her accusers' tirade. Sokunthea estimated that only twenty civilians were in the camp; she could see no soldiers, in fact, there were no men at all. The interrogator pulled Sun Sony's head back by the hair and grunted; he then left the compound, taking the old woman with him. Sokunthea sat back and waited and as the night progressed and the blackness became thicker she crawled into the compound and up to Sun Sony, who was beginning to recover.

'Sony,' Sokunthea whispered into her ear, 'don't cry out, it's me. Sony can you hear me?' She nodded slowly; as she did Sokunthea had already cut through her ropes and lowered her to the floor.

'Can you walk?' There was no response. She tried again. 'Can you walk?'

Sony groaned then nodded.

'Here, take a small drink,' and Sokunthea poured water into her mouth from her water canister. Sony began to cough. 'Shush, quiet,' said Sokunthea as she looked around, but nothing moved. Sokunthea then poured water over her head, which seemed to refresh and awaken her.

'Can you walk?'

'I've got to or I'll die,' came the clear response.

'Good; follow me, slowly.'

The two women began to crawl away from the pole and then the compound, Sokunthea in front checking for more tripwires and trying to spot any awake sentries. By dawn they were back in the forest moving down to the Prek Tnoat river; Sony, although puffy around the face and complaining of abdominal pain, had not received the beating that Sokunthea had originally thought. When they reached the northern part of the river they stopped to rest and refresh themselves.

'Why did you come back for me?' asked Sony as she and Sokunthea washed themselves in the tributary.

'I didn't.'

Sony smiled. 'I thought you'd say that.'

'I came back for everybody, I came back because people once came back for me.'

'I accept that.'

'Anyway, who would I talk to about sex?' They both laughed.

'They beat me.'

'The women?'

'Yes.'

'They only did it because they thought that's what the Viets wanted, they didn't mean anything.'

'Oh, they did, it wasn't the beatings or the accusations it was…' she went quiet.

'What?'

'I killed because I was ordered, even though I knew it was wrong and they did exactly the same; the Viets ordered it and they did it, so how are we different?'

'We're not, we're all Cambodian.'

'I don't like Cambodians anymore.'

'Okay, let's try and find some…'

'Food!' shouted Sony.

They dressed and then began the usual search for root vegetables and leaves and fruits from the trees. They had to eat these uncooked, for although they had the tools to make a fire, they had nothing to cook anything in. As they sat eating their collection Sony stared at Sokunthea. 'Sy's dead,' she said.

'I thought he would be.'

'Aren't you upset?'

'Yes.'

'Didn't you love him?'

'No.'

'But you had sex with him.'

'So?'

'Didn't that mean anything to you?'

'At the time, yes.'

'And now?'

'I have to live, get on with life.'

'They're after you, too.'

'What?'

'They're after you, the Vietnamese officer interrogated everyone about you: had we seen you, where were you headed; he's got the whole army after you.'

'I must have upset him.'

'Upset? Don't be funny, they're determined to get you.'

'Well, I'd better be careful then.'

'What's your plan?'

'Amleang and the children.'

'Are you crazy?'

'No, I'm fulfilling a promise.'

'A promise that will get you killed.'

'Maybe, but you don't have to come.'

'What, and miss all the fun?' Sokunthea looked at Sony and they laughed.

'So how do we get there?' asked Sony after a short pause.

'Well, if I remember this area, if we carry on up this tributary we will pass below Amleang.'

'Won't the valley be crawling with Vietnamese?'

'Why? They're all in the mountains looking for me.'

'I hope you're right.'

The women decided to rest for the day and begin their journey at sunset; it took two nights of careful travelling up the tributary before Sokunthea felt sure it was time to climb. On the second night of climbing they rested in a small shallow cave overlooking Amleang. Below the town of Amleang was burning brightly; the fires of the battle that had taken place were still burning unabated. Sokunthea and Sony watched their destination going up in smoke.

'What do we do now?' asked Sony.

'Mount Aoral.'

'Will it be safe?'

'It's a relay stop.'

'But will it be safe?'

Sokunthea shrugged her shoulders and suggested they rest overnight in the cave; Sony didn't need much persuading. The air was cold and a fire was out of the question so Sokunthea and Sony huddled together for warmth.

'Why don't we go down there and give ourselves up?' asked Sony eventually.

'Because they'd shoot me and hand you over to the Cambodian women.'

'Good reason to stay here.'

'Let's get some rest.'

'You know,' continued Sony, 'we're trapped; we can't surrender to the Viets because we've killed too many of them, the Cambodians believe we are Rouge murderers and you want to steal children back from the Rouge, who will not be happy.'

'You've got it.'

'They'll all be after us.'

'Let's sleep.'

'How can you be so cool about it?'

'I don't think about it. If I did, I'd head for Koh Kong like Sy asked me to.'

'Sy? But he was one of their heroes, top of his class, total Rouge, why did he plan to run away?'

'Because he'd seen enough.'

'Me too,' mumbled Sony.

By early morning the pair were moving north in search of the children; any thoughts of fighting for their country or surrendering to the Vietnamese had been irradiated from their minds. Sokunthea was motivated to find the children because of a promise; Sony wanted to prove to herself and others that she cared. Both women were strong and determined; they had learned how to survive even in battle and torture and they were determined to succeed. They kept to the open country along the Aoral ridge, not caring if they were spotted by passing aircraft or helicopters; as Sokunthea had pointed out, the pilots would have to have great eyesight to see them. By the second night they had reached the tiny village of Krang Trachak; it was deserted, like a ghost town with all its buildings intact.

As Sokunthea looked around she noted the water barrels still full, household possessions scattered everywhere and the chickens picking their way through the debris in search of food. 'Chickens!' shouted the women together. That night they ate roast chicken again and washed it down with cool, fresh rainwater.

'They must have left in a hurry,' said Sony.

'After their children,' replied Sokunthea, pointing towards deep truck tyre tracks leading out of the village.

'Where will they be headed?'

'Depends on how far the Viets have encroached.'

'Odong?'

'No, too much fighting and I would imagine the Viets have passed that point.'

'But there's no route, unless they headed to Moi.'

'Where's that?'

'North.'

'Is there a road there?'

'Sure, it goes to Leach then on to Pursat.'

'Then Moi is for us.'

After eating the leftovers of the chicken and carrying a few more carcasses for further nourishment along the way they started early for Moi. The track that was carrying the truckload of children began to work its way down the mountain and the women moved quickly after it. By midday they came across a small group of men and women squatting by the trackside.

'Did they take your children?' Sokunthea asked of them immediately.

'Yes, yes, please help us,' came the reply.

'Where are they headed?' asked Sony.

'North, north.'

'How many trucks?'

'One!' They all shouted.

'And children?'

'All the village.'

'Yes, but how many?'

'Twenty.'

'How many soldiers?'

'Two, no, three.'

Sokunthea and Sony moved on even though the group wanted them to stay to hear their hard luck story. 'We still don't know how far ahead they are,' said Sony.

'I think not far.' She gestured ahead. There was a small column of civilians moving down the track. 'I think we'll meet more of these as we go along,' suggested Sokunthea.

'Maybe we should cut across country; just following the track will take a long time.'

'Good idea,' responded Sokunthea.

They left the track and began to cut diagonally down the mountainside; the sight of the struggling groups on the track had motivated them more to achieve their objective.

As evening began they left the forest and entered a slight rise of open ground; at the top of the rise the mountain fell away sharply and as they looked out across the valley below they saw the truck.

'Okay, we've found it; now what do we do?' asked Sony.

'Take them back.'

'How? They won't just hand them over.'

'We take them.'

'But there are four soldiers down there, four soldiers who know if they return to wherever without the children they're dead.'

'So be it.'

'You're going to kill them, four soldiers?'

'Look, if you want to go down there and ask them nicely to hand over the children then okay, but I think we should handle our element of surprise differently.'

Sony squatted down. 'What's your plan?' she eventually asked.

'I don't have one.'

'Great.'

'So how we going to get rid of them?'

Sokunthea pulled her combat knife from her belt. 'This is all we have.' Both women stared at the weapon. 'This and darkness.'

They began to work their way around the cliff-face and soon found the track, which the truck had been following; they moved quickly and silently. The truck loomed up at them out of the dark and Sokunthea and Sony crouched down; they looked for a sentry but could not see one.

'They're all in or around the truck,' explained Sokunthea.

'Well, what's your plan?' asked Sony.

Sokunthea pulled out her knife, turned to Sony and cut away one of the straps to her T-shirt, which she then pulled out from her *kroma*. She then ruffled up her hair and began to rearrange her own clothing. 'You wanted to know about sex; well, it's time.'

'No way, no, I couldn't.'

'You don't have to; if there are two of them we pair up, just lead him away from me and my partner. I'll do the rest.'

'No.'

'You don't have to go all the way, just play with him.'

'Play… I don't know how.'

'Just take him away.'

'No, I can't, there must be another way.'

'Listen, men become like children when sex is on offer, they ignore everything that's going on around them, their minds are on one thing only and that's between your legs. Now lead him off into the dark, fool around with him, keep your legs closed and I'll do the rest.'

'But what if there's three?'

'I'll deal with it.'

'What if I become pregnant?'

'Then you'll have experienced the first danger of sex.'

'I must be crazy.'

'Just play safe.'

The two women, with their clothes loosened and flesh exposed, walked towards the truck laughing and pulling on each other. As they got near the truck two men appeared.

'So what have we here?' the first one said. He was a short man and fat, wearing combat trousers; next to him was a young boy in military uniform.

'Bring them here,' came a voice from behind them and the two women were ushered forwards to the truck. Beneath the truck a man lay on the ground smoking a banana leaf cigarette as Sokunthea and Sony crawled underneath to join him. Sokunthea noticed the large bowl of rice wine laid next to him. 'What are you girls doing out so late?' he asked.

Sokunthea just laughed and Sony followed.

'Where are your men folk?' asked the fat man, who had crawled in behind them.

'Gone to war,' replied Sokunthea and she giggled.

'Drink?' the smoking man asked and held up the bowl of rice wine. Sokunthea took it and drank, then passed it on to the fat man, at whom she winked; he quickly drank and passed the bowl on to Sony.

Sokunthea had already decided that she would pair with the fat man; he would be easy to lead on and then kill. The third soldier had climbed into the back of the truck, no doubt to guard the sleeping children.

'That's quite a weapon you have there,' said the fat man, pointing at Sokunthea's knife.

'That's quite a weapon you have there,' she replied, pointing to the man's crutch then grabbing Sony by the arm and giggling. The fat man slowly placed his hand on Sokunthea's knee, then began to move it up her thigh. She quickly grabbed his hand. 'Five dollars,' she said.

'No, no,' said the fat man, 'there's a war on, nobody has five dollars.'

Sokunthea took the rice wine bowl as it was being passed around again; she noticed how the second man had moved closer to Sony. 'Where's the truck going?' she asked.

'North,' said the second man.

'Okay, give us a lift to the main highway instead.'

'Sure,' said the fat man who had freed his hand and it now encamped firmly between Sokunthea's legs.

Sokunthea looked at Sony, then at the fat man and smiled; she began to crawl out from under the truck. The fat man quickly followed; Sokunthea looked back at him, smiled and headed into the darkness. She had realised that Sony was with the much more amorous soldier and with her lack of experience could find herself in difficulties; the boy in the truck could be dealt with at any time.

She reached the edge of a rice field and lay down on its bank; the fat man came running up quickly and, seeing her there, began to undress. Sokunthea remained motionless and just watched as more and more folds of fat were exposed. He lowered himself down onto her with his pelvis high into her neck and face.

'Suck me,' he said.

'No,' said Sokunthea, 'I don't do that.'

'Suck me,' and he struck her across the face.

'So you like to beat your women, I like that,' she said in an inviting voice.

'Suck me, then I'll beat you.'

Sokunthea had already released her knife and as she pulled his pelvis towards her mouth with one hand the other buried the combat knife deep into his back. He seemed to freeze across her so she quickly squeezed between his legs and stood; he then slowly fell forwards. She removed the knife from his back and quickly slit the carotid artery in his neck; he would certainly die. 'You'll not abuse any more women,' she said as she walked away.

She approached the truck slowly from the opposite side to which she had exited; she looked underneath, where Sony and her soldier were lying completely naked side by side. Sokunthea reached in and with one downward movement and slash the soldier fell onto his back, his throat cut. Sony sat up and began to dress.

'I thought you were never coming,' she said. Sokunthea pointed upwards and Sony nodded; the two women climbed up each side of the truck. In the back, amongst the sleeping children, was the third young soldier, fast asleep. They climbed back down again.

'We can't kill him,' said Sony and Sokunthea agreed.

'All right, let's check for weapons,' she said and the two women searched around, finding two AK-47 rifles, a handgun and several rounds of ammunition. They moved some ten yards away from the truck and sat on the ground.

'What now?' asked Sony.

'Wait till morning, chase off the soldier and release the children to their mothers.'

'I nearly did it,' said Sony.

'Did what?'

'Sex, I nearly did it.'

'Good job I got back, then.'

'He gave me more to drink, then I felt him loosen my *kroma* and it was off. Then he kissed me and I lost my T-shirt and underwear; I was totally naked. No man has ever seen me like that, no one. What happened to you?'

'Oh, mine was a beater.'

'What?'

'A beater; he doesn't have sex with you, he does sex to you, the more violent the better.'

'How did he beat you?'

'Oh, just a couple of blows around the head.'

'Do men do that?'

'Some.'

'What did you do?'

'I killed him.'

Sony looked back at the truck. 'I just froze; once my clothes were gone I didn't know what to do, I just froze. He could have done anything to me, I didn't know what to do.'

'Don't worry, taking your clothes off won't make you pregnant.' They walked back to the truck and Sony climbed into the cab to sleep while Sokunthea crawled in next to the dead soldier beneath the truck.

The children began to wake in the early hours as the smell of roast chicken spread over the truck; their heads rose above the sides of the truck and they stared at the fire with two women squatting cooking food. The children quickly left the truck and began to devour the food; the young soldier had joined them and it was clear to the women that the young soldier was of low intelligence, even slightly mentally handicapped.

'We can't kill him,' Sony declared, 'he's no threat.'

The soldier's name was Pen and he helped the women dispose of his two comrades; his speech was impaired and by his appearance he had recently taken a beating. Through gesture and words Sokunthea had learned that the fat man beat him regularly and that he didn't like his comrades.

As noon approached Pen reported that a group of civilians were coming down the track; Sokunthea and Sony went to see. There, getting closer and closer and moving faster and faster were the mothers and families of the stolen children. Soon the scene of united families congregated around the truck. The adults shook the hands of the women and even embraced Pen within their celebrations. As late afternoon came they began the journey back home and the women watched them go. Pen had decided to stay with the women, declaring he would protect them. That evening he demonstrated his real value by returning from the forest with a small pig and several birds' eggs. For the second night running the women could settle down to a sumptuous meal, only this time a man was doing all the work.

'How did he get involved in all this, I wonder?' asked Sokunthea.

'Ordered, like everyone else.'

'I wonder if he knew what he was doing?'

'Maybe not, but they don't want people who think.'

'What will we do with him?'

'I have no idea, he seems to follow us like a dog.'

Pen came to sit with them and with gesture and words Sokunthea asked, 'Where are you from?'

'Prsaat.'

'I think he said Pursat,' suggested Sony.

'Do you want to go home?' He shook his head and repeatedly pointed at Sokunthea.

'I think he wants to go with you,' said Sony, helping to interpret.

'We want to find children,' said Sokunthea, 'do you understand?' He nodded and pointed down the road. 'There are children down there?' He nodded again. 'Can you take us?'

He shook his head and began to shape a gun in his hand and mimic firing it. 'Soldiers, there's soldiers down there?' He nodded.

'Vietnamese soldiers?' Sony cut in; Pen didn't respond. 'Vietnamese, the enemy.' He grunted and shook his head. 'Rouge?' He nodded.

Pen began to gesture and grunt excitedly in the direction of the two bodies that had been buried, then ran his hand across his neck and pointed to his anus.

'What's he saying?' asked Sony.

'I think he's worried we might kill him tonight or have sex with him.'

'Through the anus?' replied a startled Sony.

'Maybe that's what the fat man was doing to him, so he thinks that's sex.' Sokunthea gestured the shape of a fat person then pointed to Pen and to his anus; Pen seemed to understand and nodded.

'I wonder what he would have done to the children,' Sokunthea said to Sony.

That night the two women slept under the truck while Pen slept in the back. The weapons were stored in the cab, an act that appeared to ease Pen's anxiety. In the morning the pig was finished or packed to eat later and the women began to walk down the road.

'What's up with Pen?' asked Sony. The women stopped and looked back. Pen was mimicking the movement of the steering wheel and soon all three were on board with Pen driving down the track.

'He's multi-talented,' shouted Sony above the cab noise. Pen proved to be a good driver too, meandering his way down the bumpy track and negotiating difficult obstacles.

They drove all day, not encountering any military forces from any side; when they stopped as darkness fell Pen, with Sony's help, began to fill the gas tank from the spare canisters on the back. Sokunthea had set about finding wood for a fire and soon the last of the pig was eaten. They had camped near a tributary of the Stroeng Pouthisat River and after eating the women bathed in its waters.

'Our first real bath for weeks,' said Sony.

Sokunthea just lay back and enjoyed the cool water rushing over her body. 'What were you before all this started?' she finally said.

'Just a rice girl.'

'Did you like it?'

'Being a rice girl? No.'

'There's worse things.'

'Like what?'

'Nah, you're right, there's nothing worse than that.' They both laughed. 'What about you?' continued Sony.

'Me, I was a teacher in search of a husband.'

'And did you get one?'

'Oh, yes, I got one.' She began to make her way to the bank with Sony following.

'And where is he?'

'Dead.'

'That's terrible.'

'No, what's terrible is that I'm glad he's dead.'

The women walked out of the water only to be greeted by Pen, sitting on a large rock and observing their naked bodies.

'Pen!' shouted Sony as she began to cover her body. The boy stood up and seemed not to know what to do, Sokunthea nodded at Sony and the two women grabbed the boy and threw him into the water, amidst lots of shouting and laughter. Later, as they sat around the fire, Pen appeared with fresh water snails, which they threw into the hot ashes and then ate.

'This has been a strange time for me,' said Sony quietly. 'I've never done anything like this before in my life, I've only planted rice... and killed some people, which I regret, but I was always told to shut up, that good girls don't do that, stay at home. With you I've travelled across three provinces, fought, killed, almost had sex with a stranger and sat out late at night just talking and eating different food. I don't want it to end.'

'Well, it will, one day it will.'

Their thoughts were broken as Pen came towards them carrying an AK-47. 'What's wrong with him?' asked Sokunthea.

Pen grunted and pointed the gun to the forest then pointed his finger to his nose, then to the pork.

'I think he's saying that the smell of the pork will attract animals,' interpreted Sony.

Pen nodded.

'Maybe we should sleep in the cab tonight,' suggested Sokunthea.

The night's sleep was not very refreshing to the women; the cramped cab ensured patchy, broken sleep. During one of these awake periods the sound of a tiger prowling around the now-extinguished campfire could be heard. As they set off in the morning all three travellers were still trying to catch up on sleep from the previous night.

It was lost sleep or the sound of the truck engine in the cab that stopped them from hearing the noise outside; it was only when the first of the two rockets fired by the fighter slammed into the road ahead and its accomplice smashed into the forest to the right that the trio knew they had company.

The truck passed through the cloud of dust and debris thrown up by the first rocket, then hit the ridge of the crater left in the road by the explosion. The truck jumped to the left and began to twist in the air; even Pen's driving skills could not stop it entering the forest side on and smashing into the trees. Miraculously, the twisting of the truck resulted in all the force from the sudden stop being absorbed by the rear of the truck and not the cab. The twisting and turning had thrown Sokunthea and Sony onto Pen, who received most of the injuries incurred. Sokunthea and Sony fell out of the cab and scrambled into the forest; Pen didn't move. As the fighter passed overhead, assessing its kill, Sokunthea went back to the cab and pulled Pen out. Sokunthea laid him on the ground and began to drag him towards Sony, who had sat up and seemed to be regaining her senses.

'Help me pull him!' she shouted to Sony, and her friend responded. As Pen and the women reached the edge of the forest the fighter passed over again, this time dropping a smoke bomb near the truck. 'They're bringing in choppers,' she shouted to Sony.

Sony just lay back on the ground holding her knee; as Sokunthea went to her she noticed that it was dislocated and probably fractured also. She looked back at Pen and noticed the blood coming down his nose; fractured skull, she thought. She then began to hear the sound of the helicopters coming into the valley and knew this was the end of the trio. She quickly examined Pen and realised he couldn't move, then she went to Sony. 'You have a broken leg and a disjointed knee.'

'It hurts, it hurts bad.'

Sokunthea could hear the choppers getting closer. 'I've got to leave you.'

'No,' said Sony.

'I must; if they find me here, they'll kill us all, if it's just you and Pen you're fleeing Cambodians, they'll treat your leg.'

No, I can walk.' She tried to stand and fell back.

'I must go. Remember, you're fleeing from the fighting. Pen can't contradict you; in fact, I think he's dead. Stay alive, Sony, and I'll see you in Phnom Penh.' With that Sokunthea ran back to the truck, grabbed a handgun and AK-47 and vanished into the forest.

She decided to put distance between her and the crash and quickly moved through the forest; she didn't want to lose the road, as this was her only indicator as to the whereabouts of Moi. After moving for about two hours she decided to rest and strapping the gun to her back, she climbed a large tree and wedged herself against the trunk and a branch halfway up. She lay back and listened, then sat up and looked around; there was no sound, no movement. She stayed there for the rest of the day and climbed down in the early evening; she had decided to go back to the crash site to check that Sony had been transported out. She retraced her steps easily and as full darkness fell she saw the crashed truck ahead; she approached it slowly and quickly realised that the Vietnamese had moved on. They had taken Sony but left the body of Pen lying in the grass. Sokunthea decided to rest in the cab that night and, after completing a search of the truck for food or ammunition, she retired empty-handed.

The cab, although leaning heavily to one side, was more comfortable than the tree would have been. Sokunthea arranged the seats as best she could into a bed and began to doze. While sleeping she dreamed of the children, then Tiny and Kiry, and she pictured Sony being beaten by the mothers. The faces of Sinarth and Piseth appeared to taunt her. 'Why chase children when you can't have any?' they laughed at her. Then the death mask of her father appeared, 'Stop!' it shouted. Sokunthea sat upright, sweat pouring down her face; as she did the face of the tiger loomed in the side window. She screamed as the tiger clawed at the window, then she grabbed for her gun. The tiger must have sensed the futility of its attack and dropped down from the side of the cab. It walked over to Pen's body and began to drag it into the forest. Sokunthea sat still, shivering and staring into the blackness; she remained awake for the rest of the night and waited for full daylight before she departed the cab.

She travelled along the side of the track, still determined to find the original lost children; her dreams meant nothing to her, but the appearance of her father had shocked her. On the second night she came to rest at a group of three leaf built houses; all their original inhabitants had gone, and the land around had been cleared away for rice fields but nothing appeared to be growing. As she settled down in the smallest of the houses she could hear the thud of heavy artillery in the distance. 'Moi,' she said to herself, 'it must be.' She wondered if the children would be caught up in the fighting and reasoned that if the children were to be moved away then it would be to the west. She would start early tomorrow and arc westward, avoiding Moi but picking up any trail left by the children. The night was as dead as the huts she was resting in; only a cool breeze, which ran across the flat rice fields, would disturb her. There was no water for washing and only a few drops left in her canister; she would fill it as she moved on tomorrow.

Unable to sleep, she began her journey arcing to the west while it was still dark; the dawn rose as she crossed the tributary to the Stroeng Pouthisat again, filling her canister as she went. As the morning got underway so did the artillery barrage on Moi, which seemed to grow louder with every step. The countryside was beginning to change its shape; forest had been replaced by flat rice fields and occasional rice palms. More isolated houses began to appear, and some had signs of life with smoke coming from them. Sokunthea just kept looking for the road west; there had to be one or how else would they get the children out?

By early afternoon she approached a second tributary to the Stroeng Pouthisat and decided to move forward by its cool waters. As she came slowly round a bend she noticed civilians crossing the river ahead; she approached them quickly. 'Where are you going?' she asked. No one answered.

'Are you looking for your children?'

'Yes.' A young woman stepped forward.

'Where have they gone?'

'They said they were protecting them from the fighting...'

'Yes, yes, but where have they gone?'

'Samkos!' shouted one of the men.

'Samkos in the Cardamom mountains?'

'They said they would be safe there.'

'They said we all would be safe there,' came another voice.

Sokunthea had taken a group of students to Samkos when a lecturer at university; she knew how isolated and out of the way it was. 'How long ago did they go?'

'Yesterday, before the shelling.'

'By truck?'

'No, walking.'

Sokunthea began to wade across the water. 'What about the war?' she shouted back over her shoulder.

'We don't care,' came the reply, 'we want our children.'

She reached the other bank and began to jog; she would catch them up, they couldn't move fast with small kids and no transport. 'How clever,' she mumbled to herself, 'again and again I make the mistake of thinking the Rouge are stupid, but they ain't. How clever, the Viets think the war is over once they've got the cities but they keep it going in the hearts of the people. By the time they find their kids they'll be drilled into a new army, a guerrilla army, a twenty-year army.' She quickened her pace further.

By nightfall she had passed more groups on the road after their kids. All said the same: Samkos. Samkos is a mountain near the Thailand border; if defended properly it would take an army twice the size of the Viet's to overrun it. If anything was impregnable, Samkos was. The Rouge plan was becoming plain: pull everyone back to the high escarpments at the Thailand border, regroup and wait, then take the country back, piece by piece and the people who didn't join you in the escarpments were more scum to kill.

Sokunthea slept by the side of a small Buddhist roadside shrine, which some passing Rouge soldier had kicked in; she looked down at the small, smashed Buddha, the symbol of the peace and tranquillity of the nation and wondered if it would ever be the same again.

She began to check her weapon just as Sy had taught her; as she did she thought of him and tears ran down her face. As she wiped them away with her arm she noticed a small boy looking at her. At first Sokunthea thought she was seeing things and rubbed her eyes. The boy was still there standing behind the shrine and staring at her; he was about five years old.

'Come here, it's all right,' and she held out her hand. Then the boy pointed at her rifle. 'This, you want this?' The boy shook his head. 'You don't like this, you want me to put this away?'

He nodded.

Sokunthea laid the gun behind her and held out her hand again. The boy stepped forward and took it, Sokunthea pulled him close.

'Where have you come from?' she asked quietly and softly.

He pointed to behind the shrine.

'You hid there?'

He nodded.

'Have you any brothers or sisters behind there?'

'My sister.'

'Go get her.'

The boy departed and quickly returned with a small girl aged about three.

Sokunthea looked back down the track and noticed a fire made by some of the parents following. She took the children by the hand and walked them towards the fire. As she approached people began to speak out and several mothers came running forward to check the children. There had been a second fire further down the track and word had reached there that some children had been returned. Mothers came running forward out of the dark to inspect, then turn in tears back to where they had come from. Then an old lady approached; she looked and rushed back to the second fire shouting, 'They're here, they're here!' Soon a mother and grandfather had appeared to take the children in their arms and to cry tears of joy. Sokunthea left them to their delight and walked back to her resting place.

As Sokunthea prepared to depart the next morning the mother of the two children appeared and gave her a portion of rice soup and four bananas. 'This is all I can give,' she said.

'Thank you,' said Sokunthea, following protocol.

'I hope you too return to your family one day.' Sokunthea nodded.

The rice soup and bananas were eaten on foot, and all had gone by midday. Sokunthea was convinced that the children were near, she just had to keep going. The next night and the next she spent alone, camped next to the track. The land was beginning to rise again up into the Cardamom and she knew this would slow them down further. As the third day of tracking began to close Sokunthea thought that she saw, in the murky light, a group of people sitting next to the road. She left the road and detoured around the group. As she crept by she confirmed that they were children, young children with what looked like a teenage boy in charge. She completed a full one hundred and eighty degree inspection and finally observed a soldier sat under a tree some twenty yards from the road. She approached him from the rear and slid her knife under his chin.

'Don't move,' she whispered.

The soldier twitched. 'You're in trouble now, I'm a Rouge soldier.'

'And I'm terrified, so if you move I'll kill you.' He swallowed hard. She pressed the knife tighter around his throat. 'Where are all the others?'

'What others?'

'The soldiers.'

'Oh, they're coming back; you'd better get out of here or you're dead.'

'I don't think so, somehow.' She glanced around. 'Why are you resting here?'

'We're waiting for…'

'Don't give me that crap. One more time – why?'

'They can't walk, they're too young.'

'So you're leaving them here?'

'Their parents will be along by morning. Look, I could have gone with the others, I didn't have to stay and look after them.'

'Wow, a caring Rouge.'

'We're not all Rouge.'

'Where's your weapon?'

'The boy has it.'

'And I'm standing behind you,' came a youthful voice. Sokunthea froze. 'Put down the knife and raise your hands.' She did as she was told. 'Now stand slowly and turn around.'

She did; the boy immediately saw the rifle across her chest and the gun at her waist.

'You did well to spot me,' she said to the boy.

'Oh, it wasn't me; one of the children saw you, told me someone had gone to see Uncle Poul, so I investigated.'

'Get her to hand over her weapons,' said an anxious Poul.

'So why's Uncle Poul here and not pushing on with the kids?'

'It's the commander's idea, he thinks we have to keep the mothers motivated.'

'Motivated for what?'

'To keep walking, he thinks that if we're not careful they'll just pack up and go home so a small group of us hang around and the family catches up and find the kids, a sorrowful teenager and Uncle Poul, the children's friend. We then encourage them to go further, then on and on, clever, eh?'

'Brilliant, and who's the genius behind this?'

'Commander Thalin, of course.'

'Thalin? You'd better get me to him.'

'What?' The boy was taken aback. 'You know Thalin?'

'Yes, and I suggest that you tell him I'm here or you may find yourself joining the kids, not leading them.' She lowered her hands.

'Who are you?' asked Poul.

'I'm Commander Sokunthea, I was with Commander Thalin at Bokor.'

'That's right,' said the boy, 'Thalin always mentioned you when he talked about Bokor.'

'Tell him I'm here.'

'Yes, of course.' The boy began to show signs of being unsure. Sokunthea began to walk towards the children with growing confidence.

Poul turned to the boy. 'Stop her, she may be lying.'

But the boy was convinced and followed her. 'What was Bokor like?'

'Nothing compared to Kirirom,' she answered.

'Kirirom, you… wow, you must be that woman, the one they're after, wow.'

Poul rushed to catch them up. 'Take her weapons,' he said.

'Shut up, you old fool,' said the boy, 'this is a hero.'

Sokunthea marched on towards the kids. 'How do I get to Thalin?' she asked.

'I'll take you, he can look after the kids.'

'Come, let's go.'

Sokunthea and the boy began to jog along the track leading higher into the hills; they travelled all night and by dawn approached a small village. As they approached a sentry stopped them and on recognising the boy, let them forward. They entered the village and passed houses full of adults and children; Sokunthea guessed as many as one hundred had to be in and around the houses. The teenage boy led her to the end house and sat out on its balcony was Thalin. He looked down.

'Sokunthea, Sokunthea!' he shouted and came running to meet her; he grabbed her and hugged her tightly. 'What are you doing here?' he whispered in her ear.

'Looking for you, of course,' she whispered back.

He released her. 'Great to see you again, Commander, I hope you can join us for a while.'

'Thank you, Commander, I'd like to.'

'Let's go inside and stop this crap,' whispered Thalin. Sokunthea nodded. Thalin led Sokunthea to a small room and gestured for her to sit down. 'Now, why are you here?'

'To stop this theft of children.'

'It's orders, orders from the top.'

'I'm sure it is.'

'How did you get away from Bokor?'

'I ran, what about you?'

'I don't really want that escape to be spread around; after all, I'm a hero.'

'Good, so I won't mention your cowardice and you won't mention I'm a Seventeen of April scum.'

'Hm, I'm not sure I want you here.'

'Tough.'

'The Viets are after you, there's a price on your head; if they think you are with us they'll throw everything at us.'

'Don't tell them, I won't.'

'But the mothers may.'

'I thought you had a fool proof way of getting them to follow you.'

'The lost group routine and uncle Poul?' Sokunthea smirked at him.

'Okay, so it may not work, who knows? Look, they want the mothers at Samkos and we're almost there.'

'And then?'

'I disappear.'

'I thought that's what you tried to do at Bokor.'

'It was, but I ran into the hard-liners just outside of Kompong Som and they've been with me ever since.'

'Here?'

'Even here. Maybe I should introduce a hero of the Rouge. Come,' he stood and headed out of the room; Sokunthea followed.

'Where are we going?' she asked.

'To meet An Mok and his friends.' Thalin led her outside and towards a large building: as they approached she could hear chanting: 'Death to the Vietnamese, death to the counter revolutionaries, death to the traitors.'

That's us, thought Sokunthea while looking at Thalin. They entered the building; inside was a large group of teenagers sat on the floor and at the front were three men leading the chanting. They never stop, thought Sokunthea.

An elderly man came towards them. 'Thalin, what can I do for you?'

'An Mok, I would like to introduce to you Commander Sokunthea, the hero of Bokor and Kirirom, the one we all speak of and take inspiration from.'

An Mok beamed at Sokunthea and took her by the hand; he led her to the front of the class then raised his hand and the chanting stopped. 'My revolutionaries, here is one you all would wish to meet and to imitate: Commander Sokunthea, hero of Bokor and Kirirom.' The class burst into applause; An Mok raised his hand again and everything went quiet. 'She is a true model of what Ankor stands for and can achieve and, especially for you young women in the group, a beacon of female success.' The applause rang out again.

'I'm Seventeen of April scum, you bastard,' she said to herself through smiling teeth.

As the group broke up Sokunthea guessed that the age was about thirteen; she smiled and nodded as they passed her then Thalin took her by the elbow and led her to the top table. She sat with Thalin and the three men who had been carrying out the lecture.

'You are a very brave woman,' continued An Mok. 'How long will you be with us?'

'Not long,' cut in Thalin, 'she will advise me on security, then move on to fight the enemy.' They all smiled and nodded.

'Commander Thalin is engaged on the most important mission for the future of Ankor; any help that you can offer will be appreciated.' Sokunthea smiled. 'Now,' said An Mok, 'tell us about Kirirom.'

Sokunthea recounted the battle, overemphasising the exploits of the Rouge soldiers much to the delight of the audience. She then left with Thalin and returned to his house.

'You impressed them.'

'I wonder how they would have felt if they had known that the hero of Ankor was a Seventeen of April scum.'

'They'd have shot you. Drink?' Thalin pushed a cup of clear liquid towards her. She smelt it. 'Don't worry, it's not poison, it's palm wine'

'No, thanks, I'll take water.' He shouted and a young girl of about fourteen came in carrying a bowl of water. 'I see you still have your wives.'

'They're attracted to power, all you women are attracted to power.'

'Rubbish.'

'It's true, look at you; Piseth, Thai, Van Serun, me.' She threw the water and the bowl at him. 'Okay, okay, maybe I was attracted to your power, still am.'

'Well, forget it, I'm not attracted to yours.'

'Hey, we'd make a great team; get the radio and the money, when this lot is over that money will buy half of Cambodia.'

'Forget it.'

'Why? I know what you're like already.' She glared at him and looked around for something else to throw, finally deciding to pull her gun. 'Okay, okay, I surrender.'

'Just keep your mouth shut about what you did to me.'

'Fine, fine.'

She looked hard at him. 'You didn't think about the money when you ran at Bokor.'

'Oh, I did, but to collect it I needed to keep alive.'

'And me?'

'Oh, you're a survivor, I knew you'd be all right.'

'You won't be able to run from Samkos, not with the big boys watching you.'

'I know, that's why I plan to go early.'

'Well, you'd better make it quick, because you've only four days and we're there.'

He walked over and sat opposite her. 'Why are you after the kids?'

'I made a friend a promise and I remember the last exodus you people arranged.'

'This is not the same, they need these kids for the future.'

'To fight, on you mean.'

'That's the only future the Rouge has; think Rouge or die Rouge, Ankor demands total obedience.'

'Well, not from me and not from a growing number of its previous followers.'

Thalin poured more wine and looked down to the floor. 'If this plan works and Ankor survives and returns, they'll change again.'

'More reason to stop this plan.'

'Look,' Thalin began to raise his voice, 'you've met La, the teenager who brought you here; fifteen years old and he's already killed. He's willing to die for Ankor just like the past; the school, those chanting kids aged twelve to sixteen, all wanting to die for Ankor; the plan's already happening.'

'Then think of this: if the plan works you can forget your million dollars, you can forget your plan, understand?'

Thalin stared at her, then continued softly. 'I've thought of that and I'm edging my bets; at the moment I'm the great hero, a commander, if we win I'm set up for life, a warlord amongst the peasants. If not, I go for the money.'

'Not if they get you for war crimes.'

Thalin leaned forwards again, engaging Sokunthea in eye contact. 'Nobody does that; who's going to do that? Every major country in the world has had their dirty fingers in this pile, who's going to own up to that?' He took another drink. The room fell quiet and the young girl returned, bringing more water and wine.

'Thank you,' said Sokunthea, taking the water. 'Where are you from?' she asked the girl.

She looked at Thalin who nodded. 'Kompong Speo.'

'Are your parents alive?' The girl stared at Sokunthea, then burst into tears and ran out.

'They're not all brainwashed,' she said turning to Thalin.

'They'll kill her,' he gestured to the outside. 'Why do you think she's here? If I left her to them she'd be dead by now.'

'Thalin, the killer of Tuk Meas, cares.'

'Shut up.' He drank again. 'Tuk Meas was like nothing on earth.'

'I know, I was there, remember?'

'Oh, I remember, I remember your husband trying to get you killed, I remember the educators who were going to have you killed until I dumped one into a crab hole and poisoned the other. You remember, you remember nothing.' He stood and walked over to the only window in the room and began to take in deep breaths. Sokunthea looked at him; he had lost weight since Bokor and seemed to have developed a fine tremor in the hands. Firelight flickered through the window and danced across his face and with the wine inflaming his facial scar he looked like a man fighting an internal rage.

'Okay, so I don't know everything about Tuk Meas,' she said calmly, 'and maybe all the deaths cloud my thinking but what happened there was wrong and what is happening here is wrong also.'

'Wrong, right, right, wrong; who cares? In Cambodia only power is important. Understand it, work with it and survive.'

'The power to kill.'

'No, no,' he turned from the window and regained his seat. 'The power to kill and get away with it, the power to kill, not one, but millions and get away with it, that power fixes the mind of the nation into total fear and total obedience.' He drank again. 'Maybe the Vietnamese can break that in time,' he continued, 'but I can't; those chanting kids, all but a few do it because they are terrified of the consequences if they don't. That's power and I'm drunk; go find a room somewhere in the house, there's plenty spare. I'll sober up here.' He stretched out in the chair and closed his eyes. Sokunthea stood and headed for the door.

'We'd still make a great team,' Thalin called out as she left, 'a great team.'

Sokunthea decided to take the opportunity to explore the village. As she walked down its main track she was approached by La, the teenager who had escorted her there.

'So you are the hero,' he said excitedly.

'So they say,' replied Sokunthea.

'May I show you around the village?'

'Sure.'

The boy guided her through the village, pointing out the houses for the children and the houses for the adults. 'We can't mix them, of course,' he stressed, 'they don't understand,' and he pointed to the adults' houses.

'Are your parents here?' she asked of him.

'No, they're dead, fighting for Ankor.'

'Oh, where did they die?'

He looked at her then ahead. 'I don't know, Ankor never says.'

'So they could be alive?'

'No,' he said emphatically, 'if Ankor says they're dead, they're dead.'

As they walked on the sound of human activity became louder; people appeared to be gathering near one of the houses.

'Oh, it's a beating. Great, come on,' and he grabbed Sokunthea by the arm and led her to the crowd. When they arrived they saw, kneeling on the ground in the middle of a chanting circle of mainly children, a woman. In front of her was a teenage girl of about fourteen; the girl was beating the woman with a bamboo stick across the shoulders and head. Blood was already trickling down the sides of the woman's head; the girl was in tears. As each blow struck the crowd cheered more and more.

'What is happening?' Sokunthea asked La.

'She's denouncing her mother.'

'What?'

'Denouncing her, after this she will be free, free from her parents.'

'But she's in distress.'

'No, no, they are the tears of joy, she is joining Ankor.'

'And the mother?'

'It is too late for her.'

Sokunthea marched into the centre of the circle and removed the cane from the girl; the chanting stopped. She looked around the group. 'I am Commander Sokunthea of Bokor and Kirirom,' she shouted, 'and when I fight I fight for all Cambodians, young and old, mothers and daughters, fathers and sons. If Ankor is to survive it will need all its mothers, all its children. Now go back to your houses.' She threw the cane to the floor. The crowd began to disperse slowly and Sokunthea reached down and helped the woman to her feet. 'Where is your house?' she asked. The woman led her to her house, which was full of women; Ankor did not allow the mixture of sexes or ages, and she remembered Tuk Meas. 'Take care of her,' she said to the startled women inside.

As she began to walk back to Thalin's house La appeared. 'The educators won't like that, it was a bad thing to do.'

'Beating a defenceless woman is a bad thing to do.'

'Ankor demands it, you must be pure.'

'Who decides if you're pure?'

'Ankor, of course.'

'And where was Ankor when the woman was being beaten?'

'The girl decided; her mother was talking against Ankor.'

'So the girl decided her mother should be beaten not Ankor. The girl is more Ankor than me?' she asked, raising her voice; she stopped and looked at the boy.

'No, no, of course not.'

'Then I stopped the beating because it was not pure and it was against Ankor's wishes.'

'Yes, yes, the girl should be punished.'

'You leave her punishment to me.'

'Yes, of course.'

Sokunthea entered Thalin's house. She passed the small downstairs room where Thalin was still sleeping and removed a candle that was almost burnt out. She climbed the stairs to find her own place to rest, stumbling into a room which had a small mattress on the floor, combat fatigues and weapons scattered around.

'Thalin's,' she said to herself, 'why not?' She removed her own weapons and sat on the mattress putting the rapidly diminishing candle onto the floor. She noticed a bottle and removed its cap and sniffed; it was water, and she took a long drink. There'll be trouble tomorrow, she thought reflecting on the night's events.

The candle cut out and she lay on the mattress in the dark drinking more water. She thought of the possible events tomorrow: explaining to the educators, then how she might get some of the families out; she decided the likes of La were past saving. The heat in the room was increasing and the cells in her whole body appeared to decide simultaneously to cascade sweat. She stood and opened the window, hoping for some breeze, and as she looked out across a moonlit area behind the house she saw a small group of people huddled together below a tree. Then she realised in the tree was someone hanging. 'Hanging?' she said to herself and she began to run out of her room, stumbling down the stairs and out to the rear of the house.

She charged at the small gathering screaming and they, seeing her, dispersed quickly, but not quickly enough – Sokunthea recognised La. She got to the tree and hanging there was the young girl Sokunthea had stopped administering the punishment earlier. She scrambled up the tree and cut her loose. As the body hit the floor Sokunthea had dropped down beside it; she pulled the noose away and felt for a pulse, but there was nothing; she struck the girl on the chest and began cardiac massage. 'Wake up, wake up!' she cursed.

After several minutes it was clear that the girl was dead; Sokunthea picked her up and carried her into Thalin's house and placed her in the lower room next to him. She checked her pulse again for the final time then sank down into a chair. 'The new Ankor,' she mumbled to herself.

Near to dawn Thalin began to stir from his sleep; Sokunthea, who had been dozing, woke also and both could smell the body of the girl.

'What the hell?' Thalin pulled away as he noticed the body.

'It's a present from the new Ankor,' Sokunthea mumbled at him.

'Well, get it out of here!' he shouted out and two half-asleep soldiers came rushing. Thalin pointed to the body and they removed it.

'Where the hell did it come from?'

'I brought it.'

'Why?'

'To show you how crazy the new lot are.'

'Okay, how did she die?'

'Her classmates hanged her.'

'Sure she didn't do it herself?'

'I'm sure.'

'We'll see what the educators think.' As he spoke a teenager entered the room and whispered to Thalin. 'They want us.' All three left the room and walked over to the school building; as they entered Sokunthea noticed La leaving by the rear.

'Come sit,' called An Mok, 'we have a sad event; one of our students has ended her own life and you may have had something to do with it,' he looked at Sokunthea.

'How?' cut in Thalin.

'Commander Sokunthea interrupted her scolding duty; it seems she then felt she was unworthy to be a full Rouge student.'

Thalin looked across at Sokunthea. 'I'm sure whatever Commander Sokunthea did, she did what she thought was best.'

An Mok smiled and nodded. 'We are not challenging a hero of Ankor here; the girl's death is of no importance. No, we just wish to press on you Commander, that we must begin to move on to Samkos. There is no point in waiting any more, what we have we take.'

Thalin nodded his agreement. 'I will send some of my men back down the trail to see if we have snared any from our last ploy; the rest will prepare to move. We can start tomorrow.'

'Good, that is good news, Commander.' Thalin and Sokunthea began to leave. 'Oh,' called out An Mok, 'please tell Commander Sokunthea that we appreciate that she has been out fighting alone for a long while but that in future she will not interfere with the rituals of Ankor.'

Sokunthea was about to turn and reply as Thalin grabbed her arm and walked her out of the building. 'Why did you do that?' she said once outside.

'Because you would have said something to upset him.'

'You're too right I would.'

'He let you off, so let it go. What was this ritual he was on about, anyway?'

'Mother-beating.'

'What?'

'Mother-beating.'

'Oh, that.'

They returned to Thalin's house and sat in the small sitting-room. 'So you're moving out,' said Sokunthea.

'I've no choice, I've sat here for a week.'

'How do you plan to get there?'

'Well, I could go straight up but once on top we're open to

fighters and choppers; they'll want me to go that way, of course.'

'And the other?'

'Stay in the valley; plenty of cover, food and, of course, water from the Stroeng Pouthisat.'

'Of course; I remember that beautiful river, you can get shallow boats down it and it runs right into Pursat.'

'Don't tell An Mok that; he'll surely opt for the high ground if he knows that.'

'Why?'

'The Vietnamese have Pursat and what comes down the river can come up.'

'We have to stick to the valley; tell An Mok it's easier, safer and that you could pick up more people fleeing the vile Vietnamese who are in Pursat, that should massage his ego. I'll agree with you, of course.'

'Of course.' Thalin stood and removed some maps from a desk. 'These aren't very good, they're from Lon Nol's days. The Rouge destroyed all the maps, said they were propaganda. Can you believe it? We're being overrun by a country with better maps of Cambodia than the Cambodians.'

'These will do; we'll keep to the main Pouthisat valley to where it forks at Pream Prus, there used to be a small fishing village there and that's where I'll get off.'

'Me too.'

'Okay, but I intend to take as many kids as I can.'

'Sure.'

'You'd better go and tell their majesties of your plan.'

Thalin left and Sokunthea decided to find La; she walked around the village looking out for teenagers congregating together but La was nowhere to be found. While making her way back to the house she encountered Thalin's young housekeeper.

'Are you lost?' she asked.

'No, just looking for someone.'

'La?'

'How do you know?'

'Everybody knows.'

'Where is he?'

'At the school, he always crawls around them when he's done

something wrong.'

'Them?'

'The masters; they think he's wonderful, they even let him kill…' she began to cry.

'Come, sit down.'

'He killed my mother,' she sobbed.

'What?'

'He said I wasn't beating her hard enough, took the cane from me and started hitting her hard all over the head and face.'

'So, he likes to kill old women and young girls.'

The housekeeper nodded. 'Nobody really likes him except the masters.'

'Why don't you leave here?'

'To where? I don't know this country.'

'If you could escape would you try?'

'Yes.'

'Come, let's go back to the house.' She led the housekeeper back to Thalin's house. Thalin was sitting in his room smiling.

'They bought it, you were right; the thought of maybe netting more unfortunates was too good to resist.'

'Okay, when we start tomorrow I want to go with the forward recon team, I'll need to develop a clearer plan than the one we presently have.'

'Fine, they'll agree to that.'

'Make the team small, maybe two others, and pick a couple of dumb ones – I don't want them asking where have I been or wanting to come with me.'

'Sure, I know the ones already.'

'Good, then all we need is some food and a good night's sleep and Pursat here we come.'

'I'll get the cook to work.'

Sokunthea sat back in her chair and began to doze; she needed to catch up on several nights' sleep and if she was to achieve her plan over the next few days she needed rest. Thalin returned after an hour and entered the room followed by the housekeeper. 'Let's eat,' he said. The food consisted of rice soup and one boiled egg; Sokunthea thought, If the élite are getting this, what are the others eating?

'Short of food?' asked Sokunthea.

'Isn't Ankor always short of food?'

'How will it feed everyone at Samkos?'

'Buy it from the Thais.'

'And they'll supply it?'

'Of course; it's business, you never seem to learn.'

'Maybe I find the intricacies of the main players too unbelievable.'

'Look, one last time; the Viets want a greater Vietnam, the Chinese will do anything to stop that because it will expose the atrocities that they have been contributing to over the years; the Rouge retreat to Thailand, Vietnam won't follow all the way because they don't want a war with Thailand. The Thais benefit from taking in refugees and raking in all the aid money, they benefit from selling arms and food and anything to the Rouge that the Rouge want. In the end the Viets get bored and go and…'

'Who fills the gap?'

'The people with money, you and me.'

'You make it all sound so… so inhuman, people die in this business of yours.'

'Yes, they do, so be careful; I still don't know where this radio and money of yours is, sure you don't want to tell me before you depart tomorrow?' Sokunthea glared at him, then they both began to laugh.

By late afternoon the team dispatched to find if Uncle Poul had returned; they had encountered a small force of Vietnamese soldiers working their way slowly up the track. Poul and the children had vanished.

An Mok summoned the commanders to his quarters. 'We must go, immediately,' he said.

'If we set off now, in the dark, we could lose some of the people,' advised Thalin.

Sokunthea realised the opportunity. 'But if we stay and the Viets come we could lose all,' she winked at Thalin.

'Yes, yes, she's right,' said An Mok, 'we must go tonight – we could rope the people together, that would stop them escaping.'

'Good idea,' cut in Sokunthea, 'I will arrange it.' She stood and left. Thalin looked at her in disbelief.

'Come on, Commander,' said An Mok to Thalin, 'we have to go.'

As Thalin and An Mok got outside the mothers and children were being lined up in four columns. Soldiers had begun to tie the people together and Sokunthea was concentrating her efforts on a long line of women with small children.

'Do we want the women with their children?' inquired An Mok.

'We have to have people who can generate a similar pace,' said Sokunthea, 'otherwise we'll all slow down and speed is essential.'

'Yes, yes, of course, speed.' An Mok turned to Thalin, nodding.

'I'll help you,' said Thalin and walked over to the column. 'What are you up too?' he whispered.

'Just you concentrate on leading the columns.'

'Don't do anything stupid.'

'I won't; how many men are in the rearguard?'

'None, I brought them all in.'

'Good, keep it that way.'

'Don't you think the mothers with their children may stop?' asked An Mok.

Sokunthea looked down the bustling road. 'No; anyway, we should put someone in charge who would keep them going, like La.'

'Great idea,' responded An Mok.

After a few more hours of collecting documents and further equipment to take along, the columns were ready to leave. Sokunthea had retrieved her rifle and handgun from Thalin's quarters and returned to the road.

'Come, it is time to leave,' shouted An Mok.

Then, as the columns began to move, Sokunthea stepped forward and began to inspect the ropes around the mother's group. She mimicked the tying and retying of several knots which delayed the group's departure till last. She finally agreed for them to depart and walked over to Thalin and An Mok.

'I will go and check what the Viets are up to; I should have something to report by morning.'

'Excellent,' said An Mok and as Sokunthea disappeared back

down the road, he added, 'a great fighter for Ankor, a great hero.'

'Yes,' said Thalin.

Sokunthea had chosen her group well; mixed amongst the mothers and children were a group of elderly women who began to slow the group down further. This began to irritate La and he began to beat the members of the column with his bamboo cane. Thalin had agreed with Sokunthea to leave only one soldier to help La move things along and with every step La became more aggrieved.

'I should be up front with the masters,' he kept saying to himself, 'my group should have been the best, not these idle sods. Come on, speed up!' he shouted back at the slow-moving column. 'Where's that idle sergeant, as well?' he continued to say.

He turned and looked down the column and realised it was spread out further than usual. 'What is that idle sergeant doing?'

He walked back down the column striking several mothers and children. 'Speed up!' he shouted. When he reached the rear of the column, his eyes fell on the group of elderly women who were slowing everything down. 'Speed up, speed up, you old cows!' He began to beat them harshly with his cane; the noise of his cane striking the old women and their cries were just enough to mask Sokunthea's move. Her knife passed below La's chin and she slit his throat; he sagged to the floor and she twisted him around and dropped him amongst some trees.

'He won't kill any more women,' she said to herself. Sokunthea quickly ran up the column cutting the ropes that tied the people together, then formed them into a group. 'Go back to the village; the Vietnamese will not hurt you, so go back there and wait for them.' The mothers needed no persuading. As they walked back they passed the body of La and threw stones at him; later they passed the body of the sergeant, too, who had suffered the same fate as La.

Sokunthea travelled quickly through the night and found the rest of the column resting by the side of the first Pouthisat tributary. She approached the group quickly, acknowledging a sentry then moving on to find Thalin. The camp began to stir as she approached and Thalin and An Mok were waiting.

'What's the news?' asked An Mok.

'Not good; the Viets have overrun the last group and are about a half day behind us.'

'What now?' he asked again.

'I know this country,' said Sokunthea, 'I think we should go to Pream Prus.'

'Where is that?' asked a startled An Mok.

'Due north.'

'But Samkos is west.'

'I know, sir,' said Sokunthea. 'But the problem is the enemy knows that too by now. We have to outsmart them; they will never expect us to go north. We can head there then swing west, outflank them.'

'I'm not so sure,' said An Mok. 'What do you think about it, Commander?' He looked at Thalin.

'Commander Sokunthea knows this area, sir, and she knows the Viets better than anyone; I think we should follow her plan.'

'Okay, commander, but I want you near me; if problems arise I'll need your protection.' Sokunthea smiled at Thalin.

The journey north was uneventful; Sokunthea had managed to obtain her release from An Mok by volunteering to scout ahead. Her plan was to get the group to Pream Prus and hope enough boats were there to get as many as possible down the river to Pursat.

She was still not sure how Thalin would perform when the time came to escape or if he'd join her or not; for the first time her faith lay in the radio. When she returned to the main group on the first night her desire to escape was reinforced; lying on the edge of the camp were the bodies of two women, both elderly – the old Rouge was still at work.

Sokunthea entered the camp and went in search of Thalin whom she found sitting with his housekeeper.

'Had fun?' she said, slamming down her rifle then squatting next to him.

'I'll not bore you with the old excuse.'

'Don't tell me, too slow.'

'We lost some today, even some of the teenagers; that shocked An Mok so the punishments are back. Get some food for the commander,' he said to his housekeeper.

'We have food?'

'Well, old rice.'

'Never mind, I have eggs.' She pulled from her tunic six small birds' eggs. 'Benefits of recon.'

'Commander Sokunthea.' She turned and noticed An Mok and his two assistants coming towards her. 'What do you have to report?' he continued.

She looked at Thalin then stood to greet them. 'The Vietnamese are to our west, certainly in search of us; I also believe they are in Pursat.'

'So, we are in the middle.'

'Yes; when we get to Pream Prus we'll turn west then south into Samkos, the Viets won't expect anyone coming south.'

'But will we make it, Commander? As you may have noticed, there are traitors amongst us.'

'I'm shocked to hear that, sir,' said Sokunthea dutifully, 'but I'm sure you know how to deal with them.'

'Yes, yes, of course,' said a righteous An Mok, 'but if the Vietnamese are on both sides of us won't they cut us off?' Thalin coughed and looked across the camp.

'Yes,' said Sokunthea.

'Wh… well!' blurted out An Mok.

'The Vietnamese expect to catch us on the way to Samkos,' she continued.

'Yes.'

'But they must think that either they have overtaken us, and if so they'll wait for ambush, or they think we are stupid Cambodians who are lost.'

'Yes, yes, but how do we get away from them and into Samkos?'

'Diversion,' said Sokunthea.

'Diversion.' An Mok looked at his colleagues and gave a knowing nod.

'The Stroeng Pouthisat river divides near Pream Prus; as you and the group push on I and Commander Thalin's men will set off a diversion at the southern divide. This will attract the enemy to us from both sides while you lead the group south into Samkos.'

'A brilliant plan; did you hear this Commander Thalin?'

'Yes, sir, Commander Sokunthea and I were discussing it as you approached.'

'When do we start?' An Mok turned to Sokunthea.

'Tomorrow; me and Commander Thalin's men go straight north, you and the group go north-east; when you get to Pream Prus wait one night then go south.'

'Why wait?'

'It will give us time to draw all the enemy into the diversion; we can't have you walking into a slow patrol.'

'No, of course not,' he smiled. 'Hah, I see your food has arrived; I will leave you to rest, Commander, and we start tomorrow.'

Sokunthea sat on the floor. 'Asshole.'

'What's that?' asked a startled Thalin.

'It's a word I heard used by the Red Cross staff in Phnom Penh.'

'What's it mean?'

'I have no idea,' Thalin began to laugh, 'but I do know it's bad.' She laughed too.

'Do you think of Phnom Penh often?'

'Sometimes, more of late.'

'And your husband?'

'No, never.'

'Your husband would have had you killed in Tuk Meas.'

'I don't want to know.'

'It's true; we had to kill him.'

Sokunthea slid the bowl of hot rice towards her and pressed her birds' eggs deeply into it. 'Many people have died over these past five years; I've killed some but who decides that they deserved it?' She looked at Thalin.

'What's your plan?' asked Thalin while staring at her food.

'How many men do you have?'

'Eighteen.'

'Where…'

'I know, that's the problem; it's not just the mothers wanting out. An Mok blames me, says I should discipline them; he doesn't understand that even the soldiers have had enough.'

'How many have you lost?'

'Ten over the past two days.'

'Shhh… good, the fewer the better.' Sokunthea reached down and pulled out one of the now boiled eggs. 'Keep your good ones with An Mok; he'll agree to that if it's for his protection,' continued Sokunthea.

'Best you tell him, he's losing faith in me.'

'Hmm… you'd better stay with him too, then, otherwise he may worry our diversion will become a mass escape.' She swallowed the yolk of the egg and began to eat the shell. 'I'll take half with me; if you think there's some potential deserters send them with me.' She ate a second egg. She looked at Thalin. 'What's wrong with you?'

'That's my food; I saved it for you.'

'Hmmm, okay.' She removed the remaining eggs and cracked them over the rice, mixing it all together. 'Tuck in.'

'Another Phnom Penh word?'

'Sure.'

They finished the meal in silence; Thalin went to arrange a general meeting of the educators and his remaining men before returning to Sokunthea who was asleep.

'Wake up.' He shook her gently.

She climbed onto one elbow. 'They ready?'

'Yes.' They walked over to the meeting place where Sokunthea outlined her plan.

'So to recap,' said An Mok, 'you and nine men will set off explosions and such which will attract the enemy while we wait at Pream Prus and then we all go to Samkos.'

'Yes,' cut in Thalin.

'Everyone agree?' said Sokunthea. They all nodded. 'I will lead my team out one hour after the group has started for Pream Prus.'

The meeting broke up and Sokunthea and Thalin wandered back to their rest area. 'I've given you the best,' Thalin said.

'What, I thought…'

'The best deserters,' he chuckled.

'How many will run, do you think?'

'About five.'

'Good.'

Sokunthea spent the rest of the evening checking her weapons and wondering how many she might have to kill. Thalin had departed on an inspection of his sentries before the night closed in and returned with the news that they had lost one already.

'I don't know if it's the possibility of meeting the Viets tomorrow or going to Samkos, but I'm losing men like water in a bucket full of holes.'

'What is at Samkos anyway?' asked Sokunthea.

'I don't know.'

'Does An Mok know?'

'I don't think so.'

'So why go?'

'Orders.'

'I went to Samkos when I taught at university; it's just a mountain and a few huts.'

'Impregnable though, they say.'

'Maybe, but not a place to start a comeback, and when you get there where's the food?'

'Ankor will provide,' they both said together and laughed.

'Oh, we'd make a good team,' said Thalin.

'Don't start that again.'

'Okay.'

'Remember to keep the group at Pream Prus for the night; I have to have time to reach you.'

'Then what?'

'You may have to decide which side you're on and if we really do make a good team.'

The group had set off early the following morning, much to the insistence of An Mok. Sokunthea was left behind with her small party, which had fallen in numbers due to the desertion of the previous night and An Mok's insistence that he needed extra guards; these changes left Sokunthea with three. She began to assess her comrades as they prepared their weapons and explosives and concluded that two would desert while the third was loyal. The four set off with Sokunthea setting a fast pace; within an hour Sokunthea's assessment appeared to be coming true; one soldier had disappeared already while a second was lagging far behind. The soldier Sokunthea had assessed as loyal to the cause had maintained her pace, measuring her stride for stride. By mid-morning she called a halt and sat below a large tree.

'Come, sit,' she said to her companion.

He came over and sat. 'I can't see the others,' he said.

'Maybe gone.'

'Traitors.'

'What's your name?'

'Sen.'

'Well, Sen, it looks like just you and me.'

'Huh, we don't need them.'

'Have you been with An Mok long?'

'No, they picked me up as I fled Kirirom.'

'You were at Kirirom?'

'Yes, before you came, of course.'

'How did you escape?'

'Just ran, we were caught out by the collaborators.'

'Who?'

'Collaborators, Cambodians fighting for the Vietnamese; they walked in, out of the forest, they were even dressed in our uniforms, so we relaxed, our mistake. Then the Viets came in their helicopters; they were all mates together, praising each other talking about co-operation. I managed to escape, then ran.'

'Straight into An Mok.'

'Yes.'

'Were there any Bokor soldiers there?'

'No, they'd moved on.'

Sokunthea looked down the track to see if any stragglers were coming. 'I think we had better move; it'll soon be noon.'

'And the others?'

'We can't wait.'

'Cowards.'

The fast pace was maintained by Sokunthea who kept thinking about how she would dispose of her companion; she had decided not to kill him, she had killed enough. Yet every kilometre they travelled meant that she had to finalise her plan; as the heat of the day intensified she called a second halt.

'Okay, let me outline the plan.' Sen nodded and sat next to her. 'We want to attract the enemy to this area of the forest and I believe there are two groups. The first is between us and Samkos, the second is patrolling the Pouthisat, all right?' He nodded. 'We don't want the Viets to the west blocking An Mok from getting to Samkos, or the Viets to the east blocking the river and attacking An Mok from the rear.'

'Yes, yes.'

'When we get to the second tributary of the Pouthisat we will start to plant the explosives; the fuses must be lit so we will detonate them first, then we'll release a few hand grenades and shoot the place up, got it?'

'Yes.'

'The tributary is about an hour away; we'll have a short rest here then start the action around two.' They both settled back in the cover of the trees and Sokunthea began to snooze.

'They wanted you in Kirirom,' said Sen quietly.

'I know.'

'They offered money, freedom, for anyone who handed you in.'

She rolled over and looked at him; the barrel of his pistol was pointed at her head. She rolled back and stared at the sky through the leaves. 'What now?'

'I've been thinking about that; we have our diversion and we wait for the Viets.'

'And An Mok?'

'I'll throw him in for extras; now, slide your pistol out very slowly and place it on the ground between us.'

Sokunthea obeyed. 'The only way you'll get paid is with a bullet,' she said.

'Now the combat knife. They'll honour it; they had a high-ranking officer at Kirirom, he'll honour it.'

'He's dead.'

'Don't lie. Roll onto your stomach and place your hands behind you.'

'I'm not lying, I killed him.'

'Then your price will have gone up.' He tied Sokunthea's wrists to her ankles using their belts; he then dragged her closer to a tree and tied the fuse wire first round the tree, then around her neck. He stood and looked at his work. 'That will hold you.' He began to collect both sets of hand grenades and his weapons, then he reached down and squeezed her left breast. 'I'll be back.'

Sokunthea lay still, wondering how she could have been so stupid. 'Why would someone volunteer to come with me at the last minute? I should have guessed.' She began to feel the knot tied by Sen around her wrists; he'd done a good job. 'To untie those with my fingertips would take ages; damn,' she said out loud. She began to relax and tried to clear her thoughts; the strain of keeping her head close to the tree to avoid strangulation and her wrists and hands close together began to drain her strength.

'You stupid cow!' she shouted again, 'stupid, stupid, stupid!' She began to cry. 'Stop, stop, tears are no good; think, how the hell do I get out of... the boots, my boots!'

Sokunthea realised that in his rush Sen had tied the belts around the tops of her boots, not her ankles; if she could slide the boots off she may get free. Her fingers began to search for her laces and quickly she had untied them. She then began to loosen them, trying to pull them out from the boot. As she tugged and twisted her body to loosen the boot as much as possible the wire bit deeper into her neck, but she didn't care; the boots were the priority.

The laces finally fell to the ground and, grabbing the belts tightly at the wrist, she began to force her feet backwards. At first there was no movement; the belts held the boots firm but as she pushed harder and the wire bit deeper into her neck they began to slide. She rested, taking in deep breaths and, readjusting her position in relation to the tree to which her neck was tied, she pushed again. 'Aargh, aargh! This must be like having a baby,' she said, through closed teeth. Then, with one big push, they were off. The tension in the knots around her wrists slackened and she had soon removed them, then her neck was free. She spun into a sitting position, rubbing her neck, and discovered it was bleeding. Sen had departed, leaving behind her rifle, pistol and knife. She picked them up, while scanning the surrounding forest; nothing was moving. She checked them quickly – they were usable. 'Right,' she said and began to follow Sen.

She had only travelled a kilometre when she noticed the first set of explosives pushed under some tree roots; Sen had decided not to go too far to attract his paymasters. Sokunthea left the narrow track which she was travelling down and slowly moved through the forest. She knew Sen was close as she began to smell the smoke from a cigarette; she crouched down and looked through the undergrowth. As she did, Sen's head and shoulders appeared some twenty yards in front of her; she quickly levelled her rifle and fired. Her target disappeared but it was unclear if she had hit him, so she maintained her cover and began to circle. As she moved around the target area she saw Sen laid on his front; she approached him slowly watching for any movement. Then she noticed the burning fuse wire disappearing under his body; she turned and ran, then threw herself behind a fallen tree as the explosion occurred. Others followed the main explosion as the hand grenades that Sen was carrying all began to explode; bullets began to fire from his ammunition belt and part of the forest caught fire. What a diversion, thought Sokunthea as she began to crawl away.

She made her way north then west heading for Pream Prus; if her plan was to work the Viets would have to leave the Stroeng Pouthisat, giving her the chance to move some of the mothers and children by boat to Pursat. She realised that with Sen's intervention the diversion had gone off earlier than planned and was several kilometres short of its target, but it was too late to change now.

She reached Pream Prus by late afternoon and decided to go around it and enter it from the north; the village seemed strangely quiet, although smoke could be seen coming from several buildings. When she had completed her full sweep of the village she approached her destination from the river, noticing several boats as she came. Good, she thought.

She began to push several on to the water, testing that they wouldn't sink, then resecuring them on dry land. As she tested the last boat An Mok stepped out from the edge of the forest. 'Traitor,' he shouted, raised a pistol and fired.

Sokunthea felt a lightening pain shoot down her right arm as she fell backwards into the boat; the force of her body's entry into the boat launched it away from the bank. When she woke it was daylight and she was being carried; she stared into the blue sky as her carriers talked quickly in Vietnamese, then she lost consciousness again. She regained it as water was being splashed onto her face and she realised she was lying below a tree. Squatting next to her was a man dressed in green who spoke in Vietnamese: 'Wake up, are you her?'

Sokunthea's awareness began to improve and she focused on her questioner, who appeared to be dressing her arm and side.

'Where are you from?' he asked again, 'and are you her?'

Sokunthea decided to play dumb and she lay still, letting the soldier do his work; she closed her eyes as the soldier asked more questions then felt the injection enter her left arm. She began to regain consciousness again, realising she was now travelling in a speedboat; around her were several soldiers. Her previous questioner was looking down at her. 'She's awake,' he called out. A second soldier's head came into her field of vision.

'Wake up, Commander,' came a voice, 'you're on your way to Pursat.'

Sokunthea lay still; she was going to show no sign of understanding Vietnamese. She closed her eyes and listened.

'Will we get the reward?' said one voice.

'If it's her, they must pay it to us,' said the other.

'But we don't know.'

'Only Noug knew and she killed him.'

'What about Ng?'

'Maybe, they're bringing him up from Kompong Speu to identify her.'

'Can't we pay him to say yes, then we all make money?'

'Ng, are you crazy? You offer him a bribe and he'll kill you.'

'So what if he says no.'

'Then we go back to searching for her.'

'It's her, it's got to be her.' The conversation stopped and Sokunthea began to doze with the sound of the engine and the rise and fall of the boat.

When she woke from her sleep she was again being carried, this time up some waterside steps, and was then placed into the back of a truck. Her two conversationalists joined her.

'What will you do with the money?'

'It will buy my family a small rice farm back home.'

'I'd use it to go back to university, try to become a doctor.'

'What about her?'

'Don't know, kill her I suppose.'

'But if she's not?'

'Look, I've been thinking; even if she's not it's good to say she is. I have a friend who works at command headquarters who told me they're going crazy because they can't catch this commander; the people in Phnom Penh are screaming at them every day to come up with her. They're not going to take the chance; she's dead meat whether she is or not.'

'And Ng?'

'Someone will tell him what to say.'

'Hey, this could make us heroes.'

'Heroes, hah hah hah.'

The truck stopped and Sokunthea was carried into a building and felt herself lifted into a bed, then hands appeared and began to undress her. She grabbed the hands, opened her eyes and sat up quickly. The two Vietnamese nurses were startled and stood back. 'We get you ready for doctor,' said one in broken Cambodian.

Sokunthea stared at her, then lay down; the nurses did their duty quickly and painlessly and as the covers were put over her two doctors and two officers entered the room. The doctors approached her bed. 'Do you speak Vietnamese?' asked one. Sokunthea did not respond.

'You stay here,' said the doctor to the nurse, 'tell her I am going to examine her.'

'The doctor will have you,' the nurse translated. Sokunthea shuffled up the bed looking hostile. 'Look at you, see you, eh, examine you.' She nodded.

Sokunthea relaxed while holding back the urge to laugh.

The doctor quickly removed the dressings and inspected the damage. 'Surface wound on the rear ribcage; that's where the bullet must have come out,' he said to his audience. 'The upper arm wound, the bullet passed straight through; chipped the humerus but no real bone damage. You were lucky,' he said to Sokunthea. She looked at the nurse.

'You are lucky person, no problems,' she translated and Sokunthea nodded.

'Can I ask her some questions?' asked one of the officers.

'I thought she was going to Phnom Penh,' countered the doctor.

'No, Ng is coming here; we must decide who she is before we transfer her.'

'I will give her an injection in order for her to get some rest; I think she will be ready for your questioning tomorrow.'

'She has killed many Vietnamese soldiers…'

'I am aware of that, Captain, but if she dies here due to some aftershock I will suffer the same fate.' He turned to the nurse. 'A night's rest, under guard, and the captain can have her tomorrow.'

'Yes, sir,' said the nurse.

The men departed and the nurse looked at Sokunthea. 'Are you her?' asked the nurse.

'I am Phally, I am a soldier.'

'You're not called Sokunthea, then.'

'I am Phally, a soldier.'

'Well, Phally, I must give you an insertion, a needle, ah, my Cambodian is no good,' she said in Vietnamese. She demonstrated the act of injecting; Sokunthea nodded. 'You must sleep,' she continued. 'Outside will be soldiers, I will be with you.' She smiled and nodded, and Sokunthea smiled back.

'Thank you,' she said.

The injection enabled Sokunthea to sleep until morning, something that she had not achieved for several years. When she woke the nurse had changed; on seeing Sokunthea awake she went to the door and told the soldiers outside. The two officers who had accompanied the doctors the previous day arrived quickly and sat either side of Sokunthea's bed.

'Good morning,' said the one on the right, in perfect Cambodian. Sokunthea just stared at him. 'My name is Captain Nou and this is Captain Li Min.' Sokunthea continued to stare from one to the other.

Then Li Mm said in Vietnamese, 'She appears a little dim.'

Nou looked at him. 'Remember, if this is her she can speak Vietnamese.'

'Yes, of course.'

He looked back at Sokunthea and continued in Cambodian. 'I

will ask you a series of questions; please tell the truth or it may lead to problems for you.' Sokunthea stared at him again then slowly nodded.

'What is your name?'

'Phally Mou.'

'Good, very good and where were you born?'

'Tuk Meas.'

'How did you come to be in a boat on the Stroeng Pouthisat?'

'I am a soldier, a soldier of An Mok, soldiers have rights when captured.'

'Yes, yes, of course they do and if you are just a soldier we will respect those rights. Who is An Mok and where does he go?'

'I am a soldier of An Mok; I should not tell you.'

'Yes.' He looked at his colleague. 'We're not going to get anywhere with this.'

'What did Noug report about her before she killed him?' asked the second captain in Vietnamese.

'She could speak Vietnamese, she spoke without threat, giving away valuable information, she was very intelligent and...'

'What, what?'

'He told me she was sexually attractive.'

'What did he mean?' The two captains stared at each other.

Nou looked at Sokunthea. 'Right, Miss Phally,' he said, again in Cambodian; Sokunthea nodded. 'What if I told you An Mok was captured yesterday?'

'That's not possible, he's in Samkos by now... oh!'

'Very good, very good.' He turned to his accomplice and in Vietnamese said, 'Get that information to command now.'

'Yes, sir.' He left the room. Sokunthea just smiled inwardly.

'So you fought with An Mok,' he continued.

'Yes.'

'Where did you fight?'

'I am a soldier...'

'Yes, yes, we know, but if An Mok is in Samkos it won't make any difference if you tell me where you fought.'

'An Mok always said, tell them you are a soldier and you have rights.'

'Listen,' said the captain becoming a little irritated, 'the Rouge never gave anyone any rights so answer the questions.' Sokunthea tried to put on her hurt-little-girl look and forced tears from her eyes. 'Okay, okay, you have rights, but telling me about your battles won't hurt anyone.' The captain lowered his voice.

'We fought at Kompong Som, then escaped to Kirirom.'

'Wait, wait, let me write this down; Kompong and Kirirom. Did you fight at Kirirom?'

'No, it was a relay.'

'A relay?'

'Yes, one of the many relay stations across the country.'

'Interesting, what were the others?'

'Amleang, Pream Prus,'

'And Samkos.'

'No, we fight there,' said Sokunthea mimicking enthusiasm.

'Right.' Sokunthea reached over and held her shoulder. 'Does it hurt?' said the captain. 'We can stop if it hurts.'

Sokunthea nodded and he left, to be replaced by another nurse bringing food. Sokunthea looked around her room; it had no window with the door, guarded by two soldiers, as the only way in or out. The walls were white and freshly painted and the furniture consisted of her bed and two chairs.

She ate the food, rice with chicken and an onion-flavoured clear soup; it tasted good. The nurse had moved the two chairs nearer the door and sat on one, looking at Sokunthea. After the food was removed Sokunthea indicated she wanted to urinate; a stainless steel bedpan was produced, which confirmed Sokunthea's suspicion that they were not going to let her out of there.

Before lunch the two captains returned and had decided to change their approach. 'You are Commander Sokunthea of Bokor and Kirirom,' they declared. Sokunthea stared at them.

'You will tell us,' said Li Min.

'I have spoken to your doctor and he has given permission for you to be tortured, do you understand what that means?' said Nou.

Sokunthea tried to develop a look of horror.

'She's too stupid to be frightened,' said Li Min in Vietnamese.

'We will wait for Ng; he arrives tomorrow, then we'll know.'

The two captains departed.

'Ng,' she said to herself, 'did he get a good enough look at me? I think not, but if the men on the boat are right he may call me out just to get his bosses off his back... hmm. No, no, stick it out,' she said to herself as the Cambodian-speaking nurse returned.

The rest of the day began with a roast chicken lunch, followed by a doctors' round which complemented themselves on a well-healing wound, then an afternoon nap. Dinner was served by about seven thirty and as the nurse was removing the tray the door burst open and in marched Ng.

He looked at Sokunthea, then marched straight up to the bed and grabbed her by the hair, pulling her head round forcefully. He glared into her eyes and she into his, looked at her neck, then said, 'Too fresh.' He then threw her back onto the bed.

'Commander,' said the nurse.

'Shut it,' said Ng and he looked at Sokunthea again. 'I'm not so sure at this time, lady, but I'll be back tomorrow.' He left with the two captains following.

The nurse helped to settle Sokunthea down, apologising as she did so; Sokunthea just thought how lucky she was Sen had tied her neck; Ng knew the state his men had left her in and the marks it would leave. The next morning the two guards at the door entered Sokunthea's room and instructed the nurse to get Sokunthea dressed. Although Sokunthea was naked below the sheets the guards refused to leave during the dressing process. Sokunthea decided that this was the beginning of the heavy hand approach. She was escorted from the hospital building into what to Sokunthea looked like a general barracks; at the entrance she was met by Captain Nou.

'Welcome to the Vietnamese army,' he said. He led Sokunthea down a corridor, then down some narrow winding steps into the basement of the building, then through a small door and into a cold, dark room with no windows or signs of ventilation. She was directed to a wooden chair, which was cemented into the floor. She could hear footsteps coming towards the room and as the door opened Ng and Li Min entered.

Ng stared at her. 'You look different in your combat fatigues,' he said. Sokunthea did not respond, still trying to indicate her inability to speak Vietnamese. 'Come, come,' he continued, 'you understand me, your game is up.' Sokunthea looked at him as he began to walk around her. 'Watch this woman,' he said to his fellow officers, 'she will use anything within her power to get you to drop your guard then, creeeek,' and he passed his hand across his throat. 'She is responsible for the deaths of over one hundred of my men and Colonel Noug, remember that, Colonel Noug... strap her down.'

The chair had leather straps, which could be tied around the wrists and ankles pinning the seated person securely.

'Now, what is your name?'

Sokunthea stared ahead.

'Don't think anyone is coming to help you because they are not. Now, name!'

She remained silent.

He struck her hard across the face.

'She may not understand you,' cut in Nou.

'If you've no stomach for this, Nou, get out.'

'No, sir, I mean, yes, sir, I mean I'll stay.'

The blow from Ng had started Sokunthea's nose bleeding and she tasted it as it ran into the corners of her mouth.

'Beating you is no good, is it?' continued Ng. 'You're Rouge, the real thing, death or glory. Li Min!' Sokunthea saw the door open, then heard the sound of wheels as a trolley was brought in. Ng looked at her then, placing his hands each side of her tunic, ripped it open. He sneered at her naked breasts. 'Not very big, I like them biiig!' and he reached forwards and fondled her breasts. 'Li Min!' he called over his shoulder.

The captain stepped forward holding what appeared to be paper clips in each hand, the kind Sokunthea had used in her teaching days. He then clipped them onto her nipples. Sokunthea winced.

'Hurts, does it?' said Ng. 'Good,' and he smiled and stepped back. 'Now, Li Min, now.'

The electric current rammed into Sokunthea's breast and her whole chest felt like it was on fire. 'Aaargh!' she screamed; the current was cut.

'Did you like that?' asked Ng, as Sokunthea's head dropped

forwards. 'Water, throw water on her, Nou!' and the captain obeyed. The cold water brought Sokunthea back to consciousness.

'Again,' said Ng to Li Min. Sokunthea screamed again and she began to have a minor convulsion.

'The water, the water makes the shock greater; if you're not careful you'll kill her,' said an anxious Nou.

Ng just looked at him. 'What is your name?' he shouted. Sokunthea still did not respond.

'She doesn't understand you,' cut in Non, 'she's still half unconscious.'

'I'll wake her,' said an increasingly frustrated Ng. He ripped her tunic from her body and then removed the dressings, then he lit a cigarette and drew on it heavily until its tip was glowing. He looked at Nou and, smiling, rammed the hot cigarette into Sokunthea's bullet hole. She screamed then quickly fell into unconsciousness again.

The door of the room opened and the doctor entered. 'I want my patient back in her bed now,' he said.

'I'm interrogating her!' shouted Ng.

'Your orders were to inspect her and decide if she was the woman we are after, if so…'

'I don't have to listen to you.'

'If so, she is to be returned to Phnom Penh; I would advise you, Commander, that here in Pursat I outrank you and I suggest you carry out Central's orders.'

'Damn,' said Ng and he stormed out of the room.

'Get this woman back into my hospital, Captain Nou, for if she dies we are all in trouble.'

'Yes, sir.'

When Sokunthea woke her Cambodian-speaking nurse was sat beside her bed. 'What happened?' she asked.

'Oh, the doctor got you back.' Sokunthea smiled, then felt for her breasts that were still burning.

'I've put some cream on them,' the nurse said. 'I'm used to treating burns but not on the nipples.' She looked almost ashamed.

'What next?'

'Oh, you're going to Phnom Penh, back home.' She looked at

Sokunthea. 'While asleep you spoke of your mother and living in Deum Kor; I'm sorry she's dead.' She stood and went to the door, then turned. 'And Deum Kor is a district in Phnom Penh, I know, so you don't have to deny it any more, but don't worry, I'm as sick of killing as you seem to be, so you're going home, home to Phnom Penh. Happy return.'

Return

Sokunthea began her return journey to Phnom Penh in the back of a military truck accompanied by Captain Nou. The doctor had checked her wounds that morning and declared her fit for the journey, so, chained around the ankles and handcuffed, she faced the long truck ride stretched out in the back. Sat opposite her was the Cambodian-speaking nurse who was called Phu, two guards and Nou. The truck was part of a small convoy returning to Phnom Penh to pick up more supplies. Along with its human cargo the truck carried several sacks of rice, flour and boxes of pineapples, all imported from Thailand and bound for the food-short Vietnamese encamped in Phnom Penh. The sacks and crates were stacked at the front of the truck behind the cabin with the passengers taking up the rear, Sokunthea deliberately stretching herself out on one bench so the others had to squash together on the other. In the cabin was the driver and Ng, hitching a lift back to Kompong Spue and still angry from his inability to be allowed to break Sokunthea.

As the truck's journey began from Pursat, in Phnom Penh the most senior Vietnamese general, Moc Hoa, was calling a meeting of his advisory team. This consisted of his adjutant, Colonel Tac, General Ha Tien, who commanded the ground forces in Cambodia, and Chau Thanh from the central communist bureau.

'What do we do with this woman?' asked Hoa.

'Is she the one?' asked Tien.

'We don't yet know; Ng says she is, but the report from the doctor suggests he got a little carried away,' continued Hoa.

'Ng is a good man and the only one that has seen her,' said Tien.

'Then why did he torture her?' cut in Thanh.

'Revenge,' said Tien.

'The doctor's report is accompanied by a Captain Nou's; he suggests that Ng didn't identify her, he just tried to force a confession,' sighed Hoa who then stood and walked over to the open French windows. He looked out across an open boulevard, which joined the main station in Phnom Penh to Wat Phnom. The building where the meeting was taking place had originally been the Ministry of Culture in the Cambodian government; it was in the classical colonial French style with large windows and ornately decorated rooms.

'What does the bureau think of this?' he asked over his shoulder.

'We have to be careful,' began Thanh; 'any sign that we are killing Rouge prisoners will lose us the moral ground.'

'Moral ground, what the hell does that mean?' cut in Tien, not hiding his lack of respect for Thanh.

'Well, Mr Thanh?' asked Hoa and he turned and returned to the table.

'The bureau thinks that the Chinese and the Americans are wanting to get involved in this war,' Thanh began.

'Of course they do,' cut in Tien once again, 'they can't get over the fact that we beat them, both of them.'

'The bureau believes,' Thanh continued, 'that the Americans are being kept out by public opinion; I repeat, if we start killing Rouge prisoners that could change.' He stared at Tien.

'Bah!' uttered Tien.

'So what about this woman?' continued Hoa calmly.

'This is difficult; as you know, General, there's already been an article in the Thai press about her, possibly American-inspired.'

'I told you, I told you; they're jealous, they're worried what we will find,' cut in Tien.

Thanh continued as if nothing had happened. 'Our representative at the UN has stated that we have invaded Cambodia only to stop the mass murder that has been carried out by the government of Pol Pot; many countries support our stand but they will not if we start shooting people, do you understand?' He raised his voice and focused on Tien.

'Gentlemen, please,' said Hoa. 'So what do you recommend Mr Thanh?'

'We should try to find out if she is this –' and he looked through some papers he had been holding – 'this Sokunthea of

Bokor and Kirirom; if she is, she should be transferred to Hanoi immediately, sir.'

'And if not?' Hoa continued.

'Then in common with our practice she must be treated like a prisoner of war and ultimately released.'

'And you are recommending that?' Hoa pursued.

'No, sir,' everyone looked at Thanh. 'I would recommend that she be sent to Hanoi anyway, particularly if we cannot decide; I do sympathise with General Tien here, she has killed many of our men.'

'That's right,' added Tien.

'So why bother to investigate her?' continued Hoa.

'We should try to find out her identity either way; if that is not possible then we retain her in Hanoi. If the reports of a woman fighter stop coming in, then we can say we have the right woman,' concluded Thanh.

'And if not?' said Hoa.

'We release her.' Thanh shrugged his shoulders.

'Hmmm,' murmured a thoughtful Hoa.

The meeting went quiet, then Tac said, 'But how will we find out?'

Hoa looked at him. 'Good question; how, Thanh?'

'We have someone else who knew her; we're bringing him in from the provinces now.'

'Reliable?' asked Hoa.

'We think so, sir, he fought with this Sokunthea at Bokor,' responded Thanh.

'Good. Right, gentlemen, let's get back to work. Thanh, I want you to take personal control over this situation; if we can identify her, good, if not, she goes to Hanoi anyway.'

'Yes, sir, thank you, sir,' said Thanh and the meeting dispersed.

Sokunthea's convoy had a trouble-free journey from Pursat to Kompong Chhnang where it stopped for the night. She was led from the truck into a tented compound at the local airport where Phu assessed then changed her dressings. The nurse was to share the tent to which Sokunthea had been allocated and fresh guards were posted outside.

'Do you want the left or right bunk?' asked Phu in Vietnamese. Sokunthea just stood and stared. 'Don't fool around,' said Phu, 'remember, I know.'

Sokunthea sat on the left bunk. 'Will you tell?' she replied in Vietnamese.

'Depends on you,' replied Phu.

'How?'

'You can begin by telling me why you did it.'

'You want the whole story?'

'You can if it helps.'

Sokunthea ran through the main points of her life from leaving Tuk Meas to being captured; Phu listened intently. When she had finished the nurse just stared at her.

'Phew, you had one hell of a journey,' Phu finally said.

'But nobody would believe it.'

'I do,' she said, 'I do.'

'Will you tell?'

'This war is coming to an end; just killing people for revenge is not going to help, is it?'

'I guess not.'

'No, I won't tell.'

'Thank you. Can I ask another favour?'

'Sure.'

'Let's speak in Cambodian in future; if anyone hears me speak Vietnamese I'm finished.'

'Sure, now let's be sleep.' She laughed, 'my Cambodian is not good.'

'It's good enough for me.'

The two women settled down for the night, both relieved that they had reached an understanding with regards to Sokunthea and the action Phu would take. Their night was then disturbed when a man burst into their tent and grabbed the nurse.

'Out here, you bitch!' came the drunken words of Ng, who stopped dragging the nurse when he realised who he'd got. 'Where's that cow?' he shouted angrily and turned to grab Sokunthea.

He pulled Sokunthea out of the tent and began to drag her across the runway of the airport; the nurse ran to find Captain

Nou. 'Look at this, you cow, you murdering cow, just look at this.'

Sokunthea maintained her stance of not responding to Vietnamese and therefore didn't speak.

'Come on, you bitch,' Ng continued and he headed towards the edge of the runway where he pushed Sokunthea to the floor. 'Look, you bitch,' he slurred, 'look!' and he picked up Sokunthea, then threw her down into a ditch.

The first thing Sokunthea sensed when she hit the bottom of the ditch was the smell of rotting flesh, then she could feel the limbs of decomposing bodies all around her. Nou and Phu had reached Ng standing at the side of the ditch and shone their torches down, the light exposing Sokunthea surrounded by hundreds of rotting bodies.

'This is what you lot did!' screamed Ng. 'You murderers!' He was shaking violently.

Sokunthea just sat amongst the bodies, wondering how and why; she looked down at the pile of human flesh, of men and women, of children, of the aged, and began to cry.

'Get her out!' shouted Nou. And several soldiers jumped into the ditch and began to haul her out. 'You had no right to do this, Commander Ng,' said Nou. 'It will go into my report.'

Ng stormed off into the darkness. Phu placed her arm around Sokunthea and began to walk her back to their tent.

'I had nothing to do with this,' she said through her tears.

'I know.'

When they arrived back at the tent Sokunthea asked if she could have a shower to remove the smell of the dead from her body. Phu assisted her and provided her with clean sleeping attire before they both began to retire again for the night. When they re-entered their tent Nou was sitting waiting.

'I would like to apologise on behalf of the Vietnamese army for Commander Ng's actions,' he said to Sokunthea, who just nodded and lay down. Nou watched her then turned and headed for the door.

'Who were they?' whispered Sokunthea.

Nou stopped and turned. 'Civilians, from Phnom Penh, we think; the Chinese had them building an airport. When we invaded someone killed them all.'

'Are there more?'

'Graves? Yes, three or four, all full; there must be twenty thousand bodies, maybe more.'

'All from Phnom Penh?' Sokunthea thought of her father.

'Yes, Phnom Penh.'

Sokunthea curled up and began to cry quietly. When Nou departed the sound of Sokunthea's distress grew and Phu joined her in one bed to help console her.

'He didn't have to do that,' wept Sokunthea, 'I've seen enough of that.'

'I know; you will have to excuse him, he was drunk and he thinks you are part of it.'

'Well, I'm not.' She stopped crying.

In the morning the truck took the human cargo from the airport to the Tonle Sap river landing in Kampong Chhnang town, where a military speedboat of the Vietnamese navy was waiting.

'The road to Phnom Penh can be dangerous from here onwards; the army is still mopping up. The boat is much quicker and safer,' explained Nou.

Sokunthea's leg chains were removed in order for her to get onto the boat and through Phu's insistence they were not restored. She was forced to sit inside between the two guards and made the journey staring across the small cabin space and out of a porthole. Phu sat towards the front of the boat looking back at Sokunthea and Captain Nou; she had reaffirmed to herself that she would not report this fighter, this killer of Vietnamese soldiers, this woman; her death would achieve nothing. She was still intrigued by Sokunthea's story and how she survived, a story that she, herself would like to have been involved in. Now she was and she was not going to be the executioner. The boat journey of two hours was completed in silence and, as Nou was informed that they were approaching Phnom Penh, he reattached the leg chains to Sokunthea.

The landing stage at Phnom Penh was a bustling scene of soldiers and civilians carrying boxes of supplies and munitions in and out of boats. Sokunthea shuffled between her guards onto the deck of the bobbing boat, which was still some distance from the shore. Nou followed them and he saw the official car parked with a military driver and a civilian stood watching them. The guards dropped into the shallow water and walked ashore, leaving Sokunthea in her chains standing on the edge of the swaying boat. To everyone's surprise Thanh walked out to the boat; Nou scooped Sokunthea up into his arms and passed her to Thanh, who carried her to shore. He placed Sokunthea in the back of the official car and turned to greet Nou.

'You must be Captain Nou.' He held out his hand.

'Yes, and you?'

'I'm Thanh from the bureau.'

'Ah, yes.'

'I am here to take charge of the case as ordered by General Hoa.'

'Of course. Oh, this is Nurse Phu, she is here to care for the prisoner's injuries,' continued Nou.

'Welcome,' said Thanh and shook Phu's hand. 'You will both accompany me with the prisoner... please,' and he pointed to the car. Sokunthea sat in the back with Phu and Nou and stared out of the window at her city, a city she had left years ago. The roads were empty except for the occasional military vehicle as they drove past empty house after empty house. Thanh turned in his front seat to face his passengers.

'Alas, we are in a strange situation.' Nou and Phu stared at him. 'If I begin to brief you we do not know if the prisoner will understand what we say or not, so I think it best that we wait until we reach our destination before we talk.'

'Yes, yes, of course,' said Nou.

'Enjoy the sights,' said Thanh and he stared ahead.

The car passed the royal palace then turned to the waterfront; Sokunthea knew this area but wondered where the official house was situated. The car turned into a narrow side street then turned again into a narrow covered entrance where it stopped. The passengers disembarked from the vehicle and two guards opened an iron gate, which they passed through. Ahead of them were steep spiral stairs; when Sokunthea saw them she stopped.

'The chains,' said Phu.

'Oh,' said Thanh, 'can we remove them, Nou?'

'Yes, of course.'

Within minutes they were climbing the stairs to the first floor and entered a large room, which overlooked the river.

'This will be our meeting room,' said Thanh.

'It's beautiful,' said Nou.

'Here is your room, Nou, with mine there; the ladies, I thought, would be on the next floor.' He turned and led the party up one more floor, introducing Phu and Sokunthea to a large room with washroom facilities and superb views across the Tonle Sap and Mekong.

He looked at Sokunthea and in perfect Cambodian said, 'There are six soldiers in the room opposite, four downstairs and ten on the ground floor; if you try to escape they have orders to shoot you. Do you understand?'

Sokunthea looked into his eyes. 'Yes, I understand.'

'Good. Please wash, then come downstairs for lunch.' The two men departed.

Phu looked at Sokunthea. 'This is wonderful!' she said, and walked to the window and looked out, then turned. 'Let's freshen up.' Sokunthea stood under the shower for what seemed like a day; the washroom had been fitted out with the soaps and perfumes that she had not experienced for too long. Phu had obtained the permission of Thanh to have her handcuffs removed and with warm water and soapsuds running down her body she felt human.

'Hurry, we'll be late!' called out Phu. Sokunthea emerged, wrapped in a towel, and sat on the edge of a chair. 'Just let me check your wound… it's fine,' confirmed Phu.

'You look wonderful,' said Sokunthea, looking at Phu wearing a new dress. 'Where's the uniform?'

'I've been told to wear this, and there's one for you.' Sokunthea stared at the dress Phu held up. 'Come on, let's go.'

Sokunthea dressed quickly and the two women set off downstairs; as they entered the dinning room the two men were looking out over the rivers.

'Ah, come in, come in,' said Thanh on seeing them, 'please!' and he pulled back a chair for Sokunthea to sit at the table. She sat, quickly followed by the others. Two women and a man appeared and began to lay food on the table: fish, chicken, prawns and rice, lots of rice.

'Well, I'd like from now on that we all speak Cambodian for the benefit of our guest.' Nou and Phu nodded. 'We will stay in this house until we are sure who you really are,' and he stared at Sokunthea. 'You will not be put in handcuffs or chains, but I will expect you to not attempt to escape; if you try the guards will shoot you, if you escape into an empty city we will find you and that will confirm to my seniors that you are this Sokunthea of Dukor and all the rest. Do you understand?' Sokunthea nodded. 'You will be with Phu,' he turned to Phu, 'I hope we can dispense with the nurse bit?' Phu smiled and nodded. Thanh continued, 'Who will obtain for you anything you need, within reason.' He chuckled and looked around the table. 'This large room will be the dining room, recreation room and interrogation room,' he again engaged Sokunthea in direct eye contact, 'do you understand?' She nodded again. 'Good; let's eat.'

Sokunthea stared at the prawns; she had not seen one in five years. She picked one up and slowly peeled it, then gently nibbled at its flesh. She looked around the table and noticed that everyone was looking at the tears that were softly falling down her face.

'I'm sorry,' she said and began to wipe them away.

'Not a problem,' said Thanh, 'is the food not to your liking?'

'No, it's fine.' The group ate on in silence.

'I suppose you are used to resting after lunch,' said Thanh to Sokunthea.

'Yes,' she said, 'it's been a long journey.'

'Of course, of course. Nou informed me of Ng's disgusting behaviour; I can only apologise again.'

'He made a point.'

'Yes; were you aware of what was happening at Kompong Chhnang?'

'No, I was too busy surviving at Tuk Meas.'

'Yes, Tuk Meas; who was in charge there?'

'Thalin.'

'Of course; he killed many people.'

'He did.'

'Please have more rice, the chicken is very good.'

'No, thank you.'

'How did you become a commander?'

She glanced at Thanh. 'I'm not a commander.'

'But you were at Bokor.'

'I fought at Kompong Som.'

'Kompong Som, under whose command?'

'An Mok.'

'Okay, that's enough for now.' Thanh looked around the table. 'Everyone finished?'

The diners moved away from the table and Thanh approached Phu. 'Put her to bed, then come back down.'

'She may try…'

'To escape? Not this afternoon; we put something in her water, she'll sleep.'

Sokunthea entered her bedroom, knowing something was wrong; the room had begun to spin and she seemed to be unable to stop yawning. She sat on her bed with Phu beside her then fell over; Phu quickly put her to bed then went downstairs.

'Ah, Phu, sit here. Are you ready, Nou?' Nou came to the table and sat. 'I want to outline to you our plan and to fill you in with all the details,' Thanh began. 'We are looking for a female soldier who has been implicated in the killing of about one hundred of our men and a few Cambodian counter-revolutionaries; there is a strong belief that this woman is her.' He gazed from Nou to Phu. 'General Hoa has put me in total charge and I have decided to take a gentle approach to the situation; there will be no physical torture. I believe that if she is this Sokunthea, she is a highly trained killer who will endure such an approach even to death. No, we must use our mental capacity to overcome her. Now, Nou, you write in your report that you thought she was of low intelligence.'

'Yes, sir; when we first interrogated her she seemed slow to understand what we were saying.'

'Maybe that's because she had a severe wound and was afraid,' suggested Phu.

'Maybe,' said Thanh, 'go on.'

'Well,' continued Nou, 'there's just been times when I thought she was understanding what we were saying.'

'Phu, what's your initial feeling?' asked Thanh.

'She is intelligent but afraid; I also feel she has fought in the past but now has had enough.'

'Explain,' said Thanh.

'She is obviously a fighter: her dress, her weapons when they found her; but when Ng threw her into the ditch something gave.'

'That's right,' cut in Nou, 'the graves at Kompong Chhnang did seem to affect her.'

'Okay,' said Thanh, 'it is important that we have these meetings every day; I will want you to tell me anything you have heard her say and any observations that you have. Now, detail: this Commander Sokunthea fought at Bokor then travelled north; she reappeared in a helicopter battle in the Elephant mountains and was captured, Noug and Ng interrogated her and the army left her to die. Later she reappeared at Kirirom where she murdered Noug and killed many Cambodian sympathisers. There have been other skirmishes until we captured her on the Pouthisat river – or we think we have.'

'How do we know she killed Noug?' asked Phu.

'We don't for certain, but why would anyone kill a wounded unarmed man if it wasn't to silence him? Anything to add, Nou?'

'Only her command line: she was at Tuk Meas, then Bokor, then through Kirirom to the Pouthisat; her commanders were Thalin, Thai and Van Serun at Bokor. After that we believe she was made commander of her own brigade.'

'Okay, if you hear her mention any of those places and people I want to know. Let's get some rest; I want to start interrogating after dinner.' The team began to break up.

'What will happen to her?' asked Phu.

'That's the strange thing; if she's her, she goes to Hanoi to stand trial for murder, if she's not she still goes to Hanoi because we can't afford to let her go.'

'So why not just send her to Hanoi?'

'Because the army has to be sure; it wants revenge, you see, revenge for Noug, revenge for all the dead, revenge for being outsmarted and outfought by a woman. In Hanoi they'll have their show trial in order to prove that she's not a heroine but a murderer; revenge, that's all it is.'

Phu went upstairs to her room and checked that Sokunthea was still asleep before settling down herself. Phu lay in bed thinking of Sokunthea's story and thought of the death of Noug; Sokunthea had only said she was at Kirirom and had described the fighting, she hadn't mentioned Noug's death. The thought of Noug and how he was killed inhibited Phu from sleeping; she decided that she would confront Sokunthea about the Noug incident when she woke. As she stood looking out of the window she noticed Thanh depart in the official car and reflected on his summing up; Hanoi if guilty, Hanoi if innocent. She went to a small table next to the window and poured herself a glass of water then tried to sleep.

'I can give you five minutes, Thanh,' said General Hoa directing him to a chair.

'I'm just reporting, sir, that the prisoner is already here and we have started to interrogate her.'

'Any breakthroughs?'

'I think so, sir; she has already stated that she came from Tuk Meas.'

'That important?'

'I think so; we know that this Sokunthea was at Tuk Meas but this woman didn't mention it – either she never met her, which is unlikely, or she is her.'

'Hmm, anything else?'

'Yes; Captain Nou and Nurse Phu expressed a change in her during the journey south; Nou is convinced she can speak Vietnamese while Phu thought that after Kompong Chhnang she'd had enough.'

'Enough?'

'Of killing, sir.'

'Right, keep at it, Thanh; I'd much prefer to deliver her to Hanoi having discovered the truth.'

'Yes, sir.'

'Where is your witness, anyway?'

'Coming; he'll be here some time over the next two days.'

'Time up, Tac!' shouted the general as he headed towards a

side door and his adjutant came running in carrying papers and a map and followed.

Thanh began his journey back to the house; along the way he stopped at a small café, which the military had allowed to open, and ordered coffee. He looked across the empty streets to a line of Rouge prisoners sweeping up the garbage that had been left behind by its departing citizens four years earlier.

'Emptying a whole city, a whole city; insanity or genius?'

'Talking to yourself, Thanh?'

He looked up and saw General Tien. 'Thinking out loud, General.'

'May I join you?'

'Of course.'

'Nice to have little places like this opening, makes the place more... normal.'

'I was just thinking the same.'

'I'm told you're holed up next to the river with this murderer.'

'The prisoner, yes.'

'Prisoner, murderer – Ng said it's her.'

'Commander Ng would say anyone was her; finding this woman has become an obsession with him.'

'Commander Ng is a fine soldier.'

'I'm sure he is, General, but in this matter he keeps thinking of all the men he's lost.'

'Nothing wrong with thinking of the men.'

'There is when you're after the truth,' Both men sipped their coffees.

'Strange place, this,' said Tien.

'What?'

'This city, this empty city, strange. I must be off; they will kill her, won't they?'

'Who the prisoner?'

'Yes, yes, when she gets to Hanoi?'

'If she's her they'll try her for murder.'

'And kill her.'

'I think they call it re-educate, General, then she will disappear.'

'Good, send her as soon as possible; we don't want them

rallying around a heroine, not at this late stage of the war,' and he left.

Thanh travelled back to the house as Sokunthea began to wake from her drug-enforced sleep. She sat up and Phu quickly sat beside her.

'Whew, my head,' said Sokunthea.

'I'll get you something for that in a minute.' Sokunthea began to massage her neck. 'Did you kill Commander Noug?' asked Phu quietly.

'What?'

'Kill Commander Noug.'

'No.' Sokunthea turned to look at Phu. 'Why do you, ask?'

'I need to know; they say he was shot but he had no weapon and was wounded, is that right?'

'Yes.' Sokunthea stood and walked to take water from the same place Phu had done earlier.

'But wounded and without a weapon suggests he had surrendered.'

'I think he had,' said Sokunthea turning to look at her. 'Look, we had attacked the hill station at Kirirom; men were running everywhere, there were explosions and gunfire, shouts and cries that you have never heard. I was with the commander and we targeted some men that were trying to get out; one of them was Noug. When I got to him he had been wounded and obviously couldn't escape, and Sy, the commander, shot him.'

'And you did nothing.'

'I pleaded for his life and while I did... he still shot him.'

'But a prisoner?'

'There's no prisoners out there; there's chaos, there's agony, there's instant decisions made and often later regretted. Sy thought Noug would be a burden to take and a danger to leave, so he finished him.'

'And you did nothing.'

'I cursed the stupidity of it all and thanked Buddha I was still alive.'

'It was murder,' said a now sullen Phu.

'Yes, it was.' Sokunthea turned and poured more water.

'They're going to try you for that.'

'I thought they would find something.'

'Murder,' mumbled Phu.

'Look,' said an increasingly irritated Sokunthea, 'who will try the Vietnamese soldiers for the murder of surrendered tank crews on the Kompong Som highway? Who will try the soldiers who first raped then killed the young girls at Kirirom? It's war, it happens.' She threw the glass across the room and it smashed against the door. Several soldiers instantly appeared and inquired from Phu if everything was in order.

'Yes,' she said angrily and they left. She walked over to Sokunthea and embraced her.

A knock sounded on the door and a male and female servant entered. 'Mr Thanh says dinner will be in one hour,' said the man while the woman swept up the broken glass.

Dinner was over quickly with little conversation, everybody knowing what was to come. Thanh showed Sokunthea over to a group of comfortable chairs near the window.

'I thought we could sit here,' he said. 'I will be the only one to ask you questions so I would ask you to answer only to me, do you understand?'

Sokunthea nodded.

'Everyone is keen to prove who you are; we do not want to retain an innocent person, therefore it is in your interest to answer all questions honestly, do you understand?'

'Yes.'

'Now, tell me your name.'

'I already have.'

'Again, please.'

'Phally Mou.'

'And you are from Tuk Meas?'

'Yes.'

'Have you ever heard the name of Commander Sokunthea of Bokor and Kirirom?'

'Yes.'

'When?'

'From you.'

'But not before?'

'No.'

'Who was in charge at Tuk Meas?'

'Thalin.'

'Did he have a deputy?'

'No.'

'Tell me what happened when we invaded?'

'We retreated.'

'To where?'

'Kampot.'

'And who was in charge?'

'Thai, a Commander Thai.'

'Did he have a deputy?'

'No.'

'What happened when you got to Kampot?'

'Commander An Mok took charge and divided us into two groups.'

'What did Commander Thai think of that?'

'He was dead.'

'Dead?'

'Killed crossing the bridge.'

'So An Mok took charge?'

'Yes.'

'Where did the two forces go?'

'One to Bokor and one to Kompong Som.'

'And you went with An Mok?'

'Yes.'

'Don't you think it is strange that a commander should divide his forces like this?'

'I am not a military tactician.'

'Okay, but you had not heard of a Commander Sokunthea at this time?'

'No.'

'Your commander An Mok divided his forces, but we know that the garrison at Bokor was strengthened by men from Kompong Som; why take you there to send you back?'

'I don't know.'

'When you left Kompong Som where did you go?'

'Into the Elephant mountains.'

'But why? You told us before that An Mok was headed to

Samkos, which is in the Cardamoms.'

'I don't know.'

'In the Elephant mountains you went to Kirirom.'

'Yes.'

'And at Kirirom there were lots of wounded soldiers from Bokor and Kompong Som.'

'Yes.'

'Did any of them speak of a Commander Sokunthea?'

'No.'

'After Kirirom you went to the Pouthisat river where we captured you?'

'Yes.'

'So you actually only fought at Kompong Som?'

'Yes.'

'The analysis of your weapons which we took from you at Pouthisat shows that you used them a great deal, in fact, the rifle you used was removed from a Vietnamese soldier at Kirirom.'

'Impossible.'

'On the contrary; when a Vietnamese soldier goes into battle he signs out a weapon and signs it back in when he returns. Your rifle came from Kirirom.'

Sokunthea stared down at her hands.

'How did you get shot at Pouthisat?'

'By your men.'

'No, no unit has reported any action along the Pouthisat, except some clumsy diversion – but no shootings.' Thanh paused. 'I think that's enough for tonight, you should get some rest,' concluded Thanh.

Phu escorted Sokunthea back to her room and locked the door behind them. 'You must stop this I'm-a-simple-soldier routine, he can see through it.'

'It's too late now.'

'Say you have heard of this Sokunthea, she was your heroine too.'

'That just confirms that she exists.'

'She does; it's you.'

'I'm no heroine; the people I was with don't even know what a heroine is. It's you that have made me into a heroine; sometimes I get the feeling that I'm being set up by the Vietnamese.'

'For what? Don't be crazy.' Phu began to undress.

'Look, I fought at Bokor and Kirirom so did many others. Why am I the heroine, why am I getting all the attention? Maybe they want someone to blame, maybe they know what they are going to do with me already, maybe they just want to use me.'

'I don't know what you're talking about.' But Phu's mind reflected on Thanh's words: Hanoi if it's her, Hanoi if not.

'I just hope you know your facts; if not, Thanh knows his.'

Sokunthea decided to miss breakfast; she lay in bed wondering why the Viets were making such a big play out of her war exploits. It wasn't enough that she had possibly killed one of their senior officers; as she had explained to Phu, that happens all the time in war. No, something else was happening – as a soldier of war she was a prisoner of war and was entitled to all of the rights of a prisoner.

Downstairs Thanh, Nou and Phu were just finishing their food when the officer of the guard came rushing in.

'Mr Thanh, sir!' Thanh looked up. 'General Hoa is on his way.'

'What, coming here?'

'Yes, sir; he will be here in about twenty minutes.' He then left.

'Phu, get her up; I don't care if you have to drag her here, get her here.' Phu disappeared upstairs. 'We'd better get ourselves presentable,' said Thanh looking at Nou.

'Right.'

General Hoa entered the room and looked around. 'Nice place you have found, Thanh.'

'Thank you, sir.'

'And this must be Captain Nou.' Nou stood to attention. 'Relax, Captain. Now, where is the lady?' As the general spoke Nurse Phu dressed in her uniform, led Sokunthea in. 'How beautiful!' said a startled Hoa. 'You never told me she was such a delight.' Hoa took Sokunthea's hand and led her over to the comfortable chairs near the window.

'Now, my dear,' he began, with the team standing behind and Thanh sitting opposite him in order to translate, 'we have a little problem which I know you want to solve.' He smiled. 'Everybody is now getting excited about you or about this Sokunthea, especially in the West; they say she is a heroine of the people and that we are treating her badly, that she should be released as a prisoner of war. We want to stop this; if you are this Sokunthea tell me and you will be treated like a heroine; if not, you will be treated like a common soldier and released.'

'I'm not a heroine, General.'

'Fine.' He stood up and walked to the door with Thanh following. 'This is getting out of hand, Thanh, I want the truth.'

'Yes, General.'

'Tac!' shouted General Hoa, 'give him the dossier.' Tac handed over a thick dossier as the general left.

Thanh ordered Phu to take Sokunthea back to her room as he began to read what Colonel Tac had given him. Sokunthea failed to appear for lunch so Thanh decided to have his feedback while eating.

'This Sokunthea could cause us a lot of problems,' he began. 'The western papers are writing about her and her deeds against our army, making us out to be the terrible invaders. This kind of publicity could turn our supporters at the UN against us.'

'Where are they getting their information?' asked Nou.

'We don't know.'

'But the things in that file are very accurate.'

Phu picked up the dossier and began to read. 'It says here that this Sokunthea is believed to have assisted the release of several hundred Cambodians from Rouge persecution.'

'Yes, she is quite a little heroine,' cut in Thanh as he poured more coffee.

'Look at this: it says there is evidence to suggest that this Sokunthea was engaged in counter-activities against the Rouge from within.'

Thanh reached over and took back the file. 'Yes, yes.'

'But if she was fighting against the Rouge...'

'She also killed our men.'

'Did she?' continued Phu. 'Just because you are at a battle it doesn't mean you have killed anyone.'

'We are not here to praise,' said Thanh angrily, 'we're here to shut up the western press.'

'But what about the woman upstairs?' countered Phu.

'Of course, maybe you can go and check on her.'

Phu knew she had been dismissed and went upstairs; she found Sokunthea looking out of the window again. 'Don't jump,' she said jokingly.

'I won't. Good meeting?'

'What you told me is true and we know it.'

'So why the interrogation, why the confinement?'

'I don't know, but whatever the plan is General Hoa is getting uneasy.'

'Soldiers always do when deeper plots begin to unfold.'

'They want you for a reason and it's not being a heroine or murderer.' Sokunthea sat down. 'Is there anything you've not told me?'

'If there is look in the dossier or read the Thai papers.' She pointed to a copy lying on the floor.

Phu picked it up and began to read. 'This stuff is almost straight from the military reports.'

'You read Thai well?'

'Oh, I learnt it at school.' Phu sat beside Sokunthea. 'They talk of you being a heroine of the poor Cambodians and that we, the Vietnamese, have locked you up to stop you forming any resistance.'

'Not for murder?'

'Not mentioned.'

'Why should someone build me up as a great western heroine?'

Phu threw the paper down. 'Time to rest,' she said, and they prepared for their afternoon sleep.

Thanh again couldn't rest and ordered his driver to take him to the coffee shop where General Tien had already settled down for his afternoon coffee. 'Good afternoon, General, good to see you again.'

'This girl is becoming trouble, I understand,' Tien started.

'Nothing we can't handle.'

'She could upset your bureau plans; if we don't release her or discredit her quickly your precious UN will come tumbling down round your ears.'

'We could charge her with murder.'

'In a war? Hah, they wouldn't stand for that rubbish.'

'But I thought you were all for her death.'

'I'm not stupid, Thanh,' Tien leaned forwards. 'I can smell your bureau all over this; there's bigger games at play and bigger disasters if it goes wrong.'

Thanh ordered coffee. 'How's the war going?' he finally asked.

'They're still retreating.'

'And still taking the people with them?'

'Yes, strange that.'

'Everything is strange in Cambodia.'

'Well, I have to go, Thanh.'

'Me too, General, I have a woman to interview about her travels with An Mok.'

'An Mok? No wonder Ng threw her into the pit at Kompong Chhnang.'

'Sorry?'

'Kompong Chhnang; An Mok was the commander there, butchered all those people. If she was with him she's murdered more than Noug.'

'Thank you, General,' and both men went in search of their transport.

Sokunthea attended for dinner, partly out of her hunger and partly through Thanh's insistence. When the meal had been cleared away the interrogation started.

'Now, Sokunthea, I am expecting a soldier from the Cambodian Freedom Army to join us later, he claims to know this Sokunthea from Bokor.' Sokunthea sat quietly. 'Right, you say that you first joined An Mok's command at Kampot.'

'Yes.'

'And that An Mok then led you and his men across the Elephant mountains from Kompong Som. Did he go to Kompong Chhnang?'

'No.'

'You know Kompong Chhnang, the place where thousands of your people were murdered.'

'I have discovered that fact, yes.'

'But how can you have discovered that fact? If you were with An Mok you were at Kompong Chhnang killing them.'

'Never.'

'An Mok was the commander at Kompong Chhnang, not Kampot, so if you served with An Mok you were at Kompong Chhnang.'

'I was at Kampot,' shouted Sokunthea and quietly began to cry.

'Tears from a Rouge soldier?' She glared at Thanh. 'If you were at Kampot and An Mok was at Kompong Chhnang, who did you serve with?'

Sokunthea looked at Phu. 'I served with Commander Thalin, then later Commander Van Serun at Bokor.'

The sigh in the room was audible.

'You are Commander Sokunthea of Bokor and Kirirom.'

'Yes.'

Thanh sat back and breathed deeply. 'This calls for a celebration,' he said and he sent Nou to organise the servants. When Nou returned he announced that the witness had arrived.

'Shall I bring him in?' he asked Thanh.

'Why not?'

The door opened and Ro walked in. 'Ah, Colonel Ro,' said Thanh. 'I'm very sorry to have brought you all the way from the front to identify someone whose identity we now know.'

Ro just stared at Sokunthea who then held her hands out and they embraced. 'I would not have told them,' whispered Ro into her ear.

Sokunthea looked at Ro through tear-filled eyes. 'They killed her, you know.'

'Tiny? Yes, I know, we found her body and burnt her.' Sokunthea nodded.

'Stay, Colonel Ro, celebrate with us,' continued Thanh.

'No, thank you, I must get back; what will happen now?' He looked at Thanh.

'Ah, that is someone else's decision.'

'Of course,' and with one final hug of Sokunthea, Ro left.

As the wine came Sokunthea excused herself, claiming emotional exhaustion. Thanh insisted that Phu stay with the party and Sokunthea was escorted to her room by a guard.

'Cheers,' said Thanh, and the three held their glasses together.

'What will happen now?' asked Phu.

'Hanoi.'

'And a murder trial?'

'No, that was never an option, we just tried to frighten her.'

'So why Hanoi?'

'She's a celebrity, someone who can be used against us.'

'How?' continued Phu.

A frustrated Thanh looked at Phu. 'Okay, to the simple Cambodians she is a heroine, a figurehead, someone to gather around, we can use that in order to unite the country, but to Cambodia's allies, especially the Americans, she is someone to channel resistance through.'

'But there's no resistance left in Cambodia.'

'But there is resistance outside, especially in the UN.' He looked at Nou. 'The Americans are trying to discredit this invasion; they claim it's just another Vietnamese expansion. So they discover a heroine with the pure defiant virtues of Cambodia and use her as an example in their UN debates.'

'So you're just countering the Americans.'

'Yes.'

'But how did the Americans get the information? Half of Cambodia still hasn't heard of her.'

'Time for bed, I think,' said Thanh; 'tomorrow will be a long day of meetings and congratulations.'

Phu slowly went up to her room, still puzzling this battle of credibility that Thanh had outlined. 'Sokunthea killed Vietnamese soldiers so she can't be really credible to us and the Americans – how do we discredit them?' She checked on Sokunthea, who appeared fast asleep, then retired herself, still puzzling the new dynamics, which Thanh had outlined.

As Phu turned off her light Sokunthea had already reached the ground, descending slowly and quietly down the drainpipe. She had crossed the road through the narrow riverside park and dropped down to the river; there she crouched, listening for any following footsteps. She knew where she was and began to map out in her mind the route to her and her husband's house. She realised that there would be patrols out but reckoned that her knowledge of the city was greater than that of any Vietnamese invader.

She began to head along the riverbank before coming up at the back of empty houses where she crossed a main highway and entered Wat Phnom. She rested in the pagoda for a short while then moved west, always travelling along side streets and back alleys. She was surprised at the lack of patrols and, on reflection, the ease with which she had escaped from the house, putting that down to the celebratory mood that had developed.

Within an hour she turned into the street where she and Piseth had bought their piece of luxury, now the houses had suffered the damage left behind by victorious troops and decay. She reached the gate of her house, still padlocked from the day they departed; she climbed it quickly and entered the house. Inside was debris everywhere but she headed upstairs immediately and entered her bedroom. She decided that she would sleep in the attic and quickly climbed onto the toilet and clambered through the trapdoor into the space above. She found the old bed where Piseth had treated her head after striking her and she curled up to sleep.

When she woke it was already mid-morning; she listened but all she could hear was the slight whistling noise when a gently breeze passed through the roof tiles. She moved across the attic, then crawled through a small hatch on to the roof. Immediately in front of her was the large silver water tank; she moved into its shade and looked around – nothing. She climbed up its service ladder and looked inside, surprised to see it still half-full of water after four years. 'It must have rained heavily,' she said to herself. She lowered herself over the side and down into the cool clear water, which came up to her waist. As her feet touched the bottom she kicked up mud and debris that had accumulated over the years, thinking she heard something, she crouched down into the water until it touched her chin then waited – nothing.

She began to slowly shuffle forwards, feeling through the sand and debris with her hands and feet; as she did the water became cloudy. She reached the end of the tank and apart from a rotting palm leaf that had somehow blown in there was nothing. She turned and began the process all the way back to the centre, then on to the other end. This time her foot struck a small object. At first she thought it was a house brick and decided to go on, then thought she would check and ducked below the water to bring it to the surface. The object would not move and Sokunthea had to dive down several times before she could release it from the bottom. At the surface she immediately realised that she was holding the tightly-wrapped radio. She clambered out of the water tank, sat in the shade and began to unwrap the parcel. Piseth had bound it tightly, not wanting any water damage; it was so tightly bound that Sokunthea could not release it. As she looked for an easy way in a small open pocket knife slid towards her.

'Thalin!' said a startled Sokunthea.

'Hello, my team mate.'

'How did you get away from…?'

'An Mok? Easy, I killed him.'

'You been waiting here a long time?'

'About two weeks.'

'But you didn't find this.' She held up the radio.

'No, but I knew you would come; you're a survivor, but now too famous a survivor.' He raised a gun and pointed it at her. 'Where's the money?' he asked.

'There's no money; I just told you that to get you interested.' Sokunthea began to slowly stand.

'Don't lie to me, Sokunthea, where's the money?'

'There's no money; Piseth always said the radio was the gold mine.'

'Hmm. Those numbers written on the side, they the code?'

'Yes.'

'Then I'll have to settle for that. Goodbye, Sokunthea.'

'What happened to the team?'

'You became the superstar.'

Sokunthea closed her eyes as the shot rang out but there was no pain, no violent force to throw her off her feet. She opened them slowly and saw Thalin lying in a pool of blood at her feet. She looked up. 'Sinarth!'

'Good to see you, Sokunthea.'

'But I thought…'

'I was dead? No, I could have been but then I told these guys my story.'

Thanh entered through the roof door. 'Thank you, Colonel Sinarth. Well, Commander Sokunthea, heroine of Bokor and Kirirom,' he said sarcastically, 'you're just a common spy, an American spy. Take the radio!' and two soldiers appeared from each side of Sokunthea and removed the radio. 'Shall we go?' said Thanh and Sokunthea, escorted by two soldiers, followed by Sinarth and Thanh, went down to a car waiting in the street.

'Brilliant, Thanh, brilliant,' said General Hoa as he shook Thanh's hand in his office. 'Colonel Tac, bring us some coffee!' he shouted to his adjutant. 'Now, what next?'

'Well, sir,' said Thanh, 'I'm recalled to Hanoi and will take the woman with me.'

'Ah, promotion, eh? Well, don't forget the old general who backed your plan, I retire soon.'

'I won't, sir, don't worry.'

'And the woman?'

'We needed to silence the Americans and their growing campaign against us at the UN; when Tien first mentioned this Sinarth and his ridiculous story about radios and spies I didn't believe it either. Then when he told us this woman was linked to an American radio situated in Phnom Penh... well.'

'So how come she became this heroine, famous?'

'Oh, we gave the Thais that rubbish; we knew the Americans would love the thought of a woman leading the fight against the communists. The Thais printed everything we wanted and the Americans swallowed it.'

'But we nearly killed her.'

'Yes, that bloody fool Noug. I'm glad she shot him.'

'So we build up a western heroine just to show that she's really an American spy.'

'That's it; the Americans have been increasing pressure on our friends at the UN. Every time we fed them more information about her they championed her case; what are they going to say when we portray her as a spy, with a radio, code, everything? I think our delegation at the UN will have a much easier time from now on.'

'And her?'

'Hanoi.'

'For ever?'

'For ever.'

The rain fell down as Sokunthea was led across the tarmac to a waiting plane of the Vietnamese airforce. She was handcuffed to two large soldiers, with another in front and one behind. Thanh followed with a large umbrella held over him by another guard; as she left Cambodian soil for the first and last time and mounted the steps she looked across at a small hangar. There, waving to her through the rain, was Phu; she looked at her and began to cry, then silently mouthed three words. She entered the plane and sat between her guards; as he passed her seat Thanh stopped.

'What did you mouth to Phu?'

Sokunthea stared up at him. 'Never trust men.'